The
Doomsday
Tablet

WILLIAM HENSHAW

The
Doomsday
Tablet

ISBN 978-0-473-51086-2

A catalogue record for this book is available from the National Library of New Zealand.

www.williamhenshaw.com

For G.
My lighthouse in the storm.

*But afterwards there occurred violent earthquakes and floods;
and in a single day and night of misfortune all your warlike men
in a body sank into the earth ...*

From *Timaeus and Critias* dialogues, Plato, c. 360 BC

I

Cyrus Lee climbed the two steps to the front door of the Red Lion, his fourth public house this week down by the Liverpool docks. It was another wet night, close to freezing, and his feet were aching from walking on the icy streets. As he stepped through the door, the hot stale air hit him, assaulting his senses with the vaguely unpleasant smell of the seafaring men filling the smoky rooms. He navigated the small tables that were mostly occupied with patrons playing card games, smoking their pipes and often arguing.

He strode up to the bar. "Whiskey." He nodded to the landlord, knowing he would not like the rough whiskey these men drank. He was used to a more refined spirit served in the establishments he visited in his native New York. He also knew these men were not likely to trust him unless he drank with them. The landlord had not been surprised at his American accent.

Cyrus Lee was visiting public houses like the Red Lion for a specific reason. He needed to find the right man for the special voyage he'd been planning for some years. Seeing two men stand up and don their coats, he walked over to take their place, a small, pockmarked, dark wooden table with several mismatched wooden chairs. Nestled between the bar and the

3

large fireplace, it was a good vantage point. The mood in the place was sombre and more than a few of the men were drinking alone. Winter on the docks was hard and they were in need of work, waiting for the spring tides that would double the number of ships leaving the port.

The landlord watched as the middle-aged American positioned himself near the hearth. He didn't look at all like the other regulars. Certainly, he had the look of a man as sure of himself as the ocean was deep, intelligence in his eyes, but just too well-fed and refined for the type of work the docks required. He'd accepted his whiskey in a manicured hand with no scars that the landlord noticed. The man had taken his journal out with a flourish, but he hadn't written. Instead, he watched the other men in the bar, through the dense atmosphere of pipe smoke and cursing.

Cyrus was disappointed with what he'd seen so far. He'd been seeking a first mate for this voyage, starting with the local shipping offices. The men he'd found were either poorly disciplined and looking for a voyage south towards the women of the Caribbean, or too greedy, wanting a ship bringing back valuable cargo in which they could share. There were some who were too violent, prone to fighting or brutally subduing the men in their charge. That was not what Cyrus wanted for this voyage.

He'd already chosen the master, and the master had assembled the crew, without his usual first mate, who was currently staying at her majesty's pleasure in the Liverpool Borough Gaol. Cyrus was privately pleased this man would not be first mate, since he himself was travelling as the only first class passenger on this journey, and of course as patron of this important passage. He wanted to ensure that it would not only be a successful venture, but that it would prove to be a relatively safe one.

Cyrus Lee was a man of not insubstantial means, having been successful in the emerging telegraph business. By the early 1850s, the telegraph had reached many major cities in the United States and Canada, including, recently, San Francisco on the west coast. A pioneer by nature, Cyrus believed the next important step for his telegraph was to cross the Atlantic to reach the United Kingdom and the European mainland. In

North America, the telegraph had reached Halifax a few years earlier. Lee's grand plan was to extend the cable north-east through Nova Scotia, across eighty miles of the Cabot Strait to Cape Ray in Newfoundland, then across Newfoundland to meet the Atlantic at St John's. From St John's, it was eighteen hundred miles across the Atlantic to Valentia Island, just off the west coast of County Kerry, Ireland.

The work from Halifax to St John's was planned but could not start until the spring thaw, still a month away. In the meantime, Lee had a small vessel already running cable across the Irish Sea, from Liverpool to Dublin, and his Irish gang was half finished erecting telegraph posts from Dublin to Galway. The telegraph cable terminal on Valentia Island was currently under construction.

This voyage would take the vessel around the southern coast of Ireland to meet the terminal, and start the arduous journey to lay the cable across nearly two thousand miles of open sea. Cyrus had decided to start in Ireland, as conditions around Newfoundland would continue to be particularly treacherous from sea ice and icebergs for another two or three months. This was not a journey for the faint of heart, nor was it one for those seeking riches or exotic delights from other parts of the world. The North Atlantic was rarely an easy crossing.

Cyrus Lee's musings were interrupted by the sound of raised voices on the other side of the room. He looked over through the bluish smoke of the pipe tobacco and saw the landlord moving behind the bar towards the noise. An older man with a long, reddish beard had a bottle in his hand and was yelling at the other, no more than a boy.

"... bloody chowder-headed Jack tar," was all Cyrus caught of Red Beard's shouted abuse, his voice slurred and blunted by the whiskey. The older man lurched nearer to the bar and, using the rough timber edge, deftly knocked the head off the bottle he was holding. He wielded it at the wild-eyed Irish boy who was baiting him.

"Sit down, yer drunken fecker, before I put yer down," the boy said, seemingly unafraid.

People around them had moved back and were watching as if this was tonight's entertainment. The landlord called to Red Beard to put the bottle down, but he was not of a mind to listen. He lunged at the boy, almost reaching his neck, and the growing crowd had now started telling Red Beard to calm down. His response was to start shouting at them, waving the bottle maniacally.

"Damn and bugger ye to hell," Red Beard shouted at them all.

At that moment, a young man in his twenties caught Lee's eye, as he calmly stood up from a table nearby and walked into the fracas. He had a dark beard, thick black hair and piercing blue eyes, and carried himself with an air of quiet confidence. At around five feet and eleven inches, he was also the tallest in the room. He put a large, firm hand on the Irish boy's shoulder, and the lad whirled, ready to attack. The boy stopped in his tracks as the young man stared him down and jerked his head in the direction of the door. Without a further word, the young lad downed the last of his drink, straightened his shoulders and left the bar.

"Ned, put the bottle down," said the young man to Red Beard, taking a step towards him.

Ned brandished the broken bottle at the young man, but stopped short. The young man did not move.

"Ned, I've asked you to put the bottle down," he repeated calmly, looking Ned directly in the eyes.

Ned stared back defiantly and didn't move as the small crowd looked on, but after about twenty seconds, he glanced at the bottle and put it on the bar.

"Damn insolent bugger," Ned muttered quietly. The landlord quickly removed the broken bottle.

The young man nodded at Ned, who then sat down. The audience decided the excitement was over and resumed their conversations.

As the man returned to his table, Cyrus noticed he had an inch-long scar below his right eye. He was still completely calm and looked to Cyrus to be physically strong and fit, as well as of strong character. This could be his man.

The young man did not resume his seat; instead he put his coat on, turned up the collar and went to the door. Cyrus put down his unfinished whiskey and followed him out.

"Are you looking for work?"

The man paused briefly, shrugged and walked on.

"Pardon me, son, are you in need of work?"

He stopped and turned, eyeing Cyrus up and down. "Who's asking?" he said, his breath turning to vapour in the freezing air.

"Name's Lee, Cyrus Lee. I need a first mate for a two-month Atlantic crossing. Return trip if you want it."

"I work steamships." The young man knew the sailing ship journey was eight to twelve weeks, but a steamship often took less than half that.

"It is a steamship, but there's a lot of work to do on the way. Important work that hasn't been done before," said Lee.

"Tell me more." A first mate's job would be a useful opportunity, and this was starting to sound interesting.

"Have you heard of the telegraph?" Cyrus asked.

"Aye."

"I'm taking the telegraph across the Atlantic. We'll be connecting the United States with Ireland and England, laying nearly two thousand miles of cable."

"You're mad." The young man had crossed the Atlantic a few times, and he knew how wild the weather could get.

"Son, I've crossed this ocean many times. Sure, the seas can be bad, but what do you know of deep ocean currents?" Lee asked.

The young man held Lee's eyes, waiting.

"It's much calmer below the surface. Also, we have the latest winches to allow for the worst of seas. This journey, son, could be the adventure of a lifetime."

"What are you paying?"

Cyrus named the fee, both men knowing it was a little over the odds. "A third in advance, as soon as you board. We sail in eight days."

"Henry Hobbs," said the young adventurer, extending his hand to the American.

2

Eight days later, Henry Hobbs made his way down to the Liverpool dock from his lodgings, a large canvas duffel bag slung over his broad shoulders. As he walked through the thick fog, his beard glistened with the cold moisture in the air. The fog was tinged with the usual smell of the morning's coal fires, softened by the salty sea air. The docks were quiet, not yet bustling as they would be when the fog lifted. Hobbs' senses were occasionally assaulted by the sound of unseen men loading or unloading cargoes, the smells of spoiled food, rotting fish, or the acrid tar as standing rigging was made seaworthy.

The previous night, Hobbs had met with the ship's master, Captain Kearney, and the captain had confirmed his passage as first mate. Hobbs had heard of Kearney before and while most said he was a competent seaman, some said he was also sometimes a slave to the drink.

The dank air was still. Kearney had said there'd be fog, so eat a hearty breakfast before boarding. That was Hobbs' custom anyway; he knew leaving a port could be a complicated and protracted business, so it was not unusual to have no chance for a meal of any kind for many hours after sailing. He knew, too, that the first few hours of any long voyage were important for the master and mate also, as during this time, the tenor of the relationship with the crew is set.

Hobbs located the American first, waiting by the gangway of the *City of Wicklow*, a relatively new Irish steamship with a good deal of equipment on the deck. Cyrus Lee looked out of place, wearing a hat and overcoat that seemed to be new, accompanied by an impractically large trunk proclaiming its owner's name on a bold brass plaque. Hobbs wondered how Lee had transported the trunk to the dock, since it was larger than the American himself. He assumed there must have been a carriage.

Cyrus shook Hobbs' hand, pleased to see the familiar face. "Morning, son, glad to see you here."

"Morning," said Hobbs in return, giving the American's hand a cursory but firm shake.

"Have you seen Captain Kearney?"

"Last night. Said we'd leave late due to fog. He was right."

The two men waited while the dockers loaded the last of the equipment using the dock's steam crane, the huge drums of steel cable wrapped in heavily tarred hemp. The drums had a pungent smell that lingered unkindly in the nostrils. As they waited, the rest of the crew, some thirty-two men, arrived, along with the captain. Kearney instructed two of the men to load Lee's trunk and take it to his cabin, and told Hobbs to board and meet him on the bridge in fifteen minutes.

Hobbs made his way to the first mate's cabin and dropped his bag on the small bunk. The cabin was cramped, but it was better than the shared accommodation he was used to. The sharp, tarred aroma had given way to a more subtle and familiar smell of damp and a hint of mould. The captain's cabin was next door, with the small cabins of the four telegraph engineers and the ship's surgeon across the passageway. He took a quick look around the bow and made his way through the chart room to the bridge. The fog had started to clear, and there was a brighter patch where the sun was threatening to break through. A good sign.

"Hobbs, have the men check the cargo on deck. Those cable drums are weighty, and I want to know that they're well secured and the load evenly spread across the deck."

"Captain." Hobbs nodded and set about his business.

The crew quarters were on the deck below. Hobbs walked past his cabin, through the first bulkhead and down the ladder, to find the crew's four bunk rooms divided by a narrow passageway. Six bunks per room, with a further bunk room on the lower deck for the ship's stokers and boilermen. He talked briefly to the men, making sure they were all sober, and gave his instructions.

Hobbs climbed the ladder to the engineers' cabins, passing the ship's surgeon along the way. The surgeon was an unhealthily slim man with rheumy eyes, a pale complexion and sour demeanour. Hobbs hoped he never had need of the man, especially as he had noticed the smell of whiskey on him. He located the engineers, introduced himself and asked the four men who among them was skilled in the stowage and handling of the drums. As it happened, all the engineers had expertise with telegraph cable, having worked with it for many years. One of the men told Hobbs the drums on the deck were the spares. The bulk of them had been loaded into the hold over the previous two days. They were secured upright on large, purpose-built spindles so the cable could be unfurled without twisting. The engineers' job was to ensure it was deployed carefully, and to see to it that joints were made to the required standard when one drum gave way to another. Hobbs asked two of them to supervise the crew's checks on deck, and went up with them to see for himself. As he emerged, he saw how large these drums were – almost the size of a carriage.

At the ship's stern were two large winches, each powered by its own small steam engine, and he could see that the cable had been fed up from the hold through both winches. The aft-most winch had its drums locked together firmly, holding the cable in place, and the forward winch had its large metal drums opened to a gap of about two inches for the cable to pass through. The drums on deck were all tightly lashed in place, and Hobbs watched as the men checked all their moorings.

The fog had cleared enough to let a pale sun start to show, and visibility across the water was now close to half a mile. The sounds of the dock had returned almost to normal: men shouting and cursing, the clang of iron and steel, chains being hauled.

Twenty minutes later, Hobbs reported back to the captain that all was in order.

"We're sailing on the hour. Let Mr Lee know." The ship's chronometer indicated just after 9.50 am.

Hobbs went back through the bulkhead and past the ladder to the crew deck. Just beyond were the four first class cabins. The American's cabin was the only one occupied. The others were filled with extra supplies and a small amount of equipment unfamiliar to Hobbs.

"Captain says we'll be leaving at ten o'clock."

"Thanks, son. This could be the most important voyage of the century!"

Hobbs didn't see how the telegraph was so important. Already a message could cross the Atlantic on a steamship in as little as ten days. He let Cyrus Lee have his moment, though, and didn't say anything.

3

"Quickly, cut the engine!" Cyrus Lee yelled, at no one in particular. He could see the strain in the cable, feeling the pitch of the ship shift as the seas pulled it even tighter. Lee hadn't been on the top deck much during the past two weeks as they'd slowly and carefully deployed the cable. The smell of the tarred hemp was pungent, and it all looked quite dangerous. He had come up on deck now because he'd heard men shouting and could feel the wind picking up. Thankfully, the seas hadn't risen much yet, but the wind might have been up beyond fifteen knots.

Lee knew how difficult things would be if the cable snapped. They might even have to retrace their path all the way back to the Irish coast and start over. At least a month would be lost. He looked at the winch, now locked onto the cable, and saw that the ship seemed to have drifted some way to starboard. Instead of the cable reaching out directly behind the ship, it veered off at an alarming twenty-degree angle.

Hobbs lay on the undersized bunk in his cabin. He'd been awake for a little while, having slept for only about four hours since he finished the evening watch, well after midnight. He'd been thinking about their journey so far. They'd had a smooth sailing around the southern coast of Ireland, and had reached Valentia Island a day ahead of schedule. The weather had been fine but quite overcast, and as they rounded the island, the skies had darkened further. It had taken the engineers the best part of the afternoon to secure the cable to the terminal, while the weather had quietly and ominously threatened.

The isolation of the west coast countryside was starkly beautiful and bleak at the same time. Occasional farmhouses with medieval ruins interspersed. There was little else to indicate civilisation had reached this place. Hobbs knew the potato blight had devastated Ireland a mere five years ago. He had seen many ships carrying malnourished families with emaciated children across the Irish Sea in the hope of a better life. He wondered how people in these distant rural parts had survived. Perhaps many hadn't. He'd seen a few dwellings, but no actual signs of life, except for just a few cottages with smoke wafting from their chimneys.

As he lay quietly, the smell of the sea air told Hobbs the barometric pressure had dropped. North Atlantic weather was rarely kind at this time of year. He felt the pull of the cable on the ship's motion and knew something didn't feel quite right.

"Quickly, cut the engine!" he heard the American yelling.

Hobbs climbed out of his bunk and pulled his rough oily woollen jersey over his head. He went onto the bridge and found a crewman manning the helm, looking worried. "Where's Captain Kearney?"

"He said he felt a bit under the weather," said the crewman. "The wind has just picked up."

Hobbs went to the captain's cabin and knocked loudly. No response. He opened the door and saw the captain asleep in his chair with a bottle of whiskey, almost empty, on the table next to a dirty glass. The cabin smelt of whiskey and pipe tobacco. He closed the door and went back to the bridge, thinking the captain and surgeon made a fine pair.

"Captain's unwell. What's our position?"

The crewman told Hobbs but was clearly uncertain.

"How long has the captain been gone?" Hobbs asked.

"Two hours."

Hobbs checked the charts and did some quick reckoning, determining that they'd probably drifted thirty to fifty nautical miles north of their charted course. He ran up to the deck and peered out, seeing the cable skewed off at an angle, and decided they might be more than fifty nautical miles off course. He gave the order to cut the engines to a quarter and turned the ship sixty degrees to port.

"What's happening?" Cyrus Lee asked anxiously.

"We've drifted off course a few miles. Don't concern yourself."

"The cable, it'll break if you don't do something," Lee shouted. "This is a disaster!"

"Don't concern yourself. I've taken the pressure off. Go take a look." Hobbs was keen to get Lee off the bridge and out of his way.

"Where is Captain Kearney?" Lee asked as he headed back to the deck.

Hobbs ignored him.

"Shall I fetch the captain?" The crewman was still on the bridge, unsure what to do.

"Let him be," Hobbs said firmly. "He's unwell."

Hobbs carefully steered the ship back to their charted course, with the wind putting up a moderate resistance. Far behind, the cable had reached the ocean floor, some two miles below, and it was being dragged back on its path. As they neared the planned route, it had stretched and wrenched taut. Hobbs could feel the ship being pulled backwards. *Snagged on rocks? Or an old shipwreck?*

"Fetch one of those engineers," Hobbs said to the crewman, who was glad of something to do. He looked out at the sky and could see the weather would likely worsen over the next few hours, possibly rising to stormy. He did not want to have the ship tethered to the bottom of the Atlantic during a storm. One option was to pay out more cable, and steam to Newfoundland, hoping for the best.

At that moment, the crewman returned with one of the engineers.

"How much spare cable do you have?" Hobbs asked.

"We provisioned for an additional two hundred miles," he said. "How far out are we?"

Hobbs showed him on the chart and the engineer made a quick

calculation. His face changed as he did so. "Are you sure about this position?"

"Within a few nautical miles, yes," said Hobbs.

"Then we have a problem. We are roughly halfway across the Atlantic and yet we've used three-fifths of the cable." The engineer rechecked the chart. "We may have just enough to get to Newfoundland, but I can't understand how we've used so much of it to this point."

"We've drifted maybe fifty nautical miles north, and I believe the cable is snagged on the ocean floor. That would account for a few extra miles," Hobbs said.

"What's this?" the engineer asked, pointing at a rough line on the chart snaking through the middle of the Atlantic, some hundred and fifty miles east of their present location.

"That's an undersea mountain range, discovered a few years ago. They're calling it the 'Mid-Atlantic Ridge'."

"Oh. We didn't know about that. Our calculations were based on the charts we had. Flat ocean floor. We didn't allow for crossing an undersea mountain range." The engineer hung his head. "Can you free it?" he asked hopefully. "We need to ensure we can get all the way to Newfoundland, or this endeavour will come to naught."

This was the American's venture. Lee would need to make a decision. Hobbs could see two choices: press on and hope there was enough cable to reach Newfoundland, or try and free the snag and drag it back on course, potentially freeing up an additional fifty miles or so. Hobbs was not happy with the second option, knowing the danger involved. When he was fifteen and working on the Liverpool docks, he'd seen a cable break under load. The image was as clear in his mind as the day it happened. The rusty cable had whipped back so violently it cut a man almost in half before embedding itself, along with the man's blood and flesh, in foot-thick timbers. It was a lesson he would never forget.

The wind had rounded to the north and was quite a bit colder than an hour earlier. Hobbs felt a chill in his bones, not entirely due to the worsening weather. Their options were shrinking, although perhaps if they continued towards Canada, they could get close enough to send a boat to the mainland to arrange for more cable.

"We need to talk with Mr Lee," Hobbs said to the engineer.

"I'll fetch him to the bridge," the crewman said.

Hobbs surveyed the steadily darkening sky. If the wind stiffened further, they could find themselves in heavy seas, dragged down by tons of tarred cable. It wasn't yet a matter of life or death for the ship and all hands, but if it became so, Hobbs would not hesitate to make the decision himself, particularly given the captain's apparent condition. He had also to consider the ship's provisions, including their store of coal. In the Mid-Atlantic, there was no port for emergency supplies, so their choices were to return to Galway or Plymouth, or press on to Canada.

4

Captain Kearney chose that moment to return to the bridge. "Hobbs, what's the situation?" he asked abruptly, with a slight unsteadiness in his voice.

Hobbs raised his eyebrows. "Cable's snagged, captain. I've asked for Mr Lee and his engineers to assess the situation presently. Weather's turning, too."

The captain's face belied his demeanour; he knew something had gone wrong. Kearney didn't respond immediately, instead digging out some matches to relight his old briar pipe, holding the bowl in his gnarled left hand as the stem curled up to his mouth.

"I returned to the deck an hour ago," Hobbs continued, "and found we had drifted off course about a hundred miles, so I righted the helm. The cable snagged as we dragged it back. I'd say we are still eighty miles north of where we should be."

Kearney considered this in silence, checking the charts for himself, while blueish smoke rose from his pipe. Hobbs could see the captain was having trouble focusing, but at least he seemed to have sobered up. As the captain was attempting to study the chart, the engineer returned with the American.

17

"Can you free the cable?" Cyrus Lee asked.

"Can't say. How sturdy is it?"

"It's the same cable used to tow ships," said Lee. "It should handle just about all you've got."

Hobbs' expression said he doubted it. "And if it breaks?"

Lee was clearly torn between the two options. He knew that if the cable snapped, the voyage would be a failure. He did not have enough money to start again. He'd only been able to persuade a few backers to buy into this venture – most of the capital-rich potential sponsors had told him he was mad. They said it couldn't be done. The American also knew he'd used too much of his own capital to get this investment off the ground. His engineer had quietly explained about the unexpected Mid-Atlantic Ridge, and that it appeared they'd already used up their contingency, and possibly more. They needed to free up the cable and get back on course.

"It won't break," Lee said, with unfelt confidence.

"I won't give you a guarantee," said Hobbs. "If we get back on course and run short of cable before Newfoundland, we could send a boat to get more."

"No. Free it up and we'll carry on then." Lee had made his mind up.

Hobbs was about to argue, knowing this might risk the crew's safety. A North Atlantic storm is not to be taken lightly, and he wanted to get them on their way.

"Very well, Mr Lee," said Captain Kearney. "But on your head be it."

Hobbs looked at both men for a good half-minute before giving the orders. Kearney simply stared at Hobbs, drawing on the pipe as he waited for his first mate to obey his order.

Henry Hobbs sent a crewman to get all hands below deck. He then gave the order for half power and turned the ship a further thirty degrees to port, heading directly back to their plotted course. The cold north wind was now at their backs. As they pressed forward, the cable became ever tauter. Cyrus Lee watched from the deck, well forward of the winch gear. Hobbs called to him to come inside, but he just kept watching his precious cable.

In the wind and the swell, it was difficult to determine whether they were making progress or just pulling against a firmly anchored cable. After thirty minutes, however, Hobbs felt the strain ease slightly. He looked aft and saw the cable was still tight, but he was sure they were moving. For all he knew, they'd freed it after all. They steamed ahead, still on half engines, and Hobbs hoped to get them back to their original course before the brewing storm arrived.

The engineer came back and told them there was more drag on the cable than there should be, but there was little they could do about it.

"Perhaps it's the wind," said Hobbs. It was now close to thirty knots and the seas were still rising. Visibility had dropped to well under a mile.

"Perhaps," said the engineer, but it was clear he did not agree.

The captain retired to his cabin, leaving Hobbs in command again, and Hobbs was quietly relieved. He sent for someone to man the helm and rechecked the charts and their location. He was confident they were now roughly ten nautical miles from their proper course so would turn ninety degrees to starboard soon. He then talked to the engineers, worrying about measures that might be required to pull the cable back onto its correct path. The risk of breakage and the potential backlash that could kill weighed on his mind. Hobbs also wanted to know how long before they needed to splice the cable as they changed to the next drum. 'About three hours', had been the answer, and he was not pleased. This was a complicated procedure, and he expected it would be exceedingly difficult at night. Especially during a storm. He knew also that the men would need lamps in the cargo hold to do this, and a hold full of cable coated with tarred hemp was not the safest of places for lamps.

He went back to the bridge to change course and check the weather again and was relieved to find conditions had not changed. The icy northerly wind still around thirty knots, the rain coming down steadily and the sky heavily overcast, but at least no worse. Perhaps it wouldn't escalate into a full-blown storm. If they were lucky, by nightfall, which was two hours away, they would be far enough west to have cleared the worst of it. Hobbs left the crewman with instructions to hold their course while he went to the galley for some food. The only other occupant of the galley was the surgeon, slowly eating a small plate of mutton.

"Doctor," said Hobbs, nodding in the man's direction.

The surgeon nodded back silently.

Hobbs took a large serving of meat and potatoes and sat at the bench down from the surgeon. He had half-finished his meal when a crewman rushed in to report that something was wrong. Hobbs was not surprised; he could hear the engine whining. He headed back to the bridge, after taking a large mouthful of the salty meat.

"The cable is dragging hard again, and we've stopped," said the helmsman.

"Ahead three quarters," was Hobbs' answer. Cyrus Lee had said his cable was sturdy, so now they would find out for certain. "Make sure there's nobody on deck, and fetch Mr Lee."

Ten minutes later, something gave way and the ship lurched forward. Cyrus Lee gasped and started to run to the deck. Hobbs held him back.

"Wait. I've seen a snapped cable kill a man."

After a minute or so, Hobbs let him go and he rushed to check his cable. It was now getting dark, but he could see it had apparently not broken, for it was still stretched out behind the ship, albeit not as tight as before.

"Oh, thank God!" Lee said.

The ship was now starting to pull ahead, faster than they had been able to move for some hours. Lee despatched two of the engineers to check that everything was as it should be with the cable drums and the winch gear. Hobbs cautioned them to tether themselves as they worked near the winches. The men looked concerned but did as they were told.

"Well done, Hobbs." Cyrus Lee broke the silence. "You've freed up the cable and got us back on course. This venture is going to be a success, you'll see." Lee spoke with an air of confidence that Hobbs did not reciprocate.

"Looks like we're going to be fortunate with the weather at least," replied Hobbs. "It seems the worst of it is at our backs now."

As night approached, the wind had dropped back to around twenty-five knots, though it was still an icy northerly.

After a short time, the engineers returned to the bridge, all clearly distressed.

"Something's wrong. The angle is all wrong," one of them said.

5

The phone was buzzing away on the table as Daniel put his dinner plates in the dishwasher and dried his hands. He could tell from the ring tone that it was his mother calling. He tried to visit her every Saturday, bringing her the weekend newspaper and a cappuccino. He usually stopped for a long chat, a weekly ritual, so she rarely had occasion to call him. He hoped everything was all right. The call disappeared off the screen just as he picked up the phone. He called her back.

"Hello, Daniel. I'm sorry to bother you during the week, love," said Alice Reade. At sixty-three years old, Alice still had a spring in her step, or voice, in this case.

"Hi, Mum," Daniel interrupted cheerfully. "Is everything all right?"

"Yes. Why wouldn't it be?" Alice asked.

"Oh. Just checking. What's up?"

"You've got an important-looking letter from England," said Alice solemnly.

Daniel was now thirty-four, and it had been a long time since his mail had been addressed to his parents' house. Alice and Eric Reade had bought the house when his sister Katie was born and Daniel nine years old, and Alice had worked hard to keep it after Eric's death.

22

"I'll be over on Saturday so I'll collect it then," said Daniel.

"It's registered post. I had to sign for it," said Alice, hoping Daniel would take the hint.

He realised his mother was very curious, and perhaps slightly anxious. He couldn't deny that he, too, was now wondering what could be in this apparently important letter from across the world. "Okay, I'll just finish the washing up and come over. See you in a bit."

Daniel and his parents had emigrated from the United Kingdom when he was seven, for a fresh start. Eric had quickly managed to get a job teaching history at Wellington College, and two years later they had Katie. They decided to stay in New Zealand and successfully applied for citizenship. Life was good, and Daniel looked forward to going to the 'big school' where his father taught. He could still remember those happy feelings, but sadly it wasn't meant to be. Stronger than the warm reminiscences, he could still feel the searing pain he'd suffered, as a twelve-year-old boy, when his father died of a heart attack just three years later.

Life suddenly became much more difficult, and Alice had to work full time. Everyone at Wellington College knew he was the boy whose father had died, and even the well-intended sympathies from the teachers were painful for him. Over time, life slowly got better for the Reade family, but it took some years.

As far as Daniel knew, his mother had not kept in touch with family in England. They had never gone back to visit, which he was sure was because Alice simply could not afford it, and nobody had ever come to visit them.

He threw a jacket on and went out to his car. The weather was fine and still moderately warm. October in Wellington could be cool sometimes, and often windy, but tonight was clear and calm. He drove up the motorway, through the gorge, and off at the Johnsonville exit. In a little over five minutes, he was pulling into his mother's driveway.

"I'll put the kettle on," said Alice, as Daniel followed her down the hallway to the kitchen at the back of the house.

A large brown envelope sat on the table, addressed to 'Mr Daniel E

Reade, C/- Mrs Alice Reade' in neatly typed script. It looked like it had been typed on an old-fashioned manual typewriter. It had been sent Royal Mail First Class, and had a registered letter stamp on the front, indicating a signature was required.

"The postman said I could sign for it because it's been addressed 'care of' me. Black tea?"

"Thanks, Mum, that would be great," said Daniel.

He tried to push his finger under the flap of the envelope but it was firmly stuck down. He took a knife from the kitchen drawer and slit it open.

"Have you eaten enough?" Alice asked. She thought he could use a few more kilos. He used to play rugby until a knee reconstruction at twenty-one slowed him down, but he was built more like a football player. He didn't seriously watch his weight but had a reasonably healthy diet and jogged occasionally.

"I'm fine, Mum, don't fuss."

Alice watched him as he shook the envelope, his light-brown eyes following the documents as they slipped out. She was proud of her son. At six foot tall and of an athletic build, she thought he was very handsome. Of course, mothers always think that of their boys, don't they? His wavy brown hair could use a brush, but Daniel had never worried much about that. Often on Saturdays, he would arrive with a day's beard growth, but this being a weeknight, his strong jawline and slightly dimpled chin were clean-shaven. *A handsome man indeed.* She wished he would find a nice girlfriend.

Two sheets of thick cream paper of evident high quality had settled on the table. There was a company name embossed at the top.

"Higginbotham & Marks, Barristers and Solicitors. Have you heard of them? Apparently they're in Andover, Wiltshire."

"No," Alice replied. "What is it?" Memories of her childhood started to flood back.

"It's about Edward Foxton."

"My brother. Your uncle." Daniel heard a slight sigh as she said it. "We haven't spoken in decades. He never forgave Eric for taking us to the other side of the world. I can still hear him saying 'it's just wrong'. He couldn't, no, *wouldn't* see that we just needed a fresh start."

"Mum, I'm sorry, but the letter says Edward died a few weeks ago," Daniel said gently.

His mother nodded silently and focused on making the tea.

Daniel read the solicitor's letter to her while she fussed over the teacups.

Dear Mr Reade,

It is with regret that I write to inform you of the passing of your late uncle, and my client, Edward James Foxton, of Chidwick, Andover, Wiltshire, on October 17th of this year.

Mr Foxton's wishes were that I inform you that, notwithstanding their disagreement, and subsequent losing touch with his dear sister Alice, he had never forgotten her. As his life progressed without marriage or issue, he also kept track of Kathryn and yourself, his niece and nephew.

Mr Foxton has named you as his only heir, and as such, I request that you contact my office at the earliest opportunity to discuss his estate, which includes a real estate holding and various minor assets.

Yours most sincerely,

Godfrey H. Marks

Godfrey Marks
Solicitor

"Didn't expect that," said Daniel, not quite knowing what to say. The second sheet of paper was handwritten in a less elegant hand, giving contact options and details for the firm.

Alice brought over the tea and a plate of biscuits and sat at the table. There was a tear on her cheek. Daniel went over and gave her a firm hug.

"I should have contacted him. I feel awful."

"No, Mum, you shouldn't." Daniel saw that Alice was grappling with her feelings. "He knew your address, he could easily have written. He could have visited during those tough years after Dad died." Daniel stepped back and looked at his mother, running his hands through his hair. "I didn't know him, but maybe he had regrets of his own," he added.

"But he was my brother." Alice shook her head sadly.

"Don't beat yourself up. You've had it tough enough already. My guess is he probably knew he was wrong to shun you and Dad, and this is his atonement." Daniel could see his mother was upset. She seemed to struggle with her feelings of guilt, possibly because of the way their relationship had unfolded, and no doubt with grief for a lost brother. Grief she may have carried for many years.

Unsure of his own feelings about the unexpected windfall, Daniel started wondering what he had done to deserve it. "But why me? Why not you? Why not both Katie and I? I've never even met him."

"I don't know," Alice said, pausing for thought. "He was an old-fashioned sort of man. Traditional. Except for my grandmother, who was an only child, that house has passed down the male line of the family for generations. Maybe that's his reason."

"Doesn't seem fair." Daniel shook his head slowly. "I guess I could sell up and give Katie half," he muttered to himself. He looked up to see his mother staring, the makings of a look of pride on her still-saddened face.

"We need to find out more." Daniel was resolute. "I could call the solicitor now to see what he can tell us." He checked on his phone. "They're thirteen hours behind us. There might be someone in the office."

Daniel dialled the number and waited.

6

"Higginbotham & Marks," a cultured female voice announced slowly.

Mr Marks was currently unavailable, a Mrs Ramsay explained, but perhaps she could help. Daniel relayed the details he had, and Mrs Ramsay suggested he travel to England immediately to make the necessary arrangements. She requested that he make contact again upon arrival in London to schedule a meeting with Mr Marks. All very formal. He agreed he would make his arrangements and be in touch.

Daniel and Alice talked for another hour and a half, and Alice, in her emotional state, told Daniel some of the reasons she and his father had decided to leave England.

"We were told we couldn't have another child after you, you know, but just over a year after coming here, I was pregnant with Katie. It was Edward who was wrong," she said. As she reminisced about her life in Reading, she seemed to recover some of her happier demeanour.

She talked about growing up in the Chidwick house. Her parents had moved in with her grandmother, Mary, after her grandfather passed away. She fondly remembered Mary, who died when Edward and Alice were teenagers. She hadn't been disappointed when Edward inherited the house. She and Edward had a generally happy, but sometimes rather lonely childhood in the little village, with most of their school friends living in Andover, some eight miles away. Edward was the more reserved of the two and didn't make friends easily, whereas Alice was quite outgoing, and from around ten or eleven years old, she was bored with the village and rode her bike into town on the weekends to meet her friends. "The world seemed a safer place back then," she said.

As Daniel got up to leave, he told Alice he would start planning his trip to England in the morning. He asked her if she would like to go with him, but she decided to stay home. She said she would be happy with photos and the occasional phone call. He drove back home thinking about his late uncle. That night, he lay awake for a while, wondering what might be in store for him in the UK. What would he find? He knew little about his family history. Would this be the circuit breaker he was beginning to feel his life needed?

The next morning Daniel took the bus to work. He looked at his reflection in the window. Tired, but presentable. He'd only had time for a slice of toast instead of his usual breakfast, but he was somehow energised by the prospect of where that letter might lead him. Maybe now was the right time to consider his career options. After university, he had decided following in his father's footsteps as a teacher was not what he wanted, and he joined the public service for a period. A few years ago, he started to put his degree to what he'd hoped would be better use, joining a behavioural insight consultancy firm. It started out as interesting work, relating to anthropology and sociology, which he had taken on his way to a history degree. He'd been quite successful and was well regarded by the firm's clients, but lately he felt the work had become less rewarding. There was plenty to do, but some days he worried that he was just going through the motions. He started contemplating looking for something closer to his passion for history. He knew the firm wanted him to stay on, so he was hopeful they would be flexible about his taking leave at such short notice.

Daniel arrived at the office and asked Ian, the partner for whom he worked, whether he had a few minutes to discuss his news. Ian glanced at his watch with a slightly furrowed brow, but acceded. "All right. I could use a coffee."

"Great."

As they walked in silence to a nearby café, Daniel collected his thoughts. Ian ordered coffee and they took a booth by the window.

"I've just had some rather surprising news. I had an uncle in the UK who died recently. I've never met him, but I received a letter last night informing me I've inherited his house in Wiltshire."

"Oh. That's not what I was expecting to hear."

"Same for me," Daniel said, wondering whether Ian had been expecting to hear something in particular. "His solicitor wants me to go to England as soon as possible to tidy up his affairs. I don't know what to expect when I get there."

Ian's brow furrowed again. He looked at Daniel condescendingly, drawing a breath as would a preacher about to give a sermon. "That's going to be difficult, I'm afraid. We need to put our clients first, Daniel." That did not sound promising. "Maybe when you've finished with your current clients, say nearer to Christmas?" Ian suggested, in a way that made it sound like anything but a suggestion.

"Actually, I think it's more pressing than that. I don't believe there would be a problem with handing over the portfolio to one of the others in our team; there's nothing really urgent or difficult."

"I'll have to be the judge of that," Ian said, stony-faced. "I can't allow my consultants to let the firm down."

Daniel was affronted. Of course he would ensure his clients were not let down. His boss was being unreasonable. It wasn't entirely uncharacteristic, but on this occasion, he'd hoped for better. He tried again. "How about I come up with a handover plan with one of the others?"

"Well, that would waste someone else's time, too. No, you need to rethink this. Nearer to Christmas would suit us better."

Daniel decided to press a little harder. He didn't think his request was unreasonable. He remembered Ian had taken time off without notice when his marriage had abruptly ended last year. The story that had quickly gone around the office was that Ian had got home from work and found that his wife had emptied most of the furniture and valuables out of the house. He hadn't come back to work for a couple of weeks. Maybe he had forgotten to 'put the firm first'.

"Ian, I'm asking you to reconsider. This is an unexpected family matter that needs to be dealt with. I imagine it would be done in a few weeks and I can easily arrange cover for my clients." Daniel looked Ian in the eye, with a very determined face, but his boss did not back down.

"No, Daniel, I don't agree. You could take some leave in December, as I said."

"What about last year, when you needed time urgently?" That was pushing it.

Ian's complexion became more ruddy. "That's none of your concern," he said through gritted teeth. "You work for me, and I say 'no'. End of discussion."

This was not the conversation Daniel needed. This was not the *boss* Daniel needed.

"Very well," Daniel said with muted and controlled anger. "Thanks for the coffee." He stood and walked purposefully back to the office.

Back at his desk, he typed a terse resignation letter, effective immediately, citing a pressing family matter for which leave had been sought and refused, and printed three copies. One for the office manager, one for Ian, and one for himself. He briefly explained to one of his colleagues that he was off for a family bereavement and apologised for leaving so abruptly. Ironically, his colleague said, "No problem, I can cover your clients." The office manager was surprised and said she would miss him.

Ian strolled back in, presumably after a second coffee, with a satisfied and positively managerial look on his face. Daniel handed him the letter with a wry smile as he left.

Daniel was surprised at how good he felt. It wasn't smugness, it was more a sense of relief, or perhaps of a weight lifted. His anger had subsided. Ian's reaction may well have been just the catalyst he needed. He enjoyed the interaction with his clients, and he knew he was well thought of, but he also knew, as each month passed, there was a little less of his heart in the work. Alice had observed a while ago that there was a bit less 'spring in his step'.

He stopped at the same café and decided to treat himself to a real breakfast. As he waited for his food, he turned over in his mind what he'd just done. Had he been too impulsive? Should he have given Ian a chance to reconsider, when faced with an inconvenient resignation? But he quickly decided the man didn't deserve it.

The weather was unusually pleasant for the time of year, although people passing by all looked busy and didn't seem to notice. *Liberated,* that was what he felt, he decided.

As he started his leisurely breakfast, he reflected that ever since he and Andrea had gone their separate ways, he'd felt unsettled. They had been together more than three years, but they'd had few common interests and had slowly drifted apart. They had both realised their relationship had become a habit. They had separate friends and almost separate lives. Andrea said it first, but in his heart, Daniel knew she was right. The break was amicable and surprisingly easy, he thought at the time. None of his friends were particularly surprised either. He knew Andrea now had a new man and was apparently engaged, and was happy for her.

He had known, at least subconsciously, that he should have reassessed his life back then, but he'd allowed things to drift, and told himself the work he was doing was interesting *enough*. It also had a reasonably healthy salary to go with it, so he was able to pay his mortgage a little faster, at the same time as saving a bit for ... well, he wasn't quite sure what *for* ... without having to live too frugal a life. While he ate breakfast, he set about making the necessary arrangements for his travel, starting with a one-way flight to Heathrow on Sunday.

7

"The cable is angled too far down," one of the engineers said, his face still ruddy from the freezing northerly blasting outside. Rivulets of rain ran down his cheeks from his hair.

Lee rushed up on deck and marched to the stern, the two engineers on his heels. "It's still taut, doesn't look broken to me," he said, rubbing his hands together in the cold. "But look at the angle. It should be pulling back much further. It's dropping too deep too quickly. It's as if it's not ..." His voice trailed away like he was too afraid to say what he was thinking.

"It's as if it isn't connected any more, Mr Lee," the other completed.

"But it's still taut," Cyrus repeated. "How do you explain that?"

"We're steaming ahead, Mr Lee. We could ask the captain to slow down for a short while and see what happens," said the engineer. "There's nothing to lose, other than a few minutes."

The American considered his words. The engineer was right – slowing down to see what the cable did would make little difference to the journey. But surely the man was wrong – the cable was still stretched out behind the ship, although it didn't look quite the same as before. Perhaps because it had just come back into line as they'd dragged it back on course, Lee hoped. *Visibility is low in this rain, so maybe ...*

"Sir, we need to know," the engineer implored, cutting through Lee's thoughts.

"All right, man," Cyrus said impatiently. "Tell the captain to slow down and we'll watch the cable." *I guess it's better to find out now, before nightfall.*

One of the engineers went back to the bridge. Hobbs slowed the ship to one quarter ahead and said he would keep it there for a half-hour at most. He was still keen to put the bad weather some distance behind them.

The engineer returned aft to watch the cable in the evening twilight, and over the next twenty minutes, the three men stood in the light rain watching the cable drop down at an awkwardly steep angle into the water behind them. When Hobbs came out to join them he could see in their faces that the cable must have broken.

"It's done for," said Cyrus.

"Aye," said Hobbs. "But something seems to be holding it back. Winch it back in slowly and let's see what happens."

The engineers were happy to have something useful to do and set to the winch. One went below deck to find the others. Winching cable back on board was not the straightforward operation Hobbs had expected it to be. They had to rig one of the spindled cable drums in the hold with a makeshift crank and gather a couple of crewmen to help manually wind the cable back onto the drum. Without doing that, it would have coiled and twisted, creating a dangerous mess on deck. Hobbs remembered the poor man whimpering on the Liverpool docks as he died.

When the crewmen were ready, the men on deck locked the cable back into the winch and started reeling it back in slowly. Forty-five back-breaking minutes later, the men in the hold had just about filled a drum with the damp cable when the feed stopped. Night had fallen and the half moon was largely obscured by the overcast sky, so light was poor, but as they pulled the last of the cable up, they could see it was firmly attached to the remains of a fishing net. The old net appeared to have dredged up rigging and some timbers from an ancient shipwreck. There was also some other wreckage and detritus captured by the net. As the American silently withdrew, his shoulders slumped, they decided to haul the cable in as far as the taffrail and secure the net to the stern. They would haul it all in the next morning, hopefully in a calmer sea.

Hobbs went to find the captain and Cyrus Lee. There was an important decision to make. Hobbs rapped on the captain's door, half expecting to find him drunk, but was surprised when Kearney called back, "Enter."

"Captain, the cable has broken. The engineers and the crew have winched the remnant back to the ship. There's little point in steaming ahead to Canada," Hobbs said, as matter-of-fact as ever.

"Aye, son. I thought as much when you slowed engines." Captain Kearney had sobered up. "Best find Mr Lee."

"Captain." Hobbs nodded and left, as Kearney called out to meet him on the bridge.

Hobbs knocked on Lee's cabin door several times before the American called back. The door opened and Hobbs watched as Lee trudged slowly back inside and poured himself a large measure from a bottle of bourbon whiskey. A third of the bottle was gone. "We're done," he said, as he hung his head. "I'm done."

Hobbs gave the man a minute to compose himself. "The captain wants to see you. You have a decision to make." Hobbs waited, holding the door.

"Yes, I guess I do," said Lee. He shuffled to the door and Hobbs followed him to the bridge.

"Mr Lee, this is your voyage, but it seems to me that we must now decide whether to continue to Newfoundland, or possibly Halifax, or whether we turn back to Liverpool. From my reading, Canada is a day less sailing time, but there will still be ice in the Labrador Sea to slow us down."

Cyrus Lee's shoulders seemed to slump even further as he stared through the windows of the bridge at the rain falling into a heavy grey sea.

He did not relish the prospect of returning home to the United States having failed. His backers would be furious after the promises he had made them, and his business associates would be merciless in their ridicule. They had all told him it was a foolhardy venture. Equally, he did not want to go back to England. He had no friends there, and the harshness of life around the Liverpool docks was foreign to him, yet it was all he knew in England. In the end, it was a hard commercial reality that made his decision. His contract with the ship's owners required him to pay a consideration for the crew, and to resupply the ship for the return journey from Canada to England. He knew he could avoid the additional cost if they sailed back to Liverpool.

"Mr Lee? I need to set a course. What's your decision?" Captain Kearney was firm.

"We return to England, captain," Lee said with a sad resignation and shuffled back to his cabin.

Kearney asked Hobbs to take the dawn watch, and Hobbs was glad to be able to finish the meal he'd started before, and then get some rest. The bad weather they had encountered earlier had started to give way to a cold front with light winds, and Hobbs slept soundly until just before daybreak. He quickly climbed out of bed, donning his favourite jersey again and pulling on his boots. He could see the pale early light through his tiny porthole and reckoned today's weather would be better.

On the bridge, he saw the captain off at the end of his watch and asked the man at the helm how long he'd been there. The man looked tired but said only two hours. Hobbs sent him to fetch a drink, and he returned shortly with two mugs of steaming, sweet black tea.

"I'll wake the engineers when the sun comes up," Hobbs said, almost to himself. "Need to deal with that snag."

"Already on deck, aft," replied the crewman.

Hobbs looked out aft to see all four engineers in a huddle by the winches. Two of them started walking in the direction of the bridge. The breeze was straight from the Arctic, although the sea was now moderate, Hobbs reflected, warming his hands on his mug.

"Morning," one of the engineers said, more cheerfully than their situation warranted. Hobbs nodded to them. "We can cut the cable and drop the fouled net back into the sea," he said.

"No, we'll bring it on deck. Let's see what Neptune has given up." *It will give the crew something to do, and maybe if it's an old shipwreck, there'll be something of value*. He rounded up four crewmen and gave orders to haul the net onto the deck. For the next hour, it resisted their efforts, and by then, Hobbs had ten men working to haul it in. They had decided to use the winch as well to pull on the cable, to assist them. With all hands on the net and its contents, they slowly managed to pull it over the taffrail and drag it aboard. Hobbs lent a hand near where the cable held part of the net, and as the winch pulled on it, it suddenly lurched up as it topped the rail. Hobbs felt a searing pain in his left hand as something sliced through his skin.

He released his grip but it was too late; a torn piece of copper wire had cut deeply into his palm and blood was spurting out with each beat of his heart. He cursed loudly and strode to the bridge to fetch some towelling. He went back on deck, but within minutes the towel was red with blood. He would need to wake the surgeon and hoped the man was sober enough to help. He rapped on his door until he opened it. He did not look well, but when he saw Hobbs' hand he told him to come in. The surgeon fetched his bag, found a bandage then asked Hobbs to remove the towel.

"Not good," was all he said, as he and Hobbs looked at the blood pulsing out and the visible bone and tendons in his hand. The surgeon poured a large whiskey, and Hobbs was almost relieved when the man then handed him the glass. "You'll need it," the surgeon added as he rummaged through his bag again for a curved needle and some surgical cotton.

"What are you doing, man?" The surgeon's face contorted in bewilderment when Hobbs poured the liquor onto the wound instead of drinking it.

"An old man with scars once told me to do that so as to stop the fever that follows a wound like this," Hobbs observed, wincing.

"Each to his own," muttered the surgeon, shaking his head as he drove the needle into the flesh of Hobbs' left hand.

Half an hour later, with his left hand stitched and bandaged, Hobbs ventured back out to see how the men were getting on. His hand was now throbbing painfully, but the doctor had seemed to know what he was doing. Part way through the stitching ordeal, Hobbs had decided a stiff glass of whiskey was useful.

On deck, the men had landed the old net and its contents, and had started sorting through it. There was some rigging and a few small rotted timbers, from what appeared to be an ancient sailing ship. The vessel was perhaps a century old, and no doubt another victim of the infamous North Atlantic weather. Amongst the mess were a few brass rope hooks and other small brass or copper items the crew had already started to souvenir. Some of the men seemed disappointed they hadn't dredged up anything valuable.

One item among the detritus caught Hobbs' attention. It was a piece of dark greyish-brown stone that seemed incongruous with the other odds and ends spread out on the rear deck. With his good hand, Hobbs turned the stone over and saw strange and unfamiliar writing and bizarre lines, all heavily worn and quite hard to make out. It weighed less than a sack of coal, less than half a hundredweight, Hobbs figured, but with only one hand he could not pick it up.

He had already resolved that he would not be joining Cyrus Lee on any future cable-laying venture – his injury having reinforced his dislike of the unwieldy and dangerous cables – but he decided this odd stone would make a good souvenir of this strange voyage. He directed two crewmen to take it to his cabin. They looked bewildered but complied.

The men were in good spirits, glad to be heading back home earlier than expected, and many of them were also relieved the ship was no longer attached to miles of hefty cable. With the winches and remaining cable all secured, they were steaming back to Liverpool at a good clip, and should arrive, weather permitting, within the week, Hobbs hoped.

His watch for that day was uneventful, and the seas were slight to moderate. The sun had even penetrated the cloud cover for a few minutes during the afternoon. At the end of his watch, and after a hearty meal, Hobbs retired to his cabin. The stone tablet sat on the small desk next to his bunk, where the crewmen had deposited it. It was unlike anything he'd seen before. It was somehow compelling, and seemed to draw him in.

Shaped a bit like a piece of gravestone, although only around fifteen inches wide and of similar height. Clearly part of it had broken off, and the edge had started to wear smooth. What was left of the writing on it was unfamiliar, but that added to its mystery. It did not belong in an old fishing net from an ancient shipwreck, but neither did it belong on the floor of the Mid-Atlantic, the nearest known land mass being nine hundred miles away.

8

SOUTHERN ENGLAND

The captain announced they would be commencing their descent into Heathrow in ten minutes. The flight had been smooth, and Daniel had managed to get some sleep on the second leg, after a two-hour stopover in Hong Kong. They were on schedule to land at 6.30 am, so he would have plenty of time to get to the solicitor's office in Andover by midday.

'We shall look forward to making your acquaintance in person, Mr Reade,' Mrs Ramsay had said, when Daniel made an appointment the previous Friday. She'd said it with such formality he felt he might not be sufficiently presentable for Higginbotham & Marks, Barristers and Solicitors, having neither showered nor shaved for more than a day.

Nonetheless, given his early arrival, he would have plenty of time to supplement the in-flight breakfast with something more sustaining and enjoyable and have a look around for potential accommodation, assuming he needed it. He wasn't expecting to be able to stay in his dead uncle's house; at least not immediately.

After clearing customs, Daniel rented a grey Citroën C4. It was a minor extravagance, he rationalised, and although he didn't know if he would really need the extra luggage space, it might be handy. He was soon on the road, making his way out of the busy airport. The traffic coming out of Heathrow was busier than he was used to, but at least he was driving *away* from London. He'd put Andover into the GPS and was duly informed it would take ninety minutes, at least half an hour longer than he'd expected, based on the distance. When he joined the M25, he understood why. The orbital motorway around London was heavily congested. Once he reached the M3 to the south-west, the traffic improved dramatically. The weather was clear, with a light breeze. The motorways were better than at home, though the traffic was much heavier. And faster. People here seemed to ignore the speed limit.

A growing sense of anticipation had started to overtake Daniel as he pondered what the next few days or weeks would bring. It almost felt like a life change was in the wings. His initial sense of a tentative liberation from quitting his job and stepping out into the unknown had given way to a fully fledged sense of adventure. Maybe it was partly jet lag. Partly delirium. Although, he didn't feel jet-lagged, he felt more alive than he had for some time. Some years. *Maybe I've been in a rut for a long time without realising it.*

He'd had a lot of time to think on the long flight. The house might turn out to be a chocolate-box thatched cottage, or potentially, it could be in need of extensive repairs. *Will the house be tidy and bare? Or was old Edward a hoarder, and I'll spend the next few weeks disposing of twenty-year-old newspapers?*

After watching a dull movie on the flight, he'd started reading his new book; something he'd ordered online a few months ago and hadn't yet got around to. Lately, he'd been reading novels that were more recreational than thought-provoking; perhaps in itself another sign of the rut he'd slipped into. This book, *Ancient Traces,* non-fiction, was already proving to be an interesting read, offering some evidenced, alternative views to those of mainstream historians and archaeologists.

It had started to rekindle his interest in all things ancient, especially those with some mystery to them. The debate and controversy around evidence cited, and its far-reaching implications, coupled with the *une*videnced rejection by other academics, appealed to Daniel's enquiring mind. It was another tonic for his drained imagination.

A few miles past Basingstoke, Daniel took the A303 exit to Andover. He soon reached the High Street and found the solicitor's office and a café. He kept an eye out for a nice pub with guest rooms available. It was not quite ten o'clock, so plenty of time to get a feel for the place. He had travelled overseas by himself before and was comfortable in his own company. Setting off in a randomly chosen direction, he enjoyed walking around Andover. It was a treat to explore a town with a long history, modern intertwined with medieval. And although it was cool, it was almost windless; a rare thing in Wellington in the spring.

He reflected as he wandered that it was more than two years since he'd holidayed with anyone else. It wasn't that he was waiting for anything, or anyone, it was more that he just hadn't had much of an interest in travelling these past few years.

After a hearty but not-so-healthy breakfast, it was almost twelve o'clock when Daniel arrived at the solicitor's office. It was in a grand building above a bookshop. He climbed the well-polished timber stairs and entered through the heavy door with the firm's name in gold lettering on the etched glass panel.

"Can I help you?" said a stern-faced woman who looked older than his mother.

"Yes, my name is Daniel Reade. I've an appointment with Mr Marks."

"Ah, Mr Reade. We spoke on the telephone." The woman extended a bony hand with prominent blue veins to Daniel. "Margaret Ramsay, solicitor's clerk. I'm sure Mr Marks won't be too long. Please take a seat." She motioned him to an ancient chesterfield.

"It's nice to meet you, Mrs Ramsay," said Daniel. At that moment a man who looked to be in his seventies strode out of the office towards him.

"Godfrey Marks." He extended his hand. "Come in, young man."

Daniel followed Marks into his office, and they sat down on opposite sides of the leather-inset oak desk. The armchair might have been as old as Marks himself and almost swallowed Daniel as he sat. The solicitor picked up the solitary file on the desk and thumbed through the papers. He spent the next fifteen minutes explaining everything and talking about Daniel's uncle and the property Daniel had just inherited.

"Edward Foxton has been my client for nearly four decades," Marks said.

"You knew him well?" Daniel asked.

"In a business sense, yes. Mr Foxton was quite reserved. In fact, in his later years he kept mostly to himself." Marks had a storyteller quality to his voice, enhanced by the slight reverberation in the high-ceilinged, wood-panelled office.

"He once told me his social life consisted entirely of a twice-weekly evening meal at his local hotel, the Cross Keys," Marks went on. "I'm not sure that's entirely true, he seemed likeable enough. I've been there myself. The Cross Keys. It's a lovely old place with a truly medieval fireplace." Daniel was not sure what a 'truly medieval fireplace' might look like, but he didn't ask. He was sure he would find out soon enough.

"As I said in my letter to you, Mr Reade ..."

"Daniel, please."

"Of course, Daniel. As I said in my letter, Mr Foxton, your uncle Edward, I believe had some regrets regarding losing touch with his ... with your mother. He spoke of her occasionally, not without some nostalgia. He never married but maintained an interest in the family, so kept track of his niece and nephew also. Yourself and Kathryn."

"Katie."

"Yes, quite. *Katie.*"

"May I ask, since he knew he had a nephew *and* a niece, why did he not leave the house to both of us?"

"I asked him that very question. I was mildly concerned that should you ... well, should you ... let's say were you married, and you passed away, then the house may not stay within the family." Marks gave Daniel an awkward grin. "He'd made up his mind; nevertheless, he did want it to stay in the family, but he said you would be the fifth male heir to inherit. Tradition, I suppose.

"The house was built in the late sixteenth century. Elizabeth I, the Reformation, and all that. It was once part of a much larger estate." Daniel raised his eyebrows.

"Yes, but not the main house. It would have been an outbuilding of some sort. I haven't visited for some time, but Edward told me it was in need of some work. He told me he would leave that to the next owner." Marks chuckled. "It's Grade Two listed, I'm afraid, which limits things quite a bit.

"It does sit at the edge of a delightful village. Chidwick. Less than ten miles from here. The pub I mentioned, the Cross Keys, has guest lodgings, by the way, if you're so inclined. If you'll forgive my speculation, I suggest that option because the house still contains Edward's personal possessions, and I expect you will want to work through those."

"Thank you for thinking of that. Yes, I'm sure I will," Daniel replied. "May I ask how he died?"

"Ah, yes. He died while walking to his evening meal. Stroke. I understand he lost consciousness immediately and died soon after. He did not suffer."

Daniel was pleased to hear it, and pleased his uncle hadn't died in the house, although he wasn't sure why.

Marks went on to explain that there was also a bank account, into which Foxton's pension was paid, and that after the funeral expenses and the firm's 'modest fee', there would be a little under a thousand pounds left. The solicitor took details from Daniel's passport and promised to complete the necessary paperwork by the following afternoon. He gave him directions to the house.

"Thank you very much, Mr Marks. I appreciate your help and advice."

"Not at all, it's my pleasure. Edward was a good client. A true gentleman. It's nice to have met you, Mr Reade."

"Daniel, please. Thanks again, and goodbye for now. I'll be in touch in a few days."

From Andover, it turned out to be almost exactly eight miles to Chidwick, and as Daniel drove through the countryside, the roads progressively narrowed. It didn't take long at all for Daniel to feel completely outside of modern civilisation. At first, open meadows and occasional old houses, then forest, finally giving way to a narrow country lane.

As he navigated the hedgerows near the village, he hoped he didn't meet another vehicle travelling the other way. There was no room to pass, and very few places to pull off the road or turn. Finally, he reached the picturesque village. He drove on carefully past the old thatched pub, the Cross Keys, which looked just as inviting as Marks had promised. He followed Marks' directions to the house on the north-west edge of the hamlet. Most of the homes he drove past were centuries old, punctuated by old oak and chestnut trees, and other species uncommon in New Zealand. He also passed the occasional twentieth-century dwelling that seemed out of time and place. *It really is a 'lovely little village'.*

He pulled the Citroën into the narrow driveway, and parked it under an ancient oak tree. There were no tracks on the grass, nor any evidence of a car being regularly driven through the gate, so he assumed Edward had not owned one. The house was not quite as he'd imagined. It was a simpler affair: stone and red brick on its lower level, with a whitewashed wall and Tudor beams at the upper portion of the visible gable end. The roof was thatched and looked to have patches in disrepair.

The front door sat under a small thatched portico in the middle of the house, with a large bay window immediately to its left. It wasn't quite the chocolate-box cottage, but it was still rather appealing to Daniel. Under the thatch were four small upstairs windows. There were two large chimneys, one in the middle of the house, and one at the far end.

Shaking off the cold, he hoped that if fireplaces were the only heating, there was a good store of firewood. He walked the remaining few metres down the gravel path, past overgrown flowerbeds to the front door and inserted the key Marks had given him. The lock turned, and the door creaked open.

9

"John, come have a look at this," Mary Foxton called to her husband. They were down from Oxford for a holiday weekend, having decided to visit Mary's father's house; now hers, as his only issue. Eventually, they intended to live in Chidwick, but John's work as a professor of archaeology at Oxford came with tenure and comfortable living quarters, so they spent most of their time there. Their son James, now fifteen, had decided to stay in Oxford for the weekend. Mary was in the small room, one of the quirky rooms in the old house. It was connected to the main bedroom by an anteroom, now serving as a wardrobe.

The tiny room at the back was nothing more than a storage space. Ideal for hide-and-seek games, but little else. It was dark and claustrophobic, and its only use for decades, if not generations, had been to store the things nobody wanted. Long-forgotten memories, junk that was once someone's treasure. It was little wonder it had taken Mary three years to get to sorting through its contents.

Finally, she had overcome her reluctance and had decided to start cleaning it out. In the back corner, she found an old and rather battered steamer trunk. There were fresh scratches on the wooden floor where she had dragged it across, as it was too heavy to lift. Upon opening it, she had encountered a musty aroma reminiscent of the sea, presumably the product of its contents: an ancient pair of boots and a sailor's old duffel bag. Poking out from the top of the bag was a rather incongruous, heavy-looking piece of stone.

Mary turned around, and John Foxton was standing in the doorway smoothing his moustache, a subconscious gesture he often made when musing on something. He could see the stone slab in the bag and was immediately interested. Clearly it was man-made, not unlike a section of gravestone, but it was also obviously ancient. He wandered in, picked it up and turned it over, and was astonished to see the remains of characters that looked like Sanskrit.

Mary watched as his eyes opened wider. "I remember Grandpa Henry talking about this stone tablet when I was a little girl. We still lived in the pub in Plymouth then."

John knew Mary's grandfather had been a sailor and something of an adventurer, before settling into life as the landlord of a public house. He knew, too, that Mary's father, also named Henry, as well as taking over the pub, had been a black marketeer in the illicit liquor trade. He was a likeable rogue who had made enough money to ease into an early retirement in the country.

"Grandpa Henry had it on a shelf in the pub and told stories about finding it at the bottom of the Atlantic Ocean, 'a thousand miles from any land, where it must have sat since the dawn of time'. I always thought he made it up. He was a great storyteller. He told us stories of his voyage that laid the first transatlantic cable. I think it might have been on that same voyage that he dredged up this tablet. Mother and Father must have brought Grandpa's trunk here when they moved up at the turn of the century. What do you make of it, John?" Mary was looking at him intently.

"I don't know what to make of it," he replied after a moment's deliberation. He couldn't take his eyes off it. "I doubt it came from the deep Atlantic, though. Did your grandfather ever visit Asia?"

"I don't know, but I do know he gave up his seafaring life soon after he injured his hand quite badly. He was never able to handle ropes and rigging in the same way after that. Is this tablet from Asia?"

"The text looks rather like ancient Sanskrit. From India," he elaborated as Mary appeared confused. "But it's very difficult to make out. Let's get it into a better light." John carried the heavy tablet through the main bedroom, along the upstairs hallway and into the room he'd chosen as his study. The other upstairs bedroom, Mary's room when she was a child, had been reserved for son James. He placed the tablet gingerly on the leather-inset desk under the small window and peered at the strange characters. "Very interesting. Very interesting indeed," he said, almost to himself.

Mary left him to ponder the strange object as he reached for a small brush to clean off the dust. She could see he would be busy with it for a while. She went downstairs to the small kitchen to fetch him a pot of tea and some of the lemon cake she'd brought down from Oxford. He could often be so absorbed in his work that he would forget to eat. Mary wished James had come down with them. It wasn't just that he would be a help with the garden, but she was lonely. John was reserved and often deep in thought. Sometimes she didn't know if it was his work, or the war. The Boer War was long past, but she knew it had affected him deeply, and he never spoke of it. The Great War, although John didn't serve, had brought back those memories. He would become quiet and withdrawn if anyone ever asked him about his wartime exploits.

Mary took the tea and cake into John's study and left it on the table. He was making notes in an old journal and didn't notice her enter or leave.

Three weeks later, having taken the tablet back to their rooms at Oxford in order to work on the translation in the evenings, John Foxton was no further forward. He had observed there also appeared to be images on the tablet which could be mountains, or even waves, though it was impossible to determine. It still seemed to be an exciting find, but he was beginning to feel frustrated that the tablet was not revealing its secrets, and perhaps it never would. He decided to talk with a colleague, an expert on ancient languages, and discovered that some scholars believed ancient Sanskrit could have been closely related to a 'protolanguage', the mother tongue for Sanskrit, ancient Greek, Latin and other, or conceivably *all* old languages.

'Links to Sanskrit turn up in strange places, you know,' his colleague had said. 'It has notable similarities with Lithuanian and, to a lesser extent, Latvian and Icelandic.'

John started to look for similarities to other languages, ancient and more recent, to see if that would start to penetrate this puzzle. Within a few days, and with a little help from George, he started to discern some words. 'Voice of God' seemed to appear in a few places.

He continued the painstaking work, and as the weeks became months, he found himself rather disappointed that he seemed to have stumbled upon nothing other than some ancient religious dogma. 'Voice of God'; 'uplifting voice'; 'unburden'. Nothing that hinted at its origin, aside from the fact that it appeared to be an ancient language predating Sanskrit and a handful of northern European or Atlantic languages.

News of a Great Slump in the United States arrived in England the same year, and soon after the news stories, Britons started feeling the effects of the depression. Unemployment rose rapidly, creating harsh conditions across the nation. With a tenure at Oxford, Foxton was somewhat protected from the severest of the impacts, but the whole university seemed to just focus on keeping the basics going, with all the lecturing staff having concerns about cutbacks as a result of the smaller student roll. Foxton did not want to be seen as distracted, so he took the tablet back to Chidwick and let it alone.

* * *

JUNE 1937

The years of the Great Depression and events that followed – the Spanish Civil War and the rise of fascism in Europe – propelled John Foxton into a depression of his own. The rising violence took him back to the trenches in the Transvaal and the pictures in his mind of the ranks of men, his comrades, who were marched to their deaths. He progressively withdrew from aspects of his life and family, except for his teaching, and his withdrawal continued for some years after England had pulled itself out of the depression.

It wasn't until 1937 that Foxton learned, from another professor, of the interest the new German fascists had in ancient archaeology, whether to give credence to their pseudoscience, or to find lost technologies they could pervert into weapons. That sparked in Foxton a sense of moral outrage, the beginning of his road to recovery.

For Mary, the intervening years had been lonely, especially since James had married his long-time fiancée and moved away. She knew John needed a focus, something to occupy his mind, and she remembered the old stone tablet. With Mary's encouragement, John's interest was soon rekindled. Eighteen months later, with another world war looking increasingly inevitable, he retired from his professorship and they moved to the Chidwick house permanently.

Mary grew vegetables in the garden behind the house, and John spent time reading the rather extensive library he had amassed and brought down from Oxford. He continued working on translating the tablet, while trying to ascertain where it might have originated from. The fact the ancient protolanguage had links with Baltic and Icelandic languages was a clue that its origin was indeed somewhere in the Atlantic, as Mary's grandfather had professed. Unfortunately, that seemed impossible, since there was no land mass anywhere near where old Henry had said he'd found it.

The tablet seemed to be slowly yielding to Foxton's perseverance, and he'd noticed different nuances in the words he'd previously translated. 'Voice of God' had become 'voice [or sound] of doom'. He wondered if another interpretation could be 'instrument of doom', and there was a particularly worrying phrase that could mean '... consumed itself and all around it'. The tools he was using – the texts and scholarly articles – were, of course, filled with the archaeological biases of the time. It was quite difficult to get a real sense of meaning. And some of the pieces he'd translated just didn't make sense, so perhaps he was wrong. One small portion of text, if he was interpreting the worn characters correctly, appeared to say 'unburden stones', but that made no sense.

One aspect that did seem clear to Foxton was that it was potentially a doomsday prophecy, even a record of an ancient event or a lost knowledge of some kind. It no longer seemed like religious dogma. With the unnerving interest the fascists were taking in that sort of thing, Foxton decided he needed to take precautions, and he was careful about whom he spoke with.

Mary noticed John's study had recently become much tidier. There were fewer notes on his desk, and the thick old notebook with John's finely detailed drawings tucked between its pages had disappeared. It had been replaced with a neater, smaller notebook that sat on the desk next to the tablet. When John left the house, the tablet was nowhere in sight, and Mary wondered whether he was taking it with him. Occasionally she asked how the translation was going, and he would simply say 'oh, slowly, but it's keeping me amused', never elaborating further.

By the time the Germans were defeated at Stalingrad in February 1943, John had more or less stopped working on the tablet, although he was often preoccupied and deep in thought. One spring morning, he unexpectedly announced he was going up to Oxford to see an old friend. It was something he hadn't done for years, and he didn't return for three days. Mary was worried, as bombings were still a regular occurrence.

When John returned, he told her that he had gone to review some of his notes with 'an expert in ancient languages' but would not be drawn into further discussion. Mary had kept herself busy with the vegetable garden. She was now keeping chickens too, more for eggs than slaughter, though the occasional roast bird was a rare treat for them, as were the visits from James and his wife, who had announced they were planning to start a family immediately after the war.

10

Herr Leutnant Hans Strobl received a message from an intelligence operative in England, stating a useful artefact may have been located. That could mean almost anything, Strobl supposed, but in his position in Himmler's Ahnenerbe, he was responsible for acquiring 'useful artefacts', particularly those that supported the Aryan view of an ancient master race. Such finds usually served the finder very well, and Strobl was an ambitious man. He had pushed his way into the Ahnenerbe, not because of his ideology, but because of his lust for wealth and power. Not everything that was appropriated needed to go into the Nazi war machine, he reasoned.

Strobl was a slightly built man, with a high forehead and receding hair. He had joined the Nazi party when it gained power in 1932, seeing the opportunity. He was unpopular at school and had few friends, but that had not curbed his ambition. In fact, it fuelled his disdain for others. The Nazi party suited him well, and when he'd had the opportunity, he demonstrated his ruthlessness to his superiors, securing his position in the Schutzstaffel. Soon after, he decided the Ahnenerbe was the most logical arm of the SS for him, since it focused on potential treasures and artefacts.

Personally, he felt that a lot of the expeditions conducted by the

Ahnenerbe were a waste of time and resources, such as those to Greenland and the Arctic, but it was of little consequence to him if men died needlessly. The expeditions he was most interested in were in Europe, where there was ample opportunity to appropriate all manner of valuable items.

A week later, Strobl received confirmation this particular artefact was, indeed, of interest. It was an ancient stone tablet that seemed to refer to a potential 'instrument of doom [or destruction]', therefore possibly a powerful weapon, so it had his undivided attention. He immediately despatched two men across the channel, where they would meet another on the south-east coast of England and bring back the artefact. He ordered his man at Oxford University to obtain the tablet, then get it to Folkestone, where a small boat would arrive in three days. The Oxford contact had protested that travelling far across the war-ravaged country would be difficult, but Strobl dismissed his concerns. He assumed the man just didn't want to venture to the coast and into the path of the bombers.

Strobl decided he would not alert his superiors until he knew what he had. Since Stalingrad, he had been developing alternative options, in the event that the war did not go the way they intended. Ever the pragmatist, he was not a man to fight to the bitter end. If he fled, he would leave with the gold and other acquisitions he had been covertly storing since earlier that year. He was ruthless in his procurement, supplying occasional offerings he could not sell for himself to his Ahnenerbe masters. If the war lasted another year, he would by then be a rich man, and still barely out of his thirties.

*   *   *

CHIDWICK, ENGLAND, JULY 1943

James Foxton drove his mother Mary back from Andover in his ten-year-old Rover. Mary didn't drive, and when James offered her a lift to buy the fortnightly supplies, she was grateful. It also gave her more time to talk with her son. James's father had decided to stay at home for the afternoon. She opened the front door and called out to John, as James carried the bags inside, down to the small kitchen at the back. There had been no answer; John was no doubt in the study, fully immersed in whatever he was doing.

Mary heard James close the back door and wondered why John had left it open. Perhaps it was just the July warmth. She called again as she went to put the kettle on the Aga and unpack the groceries.

"James, would you mind going upstairs to see if your father wants a cup of tea?" She started to put groceries into the kitchen cupboards, and just a few moments later she heard James cry out and knew something was terribly wrong.

II

D aniel had moved into the Chidwick house. He spent most of his time
between the drawing room and the upstairs study, sorting through
Edward Foxton's possessions and papers, trying to decide what to do with
it all. The Cross Keys was a nice little pub, and only a short walk, but he
liked the house and was getting used to setting an evening fire in the
drawing room and sorting through papers over a glass of wine. He had
disposed of all the old bed linen and bought fresh new bedding from a
store in Andover, and he'd started to restock the kitchen with the basics.

He had signed all the papers Marks had prepared and was soon to be
the legal owner of a house that he had no idea what to do with. He had
spoken with his mother and told her about it and some of the old paintings
he found stored in the little room behind the main bedroom. She had
remembered some of them from her childhood. He also told her the story
Marks had relayed of the unsolved murder of his great-grandfather John
Foxton, during World War Two. Alice remembered hearing it, although
she never knew any details. Her father had rarely spoken of it. A failed
burglary attempt was all James had ever said to her.

Daniel walked to the Cross Keys, pondering the unexpected turn his
life had just taken. Godfrey Marks had asked him what he wanted to do

with the house, and he'd said honestly that he didn't know. Daniel asked about its value, and Marks said a character, detached house like his could sell for well over £600,000. That would buy his modest home in central Wellington twice over.

The pub's landlord greeted him, and he ordered his meal along with a pint of the local bitter he'd become fond of. He took his drink over to a small table near the oversized fireplace, which was large enough for a good-sized fire, plus some wood storage, and there were even two electric lights inside the stonework to add to its imposing effect.

There were only two other people in the pub, a middle-aged couple having a hushed conversation. While waiting for his meal, Daniel picked up a book about the old village houses of Wiltshire from the shelf next to his table. He thumbed through it, half wondering whether his would be amongst them, having been built during the reign of Elizabeth I. It said that was the period in which many houses had secret chambers, the so-called priest holes, for Catholic priests to hide in during times of persecution. These secret places, often the size of a small cupboard, were commonly built into panelled walls or concealed in masonry around fireplaces. He had heard of priest holes before, but had assumed they would be rarities only associated with grand manor houses. According to the book, they were quite common, even in more modest homes. Daniel couldn't help but think of the five fireplaces and wood-panelled walls of the Foxton house.

In fact, the house had six fireplaces, if he counted the Aga and old bread oven in the kitchen's back wall. Three of those fireplaces were set into the elaborate panelling. His dinner arrived and he ate quickly, eager to get back and do some exploring. Draining the remainder of his pint, he wished the landlord a goodnight, put on his jacket and went back to the house.

He reasoned that the most logical location would be around the vast inglenook fireplace in the drawing room. A tape measure would be handy – he wanted to look for inconsistencies in room dimensions – but a quick search of the kitchen and utility rooms did not yield one.

After half an hour of tapping and pressing the panelling, he reverted to improvised measurement using a ball of string and drawing pins from a cupboard. He measured the length of the wall that separated the drawing room and kitchen, on both sides, and then, by the light of the moon, measured outside. The difference looked to be about a foot, which he decided was the depth of the old masonry. No room for a priest hole there. He then moved the heavy coffee table and rolled up the old drawing room carpet, searching the floor for signs of a trapdoor of some kind. No luck there either.

The dining room was next, and it was fairly easy to determine that there was no room to hide anything, let alone a person, in the wall. He'd already discovered the concealed door leading to the utility room at the back of the house, cleverly disguised in the panelling. That would have been servant access from the kitchen, through the original pantry. With a little effort, he managed to open the hidden door, now blocked by storage on the other side, but it was not a priest hole. Under the stairs proved to be similarly bereft, and it had been depressingly renovated – in Victorian times, Daniel guessed – to add a toilet.

Opposite the dining room fireplace was the door to a nanny or maid's room, with an even smaller room behind it, possibly a nursery. Alice had told Daniel, when he'd called her after exploring the house for the first time, that her grandmother, Mary, had moved into the maid's room soon after John Foxton had been killed. Mary had insisted, so James and his wife could have the master bedroom. Mary had used the little nursery room as a wardrobe. There was nothing in either of these rooms that suggested a possible hiding place.

The next possibility was the third bedroom, or study, upstairs. It was directly above the drawing room and shared the same chimney, so Daniel was not particularly confident. When he measured the walls, with his ball of string, he found a possible anomaly. He rechecked his measurements, and it seemed the study, from doorway to fireplace, might have been about eighteen inches too short. He was measuring the wall adjacent to the bathroom next door (which was above the kitchen), and the rooms were very different sizes. Neither did the bathroom have a fireplace, so if there were a space concealed there, it was cleverly done. He searched for joints or fine cracks in the panelling, to no avail. Then started tapping sections of walls. The space to the left of the fireplace sounded different. Not necessarily 'hollow' but it had a slightly different timbre to the other side.

The anomaly in the wall's length, coupled with the subtly different sound, had spurred him on. He'd been searching for nearly two hours now but kept going. He tried anything he could think of. There were rosettes in the panelling, along with a candleholder each side of the fireplace, so he tried turning or pulling those. One of the rosettes moved a little. Maybe just loose, but he put both hands firmly on it and tried again. It rotated a quarter turn, but there was no 'click'. No magically opening panel. *Nothing.* He started tapping again, looking for a section with anything at all different about it. When he pushed against the wall, this time it depressed slightly, and he heard a faint click. He pressed again, and the wall slipped inwards a centimetre, then came back out towards him, slowly creaking its way ajar and into the study. He gingerly pulled it open, exposing a secret space that was close to eighteen inches deep and almost two feet wide.

The secret door was cleverly cut into the panels, so as to be invisible when closed, and was almost the full height of the panelling, at about five feet. The priest hole was slightly taller inside. At some point, someone had clearly repurposed it, because its shelves were much younger than the oak panelling. On one of the shelves was a dark-brown, waxed cardboard box, in which he could see some yellowed papers and an old notebook. He carefully lifted the box out and placed it on the desk. The journal had the name John Foxton embossed onto the cover in an elegant script. It was filled with detailed notes and illustrations in a similarly elegant hand.

12

Mary Foxton quickly put down the box of flour she'd been pouring into a large earthenware jar and ran upstairs. James's face had turned pale, and just beyond him, Mary saw John lying on the floor of his study. There was a nasty wound on the side of his head and a small pool of blood on the carpet. Mary gasped and staggered backwards, James only just catching her as she fell. She wanted to go over to John, but James stopped her. He had already checked for signs of life and found John still, cold and clearly no longer alive.

Mary could not take it all in. "How ...?"

"He could have fallen and hit his head on the desk," James said, but he didn't believe it. The desk was too far away, and John's head injury looked much more serious than a desk might inflict. James ushered Mary out and into the other upstairs bedroom to sit down. They were both shocked and didn't speak for a few minutes.

"We need to notify the police," James said. "I can't believe a fall could cause that."

Mary nodded, sobbing.

James went down to the telephone in the hallway and asked the operator for the Andover constabulary.

Two uniformed policemen arrived half an hour later, accompanied by a man in a suit who introduced himself as the medical examiner. James showed them up to the study. The medical examiner inspected the wound on the back of John's head and spoke quietly to the two constables.

"Has anything been taken?" one of the uniformed men asked James.

"I'm afraid I don't know. I'll have to ask mother," he replied, shaking his head. He went to fetch Mary, who was still obviously deeply shocked. She shuddered as she saw John's body lying on the floor.

"I'm afraid it looks like it may be a burglary. Perhaps your husband disturbed them," said the constable gently.

"He should have been in the town with us," Mary sobbed.

"Has anything been taken, madam?"

Mary composed herself and looked around the room. "The stone tablet. And his notebook," she said to the mystified men. "He's an archaeologist. He was translating an old stone tablet," she explained. "Who would want that?"

"It does seem odd, madam. Was it valuable? This stone tablet?"

"I don't think so. Maybe worth something to a museum, but I doubt it would be much," James said.

"Hmm. Did he keep any money or valuables in here?"

"Not to my knowledge. He was an archaeologist," she repeated. It just didn't make any sense.

"May I trouble you to check the rest of the house, please?"

Mary shuffled off and checked her small jewellery box in the main bedroom; everything seemed to be in order. She asked James to check the silverware in the dining room. Nothing else seemed to be missing. There might have been another notebook, but she couldn't be sure.

The uniformed men completed their paperwork, and the medical examiner asked them to bring in a stretcher and carry John's body downstairs. It was all very businesslike, and Mary just watched, tears rolling down her cheeks, as they carried her husband out and loaded his lifeless body into the back of the black police wagon.

"He was obsessed by that stone," Mary said in a small voice. "Who would do this? Who would want an old stone tablet like that?"

James shook his head. It didn't make any sense to him either.

* * *

SALZBURG, AUSTRIA, SEPTEMBER 1944

The two small lorries had just arrived from the Altaussee Salt Mines, after a three-hour trip through mountainous terrain. The drivers stepped out onto the road to stretch their legs after their bone-shaking trip. The front vehicle, with the senior officer driving, had two large crates in the back, and the rear vehicle had a single crate, all concealed by green tarpaulins securely lashed down. The second lorry had started with two crates, but they had detoured through Bad Aussee, not far from the mines, where the officer had completed a transaction. The two men had loaded one of the crates onto another truck that drove off eastward, in the direction of Graz or Vienna.

Altaussee had seen a good deal of road traffic during the later years of the war. The Nazis had used the dry salt mines to store priceless valuables, appropriated from great cities like Prague, Budapest, Warsaw and others all over the occupied territory. It was unusual for goods to be leaving the mines, although traffic out had increased lately as the tide of war seemed to be turning.

The officer had conscripted the other man to 'safeguard valuable artefacts for the Ahnenerbe, in support of the Third Reich'. The non-commissioned man did not believe him but asked no questions. His superior was favoured by Schutzstaffel leaders and had recently been promoted. He knew enough to know the officer was not a man to be questioned.

They parked their vehicles outside a small house near the Festung Hohensalzburg, an eleventh-century fortress perched on a hilltop in the old city. The two men battled to get the heavy crates off the lorries and into the cellar of the old house. It was now near dark and no one was around. Nobody living in this part of Salzburg, nor most other occupied cities, paid any attention to the action of men in SS uniforms. It was best not to see, and not to be seen.

With the assistance of a wheeled trolley already in the cellar, the men managed to get the crates to the stairs then slide them down. Exhausted, they finished pushing them to the back wall, and the officer directed the younger man to bring the trolley down the stairs. He locked the external door from the inside, and as the other man stood the trolley next to the crates, the officer withdrew his pistol and calmly shot the man in the back of the head. He looked down disdainfully at the mess on the concrete floor, reached down and took the man's papers, his wallet, pistol and the keys to the second lorry. He then wrenched the dog tags from his neck, pocketing them, and wiped his hands on the man's coat.

Satisfied with a scan of the cellar, the officer climbed the internal stairs into the kitchen. He had purchased the house several weeks earlier with the proceeds of a recent black-market sale of stolen artworks. He locked the door to the cellar stairs and exited through the front door. He then drove the second lorry to the other side of the Salzach River and parked it on the roadside. On his way back to the house, across the Caroline Bridge, he tossed the keys and the driver's tags and papers into the river. He emptied the man's wallet and threw that into the Salzach too.

The man had only a few Reichsmarks in his wallet, but the major was pleased with his night's work. In his coat pocket he had ten thousand Reichsmarks from the sale of the fourth crate. More than a few years' annual earnings, from a box full of trinkets and old books. He smiled to himself. One of the books was prized by the collector who had bought the whole crate. It was a manuscript penned by Guillaume de Machaut in 1375. Machaut was a poet and advisor in the court of King John of Bohemia, Prague. The major could not read Latin, but the papers with the manuscript were in German and told him of its value, as well as alluding to some of its contents: secret knowledge, ships of light, mystical lands; the kind of medieval fanciful musings and nonsense that Himmler was so enamoured of.

Whatever the case, it had certainly proved useful. The crate was probably in Vienna by now, and the major was a wealthier man, a step closer to a comfortable exit from Hitler's Third Reich madness. He smiled again as he entered the house. With another lorry of crates would be another sale of useless antiquities, and he would move to Milan, on through southern France to Spain and then across the Atlantic. The future was bright indeed for Herr Major Hans Strobl.

13

Daniel carefully laid out the contents of the dusty waxed carton on the desk. The box had darkened over time but was still in good condition. Inside, in addition to the leather-bound journal, there were loose sheets of paper inserted inside its back cover, a thin sketchbook containing detailed drawings, several photographs that had faded to a very amber sepia, and a couple of letters.

The photographs were all of the same subject: a piece of an ancient-looking stone tablet with areas of worn symbols or text, and lines that could once have been images. It was hard to make out, and all of it unfamiliar to Daniel.

The two letters were addressed to 'Prof. J Foxton, St Dunstan Hall', from 'Prof. Geo. W Billings, Leamington College'. The script was elaborate and quite difficult to read. The letters appeared to refer, in some depth, to the etymology of ancient Sanskrit and its relationship to other languages. They would wait for now. First, Daniel would satisfy his piqued curiosity – the contents of the box were his great-grandfather's *secret* notes; a relic from the past, concealed generations ago, for reasons he hoped he could piece together from the contents.

Foxton's journal was comparatively easy to read, at least in terms of the handwriting, although the subject matter appeared at first to be impenetrable, and there was a great deal of detail. He skimmed through the pages to discover that it was a comprehensive record of Foxton's efforts to translate the text on the ancient tablet. The source of the tablet itself was less clear. Foxton's early notes stated it had allegedly been hauled up in a tangled, waterlogged mess during the laying of the first transatlantic telegraph cable. There was no further corroboration of that and no precise location.

Foxton's drawings revealed a greater level of detail than Daniel could discern from the photographs, so he assumed they must have been carefully drawn from the tablet itself. He had another look inside the priest hole but there was no sign of the tablet, or anything else, useful or otherwise.

Throughout the professor's notes were translated words and phrases, with pictures of the ancient characters next to them. It looked religious to Daniel. 'Voice of God', 'uplifting voice', then later, 'voice of doom'. And further, Foxton had written 'unburden [to somehow lighten?] stone tablets [blocks]'. About three-quarters of the way through the notebook, Foxton had written 'instrument of [destruction] ... of people and of earth. Is this a *weapon?*' Near the bottom of the page he had written 'Doomsday Tablet', underlined. Was this why Foxton had secured his notes inside the priest hole? Daniel wondered. The dates in the notebook reminded him this was all unfolding for Foxton during World War Two. But where was this *Doomsday Tablet?*

It was now after one o'clock in the morning. Daniel wearily pushed his hands through his hair. The last few hours had flown by. He'd been totally absorbed and energised by his exciting find, and the myriad questions in his mind. *Where is the tablet?* **What** *is the tablet? Why was the old box hidden away so painstakingly? Why had the translation been so difficult?* Sanskrit was a known and well-studied language. He remembered Marks' words; that his great-grandfather had been *murdered*. And his mother's recollection that it had happened during a burglary at the house. Could there be a connection?

He yawned as he scratched his head, realising he needed some sleep. Tomorrow, he resolved, he would drive up to Oxford, visit St Dunstan Hall and find out more about his ancestor.

Daniel had found a place to park, having driven up from Chidwick after a quick breakfast of fruit and toast. He'd not finished sorting through Edward Foxton's papers and effects, but the mystery around his unexpected find last night was irresistible. His uncle's papers could wait.

He slung his backpack over his right shoulder and entered the university grounds, not exactly sure where he was headed. The campus was larger and more sprawling than he expected. After more than ten minutes of wandering and asking occasional directions, he finally reached his destination. Off the High Street, a few metres down a narrow lane opposite University College, he came to a stone arch that signified St Dunstan Hall. Through the short passage and past the porter's lodge, he arrived at the front quad. The passage opened onto a manicured lawn with a fountain in the centre, and he was surrounded by three- and four-storey medieval buildings. None of them gave any indication of a visitors' office or information kiosk, or such. Victoria University in Wellington was nothing like this place. Being perched on the side of hill probably helped keep Victoria more contained, but it had signs everywhere.

Here at Oxford, he imagined, one was expected to know where one was going. He chose the most ornate-looking doorway, and it was a good guess. In the oak-panelled walls were a number of large, heavy doors, but one of them had OFFICE in gold lettering. He knocked and a woman called back, "Come in."

Inside were stands containing brochures and a handy map he could have used twenty minutes ago. There were also shelves and tables with books for sale.

"Can I help?" An attractive woman in her early twenties with a small diamond stud in one nostril and luxuriant red hair was standing in front of Daniel.

"Well, yes, I hope so. I'm looking for information about a past professor of this college, an archaeologist named John Foxton. He was my great-grandfather. Died during the Second World War."

"Oh. Come with me. I'm Tania, by the way." She beamed as he extended his hand.

"Daniel Reade."

She gently brushed past him as they navigated the brochure stands, and opened the door for him. She smelled subtly of vanilla. He followed her across the main hall and into a large, formal dining room with eight tables that would each seat at least a dozen people. She gazed around the walls, upon which were carved timber boards covered in names of former professors, benefactors, famous alumni and scores of others. On the far side she spotted the right panel. About a third of the way down, there he was in fine gold-leafed letters: *John Foxton, Professor of Archaeology, 1917–1939.*

"Your grandfather?"

"Great-grandfather," Daniel corrected. "Do I look that old?"

She just smiled at him. "From New Zealand?"

"Good guess," he answered. "People often mistake my accent as Australian. I was born here, but I've lived in New Zealand since I was seven."

"Come with me," she beckoned, leading him out of that august room and back to the office. She found Daniel a book about the college during the war years, which had references to Professor John Foxton. She also located several texts written by the man himself, but none were about a stone tablet or any similar artefact. Daniel was disappointed, although he bought the book about the college during Foxton's tenure.

"How would I find out more about his work?" he asked, as he put the book into his backpack.

"Well, as he was a senior faculty member, we would have his records in the archive. Those are in the Colchester Building. It's just next door," Tania elaborated, pointing to her right. "You might also try the researchers' rooms. They might know some of his work."

"That sounds good. How do I find them?"

"Come with me, I know exactly where we should start. It's not far."

She led him to the wide staircase, up to the landing, which had two small doors leading off from each side, then up the left-hand flight to the first floor. The doors along the wide hallway had no descriptions, just names. Tania opened the door of the Foxton Room, and Daniel followed her in.

14

"That's odd, don't you think?" They were looking at a large monitor displaying a complex graphical representation of the ocean floor.

"Yes, I think Rove has *definitely* found something strange, David," said Willow.

Rove was what they called the Remotely Operated Vehicle or ROV, that was currently roughly three thousand metres below their survey ship. Their current location was in the Mid-Atlantic, as they updated hydrographic survey data along the path of most of the transatlantic communications cables. The equipment now available yielded a good deal more detail than was possible in the last survey, completed about fifteen years earlier. That was almost a dozen years before David and Willow had commenced their studies at the University of Plymouth. Practical hydrography was part of their master's degree, but to be able to join this particular voyage was a real treat.

On the screen before them were lines that could represent man-made structures, possibly ancient ruins. The regular lines certainly did not appear to be natural features, and they had seen nothing like them previously on the voyage.

"I'll get the others," David said, leaving the workspace they'd set up in one of the large compartments below deck. Willow continued to watch the monitor, checking they were taking as wide a sweep as possible, and recording everything.

David returned with three others: Hasan, also a hydrography student; Marie, a geology student; and Owen, an archaeologist who was now studying geology as well. They looked at the monitor to see a perfectly plain and normal seabed.

"What's up?" said Owen.

"A couple of minutes ago we encountered an anomaly. Let me scroll back," Willow said, clicking the mouse on the timeline roughly five minutes prior. The screen immediately changed, and the shapes and straight lines returned.

"That's odd," said Hasan. "Where are we again?"

"About fifteen hundred kilometres from the nearest land mass," replied Marie. "In three thousand metres of water."

"This is amazing," said Willow. "How can there be ruins here?"

"There cannot be ruins here." Owen was the oldest among them, an archaeologist completing his second degree, in geology, in his late twenties. "There's never been a civilisation anywhere near here. My guess is that it's a sunken ship, or several ships. What we must be seeing is cargo strewn across the seabed, or maybe the remnants of a naval battle."

As he spoke, Willow brought up pictures on another screen, showing scale on both axes. "This is no ship. This area ..." she ran her finger around the perimeter of the geometric shapes "... is the size of a football field. Or even a whole *village*."

"Naval battle then," said Owen. "There's no way it could be an archaeological site. It's just not possible."

"And yet here it is," said Marie. "Just because archaeology says it *can't* be here, doesn't mean it's impossible. What about Yonaguni?"

The Yonaguni monument was the subject of heated debate amongst scientists of various disciplines, most notably geologists and archaeologists. Marie described its pillars, columns, straight walls and various geometric shapes cut into monolithic stones, and explained that it is heavily eroded, thus not indisputably conclusive. Some geologists argued that it cannot be a natural formation, that there are no known processes that could create it. Archaeologists (and some geologists) argued that it *is* natural and could not have been created by man, particularly given its underwater location, tens of metres below sea level in the East China Sea. Marie was implying that archaeological dogma was the foundation of Owen's view.

"Most scientists agree that Yonaguni is a natural phenomenon," said Owen, testily.

"This isn't Yonaguni," interrupted Hasan. "This is two miles below sea level, and it doesn't look like a shipwreck to me. Look at this area." He pointed at a large rectangle that was mostly intact. "It must be ten by fifteen metres. And these ..." pointing to a line of smaller features that could be the size of a refrigerator. "How would you explain these?"

"Could be anything," said Owen, somewhat defensively.

"Well not quite *anything*, in my view. Let's say it was a naval battle. How would the wreckage, having sunk *in the ocean currents* to this depth, have landed on the sea floor *in regular straight lines* like these?"

"I think we need to get this data back to Plymouth and study it in detail," Willow said firmly. "There's little point in debating a few screen snapshots here."

Marie agreed with her, and the others said there was no point in arguing.

"Yes, let's analyse the detailed data, like proper scientists," said Owen, wanting the last word. "We can all agree it's an anomaly in the seabed, whatever it may, or may *not*, be," he added pointedly.

Willow collated the data files and related charts, adding a note referencing the recording's timeline, in which she referred to it as 'David's anomaly', since he was the one who first saw it. She then uploaded the files via satellite.

15

The room was not what he expected. Gone was the dark-timber panelling, replaced by white plaster walls lined with bookshelves that were no more than a few decades old. From the high ceilings, lights were suspended from the timber beams crossing the room. The bulk of the room was taken up by benches with several people working at them. One reading, one examining some sections of ancient pottery, and a young woman studying a large screen with detailed images he couldn't make out from where he stood. They all looked up at him as Tania announced his presence.

"Daniel Reade. From New Zealand. He's researching John Foxton." She beamed at him. "Please let me know if I can be of more help."

Daniel smiled back and thanked her.

The man who had been examining the pottery wandered over to him. "Alan Richards," he said, shaking Daniel's hand. "Foxton, eh?" He nodded at an old portrait high on a wall. It was a distinguished portrayal of a man who looked to be in his fifties, with a long, slim face, brown hair neatly parted close to the centre, and a well-trimmed chevron moustache. Professor Foxton appeared deep in thought and had serious but kind features.

71

"He was my great-grandfather," Daniel explained. "I've just inherited his house, rather unexpectedly, from my late uncle, and I've unearthed some research papers Professor Foxton seems to have been working on when he died." He wasn't sure how much to say. "It seems to relate to ancient languages, or at least the text on an artefact he was studying."

"What was the artefact?" Richards asked.

"I don't know. It isn't with his notes. Perhaps it was something here." Daniel wasn't sure why, but he didn't want to tell the man too much. Was he just being overcautious because of the elaborate lengths Foxton had gone to in order to maintain secrecy? Of course, there was his *murder*.

"That's more Elisa's field," said Richards.

The young woman looked over and her eyes met Daniel's for a moment. With a click of the mouse, her screen saver took the place of the image she'd been studying, and she stood and went over to Daniel. She was wearing a grey jersey, and blue jeans with the hems tucked into low brown lace-up boots. She was around a hundred and sixty-eight centimetres tall, slightly more with the heels. Her dark hair was cut just above her shoulders, and a wisp covered her left eye until she tucked it behind her ear absentmindedly.

"Elisa Mansfield," she said, with a hint of accent from his part of the world. She extended her hand. "Can I help?"

She had a natural beauty, with a hint of vulnerability in her slightly elfin face. But her expression seemed to Daniel to say 'you're interrupting me, so please get to the point'.

Daniel repeated the explanation he'd given to Richards and asked her whether she knew of Foxton or his work. She said 'yes, a little', but couldn't elaborate much more.

"Did you say Professor Foxton was translating an artefact?" she asked, her eyes now studying his face.

"Yes. Well, I think so. I haven't found whatever it was he was working on, but I have some of his notes."

"Do you have them with you? Maybe I could take a look?" she offered.

"Ah no, I didn't bring them with me." There was something compelling in her green eyes that had caught Daniel off guard. "Do you work in ancient languages?" he asked, feeling clumsy.

"A little. Archaeology is my field, but I'm researching ancient languages as they relate to my work. Among other things," she said cryptically. "Pity you didn't bring his notes."

"Actually, I have some photos that may be helpful." Daniel took an envelope out of his backpack and showed Elisa the sepia photographs he'd discovered with Foxton's notebook. "Do you know this language?" he asked hopefully.

"It's quite hard to make out, but no, I don't think I do. Robert, could you take a look at this?"

The older man who had been reading came over to them and studied the pictures for a full thirty seconds before responding. "Odd. It's a bit like ancient Sanskrit at first glance, but then it isn't."

Daniel waited for him to continue.

"Ah, let me see if I can try to explain. Imagine if you looked at some script written in old English. With patience, you would be able to make out the letters and probably determine many of the words. Have you read Shakespeare?"

"Yes," said Daniel, as he wondered where this was going.

"Good, good. Well now, imagine if you glanced at old English text and thought you recognised it, but then you looked more closely and it turned out more than half the characters were *unknown* to you – you'd never seen them before – and as you got closer, very few of the words made any sense at all. That's where I think we are with this script. Looks a bit like Sanskrit, but isn't," the man repeated. "Do you have the object?"

"No."

"Pity," the man said, his interest beginning to wane. "I'll leave you in Elisa's hands then." He nodded to Daniel and turned back to his bench and his papers.

"Okay, thank you," Daniel said, as the man stepped away.

"Looks like you've got a mystery there," the man called over his shoulder. "Do let us know if you find the object."

Daniel looked at Elisa and shrugged.

"Do you know where it came from?" she asked.

"Professor Foxton's notes said it was allegedly hauled up from the Mid-Atlantic, a thousand miles from land and in two miles of water. Not much use, I'm afraid."

"I'm sorry we couldn't be of any more help," Elisa said. "You might try the college archive for more information about your grandfather's work."

"*Great*-grandfather," he corrected.

"Oh, yes, sorry. Good luck." Daniel felt he'd been dismissed. "Can I leave you my contact details in case ... well, in case anything comes up?"

"All right. If you want to," she said noncommittally.

She seemed to be distracted. Or disinterested perhaps, though he hoped not. As he wrote his details on the piece of paper she'd handed him, he tried to break the ice again.

"Are you from Australia?" he asked, placing the slight trace of accent.

"Originally," she answered matter-of-factly. No thawing today, apparently.

"Thanks for your help. It was nice to meet you."

"And you," she responded politely, with a half-smile.

16

Eight men boarded the vessel bound for South America. They embarked separately and did not speak with one another. Each had a good deal of luggage, which together amounted to eight large trunks and several generous duffel bags. There were also six heavy wooden crates that had required four men each to lift. The captain of the vessel had received a sum of money that would allow him to retire, and he had asked no questions of these men.

They did not have German names, nor did they wear uniforms, but the captain recognised their accents. These were not the first Germans he had taken across the Atlantic. Over the past six months, since the Allies had landed at Normandy, there had been many other voyages like this one. These men, like most of the others, had been well fed and well dressed. It was obvious they were not refugees. One of them, the man who had overseen the loading of the crates, looked at the captain on his way to his first class cabin, and the captain felt a shiver as he met the man's cold blue eyes.

Were it not for those chilling eyes, the captain might have considered killing these men and taking their cargo for himself. But his instinct told him that crossing them would be a perilous course of action, no matter

75

the value of their precious loot. *Works of art?* he wondered. *Gold? Precious antiques?*

Josef Zapomny had made the arrangements for the voyage several weeks earlier. He had paid a significant sum for their passage and had taken measures to ensure they would be secure and no questions would ever be asked. He had contemplated arranging for the murder of the captain and crew when they reached their destination but decided the men were sufficiently complicit that they would never reveal what they knew.

The eight passengers were familiar with the journey, inasmuch as they had, for a large fee, made these arrangements for others. Unlike the other voyages, however, this journey would take the eight men to São Paulo, Brazil, and not Argentina or Uruguay. Zapomny had already made arrangements in São Paulo and would soon be established as an escaped Polish businessman. The other seven had made similar arrangements. Everything was in place.

Zapomny was particularly pleased with his name. It was a variation of 'zapomniany', meaning 'forgotten' in Polish. With his cargo, he was wealthy enough to begin a comfortable new life and leave the old behind. He could soon forget that he had been born with the name Hans Josef Strobl.

17

E lisa Mansfield was still reeling from the information she had received just before the interruption. She also reflected that it seemed a remarkable coincidence. An hour earlier she'd had an email from the University of Plymouth, with images from a hydrographic survey. A geologist on the survey ship thought the images could signify ancient ruins, placed, impossibly, in the Mid-Atlantic. And then fifteen minutes later, a man walked into their research room talking about an ancient artefact dredged up from the Mid-Atlantic, with an unidentified language on it.

Elisa's life was quite orderly. She didn't believe in random coincidence. There had to be something to this, and puzzles always drew her in. Since childhood, she had been fascinated by the unexplained. Mysteries from the deep past she'd read about at school, such as the megaliths at Baalbek, were one of the things that attracted her to archaeology and history at university.

Questions filled her mind. Could it be that the hydrographic survey has located ancient ruins on the Mid-Atlantic Ocean floor? Where no known land has ever existed? There could be whole new avenues of research opening up! And more than just archaeological research, other disciplines and sciences would be needed. While she had studied archaeology, she always maintained a keen interest in the natural sciences, too. Unlike some of her academic peers, she considered anything anomalous or unexplained needed *more* investigation, not less; she was not one to dismiss or reject something unexpected as an irrelevant outlier.

The researcher from Plymouth told her that all they had so far were the images and their location. It was pure coincidence these had come her way – the head of the Plymouth archaeology department had suggested notifying Oxford, since he remembered that St Dunstan's 'had an interest'. A former colleague of Elisa's now working in Plymouth had given them her email address.

Elisa emailed her friend in Plymouth asking him what, specifically, 'St Dunstan's had an interest in', and he responded almost immediately that the department head had told him there was a professor who had been looking for evidence of a possible tectonic or geophysical event that could have submerged an Atlantic civilisation. His hypothesis was that an artefact he'd been studying had no other viable explanation. He'd been laughed at, with claims he was trying to find the mythical Atlantis, and had quickly dropped that line of investigation for fear of losing his position. However, the head of department at Plymouth had said the professor was a good man, and of course, there *was* an artefact.

The professor's name wasn't mentioned. The email stated that the HoD said 'the professor was a good man'. Had he *known* him? If so, it couldn't be Foxton. She emailed her friend again and he replied that it wasn't Foxton, it was Gillard, and that the HoD had indeed known the man. She had been just about to start researching Gillard's work when Daniel Reade arrived. Since Reade left, they all settled back to what they'd been doing before the interruption.

"Robert, do you recall a Professor Gillard?" Elisa asked her colleague.

He tilted his head to one side, in thought. "Yes, I do. I remembered him just after that young man left. Odd coincidence. Ed Gillard was a senior professor here at the hall. Died about twenty years ago. He'd taken a bit of fire, I seem to think."

"What do you mean?" Elisa was now more curious.

"During the last years before his death, he'd been under attack from many colleagues. Ridiculed and vilified mercilessly, I'm afraid. He was developing a theory that an artefact he was researching might have come from a long-disappeared Atlantic civilisation."

Elisa knew that leading proponents of the established view would usually meet any evidence that may give credence to the 'Atlantis myth' with derision at best, and character assassination, at worst. Anything 'Atlantis' threatens their view, and therefore their papers, books, curriculum material, reputations and even livelihoods. In Gillard's case, he had backtracked some distance, Robert explained, but not before contacting colleagues at other universities in his quest for more information. The damage had been done. He was barely able to hold on to his position at the university, and had it not been for his illness, he might have been let go.

"Why not take a look in the storage and archive rooms for remnants of his work," Robert suggested. A prospect that Elisa did not relish. St Dunstan Hall was established in the year 1325 as a history and antiquarian college with a religious orientation, so she expected she would find cellars and storerooms of centuries-old papers and all manner of once-valued junk. She was pleasantly surprised to learn that only the 'recent records' – those of the last hundred and fifty years or so since archaeology had become a discipline in its own right – were stored at the hall.

The storage rooms were in the basement. They were cold and smelt of dust and antiquity. The shelves were lined with boxes and odd artefacts, mementos of forgotten studies and forgotten lives. There was a disheartening melancholy about them, and the chill of dull and aging fluorescent lighting did nothing to assuage the feeling. She hoped she wouldn't have to spend too long in there, else she might inherit some of the qualities of the room.

Gillard's work, and some of his belongings – since he'd died leaving no living relatives – were, thankfully, not too difficult to find. There were six large boxes, mostly filled with notebooks and minor collections of curiosities from archaeological digs with his students. They were all neatly labelled Prof. Edgar Gillard, St Dunstan Hall, Oxford, and all dated eighteen years earlier. On one of the boxes, someone had written in large letters 'Gillard's folly' and it proved to be the one Elisa was looking for. It was unexpectedly heavy, so she had to find a cart to carefully load it onto and wheel it back to the Foxton Room.

Elisa withdrew Gillard's notes from the box and uncovered a piece of a stone tablet, or stela. It was almost 40 centimetres wide, 26 centimetres tall and five centimetres thick. It looked quite like the photos Daniel Reade had shown her, although they had degraded and it was possibly her imagination. It did have the makings of a good mystery, though. The stone had clearly been broken at the top and had what appeared to be Sanskrit characters on it, but they were quite worn so would be difficult to translate.

According to Professor Gillard's notes, he had made some progress on it. Apparently, the object had been stored for some time, having been 'borrowed' from the British Museum – and evidently not returned. The museum had acquired it from a merchant seaman for a small cash consideration, and the original notes with it had said it was found north-west of the Azores, a Portuguese chain of volcanic islands that have been slowly and steadily rising out of the Mid-Atlantic for thousands of years. There was nothing in the notes to substantiate its provenance, but neither the British Museum, nor Gillard, expressed any doubts.

Gillard's attempts at translation assumed it was a religious artefact, as is so often the case, Elisa lamented. Although he'd been far from completing it, the phrases he'd noted down included 'the songs of the waves [or seas]'; 'the overwhelming beauty [or majesty] of the ...' and 'resounding harmony'.

Whether or not Gillard's work was flawed by entrenched archaeological biases, he had, at the very least, worked out the ancient language was related to Sanskrit, as had Professor Foxton for his tablet more than fifty years earlier. It seemed likely these artefacts could be related, so Elisa started to wonder if there might be other similar objects that could help her piece it all together. Potentially, there were other institutions or museums with similar specimens. It would be an incredible coincidence if the only two artefacts in existence had both ended up at Oxford. The question was where to go next.

18

An hour and a half later, Daniel left the Colchester Building, disappointed that there was nothing of use pertaining to his great-grandfather in the St Dunstan archives. He had seen numerous references to the man – in fact, quite a long list of papers – but none of them were about any ancient tablet, the Atlantic Ocean, Sanskrit or any other language, ancient or modern. *Now what?*

Daniel followed the path back to the arched passage he had entered through, turned and looked around at the ancient buildings of St Dunstan Hall. He felt his business here wasn't yet finished, but he didn't know where to go next.

"Can I help you, sir?" A man in his late fifties wearing a bowler hat stood behind him.

"Good afternoon. I'm not sure really ..." Daniel went on to explain his story again, and at the mention of Foxton's name, the porter's interest seemed to perk up. Had he been expecting Daniel to be just another tourist?

"Professor Foxton was an important man in this college," said the porter. "I remember hearing he was murdered," he added, with a conspiratorial tone. He reached into his pocket and withdrew a small notebook. "What was it you were looking for, sir? Perhaps I can be of service."

"I'm trying to find out more about the professor's work. In particular, something he was working on when he died. A translation of an old stone tablet."

The porter raised his bushy eyebrows. "Have you tried the archives yet?"

"Yes. And the office. Is there anywhere else I might look?" Daniel asked.

"Outside of St Dunstan's, I don't think anyone could help. I'm sorry, sir," the porter said, with a polite smile. "May I take your name, sir? If anything comes up, I'll be sure to get in touch."

"Don't worry, there's no need. I'm sure I'll be in touch with the academic staff," he said optimistically. "Thanks for your help," he added as he headed out under the archway.

Daniel felt deflated. He hadn't learned anything of particular interest, and certainly nothing relating to the missing tablet. Elisa Mansfield had seemed aloof, and he felt she'd been rather dismissive. The Foxton Room had at first seemed a promising place to further his investigation, and he was still hopeful something would come of it, although he had nothing solid to base that hope on. Maybe she would give a bit of thought to Foxton's work and call him back.

Daniel walked back to his car, thankful that while the weather was cold, the rain had held off. He sat in the driver's seat but didn't start the engine. In the last few days, he'd arrived in England to take possession of a house he didn't know anything about from a deceased uncle he also didn't know anything about. He had learned his great-grandfather was apparently murdered in the house, and that the murder was unsolved. He'd found notes and pictures of a strange stone tablet carefully secreted inside the house, and couldn't help wondering if they were related to the murder. But why? Surely there must be something in Foxton's notes that would yield a clue.

The drive south to Chidwick was better than the drive up. After the thick traffic getting out of Oxford, by the time he got to the A34 it was reasonably easy going and he was home before dark. He set a fire in the living room, making a mental note to bring in more firewood tomorrow. The small kitchen was not ideal for preparing a meal, and the Aga did not warm the room. Nonetheless, he cooked himself a simple, but agreeable dinner, and then went up to Foxton's study to retrieve the manuscript.

At first attempt, the priest hole would not open, but with a little perseverance he managed it. All the material he had put back in there this morning was where he'd left it, and he wondered whether it was really necessary to lock it all away. He'd done it purely because Foxton had obviously gone to great lengths to keep it secret. But that was decades ago.

Poring over Foxton's notes with a hot cup of tea to warm his hands, he reread the translation and Foxton's journey of discovery. Foxton had at first believed he had a religious message, but after years of painstaking work had pieced together something altogether different. Daniel had a sense that Foxton was worried about what he'd unearthed, but he also felt Foxton was worried about a lot of things. In the notes there were occasional references to the war, and 'humanity at its worst'.

The tablet itself was another mystery – where was it? Why had it not also been hidden in the priest hole? From the dimensions recorded in Foxton's notes, it should have fitted on one of the shelves, although it would have to have been stood upright. Daniel had a closer look inside the hiding place, using the flashlight in his phone, and could see scratches and other marks in the middle shelf. He could also see small pieces of grit and one or two larger pieces tucked into the corners. Maybe the reason he didn't store it away was simply that moving it regularly was causing it damage, and his archaeological training overrode his caution. Or had he simply not had time when he was attacked?

On a sheet of notepaper, Daniel wrote down the translated passages from Foxton's notes. It was rather repetitive, but the phrases were starting to paint a picture:

'voice of God' or 'uplifting voice'
'uplifting voice' ... 'unburden [lighten?] stone'

<u>not</u> *'voice of God'*, but *'voice [sound] of doom' [destruction]?*
[was it] *'coveted by the few [yet] destroyer of many'*
'instrument of [/harbinger of] destruction of people and earth'
'consumes itself and all around it' [destroyer of a world?]

Foxton had evidently come to believe he was reading about an ancient weapon or technology, but to Daniel its meaning remained elusive. There was nothing in the notes that gave any sense of what Foxton thought the weapon might be. However, it now seemed quite clear to Daniel that during his last few years, Foxton was very much aware the Nazis were searching the world for ancient objects and information that would support not just their ideology, but their war effort.

It seemed possible to Daniel that this could still be a religious or a metaphorical text. He knew the story of the walls of Jericho being demolished by the sound of the trumpets, which, to the best of his knowledge, had not been interpreted by any scientists as describing a weapon. Then there was the matter of the final phrase in Foxton's notes: *'consumes itself and all around it' [destroyer of a world?].* The bracketed words, he assumed, were Foxton's musings. 'Destroyer of a world' seemed a long bow to draw, but perhaps not unreasonable from the phrases he'd deciphered before it. *But what was this destroyed world?*

As a historian, Daniel was reasonably well versed in ancient Greek texts, including Plato's *Timaeus and Critias* dialogues. Here Plato refers to the mythical Atlantis, describing it as a powerful and advanced kingdom that disappeared into the ocean around 9,600 BC. To Daniel, like many others, if Atlantis *was* real, then the story probably referred to the volcanic annihilation of Santorini, around 3,600 years ago, even though Plato clearly located his Atlantis in the *Atlantic* Ocean, not the Mediterranean Sea.

In Plato's story, the Atlanteans were powerful and warlike, but their morals declined as their power grew, until they were punished by the gods, who destroyed their island, sinking it into the sea. A quick search on his phone produced for Daniel the exact Plato quote: *"But afterwards there occurred violent earthquakes and floods; and in a single day and night of misfortune all your warlike men in a body sank into the earth, and the island of Atlantis in like manner disappeared in the depths of the sea."*

While Plato's dialogues had more than a few parallels with the stories in Foxton's notes, his hypothesis seemed just too far-fetched. Daniel could imagine a massive earthquake destroying and submerging a city. There is a reasonable amount of evidence indicating that had happened before, but those events had submerged ruins by metres. *Tens* of metres at most. *Two miles*, just over three kilometres, seemed completely impossible. It was no wonder archaeologists and historians dismissed the dialogues as fiction or allegory.

19

One by one, the men arrived in their chauffeured limousines. The drivers entered the secure underground car park of the six-storey apartment building in Alto de Pinheiros, an exclusive area on the west side of São Paulo city. The lower level was reserved for the penthouse apartment. At the rear of that level was another security garage door. Using remote controls in the cars, each driver keyed in the six-digit code as he approached the door. Inside, the second security door was a locked storage area, and a four-hundred-metre tunnel ahead. As each car drove in, sections of the tunnel automatically lit up ahead.

It took them under a small hill that was part of a private estate, ending at another security door. Inside that was another underground car park with twenty spaces. As the cars arrived, the passengers climbed out and, using PIN numbers and a fingerprint scanner, each was able to enter the double steel doors into the main building. The drivers were not permitted to leave the car park.

Through the double doors, the men stepped into a narrow corridor with storerooms and a small lift. Oversized lavish doors on the right led to a luxurious panelled boardroom. The cold echoes of the corridor, with its hard steel doors, tall ceiling and concrete floor, gave way to an eerie silence in the carpeted boardroom. It seemed incongruous against the austere entrance to the underground bunker. The room had opulent dark-timber panelling, an oversized antique table that could seat up to eighteen people, and velvet-covered antique dining chairs. Like the other small meeting rooms in the bunker, it was soundproof and electronically shielded.

Four large screens were mounted high on the wall at the far end. Today, the monitors were not in use, and, as was usual for these meetings, the table was set for eight people. The men sat as they entered, acknowledging the leader silently. He was already seated at the head of the table, scanning a folder containing some papers and photographs. He ignored the men entering, while he spoke in a hushed tone to a pale-faced man with a scar on his right cheek and closely cropped hair.

The pale man stepped back and took his place a metre behind one of the chairs. Three others dressed in black were similarly placed behind chairs. Those entering the room did not find it unusual; they knew their leader was painstakingly serious about security. They took their assigned places at the table, three on one side and four on the other. Their leader was a solidly built man in his early sixties, with an olive complexion and piercing blue eyes. His black hair was slicked back and, although the smile on his face did not quite reach his eyes, he was ruggedly handsome and charismatic, with a compelling presence.

"Good evening, gentlemen," he said, exuding a calm and pleasant demeanour. "Before we commence our usual business, we have some administration to take care of." Some looked slightly uneasy in their seats. Perhaps the extra security detail was there for a less benign reason.

"I've received some disturbing news. It appears there has been a security issue," he said, in measured but perfect English. He took a moment to look at each of them around the table. "In fact, gentlemen, one of us is not what he seems to be."

At that moment, one of the seated men reached into his jacket, but before he had a chance to complete the action, the pale-faced man standing behind him quickly stepped forward. With a swift movement and flash of steel, he drew his hand across the man's throat. Blood gushed from the man's neck as his attacker retrieved the small black pistol from inside the stricken man's jacket. Another man dressed in black entered the room with a large black plastic bag, and in less than a minute, they had forced the dying man, arms flailing, into the body bag, zipped it up and dragged him out. The remaining two security guards quickly cleaned the blood from the table and floor, and removed the bloody chair. The leader had simply sat in silence, emotionless. For all the concern he showed, the staff might have entered merely to clean up spilt coffee.

"Now," he continued in the same measured tone, "back to the business I called you here to discuss. Development of the new technology continues to move slowly forward, and we are nearing the time to conduct a test."

"Have you been able to resolve the scaling problem?" the oldest man seated at the table asked.

"There are some improvements, but they are not yet enough," the leader answered, making it clear he did not appreciate the interruption. The older man at the table had been a member of the council for forty years and was the son of one of the organisation's original eight founders. His status had emboldened him to be more direct than the others with the leader.

"The technicians are confident this test will help them amplify the effects," the leader continued. "But there is another important development, from the United Kingdom." All members of the council knew the organisation had a network of informants – usually conscripted by blackmail – around the globe. These informants included scientists and academics. Their primary function was to advise the organisation of any development relating in any way to the original source artefact: the ancient tablet found in the Atlantic Ocean and stolen from the Oxford professor during the Second World War.

"More information appears to have come to light about the tablet. It is also possible there may be other related objects that could provide further information to speed our development."

"Excellent," said another of the men. "This will make the new technology even more valuable. I assume we are maintaining our buyers' enthusiasm."

"We have potential buyers in Europe and Asia, and we have carefully leaked some information to each so they know there is competition," said the older man. He went on to further elaborate on the opportunities, and the men around the table probed the financial implications in some detail. There was a great deal of interest in the potentially vast sums this technology could yield. The leader listened, masking his impatience. These men did not need to know he had other plans for the technology.

Finally, the older man turned to the leader. "And what of the compromise to our security?"

"Gentlemen, do not worry, it has been addressed. I have also arranged for the new information from Oxford to be collected, and our interests to be protected."

The pale man returned to the room and whispered something to the leader.

"We will reconvene after the test is completed." The leader stood, smiling assuredly as the meeting broke up. He left the room and, using his PIN number and fingerprint, entered the small lift. The other men left through the insulated double doors to the car park. They noticed that neither the dead man's car nor his driver were there. There was, however, a faint, slightly acrid smell of gunpowder in the air.

The leader exited the lift on the level above and strode past the security area and control room. He again used his PIN number and fingerprint through the double steel doors, entering the ground floor commercial kitchen and laundry area of his estate. He climbed the stairs to the main floor of his home and went into the large media room. His staff had recorded his press conference of a few hours earlier.

The leader, José Zapas, sat and watched himself declare his presidential candidacy, along with his outrage at the current Brazilian government and their 'unhealthy' American allegiances. The media had been speculating for a while about Zapas's political ambitions, and he had been feeding information and stories through his companies for months. The election was now just weeks away, having been delayed by violent protests against the current president that prevented voting in some areas. Zapas had timed his announcement carefully to give the government as little time as possible to prepare to fight him.

20

Yesterday's phone calls had proved fruitless. Elisa had called the few US and Canadian universities where she knew, or at least knew of, someone on the academic staff. Nobody had any information about any possible objects with an unknown ancient language. Some had questioned her credentials when she'd asked about objects found in the Mid-Atlantic.

Unperturbed, she had been busy contacting European universities, in particular in France, Spain and Portugal, hoping for a stroke of luck. Ten minutes earlier, she'd made a call to the University of Lisbon and had received a possible lead. They did not have any such object, but the person she'd spoken to had recently been contacted by a researcher at the National Museum of Natural History and Science who had been asking questions along similar lines to Elisa. The university man had given Elisa the name of the researcher.

Elisa had also continued looking at Gillard's notes and translation. Without the burden of Gillard's biases, she had reached a conclusion that some of what he'd written was probably wrong. There were a lot of references, as far as she could discern, to some sort of sound, and she didn't believe it was about *song*.

"*Estou sim?*" said a young female voice. Elisa had been on hold with the

Lisbon museum, while they tracked down the researcher.

"Hello," Elisa said, gathering her thoughts. "Um, do you speak English?"

"Of course," came the reply, in accented but clear English. "This is Cláudia," she added.

"Hello, my name is Elisa Mansfield. I'm calling from Oxford University. I spoke with Lisbon University earlier, and I think we may have a common interest ..." Elisa went on to explain about the Gillard object, apparently dredged up from the ocean floor. She told Cláudia she considered it highly unlikely such an object would be the solitary relic of whoever left it behind, so she had been contacting institutions trying to find something similar. "The museum suggested you'd been on the same sort of quest," she finished, with some uncertainty.

"Yes. I have an object here that sounds similar to yours," came the excited response. It has been sitting here for some years, unexplained and overlooked. It was apparently sold to the museum for a nominal sum by the captain of a fishing trawler who said he'd hauled it in from the North Atlantic, near the Mid-Atlantic Ridge."

"Can you describe it?" Elisa was getting quite excited, too.

"Yes, sure. It is possibly many thousands of years old and has had some marine deposit removed previously. I am hoping the removal has not damaged it, but I can't be sure. It is 29 centimetres wide and almost 35 tall and four centimetres thick and weighs 10.5 kilograms. Some of the top and bottom has broken away, and I cannot find any other pieces. I've been studying it with various alternate light sources and scanning tools trying to make sense of the script on it, but I am not successful. All I can tell you is the text looks a little bit like Sanskrit, but it is not," Cláudia explained.

They both agreed to send photographs of the objects they each had, and exchanged email addresses. For Elisa, this was now starting to turn into a real mystery of the sort she loved. There might be something here that could seriously change established scientific thinking. Her interest in science had already drawn her into looking at archaeoacoustics, and the apparent references to sound in these objects had compelled her to look further.

Elisa hadn't talked to any of her rather conservative and cautious colleagues about her interests, but had read articles discussing some ancient monuments that had an unexpected acoustic resonance. It was still emergent science and not widely accepted, but Elisa was not overly bothered by that. Newgrange, near Slane in Ireland, and the Hypogeum of Hal-Saflieni in Malta have both been shown to have a resonant frequency of 110 or 111 hertz. An odd coincidence? In reading about Hal-Saflieni, she had come across some European researchers who had postulated that the strange acoustic reverberation properties could affect human emotions. She also remembered reading something about acoustic resonance having potential unexpected physical effects, but couldn't quite recall the details.

The email from Cláudia had just arrived. It included some photos of the Lisbon artefact, and while it exhibited a different patina, the script on it was similar to the Gillard object. Elisa surmised that the patina might be explained by it having sat in somewhat shallower water for centuries, or *millennia*. It also looked a lot like the object in the old photograph Daniel Reade had shown her. She wanted to see the alternate light source photos and scans, but maybe those had been too large to email easily.

Elisa decided yesterday's interruption had been serendipitous. These things must all be linked. She searched her workstation for the piece of paper with the phone number on it.

21

The GalizienAcht, the eight from Galicia, were meeting in an hour. Josef Zapomny had arranged for a display of the remaining promising artefacts they had smuggled out of Germany four years earlier, before the end of the war. These were objects the Ahnenerbe had coveted, objects of mystery and potential power. Some of the items they had brought with them had turned out to be of little value, other than supporting Himmler's insane ideology, something none of the eight men had cared about. They cared only about furthering their own wealth and power. If the Nazi scientists were right about any of these objects and the ancient technologies they spoke of, they had significant potential. It seemed possible to Zapomny that some may ultimately be able to be weaponised and sold for significant amounts of money. The Russians seemed like the best option, having taken over large portions of Europe, and Stalin having just ordered the Berlin Blockade, closing all routes from West Germany into his East German territory. *A world in turmoil is a world in need of powerful weapons.*

While they were still exploring the various artefacts they had stolen from the Ahnenerbe's enormous cache of looted historical objects, Zapomny considered the tablet from Oxford the most interesting. Not a technology itself, but interesting nonetheless. They had ignored Foxton's simplistic notes in the notebook found with the object; these seemed either naïve or intended to mislead. They had instead worked out much of the character set from Foxton's attempts and retranslated these sections, and, not without some difficulty, had been able to translate even more.

Tonight, Zapomny would share with the other seven the efforts of his academics. Academics over whom Zapomny had a hold because he had made it his business to know about their past allegiances in Axis Europe. They had discovered the tablet was not a religious text, as Foxton had believed. Where Foxton had written 'voice of God', they had retranslated it as 'voice of doom [or destruction]'. They had also translated that the [object?] had been 'coveted by the few' was an 'instrument of doom [destruction?] of people and of the Earth'. Zapomny felt certain it described a powerful ancient technology that could be rediscovered and exploited.

The men would be arriving at Zapomny's estate, a large house on several acres of land in an exclusive area in the west side of São Paulo city. Three years prior, he had chosen the location because of its large European community, and of course, its relative wealth. The house had served his purposes well, allowing him to easily host 'business meetings', as well as the social gatherings his new wife liked to host. He loathed the socialites but had married one of them for convenience, and tolerated the parties because they gave him a stronger social standing and greater respectability.

María Juana Lanjeira was a pretty party girl and opportunist who wanted a rich husband. She was socially well connected, and Josef's wealth was just what she needed to sustain her lifestyle. It was a loveless, but convenient marriage. Josef could be a cruel and demanding man, but he allowed her to be the socialite she wanted to be. Fourteen years younger than him, she had just turned thirty last month when she announced she was pregnant. Josef expected a son and heir early next year.

A little after dark, the men started to arrive, some in taxis and some in chauffeured limousines. The drivers waited by their cars in the large circular driveway, quietly talking and smoking. They assembled in the large dining room and Josef locked the doors. He had instructed the staff, and María that there were to be no interruptions for any reason.

As Zapomny talked about the objects he'd had brought up from the vault under the house, the council of the GalizienAcht agreed the tablet from Oxford indeed showed the most promise. The idea of an ancient technology powerful enough to destroy a civilisation and 'consume everything around it' was compelling. They agreed it had the potential to attract a vast sum of money. As Josef described the translated phrases, the idea of holding such a weapon in his hands deeply thrilled him. It was intoxicating.

The others wanted to know how the organisation could learn more about this ancient source in order to develop the technology. Zapomny told them that not only did he have trusted informants in various academic institutions, he also had scientists working on this technology now. Based on the translated text, they were confident it was a sound-wave technology and were already testing theories. His underlying assumption was that this was a technology of the ancients, and since today's science was far more advanced, it was only a matter of time. Of course, without further information, it could take years, or even decades.

22

It had been a late night, as Daniel had pored over the information he had, and he'd lain in bed while his mind continued to turn over the possibilities. After a patchy night's sleep, he woke early, breakfasted, then chopped a good-sized stack of firewood. The exercise helped clear his mind, and as he carried piles of wood into the house he pondered where he might go to next in his investigation. His great-grandfather had started a quest to solve the mystery around the anachronism that was his 'Doomsday Tablet'. That is, until he was murdered in that very house.

After his shower, as he was finishing his second cup of coffee in the front room, his mobile phone rang. "Hello."

"Hello. Daniel Reade?" a tentative female voice responded.

"That's me." He waited.

"It's Elisa Mansfield here. From St Dunstan's. We met yesterday."

The young woman who had been rather dismissive.

"Hi. Nice to hear from you. Did you find something more about my great-grandfather's work?" Daniel asked, hopefully.

"Yes, actually." A slight pause. "I'm sorry if I was a bit abrupt yesterday. I was ... well, I'd just ... Oh, it's complicated. Are you still in Oxford? Maybe we could meet for a coffee?"

He had not expected that. "I'm not in Oxford I'm afraid, I'm in Chidwick, about an hour south of you. I could get to Oxford in time for a late lunch, though."

Elisa thought for a moment. "How about we meet in Chilton? It's nearly halfway, and you can avoid the Oxford traffic."

"Sure, sounds good. Any particular place?"

"Um, the Red Lion in Main Street. I think the food is good." She had been there in the evening with friends a few months ago. There was also someone she wanted to visit in the area. They agreed to meet at 12.30. Daniel was wondering what had changed her attitude. Had she uncovered something interesting?

He looked up the Red Lion in Chilton and the map directions said it would take forty minutes to get there. He would allow fifty, since it was raining and he didn't know the area. He'd been pleased to hear from Elisa, and he decided to take his laptop with his photos of Foxton's notes and drawings.

A short time later he left Chidwick and made his way through the forest to the main road. The drive north was easy, although he had to briefly stop, soon after leaving the village, to allow some cattle to cross the road. He managed to find the Red Lion about twenty minutes early. Chilton looked like a nice little town, so he stowed the laptop under the seat, pulled his woollen jersey over his head, locked up and went for a short walk, glad the rain had stopped.

Elisa walked to her flat to pick up her car, carrying some notes and photos that she intended to share with Daniel. On the way back home, she decided to change into a silk shirt and jacket, although she wasn't quite sure why. She got home just as a light drizzle started and drove south to Chilton. It was raining now, although not too heavily, and the traffic was slower than she had expected. She was used to gloomy wet weather this time of year, but as she drove, she thought back to the warm summers in Sydney from her childhood.

She had left Sydney when she was fourteen. Her father had just been promoted to a new position in London with the technology company he'd worked for, and her mother had also been keen to move, to be closer to her family in both the United Kingdom and Spain. Elisa's grandmother, after whom she'd been named, still lived in Bilbao. Elisa had not been happy with the move across the world. As a rather geeky teenager, with a keen interest in science and history, she had often been an outsider, but that year she had made some good friends at school. For a while, she was annoyed with her parents for making her life miserable, but by the time she had finished school in England, she had regained her academic success and was easily able to get into university to study archaeology. She hadn't tried for Oxford, but had got into the University of Bristol, which she had enjoyed immensely.

She reached the exit for Harwell and Chilton and turned off. A black Mercedes SUV a few cars behind, that she'd noticed soon after leaving Oxford, also pulled onto the exit and followed her. As she navigated the roundabout onto the narrow road into Chilton, the big SUV attempted to overtake her and cut in too quickly in front. She gasped and jammed on the brakes to avoid being run off the road. Even though the rain had stopped, the road was still wet and the back of her Renault lost traction and skidded around the corner. As she fought to keep control, a truck came over the hill towards them much too fast. The black SUV was forced to swerve to avoid a collision and it slid along the grass verge into a hedge.

She had righted her car and kept going, keen to get away. She was breathing hard. It was a lucky escape. It had seemed like the black Mercedes might have been trying to run her off the road, but she couldn't be sure. She was shaken and wanted to stop the car to collect herself, but what if the SUV followed? Her heart was still beating fast.

She kept going, as quickly as she dared, her mind now starting to rationalise that these days drivers seemed to be getting angrier and more stupid each day. *Surely just an idiot in a hurry.* Slowly, she started to calm down, but kept checking the rear-view mirror all the way to the Red Lion. She saw no sign of the black SUV.

She pulled into the almost empty car park next to a grey Citroën, took a few deep breaths, checked her face and hair in the mirror and went into the pub with her folder of notes and photos.

Daniel returned from his walk right on time and saw a white Renault Clio parked next to his rental. Just a few doors down Main Street, he saw a big black Mercedes SUV with darkened windows that hadn't been there before. It was slightly out of place next to the other much smaller cars dotted along the street. He retrieved his laptop from under the seat and went into the pub.

Inside, it was dark enough that his eyes needed a moment to adjust. He spotted Elisa at a table by the fire, looking at some notes in a folder. She looked up as he reached the table, half standing to greet him. As she stood, she loosened the small scarf tied around her neck. The firelight danced in her eyes.

"Hello again," said Daniel, smiling as he pushed his wavy hair back with his fingers.

"Hi. Thanks for meeting me today," Elisa started, slightly awkwardly. I … I wanted to apologise for being quite short yesterday." She smiled her apology. "I also think we might have more to discuss. About Professor Foxton's work," she added.

"Don't worry about yesterday. I didn't call first, and you were probably busy."

"Well, I was in the middle of something I now think might be related to your great-grandfather's work." Her green eyes met Daniel's and there was an earnestness in them that appealed to him.. "And I've been working on it ever since."

"Oh? I'd love to hear more. Shall we get something to drink first?"

"Just water for me, thanks," she said.

Daniel went over to the bar and asked for a bottle of mineral water and two glasses. "When you came into the Foxton Room yesterday, I'd just received some information from the University of Plymouth about a potential archaeological site they'd found during a routine ocean survey. It's in the Mid-Atlantic, which many archaeologists would tell you is impossible."

Daniel poured the water.

"I phoned Plymouth to see if there was any more information, and I also wondered why they'd contacted us. They told me St Dunstan's had an interest in the Mid-Atlantic, through an ex-professor's work."

"My great-grandfather," Daniel finished.

"No. It was someone else. A Professor Gillard who'd done some related research around an object he had at Oxford."

Daniel raised his eyebrows.

"I found Professor Gillard's notes *and that object* in our files." Daniel could see a keenness on her face. "It had been forgotten about and was labelled 'Gillard's folly'. I thought he must have written that himself, since his talk of a potential Atlantis had caused him a lot of grief. Archaeologists generally switch off when they hear that."

"I know," said Daniel. "I'm a historian, and most of *us* react the same way."

Elisa was becoming a little more animated now, and her enthusiasm shone in her eyes. She tucked a wisp of hair behind her left ear and continued.

"That object looks like the one in your photos, and I think it's possible the language could be the same. Neither of these objects fit the establishment view so don't seem to have had the attention they deserve."

Daniel nodded. He knew what she meant; it was difficult to have *any* find accepted if it didn't support established views or theories.

"That got me thinking," she continued. "Why shouldn't there be other objects like ours? The Atlantic is surrounded by old seafaring nations. So I called anybody I could think of at universities in Nova Scotia, Quebec, Boston, New York, as well as French, Spanish and Portuguese." She paused and took a deep breath. "I found another object!" Her enthusiasm was infectious. "In Lisbon."

"Wow, you *have* been busy!" Daniel declared, wondering if he should interrupt to suggest eating. He refilled her water instead.

"Should we order some lunch?" she suggested, apparently reading his mind.

"Great idea."

Elisa grabbed her handbag off the back of her chair, and they went to the counter together. She ordered a Thai chicken salad, and Daniel a beef and Guinness pie. He would watch his weight another day. Elisa insisted on paying for their meals as an apology for her dismissiveness yesterday.

"I've already forgotten about it," said Daniel. And he had. He'd been absorbed as he'd listened to her enthusiastically describe what she'd learned. She shivered involuntarily as she sat back down at their table.

"Cold?" he asked.

"It's not that," she said. Her eyes clouded a little. "I might have a glass of wine after all. Would you like something?" she asked, gently pushing her chair back.

"Let me get that. It's the least I can do after you've bought lunch!"

"All right. Thank you. A glass of sauvignon blanc please." Daniel went back to the bar, pleased to find that the pub had a New Zealand sauvignon blanc and brought back two glasses.

"I hope you like it. It's from near where I live. Cheers." He clinked her glass.

"I'm probably still a little bit on edge." She described the incident with the black SUV, remembering how she'd felt as it cut right in front of her.

"There was one of those parked a few doors down when I got back." He told her he'd arrived early and gone for a walk, and that the black Mercedes must have arrived soon after she had.

"Probably just an idiot in a hurry." Her expression told Daniel she didn't believe it. She looked around the pub but nobody else had come in.

As they waited for their meals, they showed each other the photos they had, and Daniel explained where Foxton's notes were leading. He finished with the notion that Foxton believed the tablet talked about an ancient technology or weapon.

"Do you think you could get higher-resolution images from Lisbon?"

Daniel asked. The pictures Elisa had shown him were not great.

"Yes, I'm sure I can, these were just emailed screenshots," she replied, as their food arrived.

While they ate, they fell into a brief but comfortable silence.

"You love your work, don't you?" Daniel said.

"I do. I love a good mystery too." She paused, tilting her head slightly to one side, looking at him. "You?"

"I really enjoy history, and archaeology, *and a good mystery*, but that's not my work. I'm a consultant," he said, and then grinned. "Or I used to be – until last week." He briefly told her how his employment had ended. "It's quite liberating," he finished. She was easy to talk to. And she seemed genuinely interested.

"I mentioned I'd discovered my great-grandfather's notes in the house. They were hidden away carefully. In a priest hole in his study."

Elisa took a breath as if to speak, but instead looked at Daniel and waited, her expression asking 'how ...?'

"Well, the house is the right age and I just hoped I'd find one." As he said it, he realised it sounded silly. "I can still be a bit like the inquisitive little boy I used to be."

The look on her face invited *tell me more*.

"Eventually I found it by looking closely at the panelling around all the fireplaces. I don't know what I expected, but it wasn't a journal about a 'Doomsday Tablet'. That's what he'd written. Since I've been here I've also learned he didn't die of natural causes, he was murdered. In the house."

"*Murdered?*" Her eyes grew larger.

Elisa could see the fervour in Daniel's face as he told the story. There was a warm sincerity to him that made her feel relaxed and comfortable. She'd forgotten how on edge she felt when she arrived.

Neither was in a hurry to finish their lunch, and they enjoyed a leisurely conversation, stopping only to order coffee.

After they finished their drinks, Elisa mentioned she had a colleague whom she wanted to talk to on her way back to Oxford. "He's in Harwell, just up the road, and something of an expert in the use of alternate light sources and scanning of ancient objects. The woman in Lisbon said they had used similar techniques on the artefact they have."

They went out into the cold together and theirs were the only two vehicles in the car park. Elisa noticed Daniel's had a flat tyre, pointing out the right front wheel.

"That's not ideal," said Daniel, stating the obvious. He opened the back to find the spare, while Elisa put her folder into her car. The spare tyre was also flat. "Looks like I'm stuck here for a bit. Thanks for a great lunch, and great conversation. I really enjoyed it. I'm glad you phoned."

"Me, too. If I can get more information from Lisbon, let's compare notes and see where we get to," Elisa replied.

Daniel said that would be great, as he locked the car. As he did so, he thought maybe the rental papers had been moved. He was fairly sure he'd left them tucked between the seat and the console, and now they were sitting on the passenger seat. He let it go, deciding he must be mistaken. He felt Elisa still looking at him.

"Do you want to come to Harwell to meet my friend? If you leave the keys with the landlord he could give them to the RAC."

"Oh, thanks, that would be great," Daniel replied, after a brief moment. He realised he didn't want their lunch to end just yet. He made a call to the rental company and left the keys with the landlord. He glanced down the street and saw that the black SUV was no longer there. He climbed into Elisa's passenger seat, noticing her perfume as he sat next to her.

23

José Zapas's mobile phone vibrated on the table. Recognising the number, he took the call. "Yes?"

"There is some interest here in the artefact, and it seems there may be other related objects," said a clipped voice with a hint of a German accent. The man did not bother with pleasantries, and Zapas did not expect any. He waited in silence for the caller to continue.

"The woman is not alone. She has a colleague."

This was unexpected. The pale man had arrived in England early that day and followed up the information Zapas had supplied. He had been told the Mansfield woman was the only one investigating the tablet. His instructions were to find her research and, if warranted, interrogate and dispose of her. Methods were, as usual, his choice, as long as it could not lead back to the organisation.

"Name?"

"Daniel Eric Reade. Arrived from New Zealand a few days ago." Anton Rigo had found the car rental papers most informative. More informative than Rigo's own rental car papers, since they were not in his real name, the name in which he had served the East German Stasi. Rigo regularly changed his identity so that no one living could identify him.

"I don't yet know what the connection is, but they have spent some hours together since he met her at the university," Rigo said, pausing for Zapas's instructions.

Zapas considered the new information. New interest in the stone tablet. From where? And another person involved; that did not please him. But the most interesting news was that there may be other related objects. This could be helpful.

"Find out more about Reade and what he knows. He might be useful." Zapas cut off the call. He sat back and wondered how this related to the phone call he'd taken just a few minutes before Rigo's. The organisation's informant in Oxford had relayed another interesting development, and Zapas did not believe in random coincidence. He dialled another number.

"The University of Plymouth has a survey ship currently working in the Mid-Atlantic. They have discovered something that might link to our tablet." Zapas supplied the scant details the Oxford man had given and ended the call with a curt 'find out more!' Then he punched another number into the phone.

Two levels below the room in which Zapas was sitting, underneath his mansion, the engineer angrily stubbed a cigarette out and picked up his phone.

"Días." He took off his glasses, wiped his brow and pushed his receding hair back. As chief architect and engineer in the organisation's underground laboratory, Doctor Henriqué Días was accustomed to unusual demands.

"I want the test done tonight."

"We are not ready. I cannot guarantee results," said Días as he lit up another cigarette. "I need more information about this technology."

"Do it tonight. You'll get more information by testing it. Make sure it is decisive, and report back when it's done." Zapas ended the call.

José Zapas rarely got involved in the operations of any of his businesses, whether public or covert, but any matter related to the technology they were developing he directed personally. None of the other council members, nor anyone but the most trusted of his security personnel, knew that the development laboratory was only fifty metres from the underground boardroom in which the council met. *This will be Zapas's triumph.* The thought of a weapon in his hands that could destroy an entire civilisation was thrilling.

24

HARWELL, ENGLAND

There was no sign of the black SUV on the short drive to Harwell. As Elisa drove, Daniel told her what he remembered about his early childhood in Reading, and the family's move to Wellington.

"Did you miss your friends?" she asked. "That was the thing I remember most about leaving Sydney to come here. I suppose it was a bit different as a teenage geek."

Daniel was surprised to hear her describe herself as a 'geek'. "I think so, but it's not a strong memory. Why do you say 'geek'? If it's because you were interested in archaeology or science, then I guess that's me too!"

"I was an awkward teenager. I didn't have many friends, and boys thought I was a geek. It was hard to fit in when I moved here," Elisa replied, surprising herself with her openness.

"I think I understand," Daniel said. He told Elisa about growing up in Wellington, and the shock of his dad's sudden death when he was twelve and how it had turned life upside down. Elisa gave his forearm arm a gentle friendly squeeze, as she eased the car into a space outside a monolithic white building with dark, mirrored windows. Daniel reflected that he hadn't spoken about these things to anyone for many years.

"Shall we?" he said, not knowing what else to say.

"Let's." She climbed out of the Renault, retrieving her folder and the small brown handbag from the back seat. Daniel picked up his laptop, and they walked to the doors as Elisa texted her friend. It was one of those buildings with internal security access, so she told security at reception they were expected and her friend was coming down.

At that moment, a man of about thirty with a beard and earring swiped his access card and came through security. He gave Elisa a beaming smile as he drew her in for a hug and kiss on the cheek. "Elisa! You look as stunning as ever!" He let go of her hand.

"Mark. Nice to see you, too. Thank you so much for making time to see me. I don't get down here often enough," Elisa said, as Mark looked at Daniel for the first time.

"Daniel Reade. Pleased to meet you."

"Mark Nicholson." He shook Daniel's hand cursorily and returned his attention to Elisa. "You mentioned you wanted to talk about alternate light frequency techniques and the like. How much time do you have?" Mark said, turning on the charm.

"I'm not sure," Elisa said, looking searchingly at Daniel.

"Don't worry about me," Daniel said, wondering if Mark wanted Elisa to himself.

"Well, I've got about half an hour," Mark said, neatly solving the problem. "Come with me and I can show you some of what we do while we talk about it. What sort of artefact do you want to scan?"

"It's a stone tablet, at least a few thousand years old, heavily worn, and we think it's been under the sea for most of that time," Elisa replied. They'd had visitors' passes issued and gone through security, and were now entering a small lab without windows. Mark led them to a bench with a small gravestone lying on it.

"This stone is only two hundred years old but it's limestone so hasn't weathered well." They could see that the text was barely visible in many areas and completely gone in others. Above the gravestone there was a piece of equipment neither of them recognised. "That's our latest toy."

Over the next ten minutes, Mark deployed the equipment to take successive images at different light wavelengths, many not visible, and from slightly different angles. He then let the software analyse and process the images then overlay them to reveal a very different view. On the screen they saw the gravestone, and even the areas where no text was visible to the naked eye were now clear and unmistakable.

Remarkable, Daniel thought. The technology had revealed the lost text in full.

"With a bit more time, and some different filters on the lighting, we can sometimes do even more. Soon we won't need archaeologists," he said, winking at Elisa.

"Who would you have to show off to then?" she quickly replied.

"Agh, mortally wounded." He put his hand on his heart and feigned a look of distress.

"Oh stop it," she said.

"What if all of the surface has been ground down by years of ocean currents and sand, not just rain and wind?" Daniel interjected, feeling slightly surplus.

"Good question," Mark said. "This clever bit of tech also uses higher frequencies than visible light. It can more or less X-ray the surface to 'see' the layers just below. If there's any evidence below the surface of the impacts that created the original text or images, such as chisel or stone tool marks, then there's a reasonable chance we'll see those too." Mark checked his watch. "Sorry, but I've got people waiting for me upstairs. I'll have to throw you out."

"Thanks, Mark, you've been really most helpful," Elisa said.

"Thanks a lot. Nice to meet you," Daniel said, as Mark took them back out through security.

"Pleasure. Elisa, you can owe me a drink or at least a coffee!"

They stepped outside and hurried back to Elisa's car in the light rain.

"You'll want to get back to your car," Elisa said, with the hint of a question in her voice.

"I'm sure it will be fine. If it's all right with you, I'd like to see the piece of stone you have. I've never seen Foxton's stone, only the drawings and photos. Would you mind?" he asked, hoping she would agree. "I'll sort my car out later," he added.

"Okay. I don't mind at all," she said. She seemed pleased he'd asked although didn't say so. "Oxford it is," she added, fishing her car keys from her handbag.

As Elisa drove, Daniel told her what he believed Foxton had discovered about the tablet; about his fear that he'd uncovered something that described an ancient weapon, something potentially powerful enough to destroy a whole civilisation, including its entire land mass.

"Did I tell you the strangest thing I've learned about my great-grandfather's murder?"

She waited for him to continue, as seemed to be her way.

Daniel obliged. "In the burglary, the only things taken were apparently his notes and the tablet. Other valuables in the house had been left untouched. Someone apparently wanted the tablet very much."

"And now you have his notes," she completed.

Elisa told Daniel she had a strong feeling there was something more to it than what she'd gleaned from Gillard's notes. She felt the translation referred to sound in a way that didn't quite gel, and it certainly did not appear to be a religious text. "As a trained archaeologist, I shouldn't say this," she said, "but what if this *is* somehow linked to the Atlantis story? Professor Gillard believed that, and it almost destroyed his career. I'm not saying Atlantis is real, but maybe the story is based on something as yet undiscovered?"

"As a trained historian, I shouldn't agree with you," Daniel countered, smiling at her. "But I do. It's hard to ignore. How well do you know the original Atlantis story?"

"Plato? Not in great detail," she replied.

"Most people seem to think it probably refers to the destruction of Santorini, or Thera, around 3,600 years ago," Daniel explained. "Generally speaking, that's been my view, too. But there are problems with it. Plato was clear that the events he described occurred 9,000 years earlier, roughly 11,600 years ago. He also described his Atlantis as a large island 'beyond the Pillars of Hercules'. That seems to make it clear it was in the Atlantic, and not the Mediterranean.

"Plato wrote that as the Atlanteans grew more powerful their ethics deteriorated, they became increasingly warlike and, by way of divine punishment, the island was beset by earthquakes and floods, and sank into the sea *in a day and a night!* Professor Foxton had seen similarities in the dialogues and his translation of the first tablet, but there's no clue as to what could have caused the cataclysm. If it was a weapon, as he suspected, it must have been the mother of them all. There's nothing today, thankfully, able to wreak that sort of destruction.

"So, I've been trying to work out what else, then, could realistically cause a land mass to sink two miles to the ocean floor so quickly. Some sort of massive volcanic event? An asteroid or comet? Geophysics and geology are not my strengths, but I'm fairly sure there have been no such events since the age of man. If there had been, surely there would still be ample evidence. It would have to have been an almost global cataclysm. It's pretty certain, to me at least, that the slow movement of plate tectonics, a few centimetres per year at most, just can't come close to explaining it."

Elisa considered his words for a moment. "So we're left with stone tablets that shouldn't exist, and a possible archaeological site in the Mid-Atlantic that's actually *not* possible."

"Good summary," Daniel replied cheerfully.

Elisa parked the car as close as she could to the campus. They walked between buildings until they reached St Dunstan Hall and as they entered, the porter rushed out to greet Elisa.

"Ms Mansfield! And Mr ...? We meet again."

"Hello, Mr Hearne," Elisa said.

"Daniel Reade." Daniel extended his hand.

"How goes the search for Professor Foxton's work?"

Elisa raised an eyebrow at Hearne's question, and Daniel explained that he'd spoken with him on the way out yesterday.

"It's very interesting, Mr Hearne. See you later," Elisa responded, almost without breaking her stride.

Daniel followed her, nodding to the porter. Elisa explained that he seems perfectly nice, but he loves to chat. "Sometimes it can be hard to get away."

Elisa led Daniel upstairs to the Foxton Room. There was no one else there, and he followed her to the storage shelves where she showed him the Gillard stone. It was less exciting to look at than he had expected. The text was hard to discern, and the characters he could see were incomprehensible. The stone seemed to come to life as Elisa explained it to him. The patina, the language, the fact it was an artefact of an *unknown* culture all served to increase the mystery. Elisa's words made it more appealing to him. Next to the stone were printed images with clearer text, and she explained that they, too, had alternate light source scanning technology, although not as up-to-date as Harwell's.

"I have an idea," she said. The enthusiasm on her face was almost conspiratorial, immediately drawing Daniel in.

25

President Médici had just announced another record year of economic growth for Brazil. By contrast, to the north, the Nixon administration had launched an invasion of Cambodia, creating significant unrest and protest. Civil rights also remained a festering sore for the government, with the Voting Rights Act due to expire in August.

For Zapomny, business was exceptionally good in virtually all of his interests, and São Paulo was experiencing the fastest growth in all of Brazil. Construction was under way on the new mansion on his estate, sixty metres from the current house. When completed, it would provide the facilities for Zapomny to direct his business ventures, as well as luxury accommodation for himself, his son José and their staff. María Juana had died six years earlier after years of drug and alcohol abuse. She had been deeply depressed, and Josef was glad to be rid of her. The awful parties had stopped, and, to his slight surprise, becoming a widower had further increased his respectability.

Josef's interest in the ancient artefacts had narrowed to a single piece, the only one with remaining promise. He knew the rest of the GalizienAcht had by now lost interest in all of it, focused only on amassing wealth and power for themselves and each other. They had enjoyed great success through covertly manipulating the economy and the government, to support each other's business interests. They had disabled competitors, undermined non-advantageous deals and manipulated stock prices, using any nefarious means available. For most of the eight, the artefacts were relegated to the realms of old ideals, curiosities or simply nothing more than memorabilia of the Nazis' madness.

But the Oxford tablet spoke to Josef of an ancient power he believed had been real. He also believed that since it had once existed, it could be recreated, and what a power it would be! It had destroyed an entire civilisation. One day he, or José, would wield it.

José was now twenty-one and had grown into a tough, brutal young man. The years of education, and preparation, from those carefully chosen tutors and trainers had paid off. Josef believed his son's lack of self-control would be tamed as he got older, and in the meantime, if channelled well, would build his reputation as someone to be feared. The incident with the prostitute had occurred a few weeks before his twenty-first birthday. 'She should not have defied me,' José had said. Josef had sent his senior security man in to clean up, and he reported back that the woman had been brutally beaten with a wooden chair, as well as José's fists, and was barely recognisable. She had bled to death from internal injuries.

Josef contemplated the report with distaste. He had always deplored lack of self-control as weakness. He did not blame himself, though he had been as distant a father as he'd been a husband; he was not interested in children. His interest lay in ensuring his empire had an heir who was capable of leading it.

José's early childhood was lonely and unhappy, with a cold and uncaring father, and a mother who was increasingly driven to depression and substance abuse. José had learned early that by imposing his will on others through whatever means available, whether by instilling fear in the people around him, blackmail, or just the crude use of his wealth, he was almost always effective at getting what he wanted.

Josef had been mildly surprised when José had informed him he would be changing his name to 'Zapas'. He wanted a name that was more

Brazilian, and Josef did not object. The boy had partly said it to challenge Josef, but Josef saw it as a good strategy. Perhaps it was time Zapomny was 'forgotten'. José looked more Brazilian, too. That was something María had been useful for. He was a handsome young man, with thick, almost black hair, an engaging smile that belied the danger behind it, a strong personality and steely blue eyes.

José did not care for his father, but he admired the fact that the old man got whatever he wanted and had amassed great wealth and power. Some days he held a grudging respect for his father; other days he wished him dead. José knew one day he would inherit it all. Or maybe he would not wait ... Since José's mother had died, the old man had become more obsessed and more secretive. José never knew why, but when he reached his eighteenth birthday, the old man had shown him his great obsession.

At first, José thought his father was a fool. He did not believe in it the way Josef did, but after a while he began to see the potential *if* the old man was right. *Let the old man pursue it.*

José decided there were more important things to do. He was beginning to enjoy the power that came with being Josef's son, and he savoured the fear people felt when he made unreasonable demands or threatened them calmly and coldly. He would progressively take control of the organisation, the GalizienAcht, and make it his own. When the time was right, Josef Zapomny would be expendable, as would the organisation's old name. And if the old man's obsession paid off, so much the better.

26

"I have an old friend," Elisa said. "A semi-retired professor of physics and geophysics. He lives on campus, not far from here. He might be able to help us."

Daniel wondered why but was prepared to trust her instincts.

Now almost five o'clock in the afternoon, it was getting quite dark. Elisa led the way, about three hundred metres, to another college within the main campus grounds. Through the main hall, they climbed the stairs to the first floor. About halfway along a dark, panelled corridor, she stopped at a door with a brass plaque announcing Professor Avery Compton.

Daniel heard a voice as Elisa knocked. A moment later the door opened, and a man of about seventy smiled at them.

"My dear Elisa, wonderful to see you!" beamed Avery Compton, peering over his wire-framed reading glasses. "Do come in, both of you." He walked with a slight stoop, smoothing his full head of silver-grey hair down with one hand. "Please sit. Can I offer you some tea?"

"This is Daniel Reade. His great-grandfather was John Foxton, namesake of my research room. He taught here between the wars."

"Fascinating," said Avery. "Are you also an archaeologist, Mr Reade?"

"Daniel, please. And no, I'm a student of history mostly. Right now I'm studying my great-grandfather's history."

"Oh?" Avery asked. "Tell me more, while I put the kettle on."

"Well ..." Daniel started, looking over at Elisa. She nodded her encouragement. "We've uncovered a bit of a mystery." Daniel went on to explain about Foxton's research notes in the Chidwick house, his incomplete translation of the ancient language and the messages in the text suggesting a lost technology. Elisa continued the story with the artefact Gillard had studied, and his interpretations.

"I remember Gillard," Avery said. "Nice chap, but he had quite a bit of trouble when he started talking about an ancient Atlantean civilisation. That was very nearly the road to his ruin." Avery served tea on a silver tray.

Elisa went on to explain that the Gillard fragment was written in the same unknown language related to Sanskrit, and that it, too, was reportedly dredged up from the Mid-Atlantic. She explained that they had enough of a translation to suggest the lost technology these objects described appeared to have something to do with sound, and may have been powerful enough to cause a catastrophic event.

"My great-grandfather was worried he'd found a key to a powerful ancient weapon the Nazis might want," Daniel concluded.

"There are a lot of people now theorising about lost ancient technologies, you know," Avery said in a measured tone. "And some of them do relate to acoustics. Elisa knows I'm drawn to mysteries, just as she is. As a physicist and geophysicist, my training tells me to ignore things that don't comply with the known laws of physics, but I've come to the view that not everything can be satisfactorily explained within the known laws. There are things we do not fully understand." Avery drained his teacup. "Some of these things relate to acoustics, and some go back millennia."

Elisa was on the edge of her seat, listening to every word, her cup of tea untouched.

"More than two thousand years ago, Pythagoras spoke of the 'music of the spheres'. He believed the planets and other celestial bodies made 'music'. That is to say, they have resonant frequencies and emit sound. Most people dismiss that as a rather romantic notion, but over the past two decades NASA have confirmed Pythagoras was correct!" He paused for effect. "It's remarkable, isn't it? How could Pythagoras have known that?"

Elisa said she recently read about resonant frequencies in ancient monuments like the Hypogeum of Hal-Saflieni.

"Ah yes, the Hypogeum. A strange case," Avery said. "Did you know there are physicists studying that very edifice? Have you heard of fractal non-linear resonance?"

Daniel and Elisa both shook their heads.

"Well, it's rather complicated, I'm afraid, but let me try to explain," Avery said. "Most sound waves are linear. Musical notes, for example. They are broadly symmetrical and follow a pattern. Generally speaking, they are pleasing to the ears, even at louder volumes. Linear sound waves can resonate, say, in a small room, causing vibration. They can make dust collect in the pattern of the wave. These 'standing waves' – resonating sound – are perfectly normal phenomena. However, they can also have unexpected effects. For example, research suggests that low frequency standing waves can result in people feeling disoriented and nervous. But these are often linear in nature. Non-linearity is much more interesting.

"A sharp change in frequency and intensity can force part of the wave to move faster than the rest, distorting the wave, and can add *non-linear* components to the sound. The louder these sounds are, the greater the propensity to introduce non-linearity. These non-linear waves travel through air or water or *objects* in a different way to linear waves. We *hear* them differently." Avery went back into his small kitchen, returning in a moment with a plate of shortbread.

"May I offer you a biscuit?" He passed the plate to Elisa. "Now, where was I? Oh yes, non-linear sounds are often unpleasant. Non-linear effects can also combine. A sonic boom, created when a jet travels faster than the speed of sound, leads to the sound waves collapsing into themselves, becoming *non-linear* and travelling great distances as they amplify each other. Up close, a sonic boom is incredibly loud and would damage your hearing. Are you following me?" Avery asked patiently. Daniel and Elisa said they were.

"Do you remember the shower scene in *Psycho*? The screams and the loud staccato violins have non-linear components. It's been proven that these sorts of sounds can cause an emotional response, like fear. The loud wailing of a baby also has non-linear components. Shall I pour another cup of tea? From here I'm afraid it starts to get a bit weird." Avery paused to pour another cup for himself, after Daniel and Elisa both declined.

"Physicists have developed high-powered transducers that generate non-linear sound waves powerful enough to overcome gravity, at least for small objects. Using two or three of these transducers has allowed small test objects to be *levitated* and moved around. I've seen such an experiment, made all the more strange by the fact that these transducers are silent. The loud sounds they generate are above the human ear's frequency range.

"Elisa, my dear, you mentioned the Hypogeum in Malta earlier. We now have new research that it has a fractal non-linear resonance of its own. These are the kind of acoustic effects researchers sometimes find in houses and buildings deemed to be 'haunted'. There has also been recent theory that the kind of non-linear resonance the Hypogeum exhibits, and the way it travels *through* the stone walls, has the potential to *alter matter*." Avery paused and sipped his tea as he waited for those last words to sink in.

"Now, don't get too excited," he went on, "this theory is well outside of the mainstream and may turn out to be debunked, we just don't know yet."

"What do *you* think about it?" asked Elisa.

Avery hesitated for a minute then climbed out of his chair and retrieved a book from the large overcrowded bookshelf near the door.

"Imagine if powerful non-linear acoustic levitation technology existed in ancient times. It could explain the construction of seemingly impossible monuments. Have you ever seen pictures of the walls of Sacsayhuamàn, in Peru?"

"No," Elisa and Daniel said in unison, wanting the professor to continue.

"It's built from large stone blocks, each weighing between a hundred and twenty and two hundred tons. It doesn't seem possible that a relatively primitive people could have built it, but the weight of the blocks is not the strangest thing about it." He thumbed through the well-used index of the book then located the right page and handed it to Elisa.

Daniel moved in closer to have a look and gently brushed her arm with his. She turned the book so they could both see the picture in the weak overhead light of Avery's sitting room. They stared at the high-resolution photograph of a huge stone wall that appeared to have been made from blocks that were *moulded* rather than cut. It was as if they had been put in place *while soft* and pressed together to make impossible shapes and joins. It was truly bizarre.

"There are other ancient sites like this one. Let's imagine, for a moment, that the ancients had this acoustic technology. Suddenly these megalithic structures make more sense, don't they?"

Avery talked for another ten minutes about quantum physics theories, including string theory and quantum gravity, which, although highly theoretical, were beginning to suggest that matter may not be as we think it is. That all matter might be made up of *strings*, or vibrating energy. He could see Elisa and Daniel's interest was beginning to wane, however, so he suggested if they wished to discuss 'life and the universe' any further with him, he would not be going anywhere. They thanked him very much for his time and went back out into a cold but dry evening.

"What do you make of all that?" Daniel asked Elisa.

"The idea of an unknown ancient technology makes sense to me. There seems to be so much unexplained evidence. Maybe we will relearn lost knowledge."

"Which makes me wonder whether modern humanity is wise or enlightened enough to use such powerful technology well," Daniel said. "I don't think we are, and it's a frightening thought." They walked on in silence to Elisa's car.

"I should drive you back to your car," Elisa said. It was a kind offer, but Daniel was famished, so dinner in Oxford seemed like a better idea.

"That's very kind of you, but I don't want to put you to any trouble. I can get the car later. I'd really like to get something to eat. Can you recommend somewhere nearby?"

"Well, yes, actually I can," Elisa said.

Daniel thought he might stay in town tonight if there was a pub with rooms nearby. It would be easier. "I know it's getting a bit late, but if you haven't any plans, would you like to join me for dinner?" he asked. "I feel like our conversation isn't quite finished yet."

Elisa paused for a moment. "I'm sorry but I can't tonight. I have a Taekwondo class I'm afraid. I've been doing it for two years now, and my instructor doesn't like me to miss classes," she explained.

"Oh, okay." Daniel felt disappointed but tried not to show it. There was more he wanted to discuss. "Would you mind if I call you in the morning? I feel like we're starting to get somewhere with this mystery."

"Yes. I mean no, I don't mind." Elisa smiled as she said it. "And this *is* getting interesting." She pointed out the pub down the street, and they parted ways.

Elisa drove the short distance back to her flat. She was still unsettled by the incident on the road near Chilton earlier and was more than a little weary. Briefly she considered not going to Taekwondo tonight but quickly dismissed it. She had said 'no' to dinner with Daniel, so she resolved that she should go.

She opened her front door to the sound of Mango, her cat, lecturing her loudly for being out all day. Elisa didn't like leaving him alone for long periods, but she had a good arrangement with her neighbour so she didn't need to worry. She always made sure Maggie, now retired, had plenty of cat food, and she knew Maggie also enjoyed the company. Elisa changed her clothes and headed out to her class.

27

NIGHT CLUB DISTRICT, SÃO PAULO, BRAZIL

The Club Na Beira was heaving. At 12.30 am it was full. Security out front were turning people away. The music was loud enough that people had to shout into each other's ears to be heard. The dance floor was overcrowded, and with flashing lights all around it, tonight's patrons had barely noticed the lights occasionally dimming unexpectedly. The DJ had noticed they were behaving strangely, but the drinks were flowing and so were his tips, so he didn't much care.

Tonight's customers were the usual sort of crowd. Young people out for a good time and looking to hook up, some groups partying on the dance floor, others for drinks with friends, and a few couples dancing close, a little more suggestively.

A young, scantily dressed girl stood at the bar, playing with her hair and flirting with the barman. As he poured her drink, he grinned at her and was about to ask for her number, when the floor seemed to start vibrating. It caught him off guard. The cause of the vibration did not seem to be the music. It was more as though heavy machinery was operating nearby. The girl had started to hand her money to him, but the notes fell to the floor, as the smile suddenly disappeared from her pretty face.

Blood started streaming from her nose. She stared at the barman, her expression saying 'help me'. His shock quickly gave way to horror, as her face contorted in pain and she fell to the floor.

Nearby, the DJ looked across, dumbfounded, to see some people standing holding their heads, and some on their knees, close to others still dancing. He cut the music as people around them started screaming.

* * *

OXFORD, ENGLAND

The next morning Daniel had awoken early after a patchy night's sleep. He'd been tired, but the day's conversations were still swirling in his mind. The discussion with Avery, the new Lisbon artefact, strange acoustic technology. And Elisa. Her enthusiasm, her refreshing curiosity, her green eyes.

He hadn't thought through staying in Oxford and had neither fresh clothing nor toiletries. Waiting for clothing stores to open, he'd had a light breakfast and then spent nearly an hour searching the Internet for anything helpful about the tablet, mostly finding random Atlantis theories and speculation. It seemed to be a crowded space, and he'd seen nothing helpful.

Not long after the stores had opened, he was back at his room changing his clothes. He called Elisa and got a busy tone, so he went downstairs and settled his account, with yesterday's clothes in the shopping bag. A few minutes later Elisa phoned him back.

"Hello."

"Daniel, hi. Sorry I missed your call."

"No problem. I've been thinking more about what we found yesterday, particularly the alternate light scanning stuff. Do you think your friend Mark would be able to get more information from your tablet?"

"Maybe. I think the Lisbon stone could be more promising. They were examining it with the same sort of tools," she replied. "I'd love to see that."

"Why not go and take a look?"

"To Lisbon?" She sounded surprised.

"Sure, why not? It's only a couple of hours," he said. "We could both go." She seemed taken aback.

Be careful. Don't crowd her. "No pressure. It's just an idea," he added.

A brief silence at the other end.

"Well, when you called earlier, I was talking to Cláudia at the Lisbon museum and said she'd be delighted to show us what she has. I told her no thanks, but now I'm wondering whether we should just go. *Why not?*"

"*Really?* That would be great! Oh, dammit, I'd have to get my passport," Daniel said. "And my car. Looks like the car is about an hour away by train, but I can leave now.'"

They agreed the best approach would be for Elisa to pack, while Daniel booked their flights and walked around to her flat. Then they would book a ride down to Chilton and drive Daniel's car to Heathrow, via Chidwick to collect his passport and backpack.

Half an hour later, Daniel pressed the intercom button for Elisa's flat.

"Be right down," she said, and momentarily she appeared wearing blue jeans tucked into brown leather boots, and a dark, quilted jacket zipped nearly all the way up. "Aren't you cold?" She was towing a small green overnight bag with wheels, and the narrow leather strap of her handbag was slung over her shoulder.

"Yes. A bit." Daniel was wearing only a T-shirt under his jacket. "I probably should have bought a new shirt as well."

"It's only three degrees," she observed, helpfully. "Our ride should be here in a minute. White Toyota. Hopefully a warm one. You're making me shiver."

Their car arrived and as they travelled to Chilton, Elisa phoned St Dunstan's to let them know what she was doing, and searched for a hotel, insisting on paying for that, since Daniel had paid for the flights. He told her he was happy to pay, since he'd just inherited a whole house and furniture, but she wouldn't have it.

A little over an hour later, they arrived in Chidwick. Daniel had been happy to observe that they could fall into a contented silence from time to time as they drove down. When he pulled into the driveway, he thought there might have been some tyre tracks that were not there before, but couldn't be sure. There could be any number of reasons for those – tourists occasionally drive through and could simply have been turning around. Or he could be mistaken. He didn't want to alarm Elisa, so didn't mention it.

Daniel invited Elisa to take a seat in the front room while he repacked. He apologised for the coldness of the house and ran upstairs to retrieve his passport, pull on a jersey and throw a spare shirt and the basics into his backpack. Elisa waited, sitting on the old chesterfield sofa, admiring the timber beams, the wide oak floorboards and the inglenook fireplace that occupied almost a whole wall.

Daniel ran down the stairs and found her looking thoughtful, with the makings of a smile on her face.

"I love this room," Elisa said, grabbing her handbag. "It just needs a big fire."

Daniel locked up and they left for the airport.

* * *

"They're going to Lisbon," said the caller, an older man with a crisp English accent.

"When?" demanded Rigo, sitting in his rented SUV, just outside central Oxford.

"Now," the informant replied. "You ..."

"Why?" Rigo cut in.

"They've found something at the Museum of Natural History and Science. I don't know what it is."

"Send me a name. I want to know who they are meeting."

"You're not ..."

Rigo ended the call. He was not remotely interested in the man's view of what he would or would not do. Anton Rigo was, in fact, looking forward to what he was going to do.

28

Thirty seconds later, the vibrating stopped as abruptly as it had started. Security staff ran to the dance floor, wondering where the fight was. Panic had started to take hold. The DJ could see some had blood running from their noses and ears. Near the edge of the dance floor, there were some people on their knees vomiting, and others just holding their heads. The barman was staring in horror. Something terrible had happened, but no one seemed to have any idea what it was.

The DJ could see that the carnage seemed to be contained to a portion of the dance floor, those stricken being more or less in a narrow band, two to three metres wide, across the floor, spanning from the brick side wall across to the bar. The ones who weren't moving were all in the middle of the area, nearer the brick wall. People all around were just staring, dumbfounded. The security staff did not know what to do. The bar manager called the police.

Within ten minutes the police had arrived, complete with riot gear, apparently expecting there had been some sort of terrorist attack. Paramedics ran in, taking the survivors out to waiting ambulances, and it was now clear there were more than a dozen dead. The injured who could still speak told the police stories that did not make sense. Some had heard incredibly intense sounds exploding in their ears, although nobody else in the club seemed to have heard anything other than the music. Others had felt the floor vibrating, and some reported the vibrating had made them physically sick. Others still had blinding headaches that hit them suddenly, and had affected their hearing, but no other apparent effects.

To the police interviewing people, many seemed disoriented and unable to clearly recall what had happened. One of the stranger things they had noted was that nobody was angry – in a gang or terrorist attack there are always some who are angry at the senselessness of it; angry about the innocents caught in the crossfire. Not tonight. Everyone was just bewildered.

The DJ and the barman explained to the police what they'd seen and felt, as best they could, and the police had searched the club for any evidence of what had happened. There was nothing. The doors were closed and guarded while they interviewed staff and customers, but there simply was no logical explanation. An hour later, the traumatised partygoers were allowed to leave the club, and they went out into waiting media to tell their baffling stories.

29

"Last time I came here it was like this," Elisa said. The wind was buffeting the plane from side to side.

"It's just like landing in Wellington," Daniel observed. "When were you here last?"

"Two and a half years ago," she answered, a little self-consciously.

Daniel could tell from her face there was something more to say. He waited.

"It was my last holiday with Will." She decided she trusted Daniel enough. "A week after we got back home I discovered he'd been cheating on me with someone I'd considered a friend. I didn't think I'd ever come here again. That was part of my reaction to your suggestion last night."

"I'm really sorry to hear that," Daniel said, shaking his head. "The man must be a fool," he added, half to himself. The look of vulnerability reappeared briefly in her eyes, and disappeared as quickly as it had come. Daniel wondered if he'd said too much. "Sometimes I guess things just don't work out how they should," he said.

Earlier in the flight, Daniel had told Elisa about how his father's death had affected the family, his mother taking years to recover from her loss. About how it had affected both him and his sister differently. He'd also told her about he and Andrea going their separate ways two years ago.

"After Will, I just threw myself into my work," Elisa went on. "I decided it was time to take my career more seriously."

Daniel was pleased she felt comfortable to confide in him.

The plane touched down with a bump, and Elisa was relieved. They retrieved their bags from the overhead locker. As they exited the plane the temperature in the air bridge felt like mid-twenties, so Daniel slung his jacket over his shoulder, feeling slightly underdressed next to Elisa in her silk shirt and tailored jacket.

They quickly navigated their way out of the terminal and took a taxi to the hotel. It was still a lovely twenty degrees, although it was now quite dark. Elisa had booked them into a small hotel on Rua Castilho, a leafy street roughly a ten-minute walk to the museum, according to the website. It looked to be a good choice to Daniel.

They'd been lucky. Cláudia was happy to meet them the next day, Sunday. Elisa had checked with her before they left Oxford, once they'd worked out they wouldn't be able to get to the museum until well after six in the evening.

They checked in and deposited their bags in their rooms – Elisa had booked adjacent rooms – and decided to go for a walk to find somewhere to eat. Seven o'clock was early for dinner in Lisbon, so they found a bar for a drink first.

"It's been an amazing few days for me," Daniel said, sipping an ice-cold beer. "A week ago I had no idea I'd inherited a house, nor that I had a murdered archaeologist as my great-grandfather, a *Doomsday Tablet*, or any of this."

"For me, too," Elisa said, smiling at him. "I did say I love a good mystery! I'm looking forward to seeing what Cláudia has tomorrow. I feel like we need to piece this together."

The mystery of the tablets kept them talking enthusiastically through dinner, and neither was in a rush for the night to end. But it had been a long day, and both were starting to feel tired.

As they returned to the hotel, Daniel was tempted to ask Elisa if she wanted another drink, but he was still conscious he might be crowding her. They took the elevator to their floor and as Daniel reached his room and said goodnight, Elisa unexpectedly gave him a kiss on the cheek.

"Goodnight, Daniel." She turned and went to her room next door.

Elisa started getting ready for bed, feeling slightly embarrassed for having kissed Daniel on the cheek. It was spontaneous, just an impulse. They'd had a wonderful day. He was so easy to talk to. So easy to just *be with*. She recognised in herself the feelings developing for him but was worried she'd only known him a few days, and, since Will, she hadn't felt confident about her judgement in men. But more importantly, Daniel lived in New Zealand and would probably be going home soon. Whatever she was thinking, it seemed to be doomed by distance.

As she lay awake, she wondered if her impulsive kiss was a mistake. It was well after midnight before sleep finally overtook her busy mind.

Daniel woke just after six the next morning. *Too early to text Elisa.* He took a leisurely shower, dressed and went out for a walk. It was another nice day, although at six-thirty it was still a little dark. The air was crisp, although warmer than Oxford. He went past a few cafés, though none were open yet, so it seemed a hotel breakfast would be in store for them. As he stepped into the hotel lobby just after seven, his phone chimed. *Elisa.*

Hope I'm not too early. Breakfast soon? her text said.

Perfect. How soon?

Half an hour?

Okay. See you in the lobby.

Daniel went back to his room to pack, since they would need to check out this morning. He was back in the lobby by seven-thirty and Elisa was waiting for him.

"Good morning!" she said with a welcoming grin. She noticed he hadn't shaved.

"Yes, it is," he replied, noticing her look and stroking the stubble on his chin. "Forgot to pack my shaver." She was wearing a pale pink T-shirt under her navy jacket. "You look radiant! There are no cafés open yet so it's a hotel breakfast for us."

"That's fine with me."

They went into the small restaurant and chose a table by the window.

"Did you arrange a time with the museum?" Daniel asked, as they sat down with glasses of juice, and some fruit and toast to share.

"They open at eleven, but Cláudia said she would meet us at ten, so we have plenty of time." Elisa's hand brushed Daniel's as they reached for some toast.

They finished breakfast with coffee and returned to their rooms to pack. Keen to find out more, by nine-thirty they were checked out and ready to go.

They walked along the Rua do Salitre and turned left into Rua Nova de São Mamede, past the elegant residential buildings and the occasional café. Then another left turn onto Rua da Escola Politécnica. Daniel marvelled at the elaborate street names.

A hundred metres further along, they arrived at the grand front entrance of the Museu Nacional de História Natural e da Ciência, the Museum of Natural History and Science. It was just a few minutes before ten.

As they peered through the front doors, they saw a young woman crossing the wooden floor to greet them. "Hello! Elisa?"

"Yes, hi. This is Daniel."

They all shook hands.

Cláudia opened one of the doors, ushered them in, and arranged visitors' passes for them with her colleague at the information desk. She took them upstairs and along a corridor to doors marked 'Staff Only' in English and Portuguese. She swiped her access card and took them into a room reminiscent of the Foxton Room at St Dunstan's. Daniel and Elisa waited while Cláudia went to retrieve the tablet. She soon returned, reverently placing a box on the table and slowly removing its lid. The stone tablet inside was somehow captivating. An ancient relic or harbinger. It was similar to the one at Oxford, and the pictures of the first Foxton tablet, but not quite the same. It was not as thick and had a greener patina, with the remnants of what Elisa supposed was marine growth.

The text on it was a disappointment, having worn away even more than the stone at Oxford. Cláudia explained that she was quite excited about the results of the alternate light scans. She showed Daniel and Elisa the scans on a large screen at her table, and the results were indeed impressive. The text appeared to cover most of the object, and it was clearer where the bottom section and some of the top had broken off.

"The characters look consistent with the ones on our tablet, don't you think?" Elisa said to Cláudia.

"I think so," replied Cláudia. "It is not easy to be certain, but yes. We do not know this language and have no success translating. It is not Sanskrit. I must admit that we do not know how to classify it, and it has not had much attention."

"Would it be possible to get copies of these scan files? Or high-res prints?" Elisa asked.

"Of course," said Cláudia. "The files are too large for our old email system, so I have copied them for you." She retrieved a USB flash drive with MUHNAC printed on one side, and handed it to Elisa.

"That's very kind of you," said Elisa.

"It looks different to the one at Oxford. Do you know where it was discovered?" Daniel asked the question that was in Elisa's mind.

"We can't know for sure, but supposedly south of Iceland, near the Mid-Atlantic Ridge. The marine growth suggests it was in water not deeper than five hundred metres," Cláudia explained.

"I hope you don't mind me asking, but do you think it would be possible for us to borrow it? My college at Oxford would love to study it. And return it to you, of course." Elisa hoped she did not offend Cláudia, but she was keen to understand more about where it came from. She was sure her colleagues would like to see it, and maybe marine biologists could shed some light on its provenance.

Elisa and Daniel could see in Cláudia's face that she was surprised by the request.

"If it would help, I'm sure I could get my department head to send an official request to your curator," Elisa added. "And if not, please don't worry, I understand."

"A brief loan might be allowed. My curator is not in until one o'clock today, but I will ask her then. I will be very interested if you can help to translate this," Cláudia said. "For us it is a new language."

"For us, too, but we've made some progress with the artefact we have," Elisa replied. "Thank you so much, Cláudia. You've been a great help. We'll come back a little after one o'clock?"

"Perfect," Cláudia agreed.

They shook hands, and Cláudia escorted Daniel and Elisa back to the public area, saying she would find a suitable transport case for the flight home. In the museum's main lobby, Elisa called Alan to ask him to email an official request to Cláudia, and he promised to log on and do it right away.

"We've got a few hours to kill. Shall we have a look around?" Daniel asked, as he produced a museum map he'd picked up while Elisa made her call.

After a tour of the museum, they took a short walk around Lisbon's narrow cobbled streets. With the help of Daniel's phone and Elisa's memory, they had managed to find the Miradouro de São Pedro de Alcântara, a beautiful garden terrace that overlooked the city. Even for the time of year, it was quite busy, with many people sitting on the benches under the shade of the large trees.

"The weather here reminds me of Sydney in the spring," Elisa said.

"I'd love to spend some time here one day, it seems a beautiful city." Daniel saw Elisa's face cloud momentarily, perhaps remembering her last time in Lisbon. He didn't know what to say.

They arrived back at the museum at one-fifteen and climbed the front steps, dismayed to see the front doors blocked by a police cordon.

30

Josef Zapomny had summoned his son. He felt it was time for José to step up. Not just because Josef was eighty-two years old, but because he felt it was time he had to let go. His will was still strong, he could still control his empire, and he could still instil fear, but physically he was becoming frail. Others could see weakness emerging. They would find ways to exploit any weakness they found. There was also the inconvenient matter of Josef's heritage. The Jew, Wiesenthal, was still relentlessly pursuing Nazis, and the previous year had forced the exhumation of the body of Mengele, the Auschwitz Angel of Death, in São Paulo.

Josef reflected that his life had not gone in the direction he had been conditioned to expect as a child. None of it had been mediocre. In fact, it had been a very successful life indeed. He had amassed a great fortune, and he had ruled his organisation with the rigid force he'd learned to master when he was in the SS. He expected the same of his son. Josef was the last survivor of the original eight from Galicia. His son was his legacy and would continue his empire, which already controlled a large portion of South American commerce. José was ready. When the breakthrough came, the new technology would make José Zapas, son of Hans Josef Strobl, the most powerful man in the world.

A member of the house staff knocked on the door of the second-floor lounge room where Josef was relaxing in his favourite chair. "Enter," he said in a clear but slightly raspy voice.

"Mr Zapas's car has arrived, sir."

"Good. Bring us some tea."

José lived in a large house that Josef had always hated. It was excessive and opulent. The house was ten kilometres from the Zapomny estate, in another exclusive part of São Paulo. Josef believed José had chosen it simply in defiance, because his father didn't like vulgar displays of wealth. The Zapomny house was certainly not small, but the grounds were fenced and the house itself not visible from the street. The gardens and grounds were large, but that was more for security for Zapomny and the organisation. The house, like the grounds, was large and functional, but it was not ostentatious. José would have to choose where to live when he inherited the estate. Hopefully, he would make the right decision and choose the more respectable and dignified family estate. *Greater privacy for my son's excesses would prove useful also,* Josef thought distastefully.

"You wanted me." José announced his presence as he strode in.

"Yes, my son, I did. I'm pleased you could drag yourself away from whoever it was today," the old man said, contempt ringing in his voice.

José had had a string of short-term relationships with young women, many of them ending violently. He had not made even the slightest pretence of respectability. It would not serve him well in the future.

"You're still alive then," José said, throwing the disrespect back.

"You are fearless. I like that. Soon this will be yours. You will lead the organisation, and you will lead my businesses. You should try to be more respectable. Take a wife."

"Why would I take one when I can have many?" Always the barbed response.

"One day you will understand. You have all the money you could want, but you have not tasted power yet. Not like I have." The old man lay his head back and took a slow, disappointed breath. "The technology is almost ready."

"It has been 'almost ready' for decades," José shot back contemptuously. "You're a fool to be so obsessed by it."

"There have been difficulties, yes, but we know it has existed before. The only obstacle now is the power source. We know it can be done. It will be done." The lust for power still gleamed in the old man's eyes. "With it, you could become the most powerful man in the world." Zapomny paused for his son to think about that. "Those women are a weakness. Take a wife."

"Like my mother? Don't tell me what to do, old man," José snapped. He remembered how Josef had destroyed his mother. José had watched her waste away, through years loneliness and depression. He vaguely remembered the good early years, too. Playing together in the old house when he was a small boy. Josef had destroyed that house, too. Josef had made him all that he was today.

"Soon you will have all of this. You need to learn to be a man." Josef spat the last words out as if they were poison.

José bristled. *I will not be spoken to like this. Not by anyone.*

Josef watched without any fear in his cold blue eyes as José marched across the floor. He made no attempt to move. He expected his son to strike him. A defining moment for the thirty-six-year-old. The son becomes the master. José had something else in mind, however.

"Actually, I'll have it today, old man." He reached his father's chair, ripped a pillow out from behind his father's head and forcefully pushed it over his face. The old man was no match for his son. Thirty seconds later he was dead. José Zapas was not just *a* man now, was *the* man. He smiled at the thought. He put the pillow roughly back behind his father's head and left the room.

"He's dead," José said to the servant standing outside with tea on a tray. He heard it crash to the floor as he walked away.

31

E lisa grabbed Daniel's arm and squeezed nervously as they approached the doors. They were allowed to enter, but the cordon closed off part of the ground floor as well as access to the lifts. She went over to the information counter, Daniel close behind. The young man remembered her. He told her Cláudia had been attacked by a maintenance worker, just half an hour earlier. He was shocked such a thing could happen in the museum, particularly in Lisbon, a safe, friendly city. The young man had no idea of motive, since it appeared the only thing that might be missing was the stone tablet she'd been working on. Of course, it may yet turn up, and it might have just been a random attack.

"Is Cláudia all right?" Elisa asked.

"I don't know," he said with dismay. "She was unconscious when they took her away." Elisa touched his arm in sympathy.

The man was visibly upset and wanted to talk. He explained that the staff had told police the stone tablet was an interesting old artefact but had little, if any, intrinsic value. They did not consider it a motive and had started asking questions that suggested they thought the motive could be a spurned lover, or would-be lover. "I don't believe that," he said.

There was talk that a maintenance man carrying a toolbox had been working in the area and now could not be located, but nobody remembered what he looked like other than he'd been wearing a red baseball cap. The young man said it was strange, because the front desk hadn't been notified there was a maintenance crew working today, although he also admitted it wasn't the first time that had happened. Two police officers came over to the information desk, and Elisa drew Daniel away as they starting speaking in Portuguese.

"I just knew it would be about the tablet as soon as I saw the police," Elisa whispered into Daniel's ear. The distressed look on her face said it all – *did we cause this?*

After the police officers had gone, Elisa went back to the young man. He told her that apparently Cláudia was in a serious but stable condition and had regained consciousness. They were optimistic of a full recovery. He also explained he'd heard one of the police officers say, as they left, that she hadn't been able to help, having been struck from behind and not seen the attacker. Daniel and Elisa were thankful Cláudia was going to be all right. Perhaps she was lucky she hadn't seen him.

They weren't keen on getting involved in the police investigation and felt there was nothing they could add anyway, but nonetheless made sure the young man had their names and contact details before leaving the museum.

"What if the man in the cap is still around?" The thought chilled her.

"If he came for the tablet, he's got what he wanted. I think he'll be long gone," Daniel replied, hoping he was right. The attack had been only half an hour ago. *If we'd come back fifteen minutes early, instead of fifteen minutes late …*

A shout from across the street startled them both, and Elisa grabbed Daniel's arm in fright. A man with a cropped haircut waved in their direction, calling loudly. They were about to turn and run, as a woman behind them called back in Portuguese and waved at the man.

"Can we get out of here?" Elisa asked anxiously.

"Good idea. Let's get an earlier flight."

They hurried back to their hotel, and Elisa started checking flights on her phone. It was clear to both of them that someone was very interested in the information contained in these ancient tablets, and that their intentions were obviously not good.

"I've got a bad feeling this *is* all about an ancient weapon, a very dangerous one, just like my great-grandfather wrote," Daniel said.

"We really need to figure out what these tablets are telling us," Elisa replied, with a determined look.

"Yes, we do. The other thing in my mind is that this looks like it's been going on since the murder of my great-grandfather. It seems crazy – his death was more than seventy years ago – but it all seems connected."

* * *

Thirty minutes earlier, Anton Rigo had handed his toolbox to a man at the Lisbon air cargo terminal. Zapas's security people had sent the details and made the necessary arrangements. The new tablet would be on its way to São Paulo by now. Zapas had demanded that Rigo send it immediately. He hadn't explained why, though Rigo knew the lab men were desperate for more information as they worked to scale up the weapon.

Waiting to board his flight back to London, he found a quiet space to make a phone call. "It is done," he said.

"You did not kill the woman. Why?" A moment of silence. "Do not be concerned. She did not see me. Nobody saw me," Rigo said through his clenched jaw. He was disappointed he hadn't hit her hard enough. "There is no possible link to you." He didn't know how Zapas had received the information so quickly, since it was less than an hour since he'd left the museum with the tablet. A reminder of the organisation's formidable network.

"Reade and Mansfield were at the museum ahead of you. You should have killed them all." Zapas was angry.

"And escaped unseen? I doubt it. That would have been unwise."

"You are challenging me?" Zapas's voice was rising.

"I am doing my job."

"Do not push me," Zapas snarled.

Rigo knew what the man was capable of, so he backed off. "Of course not."

"Then get back to England and find out what they know. We now understand there's another stone at Oxford. I want that too," Zapas directed. "And this time, clean up your mess properly."

José Zapas slammed the phone down on the table. If his pale-faced killer hadn't been so effective in the past, Zapas would have ordered his execution and replacement. But he decided to leave it alone, for now.

As his anger subsided, he picked up the remote control and pressed 'play', resuming the recorded press coverage of his previous social media comments. He'd been pleased with the editing his media organisations had done. It was a useful way to undermine the current government, strengthening his position as challenger, but more importantly it also gave potential buyers a demonstration that the technology was real. Having others hint at collusion with the United States was just a fringe benefit.

The next demonstration would be unequivocal and terrifying proof of its power.

32

By mid-afternoon, Elisa and Daniel were at the airport, having managed to change to an earlier flight, collect their bags and grab a taxi from the hotel. As they made their way through the airport, they scanned the crowd anxiously, not knowing what Cláudia's attacker looked like and both hoping Daniel's earlier guess was right. It seemed sensible that the man would have left quickly after he'd got what he came for, but there was no way to know.

Daniel turned to Elisa. "I've got a bad feeling about all of this. It's not just Cláudia; there've been other things too. Outside my uncle's house, I saw tyre tracks in the driveway. At the time, I thought it might have just been tourists or something, but now I'm not so sure. Your encounter with the black SUV, too."

"That could have just been a crazy driver," Elisa replied.

"Or not. In my car outside the pub in Chilton, I was pretty sure the rental papers had been moved. I don't think I imagined it. And now Cláudia."

"I hope she is all right." Elisa bit her lip.

"The police said she'd regained consciousness. Let's check with the museum tomorrow," Daniel said.

They boarded the plane in a sombre silence, stowed their luggage overhead and took their seats. A flight attendant handed out newspapers, and Daniel took one, more as a distraction than anything else.

"Let's hope Cláudia's information tells us something new," Elisa said, trying to look forward. "I *am* worried, but if we analyse this logically, all we really have is a *possibility* the tablets are talking about a technology. We need new information. Without it, maybe we're reading too much into the text we have. It still could just be religious doomsday warnings."

Neither of them believed that, but neither one said so.

After take-off Daniel opened his newspaper, *The Portugal News*, the only Lisbon paper in English, asking Elisa if she wanted a section to read. For Daniel the distraction was welcome, but Elisa was feeling quite tired and said she would try to rest. And try to think about something else.

"Next time I fly across the channel I should visit my grandmother," she said, almost absent-mindedly. "She's in Bilbao. We have the same name. Elisa is Spanish. I used to get called 'Lisa' at school all the time and almost changed it, but I didn't want to offend my grandma."

"Well, you're *Elisa* to me. It's a beautiful name." *Is that the hint of a smile on her lips?* Her eyes were closed. Daniel went back to his reading.

Moments later, on page seven of his newspaper, Daniel spotted a headline that grabbed his attention. BRAZILIAN GOVERNMENT ACCUSED OF TESTING A SOUND WEAPON ON CITIZENS.

"Look at this!" he exclaimed.

Elisa opened her eyes, leaning into Daniel, nudging his emotions into overdrive. She didn't seem to notice.

"Sorry, I didn't mean to wake you," he apologised.

"I was just dozing," she replied. "What is it?"

"I'm not exactly sure, but ..."

He pointed out the article and her eyes opened wide. The article itself was not as strong as the headline, but it was nonetheless shocking:

São Paulo police are investigating a baffling tragedy at the Club Na Beira in the early hours of this morning. Thirteen people are dead and a number of others injured in an alleged attack that remains unexplained. Survivors and witnesses reported a variety of effects including deafness, bleeding from eyes, ears and nostrils, disorientation, nausea, all accompanied by a strong shaking or vibration. A source at São Paulo morgue told reporters the dead all had signs of brain haemorrhage, and their internal organs had been liquefied. Police and coroner are yet to make an official statement.

Presidential candidate and leading businessman José Zapas has lashed out at the Brazilian government for failing the people. 'This is what happens when a weak government is soft on crime!' Zapas said. Other unconfirmed sources have claimed that 'the government, in collusion with their American friends, is testing some sort of weapon on the good people of São Paulo'.

"Could it be ..." Elisa's voice trailed off as she started to say what Daniel was thinking. *So someone does seem to be developing this ancient technology. That's why they want the tablets.*

The implications were shocking. Terrifying. But aside from the imminent threat, they couldn't help but think that it added weight to their theory; that there *was* an ancient Atlantic civilisation that may have destroyed itself with its own advanced technology. Plato's story, dismissed by academics, scientists and scholars as fantasy, could actually be true. But how was this possible? Where was it? And how could it have vanished so completely, thousands of metres below the ocean?

"And it looks like this has been going on since the Second World War," said Daniel, repeating his earlier observation. "It just seems too far-fetched."

"I know," Elisa replied. "I want to get this new tablet translated. Let's hope Cláudia's images are sharper than those screenshots. We need to know more."

As they began their descent into Heathrow, they both noticed the weather in London was decidedly worse than Lisbon. It was getting dark already, but they were going through thick cloud and heavy rain. By the time they made their way through the terminal and out to the car park, it was nearly six o'clock, and a cold six degrees. Elisa said she would catch the train, but Daniel persuaded her that it was no trouble to drive her home. Traffic on a Sunday evening shouldn't be too bad, and he didn't want to leave her alone.

Elisa was eager to get to the images of the Lisbon stone to try to start deciphering it. Daniel was keen to see what they had, too, and had an idea. "Another option is to go back to Chidwick and lay out Foxton's notes and drawings next to Cláudia's and see if that helps. I'm happy to drive you back to Oxford afterwards. There's also a spare room, and the pub has rooms, so plenty of good options." Elisa didn't respond immediately. "Please don't feel pressured. My curiosity is just getting the better of me. I'm very happy to drive you home now, if you prefer."

"No, Chidwick sounds like a good option. I'm curious too. Let's do that," she said.

The weather was steadily worsening as they reached the M3, heading south-west. The windscreen wipers rhythmically beat away the rain. Daniel suggested a dinner at the Cross Keys, in front of a nice warm fire, and Elisa agreed. The wind was picking up, and driving had become more difficult.

Forty-five minutes later, they took the exit to Andover. After they skirted around its outskirts, the road progressively narrowed and gave way to meadow, and then the familiar forest. They drove through the village and past the Cross Keys to the house, through the pouring wind and rain. Daniel stopped the car inside the yard and reached into his backpack to dig out the house keys.

"Give me a minute to open the door," he said, leaving the backpack as he climbed out of the car. He ran over to the door and opened it quickly, and Elisa followed close behind. Shaking off the rain, they hung their coats in the hallway. The house seemed colder than usual to Daniel, and there was a subtle chill wind coming from the kitchen. He went through to the back of the house and saw the back door ajar. Elisa followed him in.

"Someone's been here," he said in a hushed voice, pointing at the door. The kitchen had been searched and some boxes moved in the utility room. His heart was beating a little faster, and his first instinct was to rush upstairs to check Foxton's papers, but Elisa already had her phone out.

"I'm calling the police. What if he's still around?"

As she spoke, her eyes opened wider as a very pale man dressed in black silently entered the kitchen, through the hallway door. He had a pistol pointed directly at her.

33

Felipe and Paulo, two of the engineers in the organisation's underground laboratory, returned through the long tunnel, having taken a break for lunch and some fresh air. As they arrived, they knew something was wrong. They could hear the low hum and feel the vibration of the device.

"Mãe de Deus!" Felipe exclaimed, as he panicked and raced to the control panel to turn it off. He knew Zapas had killed men for lesser mistakes. The two men waited for the vibration to stop, hoping no damage had been done. If the weapon had been compromised ...

When the vibration stopped, they entered the reinforced test room and checked the equipment. Paulo thanked God everything seemed to be in order, but just as he did so, a cracking sound came from the steel- and concrete-reinforced back wall. It was towards this wall that the device, for safety, had been directed.

The two men stared at the wall. Something just didn't look right. The concrete blocks of the inner wall had somehow sunk. They were *a different shape!* They had bulged out considerably in the middle and were flatter than the unaffected blocks. At the top of the wall there was a gap of around ten centimetres through which the men could feel a slight breeze.

Paulo brought a chair and stood on it. He could see through the wall to the earth behind, and a sliver of light penetrated from above. The whole wall seemed to have *compressed*. Felipe pushed the bulging mid-section concrete blocks, and they were soft like thick mud. They ran out excitedly and called for Días.

When Henriqué Días returned, he berated the men for an unauthorised experiment but soon calmed down when he saw what had happened. He wanted to know whether there had been any similar effect at the nightclub. That could be a useful development.

Días phoned Zapas with the news, and Zapas was down in the lab before Días finished his cigarette.

"Show me," Zapas demanded.

They showed him the test room wall, and when Felipe pressed the concrete block it was now hard, as if it had been set in a compressed bulging shape. Zapas could see finger-shaped indentations in the block. "How long did this take?"

"One hour," said Paulo. "We were testing whether the device could be operated for a sustained period," he improvised.

Zapas considered the new information. "I want to know how far this effect can penetrate rock," he demanded.

Días suggested examining the nightclub site further, as a next step. He also pointed out that further testing here could damage the Zapas estate.

Zapas directed them to pack the device ready for transport and said they would be notified when and where. "Also, doctor, you said you needed more information, so now that you have another tablet, I expect faster results," he added.

Días lit another cigarette and adjusted his glasses, as he wondered what Zapas might do if he failed to meet these expectations. He wanted to tell Zapas that what he needed most was some information explaining the power source, though he knew he would not care.

Half an hour later, Zapas's senior security officer contacted Días with the location for the tests. It was a recently decommissioned copper mine owned by a Zapas company. It had been closed down by order of the government for the acid rain it produced, which had caused significant damage to the surrounding vegetation and property. An order Zapas would rescind when he became president. He had also learned that one of his companies currently had a maintenance detail working in the nightclub district, so he would soon have some information regarding any similar effects near the site.

As José Zapas assessed this interesting new development, he imagined its possible uses. Surgically precise destruction of buildings, or even whole city blocks. Maybe it could undermine and destroy whole cities. He thought briefly that the old man had been right to covet and obsess. He would have more power than the president of the United States, and it thrilled him to the core.

34

"Ah, Ms Mansfield. Please put that down," he said, nodding in the direction of the kitchen bench. Elisa put her phone down. The pale man then directed them back to the utility room, while he checked her phone to make sure no call had been made. "I want all your work on the stone tablets," he said, in a faintly German accent.

Is this the same man who attacked Cláudia? Elisa's mind was racing.

"It's not here," Daniel improvised.

"Mr Reade, please. I know it is here. Get it now, or perhaps I should shoot Ms Mansfield." Rigo pointed the gun directly at Elisa's face. She recoiled, and Rigo saw a vulnerability in her face that he would enjoy later.

"Okay, okay. It's upstairs," Daniel said hastily, willing him to point the gun somewhere else. The fact that he knew their names made it all the more menacing.

"Show me. Both of you." He motioned them to the stairs. As Elisa passed the open back door, she noticed a fuel can sitting just outside. In her gut she knew this man wasn't going to just walk out of here and leave them alive. When he got what he wanted, he would kill them. Her mind was still racing as she stepped into the hallway ahead of Daniel.

Rigo pointed the gun at Daniel, signalling him to go up the stairs first.

151

Then he nodded his head to the stairs for Elisa to go after. A few steps behind, he followed. He thought he'd seen real fear in the woman's face, and it excited him. 'Clean up your mess,' Zapas had said. He would obtain the notes and anything else these two had, then kill Reade. Painfully. That would ensure the woman's compliance. The fire would clean up the mess later.

At the top of the stairs, Daniel pushed the study door open, and Elisa stepped out of the way into the doorway of the small bathroom.

"Both of you, in there!" Rigo signalled towards the study with his pistol.

Daniel turned, and while Rigo watched him, Elisa chose her moment. She lashed out with a strong kick at his groin. Rigo avoided the brunt of the kick, but had to turn awkwardly on the small landing. He was angry with himself for underestimating her, misreading her look of vulnerability as weakness. He regained his balance and pointed the gun at her chest, with the beginnings of a cold-eyed smile on his pale face.

Daniel instinctively lashed out at the weapon and grabbed it with both hands, pushing it to the side as Elisa unleashed another kick, this time to his stomach. The kick was on target, surprising Rigo enough that Daniel managed to wrestle the gun away from him. But Rigo was fast, he produced a knife from nowhere, and slashed Daniel's arm, causing him to drop the gun.

Daniel kicked hard at the man's left knee, not fully connecting, but enough for Rigo to start to lose his balance. Elisa shoved him backwards as hard as she could, and his foot caught in the threadbare carpet on the landing. Elisa watched speechlessly as Rigo stumbled back and fell down the top flight of stairs, his arms flailing wildly as he dropped the knife to grasp at the balustrade. His fall came to an abrupt stop on the lower landing as his head struck the masonry wall with a sickening crunch. He did not move.

Daniel and Elisa were still in shock and breathing hard, as Daniel retrieved the man's knife and gun. Not knowing what to do with them, he took them both into the study and put them on a bookshelf near the door.

Elisa followed him in. Daniel pulled his phone out of his jeans and dialled 999 breathlessly.

"Police," he said as the call answered. Elisa said 'ambulance too', looking at the blood dripping from Daniel's right sleeve. He finished the call with address details. "They said fifteen to twenty minutes."

"Are you okay?" she asked.

"I think so. You?" They were still running on adrenaline, breathing hard. Daniel went back out to the stairs to see if the man was dead, wondering how they would tie him up if he was still alive. But he was gone!

Daniel took the gun from the bookshelf, assuming it was not safety locked, and searched the house quickly but cautiously. He wasn't sure exactly what he would do if the man was still there, but he was in no doubt that if the man got the upper hand again, he would surely kill them. He checked the whole house, even the tiny bathroom under the stairs. There was no sign of him, so he securely locked both the front and back doors, and went back up to Elisa.

"He's gone."

Elisa was busy in the bathroom looking for supplies to tend Daniel's wound. She found a bandage and some tape, and told Daniel to take off his shirt. The wound was on his right forearm, near the elbow. It was still bleeding profusely but Daniel said he didn't think it was too deep. He flexed his right hand as if to prove his point but winced slightly as he did so. They were both still shaking, from nerves or the adrenaline rush, but Elisa managed to bandage the wound and slow the bleeding. Her touch was gentle, and she kept glancing at Daniel's face as if to make sure she wasn't hurting him.

As she worked, she remembered the jerry can. "Did you have a can of fuel outside the kitchen door?" she asked.

"No." Daniel looked mystified.

"I saw one when we were in the kitchen. I knew he was here for more than burglary."

The reality of their situation started to hit home, as the shock slowly dissipated. They were still standing at the top landing, Elisa's hand on Daniel's bandaged arm, when there was a loud knock at the door. They jumped. Daniel went downstairs, Elisa following, and through the small side window saw a man in an overcoat standing outside in the heavy rain. Lightning flashed as Daniel opened the door and quickly ushered the two policemen inside.

The man in the overcoat sent the uniformed constable back outside to check the house and grounds. Overcoat introduced himself as 'DI Mander'.

"Daniel Reade." Daniel shook the DI's hand. "Visiting from New Zealand to deal with my late uncle's estate. This is his house," he added by way of explanation.

Elisa introduced herself and DI Mander jotted notes on a small pad while he interviewed them both. The ambulance arrived as he was wrapping up his questions, and the paramedics replaced Elisa's handiwork with a surgical dressing and some tape, after applying some antiseptic.

"You're lucky," one of the paramedics said. "Nothing important nicked, and you shouldn't need stitches. Tomorrow you should go to a medical centre and get that checked again." The paramedics left him with another large adhesive bandage.

The constable had returned with a jerry can and a small kerosene heater from outside. His clothes were dripping wet. "Are these yours?" he asked.

"No, I've never seen them before," Daniel replied.

"These little heaters are the cause of a lot of house fires in this district," DI Mander explained. "The houses are often poorly heated, and these things are far too common." He unscrewed the cap of the jerry can and smelt it. "Kerosene. My guess is this was a burglary and he'd planned to cover his tracks with arson."

Daniel wanted to tell the man it was no ordinary burglary; the attacker knew their names and knew exactly what he wanted, but he checked himself. DI Mander would want their notes. Now, more than ever, Daniel knew they needed to work out what this was all about. They needed to translate the tablets and understand what they were facing. Only then could they get some real help.

The constable had stopped dripping on the floor. He told his DI there was no sign of any vehicle, but there were shoe tracks from the back door into the forest. Daniel knew most of the tracks led to other roads near the village.

"The man was armed, too." Daniel took them upstairs to show them what had happened. He retrieved the gun and the knife from the study bookshelf and handed them to the detective. The line of questioning changed slightly. The DI wanted to know what Daniel and Elisa did for a living; did they know anyone who might wish them harm; was there money or other valuables on the premises?

A short while later the policemen left, but not before reminding Daniel and Elisa it was possible the man might return. A prospect they had already considered. The detective agreed to send a constable back to keep an eye on the house but suggested they might want to stay somewhere else tonight. As he'd said it, lightning flashed ominously and a loud crack of thunder followed a few seconds later.

"We need to get out of here," Elisa said, still clearly shaken.

35

Daniel quickly retrieved Foxton's notes and grabbed a few things from his room, keen to get away from the house. They were soon back on the road and driving into the storm. "Oxford?" he asked, unsure.

"I don't know. He knew our names. He knew where you live. He might know where I live, too., Elisa said, thinking quickly. "I think we should assume he's the same man who attacked Cláudia. He seemed to know a lot."

"Hmm. Andover then? It's in the other direction, at least, and it's a big enough town," Daniel offered.

"All right. Let's see if we can find somewhere with a parking garage, in case he's looking for your car as well."

It wasn't much of a plan, but just *having* a plan helped to calm their nerves.

"We need to finish the translation and figure out what we're up against," Elisa said.

"Yes. That's why I didn't tell Mander about the notes. He might have taken them as evidence."

"Mm, I thought so, too. Well, we have it all with us. Do you still have your laptop?"

"Yes."

They drove the remaining few miles to Andover mostly in silence, as the windscreen wipers swished back and forth. After a brief drive around the town centre, they found a fairly new pub with accommodation and a fenced parking area at the back. Daniel drove in and parked up against the back wall of the pub, ensuring the car couldn't be seen from the street. They climbed out, quickly grabbed their bags and ran inside. Thankfully, there were vacancies.

It was well after nine o'clock when they settled into their rooms, but both were drained and didn't feel much like going out. Elisa had changed out of her wet shirt and jacket into a more casual fleecy top. She grabbed a brochure from a local takeaway house offering delivery and knocked on Daniel's door. She was glad he was close by. She didn't want to be alone just yet. He opened the door as he finished pulling on a T-shirt, wincing a little as he put his right arm into the sleeve.

"Pizza?" She said it lightly, but Daniel could see she was just as anxious as he felt. Neither had any idea who the pale man was; all they knew was that they had something he wanted.

"Perfect. Come in," he said, with an unconvincing smile.

Elisa ordered the pizza sitting at the solitary chair in the room, the spindly, wooden variety common to English pubs. While they waited, they started to reassess their situation. They still had all the notes, but there were likely now two related stone tablets in the hands of whoever they were dealing with. There was still Gillard's stone at St Dunstan's, so it seemed the bad guys didn't know everything.

"That's one positive, at least," Daniel mused.

Elisa watched him as he ran both hands through his short hair. The muscles in his upper arms flexed as he did it. "Are you all right?" she asked gently.

"I'm okay. How're you feeling?"

"I don't know. A bit numb, I think." Her voice sounded small and vulnerable.

"Those kicks, by the way, amazing. I'm so glad you do Taekwondo," he said, in an attempt to lighten the mood.

"Teamwork ..."

They both jumped at a knock on the door. Daniel answered it, as Elisa cleared their papers off the small table and pushed it towards the bed. They sat next to each other, Elisa in the chair and Daniel on the edge of the bed. They hadn't realised how hungry they were until the pizza arrived, and ate in silence while listening to the storm outside.

As they finished their meal, Elisa delicately reached over and touched the bandage on Daniel's arm. Her touch was soothing and yet electric at the same time. Lightning flashed again, followed three seconds later by explosive thunder that shook the walls.

"One kilometre ..." they both said at once, stopping mid-sentence, Elisa looking quizzically at Daniel. Both had worked out that a three-second delay meant the lightning was one kilometre away.

"Geek," Daniel grinned.

Elisa smiled, remembering their conversation a few days ago.

Then she stood and went to the tea tray in search of a glass. There was only one, and there was nothing in the small refrigerator. She went into the bathroom and filled the glass. "Cheers." She took a sip and handed it to Daniel. He drank a little and put the glass down. She looked more relaxed, but he could still see worry in her eyes.

"We'll be okay," he said, with as much conviction as he could muster. There was another flash of lightning, giving them both a start.

"I want to believe you." She shivered involuntarily and Daniel's immediate instinct was to hold her close, but instead he reached out to touch her cheek and tuck a wisp of hair behind her left ear. As he did, she put her hand on his and held it to her face for a moment. It was a simple, sweet gesture that set Daniel's heart racing. He was about to lean in and kiss her when she broke the moment.

"I need to get some sleep," she announced, getting out of the chair. "Thank you for ..." she paused to search for the right words, "... for just being here," she finished clumsily. "Goodnight," she added, as she closed the door.

"Goodnight, Elisa," he said to himself, realising he'd just sat there in silence as she'd left.

Elisa felt like the awkward teenage girl she once was. *What was that? Did I just run away?* She remembered his words to DI Mander: *'visiting from New Zealand to deal with my late uncle's estate'*. There was something indefinably attractive about Daniel. She felt drawn to him, but maybe it was just the way they'd been thrown together, the danger they were in. Lightning flashed again, followed by more thunder that made her jump. She rushed to her door, ready to go back and knock on his, but stopped herself.

36

Anton Rigo sat in his newly rented dark-grey SUV, tucked around a corner half a block from Elisa Mansfield's flat. He'd picked up the new car from the airport that afternoon, renting it in a new name. His head ached and his left ankle was mildly twisted, but at least nothing was broken. He had admonished himself for the lapse in discipline, disappointed in himself that he'd let his desires sway his usual meticulous execution.

The car was partly concealed by a large tree on the corner, but he could see the building's front entrance clearly enough. The weather in Oxford was better than in Chidwick and visibility was adequate. An advantage of the rain was that nobody else was on the streets.

Reade and Mansfield had been lucky. After he had tripped down the stairs, he'd quickly regained consciousness and realised they had taken the knife and his Glock, so he decided to get out of the house. He would get his retribution soon enough. He'd managed to get out the back door quietly and run back to his vehicle through a forest track on the edge of town, occasionally stumbling in the brush. His shoes were muddy and his feet cold, but his clothing had dried sufficiently on the drive back to Oxford. His anger had solidified into a cold and brittle resolve to get the notes, then kill Reade and Mansfield before he had to report back to Zapas tomorrow.

Rigo had been confident they would return to the woman's flat after their lucky escape, so he had hurried back to Oxford. At his rented accommodation, he picked up another knife and a cleverly made wire instrument that looked like an ornamental necklace, but was, in fact, a garrotte. They would not get the better of him again.

But they should have arrived an hour ago. He was sure they would not have stayed in Chidwick. He'd seen fear in their eyes. He'd expected them to go to the woman's flat. They had nowhere else, as far as he knew. And. they were amateurs. She would need clothing or other things, he'd reasoned. *But where are they?*

He started the engine and slowly drove into her street, past her unlit flat, and on to his own modest flat. In the morning, he would collect his spare pistol, a Glock 9 mm like the first, from the locker at Oxford railway station. He had business to transact at the university tomorrow. *Perhaps I might be fortunate enough to find them there.* The thought pleased him.

* * *

ANDOVER, ENGLAND

Daniel awoke with the dawn light streaming through the curtains. He hadn't slept well. After Elisa had abruptly left last night, he wondered whether he'd been too forward or had simply read the signals poorly. He looked at the clock on the bedside table. Six thirty-five. He climbed out of bed and pulled the curtain to one side. *At least today's weather is better.* Soon after he'd showered, shaved and dressed, his phone chimed as a message arrived. *Breakfast?* was all it said. Instead of texting back, he went next door and knocked gently. The light slipping through the spyhole momentarily disappeared.

"Hi," she said, smiling warmly at him as she opened the door. She looked as though she'd slept better than he had. She was wearing a V-neck

T-shirt tucked into a pair of grey jeans. "You could have just texted back."

"I prefer personal service." *And I wanted to see you.*

"I need another ten minutes. I'll see you at breakfast."

"Sure, okay."

Elisa closed her door as Daniel made his way to the lounge.

Less than ten minutes later, Elisa entered the small breakfast room, wearing the same fleecy top as last night. They settled for a simple breakfast, with fruit juice and coffee. Apart from the young boy on duty, they were the only two in the lounge.

"We should work on the tablets. We need to figure out what this is all about." She seemed determined.

"Yes. Maybe we should go up to Oxford and work there."

"I don't know. He might be there. I think we're safer here for now."

She's got a point, Daniel thought. *And a few hours' work might just decipher this mystery. If we're lucky.*

Without asking, Elisa took their coffee cups to get a refill and returned to the table.

"Thanks," Daniel said.

"How's the arm this morning?" she asked.

"It's okay."

"Do you want me to help change the dressing? It must be tricky with only one hand."

"The dressing the paramedics put on seems to be waterproof, so I'll leave it today." He remembered how her touch had felt on his bare skin. "Maybe tomorrow? And thanks for offering."

"Well, I'll be happy to do it, just let me know."

She finished the last of her drink and looked straight at Daniel.

"Should we work in one of our rooms?"

"I think so," Daniel replied, as a couple with a toddler came in, the youngster requesting sausages quite loudly.

On the way back, Elisa asked at the hotel desk whether they could check out a bit later, agreeing they only needed one of the rooms. The receptionist told them they could probably have until noon, and if the cleaning staff needed it sooner he would let them know.

By eight o'clock, Elisa had returned to Daniel's room with her bag packed. They laid the notes on the bed, Daniel took out his laptop and opened the high-resolution photos of the Lisbon tablet. Within an hour Elisa had identified a few words that matched translated parts of the earlier tablets, using Foxton's and Gillard's notes as a guide. On a large notepad Daniel had fished out of his backpack, she had carefully drawn each line of characters, leaving a space beneath. The tablet's characters were in ink and the few translated portions were below in pencil. Her knowledge of Sanskrit was limited, and she'd had to rely heavily on her predecessors' work.

"You've done this before!" Daniel said, genuinely impressed with her progress as he looked on.

"Yes, but more by trial and error than good training." The words she had picked out were 'creator ... of doom', 'resounding harmony', 'overcome by seas [waves]', 'voyage' and 'fury'. It seemed a good start, but no clear meaning was yet emerging.

"This is frustrating," Elisa said. "It looks like more of the same." She shifted her position on the edge of the bed and rubbed her neck.

"Tea?" Daniel asked.

"Good idea." Daniel found a tray in the cupboard with a kettle, two teacups and some English breakfast teabags.

He set the two steaming cups down on the small table and pulled the wooden chair over next to Elisa. Leaving the tea to brew, he picked up Foxton's notebook. After a few minutes of studying his great-grandfather's translations, or, more particularly, his detailed drawings of the ancient text, Daniel noticed there was something different about the Lisbon tablet. Something about its text.

"Look at this," he said, pointing out Foxton's translation of the word 'doom [destroyed]'. Look at the tablet text, then look at the Lisbon version.

Elisa leaned forward and studied it intently. Then she saw it. "They're not quite the same! The last character is definitely different." She gave Daniel's good arm an encouraging squeeze. "I think you're onto something!"

They both studied the ancient characters and the words Elisa had written in pencil. After close examination, they decided that what they probably had was, in some cases, like the difference between 'destroyed' and 'destroyer'. Possibly, in other cases they could have been completely different words, like doom and door. One character can make all the difference.

By late morning they needed a break. They had got some way further, and a different meaning was just beginning to emerge, but it was painstakingly slow. The pages in front of them had many eraser marks and needed rewriting. The words they had still didn't make enough sense:

'Lifting [or carrying] sound' ... 'builder of [obscured] is become destroyer' ... 'returned from/ to the sea' ... 'mother[land?] doomed/ [destroyed/ destroyer]' ... 'arrogance of majestic [rulers?]'. Then in another passage further down, 'song [sound] in increasing harmony' ... 'mother [earth?] trembling and turning to water [liquefaction?]' ... 'overwhelmed by seas [waves/ tsunami?]'.

On a separate sheet of paper, Elisa had tackled part of an earlier section a different way. She had written 'returned [fleet] found no harbour', and 'days and nights of fury ... there was nothing'. Daniel looked over her shoulder.

"Are we looking at a historical account written by survivors? People who had settled somewhere else after the disaster?" Daniel asked. "Could that explain why it was discovered nearer to Iceland, in shallower water?"

Elisa turned to face him, and her face slowly broke into a smile. "I'd say that's exactly what we've got here! You're not so bad at this yourself!" Her smile and her enthusiasm lifted Daniel's spirits. "That would help to explain the link between Sanskrit, Icelandic and Baltic languages. I think it's possible this could potentially be the protolanguage that influenced all of those languages. But there's still a big problem. There's nothing in this world, or at least *nothing known today*, that could cause an entire land mass to sink literally two miles under the ocean, in a few 'days and nights of fury'. It's time to talk to a geophysicist," she concluded, reaching for her phone.

"Why don't we go and see him? We could pick up the rest of your notes at the hall and maybe risk a quick stop at your flat so you can pack some things." Elisa bit her lip as she pondered his suggestion.

"All right, let's do that," she said, with some uncertainty.

They were soon on their way north. The weather had cleared, and a short while later, as they negotiated the A34 on-ramp, a black Mercedes SUV loomed up behind them. Elisa noticed the alarm on Daniel's face as he looked in the rear-view mirror. She turned and looked around as the vehicle started to overtake. Fear suddenly gripped her; an unreasoning knot of fear deep in her gut, and her blood ran cold as she saw the familiar SUV. She strained her neck around but couldn't see the driver. He was obscured by the right rear bodywork of the Citroën. The SUV was less than half a metre from the side of Daniel's car, its front grille almost touching the rear side window of the Citroën. The Citroën was no match for this monster of a vehicle. Her heart started racing – were they going to get rammed off the road? Would he shoot them as he drove by?

Elisa held her breath as Daniel hit the brakes to let it quickly pass, and as it did so a small face appeared in the rear window. A little hand waved at her. A girl of around eight years old was smiling at her. The black SUV drove past and it was a full minute before Elisa was able to speak.

"I thought it was him," she said in a tiny voice.

"So did I."

She reached for his hand and held it firmly, as they drove on in silence for another few minutes as the adrenaline settled.

"That poor little girl, I must have frightened her."

"She probably just thought you were surprised," Daniel suggested.

"Yes, I suppose you're right. I hope so. I guess I overreacted."

"We're still on edge, I'm sure. Do you still want to go to Oxford?"

"I can't think of anywhere else," she replied.

"Okay, shall we go to St Dunstan's first and then call in to your flat?"

"All right." She was still holding his hand firmly.

Within twenty minutes they were back in Oxford. Daniel parked as close to the hall as he could, grabbed his backpack and locked the car. He looked at Elisa, trying to read her expression.

"Are you sure you're okay?" he asked. She nodded.

As they walked between the buildings, they looked all around them, scanning the faces for the all-too-familiar pale man. Gone were the benign ancient and leafy environs so familiar to Elisa. She felt a pall of trepidation had settled around her, following wherever she went. Danger seemed to lurk at every lane and behind every hedgerow. She was glad Daniel was with her.

Finally they made their way to the St Dunstan's entrance just off the High Street. As they approached the archway they saw something all too familiar. Blue and white police tape. Their hearts sank.

37

An hour earlier, Anton Rigo had been sitting at the small laminated table in his rented accommodation. He rubbed the bruised swelling on his head and deliberated over the call he was about to make. He had decided to be circumspect in his report back to Zapas. He knew he would be a fool to lie to him, but there were things his employer did not need to know.

"I am in Oxford. They haven't returned to the university yet."

"What about the woman's home?"

"I waited for them last night, but they did not return." There was a brief silence, and Rigo hoped he was not asked about Chidwick. He'd already been out that morning, looking for Reade's Citroën, without success. Mansfield's car was parked in the street outside her building.

"For the moment you have another priority. There is another tablet, in the archives at St Dunstan Hall. I want it sent here urgently, along with any notes. Our carrier is on his way to you now." Rigo knew the man, he'd arranged delivery of weapons and other supplies in the past. The driver would wait at Rigo's flat, as per usual. This would need to be a quick and surgical operation, like Lisbon.

He'd been about to put the phone down, since he was accustomed to

Zapas ending the call as soon as he'd given his orders, but the line was still open. He waited.

"And search their homes and cars. If they see you, kill them." Click.

Yes I will.

He looked at his appearance in the narrow mirror. He would need to hide the bruised lump, or it would otherwise be a feature someone might notice. And it was going to last for a few days. He changed his clothing again and took his time to carefully apply a toupée, paying particular attention to the back and sides. The front would be obscured by his baseball cap.

He left his flat, his left ankle still aching from the previous day, and climbed into his dark-grey SUV. He'd stuck with the same model because of its power and also because it was not uncommon to see this particular make of vehicle with darkened windows.

Rigo drove into central Oxford, to the university, pleased with his orders.

38

It was just after eight o'clock in the morning in São Paulo, and José Zapas was angry. He had sent Antônia out for the morning; he didn't care where, just as long as she did as she'd been told. Today would be a turning point, and he wanted no interruptions.

Early in the previous year, when he'd decided he would run for president, José realised his father had been right, all those years ago. He needed to show respectability. He needed a wife. It had not been difficult to find Antônia. As always, his money got him what he wanted. He would need her later for his next press conference, where he would thank her for her support of his candidacy. The Brazilian public lapped up that sort of thing. For now, though, he wanted her out of his way. She'd learned quite early that it was best to do what he wanted.

His focus was on the implications of the news from the University of Plymouth survey ship. It had reported back details of a probable archaeological site in the Mid-Atlantic. He knew enough from the tablets to know this could be the origin of his technology, and he needed to ensure the weapon was perfected *before* anyone else uncovered the ancient technology. His strategy was a simple one. It was another thing he'd learned from Josef. There's only so much money and power in the world, and the best way to get more of either was simply to make sure that others had less. His technology must be used to weaken anyone else before they had any chance to develop it for themselves. If the tablets revealed the source, or the nature of it, he would lose the upper hand.

Zapas had considered sending his own ship in to retrieve any useful artefacts but decided it would take far too long. It was time for a *real* demonstration. He would not allow decades of work to come to nothing. He also toyed with sending a ship to destroy the site, to ensure no one else obtained this technology.

Reports from Días at the copper mine were, at least, encouraging. They had quickly determined that the weapon's effect could travel through hundreds of metres of rock with minimal loss of intensity. Días was convinced more power would equate to more distance, and so had adapted the weapon's power supply to take the high current grid power source available at the mine. Testing was now due to finish.

A cursory report from the nightclub site had confirmed there was unusual damage to brickwork in the three buildings adjacent to the Club Na Beira. It had taken a while to track the path of the acoustic beam, slowed further by the fact that only one man, one of Zapas's security people, knew what they were looking for. But eventually he had found it – oddly damaged masonry. Bricks that had bulged outwards and separated from their mortar – up to a hundred metres away from the test site, and all sitting directly in the path of the weapon.

Zapas's phone rang. "Yes."

"There's been a problem." Días sounded flustered and nervous. Zapas waited impatiently for more. "The power supply overheated. We've repaired it, but we'll need to make some modifications for future high-power use. It's not stable."

"The test?"

"It destabilised a mine tunnel and part of it collapsed. We confirmed positive effects just over one kilometre from the source before it failed. That was in just four minutes of high-power operation. It was pure luck nobody was killed in the collapse," Días explained.

"How quickly can you modify the power supply?" Zapas asked.

Días quickly assessed how much time would be needed, and added a small buffer. "A week," he ventured boldly.

Zapas cursed him. "Not good enough. I'll give you three days."

Predictable, Días thought. Being unreasonable had got Zapas a long way.

"Don't disappoint me." Zapas made it clear he would not tolerate failure.

Días knew it would be tight, but he was confident they could make it. He was wondering what Zapas had in mind for the test. Whatever it was, he expected it would be decisive. Zapas was not a man for half measures. He lit another cigarette and went over the redesign he'd started for the modified power supply, wondering how the ancients might have powered the technology.

As he smoked and worked, Días wondered what sort of president Zapas would make. He was tough and ruthless, and Brazil needed a tough leader. Brazil was no stranger to far-right politics, and Días had no time for the socialists. The presidential election was only six days away, and Zapas was gaining ground.

His employer's masterstroke had been to accuse the government of being weak on law enforcement – not protecting the people – while he'd made sure that 'other sources' pointed the finger for weapons testing on the people of São Paulo. The media lapped it up, and the story lifted Zapas in the polls. He was now the leading opposition candidate. The way things were going, it seemed likely to Días that he would soon work for President José Zapas.

39

E lisa showed her college ID and they were allowed to pass the cordon. She looked for Mr Hearne, the porter, to see if he knew what had happened, but he was nowhere in sight.

A policeman approached them. "Good afternoon ma'am, may I have your name please?" It did not sound like a question.

"Elisa Mansfield. I work here. At St Dunstan's. What's happened?"

"And your name, sir?"

"Daniel Reade. Visiting from New Zealand."

Daniel and Elisa both stared at the constable, waiting as he wrote their names in his notebook.

"I'm sorry to have to tell you Mr Hearne died a short while ago. He fell from a balcony on the third floor," the constable explained gently.

"I don't believe it," said Elisa, without thinking.

"I'm very sorry, ma'am. You knew him well?"

"Yes, he is, *was*, porter at the college. He's been here longer than I have ... But you don't understand. I *really* don't believe it. Mr Hearne was desperately afraid of heights. He wouldn't have gone anywhere near the balcony voluntarily." Elisa looked stricken.

"Yes, ma'am, we've been told that already. The DI will want to talk with both of you before you leave." Elisa wanted to go to the Foxton Room. She wanted to know this wasn't related to other recent events. She wanted to know her colleagues were all unharmed. And she wanted to know that she and Daniel had not somehow been the cause of these events.

The constable allowed them through, pointing out the building the DI had disappeared into. Elisa's building. A sense of foreboding hit as she rushed to the Foxton Room, Daniel in tow.

There, she saw Robert talking to a serious-looking man in a navy-blue suit. She looked around but didn't see Alan.

"Elisa," Robert beckoned. He introduced Elisa to Detective Inspector George, but he didn't know Daniel's name. Before Daniel had the chance to introduce himself, Elisa interjected.

"Where's Alan? Is everything okay?"

"Don't worry, he's fine. It is odd, though; we came back from lunch and somebody had been here. Papers were out of place and your stone is missing. Gillard's Folly."

"What is Gillard's Folly?" DI George asked.

"Well, I was just getting to that," Robert started to explain.

Part way through his explanation the DI interrupted him. "Is it valuable?"

"Probably only to archaeologists. And even that's dubious. Nearly destroyed a man's career twenty years ago."

"Was anything else taken?" DI George asked, losing interest in the old stone.

"Not as far as we can tell. But a full inventory will take a bit of time," Robert advised, as Alan came back in.

"I can't be sure, but I don't see any evidence of anyone searching the storeroom," Alan said. "Why on earth would anyone steal that old stone? And *why kill Mr Hearne*? It just doesn't make any sense."

"We can't be sure these events are linked, sir. Nor are we certain Mr Hearne was murdered."

"Nonsense. He couldn't go near a balcony," said Alan firmly.

DI George went on to take statements from Elisa and Daniel. He wasn't convinced the stone had anything to do with the porter's death. Nor did he seem convinced Mr Hearne was murdered; he asked repeated questions about the porter's well-being and state of mind. The DI's final question gave Elisa little confidence that anything would be done.

"Is there any chance you're mistaken about that stone being missing? There appears to be no possible motive for stealing it," the DI asked, having closed his notebook.

"It's possible, I suppose. Someone else could have moved it," Elisa said.

"Well, let me know when you've done the inventory," he said to all of them as he put his coat on. He took a card out of his pocket, handed it to Elisa then left.

"Excuse me," Elisa called out. He turned and waited.

"I think there's more to this," she went on. "The stone that was here isn't the only one. We were attacked last night by a man who wanted to take our analysis and notes on the first tablet." Her energy trailed off as she realised this was not going to sound like a coherent story. And if she mentioned *Atlantis* ...

"So there are more of these tablets? What are they?" DI George asked patiently.

"They date back thousands of years. They might be a ... doomsday warning," she finished weakly.

"But they have no real market value." The DI's face remained blank. "What about this attack last night?"

"A man with a gun broke into my house and demanded we hand over our notes. Archaeological notes." Daniel could see they were getting nowhere.

"Did you report that?"

"Yes. To DI Mander in Andover. The house is in Chidwick."

"And what did he make of it?"

"He thought it was most likely just an ordinary burglary." Daniel realised he would have to let it go. They hadn't told Mander about the notes.

"Can you be sure these events are related?" the DI asked.

"No. Unless anyone saw the man who was here."

"Nobody saw anything unusual."

"Who would want to steal archaeological notes and old stones with no real value?" DI George had a valid point. "A doomsday message, you say. Are you suggesting a religious cult might be involved?"

Daniel shook his head. There was little point in continuing. DI George seemed to think they might be delusional. Daniel contemplated suggesting the DI contact his counterpart in Andover, but George hadn't reopened his notebook since Elisa had called him back. He wasn't interested.

"Well, please let me know when the inventory is done, and if any *evidence* turns up," George said pointedly.

"I don't believe this isn't related," said Elisa to Daniel quietly, after DI George had left, as she put his card into her handbag. "Let's make sure Avery is all right."

They went downstairs and quickly exited the building, jogging the three hundred metres to Professor Compton's rooms, through a light drizzle that had just started.

They climbed the stairs, noticing as soon as they reached the first floor that Avery's door was ajar. The daylight spilled into the dark corridor. They ran over and Elisa knocked loudly. No answer. She was worried and started to go in. Daniel instinctively held her back and went in first, just in case someone was in there. They knocked loudly on the inside doors but still no answer. Elisa texted Avery, and a few seconds later his phone chimed on the bookshelf, although there was no sign of the professor.

"Oh. That's not good." Daniel said.

40

A white van was parked outside Rigo's flat. The man sitting in the driver's seat read a newspaper while he smoked a cigarette. The window was open a few centimetres and an occasional waft of smoke escaped into the light rain outside. The driver watched as a man wearing a red cap drove up and parked his four-wheel-drive wagon. The man got out of his car, reached into the back seat, and slung a heavy-looking backpack over his right shoulder. He straightened his cap and walked to the van with a slight limp. His pale face was familiar to the driver, although the longer hair was not.

Anton Rigo opened the passenger door and climbed in, looking distastefully at the courier's cigarette. Smoking was a weakness that Rigo disliked. The van stank of cigarettes and stale sweat. The driver had most likely come straight to Oxford from one of London's airports, and would no doubt soon be driving back to the same place. He handed over the backpack.

"Zapas wants this sent now." Rigo disliked the driver, and the feeling was reciprocal. The courier peered inside the backpack, and into the back of the van. Rigo glanced over and saw an empty, clear-plastic document protector sitting on the back seat.

"I was told there would be papers, as well as this stone slab. Where are they?"

"There were no papers," Rigo snapped. He had quickly searched through loose papers sitting on Mansfield's bench, but there was nothing related to the stone. They would have all their notes with them, he was sure, making it all the more important that he found them soon.

"He will not be pleased."

No, Zapas is never pleased. Perhaps except when he was beating a prostitute. Rigo had cleaned up Zapas's mess on more than one occasion over the years he'd been in the man's employ. Usually they were better off dead.

"You'd better tell him," the man added, exhaling smoke in Rigo's direction. Rigo slapped the cigarette out of his mouth.

"Don't ever tell me what to do. I could kill you now, and no one would care," Rigo sneered. "Just send it." He stepped out of the van and slammed the door.

The driver picked up his cigarette. *I hope Zapas is very displeased,* he thought angrily.

As Rigo opened the door to his flat, he reflected that Zapas also would not be pleased their Oxford contact was now dead. But the man had become a liability, in Rigo's mind. He was weak and afraid, and would not have lasted more than a few minutes under even the mildest police probing. Seconds, at most, under Zapas's interrogation. The contact had given Rigo directions to the Foxton Room and told him where to look for the tablet. But he was a coward, clearly terrified in Rigo's presence. His face had a sheen of sweat within seconds of Rigo finding him.

Knowing the organisation's methods, it was Rigo's assumption that he was an unwilling recruit, no doubt coerced when they had uncovered something to blackmail him with. Very likely some sort of distasteful sexual dalliance the man wanted to keep buried. The man had been useful but had started to tell Rigo he wasn't to hurt the woman. Rigo was incensed. How dare this weak man challenge him. He decided to teach him a lesson, so he forced him up the stairs at gunpoint to the balcony. His plan was to threaten to push him over edge until he'd learned some respect.

But as he had marched him to the edge, gun pressed into the back of his neck, the man had stopped involuntarily, wet his pants and started screaming like a little girl. Rigo could not shut him up so quickly and brutally shoved him over the side. The screaming stopped before he hit the ground. Rigo now needed to work out how he would explain that unfortunate turn of events to Zapas.

Back inside the flat, he carefully removed the red cap and toupée, wiped the adhesive residue off his cropped hair, then changed his shirt and jacket. He looked at himself in the mirror. Different enough, although the bruise was still a problem. He retrieved a black wool watch cap from his bag and pulled it on. It would suffice.

He drove back towards the university and Mansfield's flat.

41

"He often forgets his mobile," Elisa rationalised, trying to calm her nerves. She stood in Avery's front room, looking at the phone, as if it could somehow summon its owner.

"He might have just stepped out for a minute," Daniel reasoned. "He has no connection to the tablets."

"But he's connected to *us*," Elisa said, with a look somewhere between concerned and annoyed.

At that moment, Avery Compton came back into his rooms.

"Well, hello. This is a pleasant surprise!" he said amiably. "Lovely to see you both again."

"We were worried about you! The door was open, so ..."

"Oh, I was just dropping off some papers down the hall," Avery said. "Tea?"

"Yes, thank you," Daniel and Elisa agreed.

"Terrible business about the porter, poor man," Avery observed as he went into his small kitchen. "Nasty fall, by all accounts."

"Yes, it's awful," Elisa called, deciding not to share their fears with Avery. At least, not yet. She shot Daniel a look that told him she was annoyed with him. He remembered he'd barged in front of her at the door.

"I'm sorry I pulled you out of the way before," he said, with both apology and concern written on his face. "I just thought of Cláudia being hit and almost killed, and my manly protector instincts took over," he said with a tentative grin. "Sorry."

She gave him the same annoyed look, although it had softened in her eyes. "It's all right. I guess I'm just on edge. I don't need a 'manly protector', though. I'm perfectly capable." Her face broke into a weak smile.

"I know. You could kick for the All Blacks," Daniel said.

"Wallabies, please."

"He was just asking after you the other day," Avery called from the kitchen. "Mr Hearne. He was interested in your work, and where you were travelling to. Nice, friendly chap." He poked his head into the sitting room. "Biscuits?"

As Daniel turned to face him, he noticed some framed old maps on the wall right in front of him. Curiosity drew him to them and he took a closer look. The one on top was a brown map of an ocean between two coastlines, with a corner missing. It had ornate drawings of animals and birds on the two land masses, and elegant tall ships sailing the ocean between.

"That's the Piri Reis map. Quite famous now." Avery had returned with a tray containing a teapot, small china milk jug and three cups. "I'll just get the biscuits. Have a closer look at the coastline on the right-hand side," he called. Elisa joined Daniel and they studied the map together.

"That's reckoned to be the Antarctic coast," Avery said. "It's a true enigma because this map dates back to 1513, three centuries before Antarctica was discovered. The coastline drawn by Piri Reis quite accurately depicts the Antarctic coast *without the ice*. Remarkable, isn't it? It's believed he compiled this from numerous much older sources that have never been found.

"The next map down may interest you more, though, given your current line of enquiry," Avery continued.

They leaned in together and studied the next map. At the top it stated 'Carta da navegar de Nicolo et Antonio Zeni. Fvrono in Tramontana l Ano MCCCLXXX'.

"Loosely, it means Nautical chart of Nicolo and Antonio Zeno, Year in the North, 1380. Oddly, the title is half in Portuguese and half in Italian," Avery said. "Can you work out where it is?"

"I think I see Greenland, Iceland, Great Britain and Scandinavia. But what is Frisland?" asked Daniel.

"Exactly. It's clearly the North Atlantic, and most people agree with you about those other places. Is there anything unusual about Greenland?" Avery was now in full lecturing-professor mode.

"The mountain ranges?" Elisa asked.

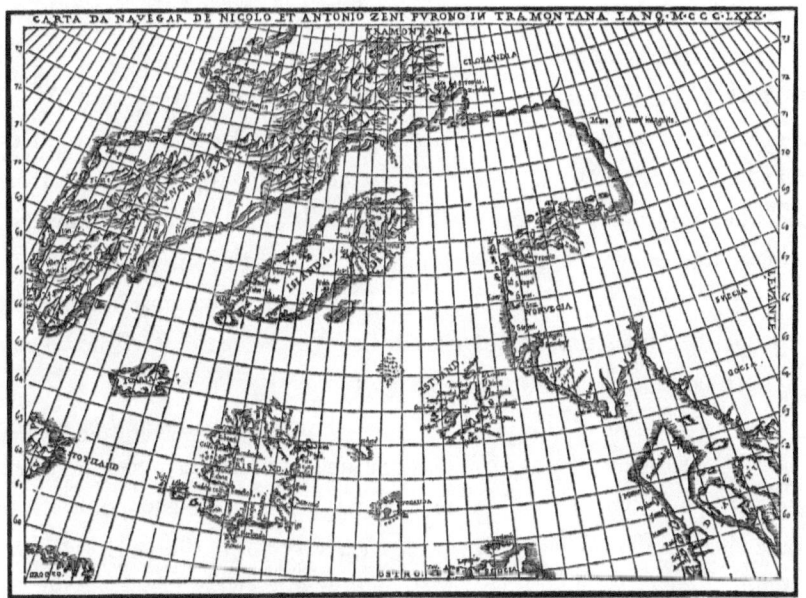

Map of the North of the Zenos, printed in Venice in 1558. (Orig. size 380 X 284 m. m.).

"Well done! It is Greenland *without* the ice sheet. Another interesting enigma." Avery paused for effect. "The ice sheet is, on average, about a mile and a half thick, and is supposed to have been there for millions of years, and yet here we have a six-hundred-year-old map showing mountains, rivers and a detailed coastline."

"And Frisland?" Daniel enquired again.

"Yes. An *imagined* island, scholars would have us believe. An imagined island that's larger than Portugal, also with a detailed rocky coastline, numerous small offshore islands, and even a possible city with a port. Right in the middle of the Atlantic. The Zeno family were prominent, respected and wealthy Venetian seafarers. It's understood that this map, like the one above, may have been created from much older source maps. No one has ever found any evidence of the older sources, though." Avery was enjoying himself.

"Frisland looks like it's in the right location to be the potential source of our tablets, at least the first two," said Daniel. "It would have been directly in the path of the transatlantic telegraph, and probably all of the current modern undersea cables."

"But what could have caused it to disappear?"

"Well, I believe you two are on to something here," Avery said. "As for the pertinent question – *where did it go?* – there are some possibilities. You'll no doubt know a little about the structure of our planet. Apart from the small inner core, the crust is the only solid part, and it accounts for only around one per cent of earth's mass. The mantle is about eighty-four per cent, and it is *viscous*, not solid. It's always moving. I imagine it's possible the Mid-Atlantic Ridge is the key. You've heard of it?" he asked.

Both nodded.

"It's a very large rift in the earth's crust, and magma, or *mantle*, has been pouring out for thousands of years, creating the undersea mountain range that is the ridge. This flowing magma must obviously come from somewhere under the crust. It must leave a large void." The professor gave them a moment to process that information, as he would with a group of students.

"Now, imagine the immense weight and pressure of the ocean surrounding our mythical island of Frisland. What might happen if that large void in the magma was directly underneath the island?" He paused for effect. "I believe the crust would quickly collapse under this colossal pressure, the ocean pressing in from all sides, and soon from above. This process could certainly be capable of swallowing an island, over time."

"But Plato said it sank in a day and a night," Elisa countered.

"But possibly it did, my dear. Their technology could have triggered an earthquake or volcanic activity, and perhaps their island suddenly sank, let's say, *tens* of metres. That would be enough for the cataclysm Plato describes. It's certainly enough to cause major earthquakes and tsunamis. Frisland may then have slowly sunk to its current depth over the next thousand years. As a geophysicist, I think that's a plausible scenario," Avery added.

"It makes perfect sense," he concluded, "but please, gather your evidence carefully and remember those who have gone before you."

Daniel looked surprised at the sudden change of tone.

"Theories about mysterious advanced ancient civilisations have been the ruin of many a good academic. Even just presenting factual evidence can draw fire, and our scientific establishment can be merciless. Professor Gillard probably got away lightly. Simply mentioning a potential civilisation in the Atlantic caused the anti-Atlantis zealots to go into a frenzy. They nearly destroyed him, and he had an authentic artefact to defend his theory!"

Avery started to clear away the teapot and cups, and Elisa gave Daniel a subtle nudge.

"Thank you so much, Avery. As always, you've been a fantastic help," she said, as Daniel stood.

"Not at all, my dear. It's been my pleasure," said Avery, patting her arm.

"One more question, if I may," Daniel asked, as he shook the professor's hand. "Our imagined technology, this acoustic weapon that might have caused the destruction – what do you think it might do to humans?"

"Difficult to imagine, young man, but it can't be good. If it can change the molecular structure, or molecular bonds, to soften rock, then I'd probably expect serious tissue and organ damage and likely death. A weaker version might induce haemorrhage, tissue damage, and at the very least, significant discomfort. Mind you, I'm not a biologist."

Daniel was lucky enough to find a parking space just a few metres from Elisa's flat. They had kept an eye out for the pale man and his black SUV, and were still nervous about calling in. But with no sign of the SUV, they had decided to risk it, planning to be in and out within a few minutes. It was now mid-afternoon, and they wanted to get out of Oxford to find somewhere to try and finish the translation.

As they stepped into her flat, Daniel took in the tasteful and understated furniture and décor. There weren't many pictures on the wall, although one caught his eye. It was unmistakably a prehistoric rock painting of many hands painted in silhouette.

"Where's the cave painting from?" he called. He'd seen pictures from the caves in Altamira in Spain and Lascaux in France, but not this one.

"It's the Cueva de las Manos, in Argentina. It dates back to sometime between 11,000 and 8,000 BC. The name means Cave of Hands." She came back into the living room with her green overnight bag in tow, carrying a coat and scarf. Her cheeks were somewhat flushed – from the hurry they were in, Daniel supposed. A dark tortoiseshell cat with pale-orange front paws calmly followed her, then sauntered over to Daniel to brush past his legs, purring.

"That's Mango," she said. "He's just come back from Maggie's next door." Daniel picked him up to the sound of loud purring. "He's a people cat. When I'm not here, he's in next door looking for a comfortable lap." Elisa came up close to Daniel and stroked Mango. "I'm sure I've probably forgotten something in the rush," she said as she picked up her handbag, "but let's get out of here."

Daniel put Mango down, and offered to carry her bag.

"I'm fine," she said, handing him her coat and scarf as she locked the door. A group of some twenty or so school children were walking down the footpath to Elisa's building, one teacher in front and another behind. They had brightly coloured vests on. An old woman was standing on the path outside the building next door, presumably waiting for someone. She was watching the children, smiling. Daniel opened the back of the Citroën and stowed Elisa's bag. As he did so, Elisa saw a face she had never wanted to see again. Her sharp intake of breath was enough to put Daniel on alert.

"It's him! The pale man!" she gasped.

Daniel looked up and saw him start running directly at them. As they made eye contact, the man reached into his jacket.

42

A plain black folder sat on the large carved table. It was the only object on it and seemingly out of character with the room, whose only occupant stood by the window, surveying the extensive rear garden. He had rehearsed his press conference speech and was now perfecting the surprised and mildly offended look he would give to the media this evening. The event had been carefully choreographed. He would be asked about the recent speculation that he would take Brazil back to dictatorship if he were elected president.

José Zapas's media advisors had told him the rumours had started a few days ago, fuelled by his nervous opponent, the incumbent president. Zapas was mildly amused at the thought; the conjecture had more likely started because it was true. His own media companies would not touch the story, of course, but publications and other sources that were not part of his empire had started to pick it up. His advisors had told him he should answer the question now and have his newspapers ensure it was reported in the right way, thereby negating the incumbent's ability to make a meal of it.

A reporter on the Zapas payroll was going to ask the question this evening. José would smile and make light of it. He would not take the bait to repeat the accusation back to the reporters. Instead, he would spin it to his advantage.

"Ah, yes, that nonsense," he smiled broadly at his reflection in the glass. "I've heard my opponent's speech writers are in fear of losing their jobs." He nodded slowly then paused for imagined laughter. "But in President Zapas's Brazil, the economy will be strong, and no one will be in fear of losing his or her job!" He looked around the imagined press gallery, then leaned closer to where the microphone would be. "My focus will be on prosperity and growth, and improving the lives of *all* Brazilians." His face changed to a concerned and piteous expression. "Sadly, our beloved nation has not seen this focus for the entire term of our current, *and apparently desperate*, president!"

That was the moment at which Antônia would step forward to the podium, smiling, and link her arm in his. They would smile for the cameras, and tomorrow the benevolent faces of the happy couple, the next president and his wife, would be on the front pages of the newspapers.

He reflected that it was fortunate he had not struck Antônia this morning. She had returned earlier than planned. As she'd opened the doors of the second-floor lounge, he'd taken several menacing steps towards her. She rarely entered the room when he was at home, knowing it was his favourite. It had been his father's favourite, too. José remembered the day he'd inherited his father's empire. As he strode over to her, she had run out of the room, retreating to the master suite across the wide hall. He'd let her go. Tonight, Antônia would need to look beautiful for the media.

Although she was now in her early forties, she had retained her model's figure and still had a face the camera seemed to love. José had no doubt she would play her part. She understood her role, and she understood there was no possibility of leaving him. If she was ever foolish enough to attempt it, she knew she would soon disappear tragically, and in doing so, would helpfully engender the public's sympathy for her grieving husband. In fact, if she ever outlived her usefulness, he reflected, he would play the grieving husband even sooner.

Zapas stepped back from the large window, satisfied he was ready for tonight's performance. He took a deep breath, slowly exhaled and sat down in an armchair close to the table. It was his favourite chair, located in the exact place he had ended his father's life many years earlier. *The presidency is mine. I am in control.*

He reached for the black folder. It had been delivered quietly, fifteen minutes earlier, by his security chief. He had asked for a full report on the troublesome pair from Oxford, Reade and Mansfield. Despite authorising Rigo to kill them at his convenience, it had occurred to José that it was *because* of these two the organisation had become aware of two more ancient stone tablets.

He opened the folder and scanned the contents. A brief report and several photographs. He read the short text describing Reade and Mansfield. They were just ordinary people, according to the dossier. A visiting historian and an archaeologist. Reade had stumbled into this by inheriting his uncle's house. The house where José's father had arranged a burglary and murder during the Second World War. It had taken a few days for the security people to discover that fact from Josef's old records.

Reade did not look to Zapas like he posed any kind of threat. He did not have the face of a man who could kill another. The woman, however, was much more interesting. An archaeologist who had understood the significance of the original tablet, and who had unearthed two more within a matter of days. Something his own organisation had failed to do over many decades. She was clearly resourceful. Zapas flipped pages until he found a full-sized picture of her, and he smiled. He liked what he saw. *Perhaps I will interrogate you personally.*

43

Elisa saw the pale man reach for a gun and stifled a scream. The school children stared at her in surprise as they walked by. He was about fifty metres along the road, rapidly gaining ground.

"Get in!" Daniel shouted.

Within seconds, they were both in the car and Daniel had the engine running. He could see in the side mirror that the pale man had changed tack. He was now running away from them, presumably back to his vehicle. As Daniel pulled out into the road, he assumed the man hadn't fired at them because of the children. Or maybe because there were too many witnesses.

The children were still staring at them, open-mouthed, as the teachers started to corral them across the road. The two teachers stepped onto the road, each facing in the opposite direction, and beckoned the children to cross quickly.

From the footpath, the old woman watched as the children started to cross. The teachers had to herd them, like sheep. Or cats. The couple in the grey Citroën had pulled into the traffic at a dangerous speed, and had just swerved around a bus. Now, a dark-grey four-wheel-drive was bearing down on the children, accelerating. *What in the world is wrong with drivers these days*, she wondered, shaking her head. *Everybody is in a mad rush.*

The teacher facing the oncoming SUV screamed in alarm and tried to grab the straggling children and get them out of harm's way. A little girl had seen the big vehicle and run back to the kerb. The old woman started waving her arms at the driver of the SUV. He was almost upon the children when he slammed his brakes on and hit the steering wheel with both hands, blasting the horn. The last remaining children and the two teachers scurried to safety while the old woman held the hand of the scared little girl.

"Idiot," she shouted at the SUV driver, who ignored her and sped off down the road. She tried to get a photo of his licence plate in order to report him, but she was too slow.

Rigo's focus was singular and unyielding. They were not going to escape this time. He was sure he could see the grey Citroën just a few cars ahead of the bus he was now stuck behind. As the bus pulled off the road into its next stop, he manoeuvred his big car around it, momentarily wishing he'd opted for something a bit less bulky. There were too many cars for him to push his way past, so he just had to stick with them until the open road. *Then they are mine.* The Citroën would be no match for the muscle he was driving.

"Let's hope he's stuck in the traffic back there," Daniel said. "Any idea which way we should go?"

"No. Not the A34, though. Somewhere he won't guess," Elisa said, rushing her words together in panic.

"Okay, let's get out of here. I'll get us past the turn-off, and hopefully he'll assume we've taken that."

Daniel drove down St Aldates as fast as he dared. They crossed Folly Bridge on the Abingdon road. Still in a residential area, Daniel didn't want to push the speed too much, but was well over the speed limit. Elisa kept looking nervously behind them. Daniel thought he might have spotted a dark-grey SUV some distance back, but there was no way to be sure it was the pale man. It wasn't the same black SUV he'd seen in Chilton, but he could have easily changed vehicles. And its driver was driving dangerously around other traffic, seemingly in pursuit.

Rigo was frustrated he could not get closer to them, but as they started to leave suburbia behind, he knew he would be able to get to them more easily. He was sure he still had the Citroën in his sights, but there were cars, a truck and a bus now between them. He was angry, but a confident driver, and a man who knew how to use a vehicle as a weapon. He would be able to overtake and run them into a ditch or fence. Then he would stop under the pretence of assisting, in order to kill them and take the notes. Nobody else would stop. City drivers never do.

44

Willow was deeply annoyed. Owen was being as difficult and obtuse as he could be. She knew they had enough data to garner support for a further survey of David's Anomaly.

"I don't agree," Owen said. "It's a crazy idea that there would be ruins there. I still say it's a naval battle, and that's going in the report."

"But you can't seriously tell me all those symmetrical lines, in such a large area, could be debris that's sunk over two miles in an orderly enough manner to lie as we saw them. That defies logic."

"So does Atlantis." *And there it is.*

"Ah. So that's it. You don't want to be associated with Atlantis hunters."

"No. It's not that. I say the data doesn't support your idea."

"You're *impossible*," Willow said in frustration. She marched off to find the others.

David and Marie were in the kitchen downstairs drinking coffee.

"Owen is impossible," Willow lamented, joining them at their table. "David's Anomaly needs to be properly investigated. It can't be ship wreckage. It just can't."

"Well, you know we agree with you," Marie offered.

"I know. And I appreciate it, but we're going to need more support than that. Especially as we're not unanimous."

Marie rolled her eyes. "Owen's too conservative."

"What about the Oxford connection?" David asked.

"What Oxford connection?"

"My friend in archaeology told me this morning they'd sent a copy of our bathymetry to Oxford. Apparently, a researcher there is looking into ancient artefacts and had an interest in it."

"Why didn't you tell me?"

"I thought you'd left. I was about to go home myself. I'd have told you tomorrow." Their survey voyage had returned to port well before dawn, and none of them had been home yet.

"Can you call your friend? I want to know more about this. We need another ally!" Willow was getting excited now.

"Sure," David said, trying the number. "Voicemail," he said, covering the phone. He left a message asking for a call back about the Oxford researcher. He yawned, and the other two followed suit. "Time to go home," he said.

"*Please* call me as soon as you hear back. I want to talk to this researcher urgently!" David said he would, and they went their separate ways.

Back in her flat, Willow contemplated what they might do. She could approach the head of the archaeology department, whom she knew moderately well, but first she wanted to wait to talk to the researcher. She reasoned that if there was an ancient artefact involved, something *archaeological*, she would stand more chance of getting support. *David'll be in touch soon,* she told herself.

She waited, exhausted, in the afternoon's slowly fading light, willing her phone to chime, but there was no message, and in the end, she gave in to tiredness and went to bed.

45

As Daniel pushed on, the large houses gave way to fields to their left. He passed several buses, with one of the drivers waving his arm out of his window and shouting something. As Daniel overtook, he looked in his mirror and saw an old couple walking in front of the bus. Had they been a little faster, Daniel might have hit them. He eased his foot off the accelerator just a bit. He navigated roundabouts, not sure which exits to take, and ended up on Hinksey Hill. He'd avoided the motorways, where he knew he'd be no match for the big Mercedes. The houses and fields had been replaced by a quieter wooded area.

Elisa was happier now they were off the main road, and the woods around them meant they could not be seen from a distance. She wasn't quite sure where they were, but at least it seemed safer. A small road sign indicated Boar's Hill, and just over a rise, she saw a sign for a pub, a big old building shrouded by trees. She pointed it out to Daniel. "What do you think?"

He wondered whether they should try to get further away, or was it best to get off the road sooner? He chose the latter. "Okay. Let's take a look. If they have rooms, and somewhere out the back to park the car, it might do nicely."

Daniel negotiated the narrow driveway around to the back of the building and pulled into a space sheltered by a large alder tree. "I think this is good." He climbed out and surveyed the car park until he was confident they could not be seen from any road. They were both shaken and still running on adrenaline. "Shall we see if they have rooms?" he asked, trying to sound less anxious than he felt. Elisa simply nodded.

They left their bags in the car and went in through the side entrance, into a lounge with timber panelled walls and old beams.

A woman came over to greet them. "Table for two?"

"Maybe later. Do you have guest rooms available?" Daniel asked.

"Yes. I can give you a double, or a larger one with a table and chairs."

"How about one of each, if they're next to each other?" he suggested, looking at Elisa awkwardly. "I'm thinking one we can work in could be useful?" he said to her tentatively.

"Yes, I can do that," the woman said, looking at them curiously. They did not seem like they were here on business.

Elisa checked them both in while Daniel fetched their bags. They chose Elisa's room to work in. It was a lovely, generous space with a large table and comfy chairs. Daniel had insisted on taking the smaller room.

He took their notes from his backpack and dumped them on the table along with his laptop. He was tempted to suggest getting a drink first to calm their nerves, but then it occurred to him that they may have to leave again in a hurry.

Elisa slumped onto the sofa, energy drained. "Do you think we could have tried harder to get DI George to understand?" she asked.

"I'm not sure what else we could have done. He's a policeman, and we're talking about a conspiracy involving an unknown, and apparently international criminal organisation, and an unknown technologically advanced civilisation that may be Plato's Atlantis. If we'd tried any harder, he might have taken us in for questioning."

"Yes, I suppose you're right. But what can we do? What happens if these people use their weapon again, like in that nightclub?"

"I know. But to be honest, we can't even be sure these things are linked,"

Daniel said matter-of-factly. "We don't have any proof. Even the tablets are gone – all we have are photos and handwritten notes." He sat on the sofa next to Elisa as she sighed softly. They were safe for the moment, but what next?

"We should work on those," she said, pointing at the notes, although she made no attempt to move.

Daniel wasn't sure either, but it would be good to have *something* to do. "Yes, we should. Maybe there's more about this ancient technology. More importantly, we need to find something that could help us get the attention of the police," he said. "Or somebody in intelligence, or something."

They spent the next hour going over the notes, checking back to Foxton's original work and drawings, but the enigma of the ancient tablets was unyielding.

"This is getting us nowhere. All we've managed to do is fill in a few blanks without actually finding new information. Let's take a break," Daniel said. They had both started to relax since they'd arrived, but they knew things could change at any moment. Daniel picked up the car keys. "I'll just check I locked the car."

He walked out into the dark of the evening and around to the car park, which was aesthetically but passably lit. His heart missed a beat as he spotted a dark-grey SUV parked behind a tree, the only other car there. Could it be? Could the man have found them? His instinct was to race back inside and make sure Elisa was all right. But surely this was just a coincidence? And he didn't want to alarm her unnecessarily. *Check that car first,* he told himself.

Satisfied there was nobody in the vehicle, he took a closer look. It was not a Mercedes; a small comfort, but he couldn't be sure the pale man's new vehicle was the same make as the black one. Peering inside cautiously, he saw it had two child seats in the back, and the windows were not heavily tinted. His nerves settled, and he checked the Citroën, then went back to their room. A family of four passed him in the hallway, presumably on their way to dinner.

"What's wrong?" Elisa could see from Daniel's face that something had happened.

"Nothing. But I saw a dark-grey SUV in the car park and thought the worst for a minute." Her eyes opened wider. "But it wasn't him."

"How do you know?" Daniel explained about the child seats and the windows, and she relaxed a little.

"Let's leave this and have something to eat," Daniel suggested.

Elisa sighed heavily and stood, stretching her legs.

46

The restaurant was reasonable, but dinner was a lacklustre affair, more because of the way they felt than the food. The reality of their situation had started to bite. The pale man knew their names and where they both lived. His intent seemed clear, and he'd most likely killed poor Mr Hearne and tried to kill Cláudia in Lisbon.

Elisa could not forget the cold look on the man's face when he'd been about to shoot her at Daniel's uncle's house. If Daniel hadn't lashed out so quickly, she would be dead.

"I wish I knew what's going on," Elisa protested. "How does that man fit into this?"

They had no idea who he worked for, but they knew whoever it was probably had all three stone tablets and had recreated the ancient technology. There was no proof of a connection, but they felt sure the nightclub incident in Brazil must be linked. Reports in the media all seemed to point to the idea of an acoustic weapon.

But why Brazil? What is the connection? Who are these people? And if they've worked out the technology already, why are they still so intent on getting more information?

They hurried through their meals and headed back to the room. As they reached Elisa's door, she stopped Daniel. "Do you think we should pack everything away now?" she asked. "Just in case we have to leave quickly," she added in response to Daniel's questioning look.

"Yes, I think's that's probably a good idea."

They gathered up the notes and Daniel's laptop. Neither in a hurry to leave the table. Or each other.

"These people who are chasing us, they must still be developing and perfecting the technology," Elisa said, thinking aloud. "That's why they want the tablets and our notes." Daniel could see she was still just as deeply worried as he was. "Or they want to make sure nobody else works it out," she finished grimly.

"If that's all it was, then why demand the notes? They wouldn't need them."

"We must find a way of convincing the police." Her nerves were still on edge.

"Or the government," Daniel said.

"Oh, this is so frustrating." She buried her face in her hands for a moment.

Daniel didn't know what to say, and let his instinct take over. He reached out to her and pulled her to him, holding her close.

"I'm sorry," she said, "I just feel so ... powerless. People's lives are at stake and ..." Her voice trailed away and she held him tightly. Then she pulled back a little to look at him, her worried eyes searching his. He could see her frustration but also her determination. He didn't want to let go. Then she slowly moved closer, opened her mouth and kissed him. It was soft and tender at first, but as he responded, her kiss soon became much more urgent.

With his arms firmly around her, he lifted her out of the chair and to the bed, still kissing her. He had a fleeting thought of asking if she was sure about this, but her kisses were as hungry as his, and her hands were taking his shirt off.

They were awoken by an insistent call to Elisa's mobile. It was just after seven in the morning, and Elisa picked up the phone as the caller tried a second time. The number was withheld, but she answered anyway. "Hello," she said sleepily.

"Hi. Sorry to call so early. My name is Willow Peters, and I'm studying hydrography at Plymouth. The archaeology college gave me your name and number." Willow had woken at five o'clock to find a brief message on her phone giving Elisa's name and number. She'd used all her reserves of patience to wait until seven to call. "I wondered if we could meet. I understand you've seen our ocean floor bathymetry of the anomaly in the Mid-Atlantic. Our ship just got back to port yesterday, and, well, you've seen the images. I understand you're researching a ... um ... potentially related artefact."

The girl was clearly exuberant, but nobody ever wanted to suggest 'Atlantis' out loud.

Elisa nudged Daniel gently, though he was already awake and listening. "Plymouth University," she whispered.

"Um, yes, hi, Willow. Yes, I would like to meet you. I'm interested in what you've found. It was the email from your department which led me to the artefact, and now there're others we're quite confident about too."

"This is amazing. I'm trying to get my department to commission a full survey of the area, but they want more evidence. There's a debate going on here about whether it's really an archaeological site or just some shipwrecks or wartime debris. Personally, I'm convinced it can't be wreckage." Willow's enthusiasm started to infect Elisa, too. "I can come up to Oxford today, if that would work for you," Willow added, hoping Elisa would agree. Daniel was smiling at Elisa, genuinely pleased to see her confidence returning.

"Can you hold for just a minute?" Elisa covered the phone with her hand.

"We need to go to Plymouth," she told Daniel, enthusiasm and determination written all over her face.

"Okay." Whatever the reason, he knew that getting further away from

Oxford and Chidwick was a good idea.

"Hi, Willow, I'm not in Oxford right now. We'll come to you. Say, late this morning?" Elisa calculated that Plymouth was between three and four hours away.

"Oh, that would be brilliant," Willow said. "I'll text you directions to our building."

Elisa put the phone down and gave Daniel a good morning kiss. "This could confirm our site. It could be the evidence we need to get someone's attention! Let's go."

Daniel was happy to see that some of her eagerness had returned.

"In a minute," he said, wrapping his arms around her warm, naked body. "Maybe longer."

Daniel returned to his room to quickly shower and dress before returning to knock on Elisa's door.

"Come in," she said, heading back into the bathroom. "I'll just be another five minutes or so."

Daniel put down his backpack, opened it and pulled out a creased shirt. He checked the wardrobe, hoping to find an iron, and was pleasantly surprised. There hadn't been one in his room.

Elisa returned as he was admiring his handiwork. "That'll do," he said.

"Good to see a man who does his own ironing," Elisa observed. She liked the way he looked in a T-shirt and gave him a kiss on the cheek. She also noticed the area around his dressing was red. "You should change that. Do you still have the other dressing the paramedic gave you?"

Daniel rummaged around in his backpack and found it. He gingerly pulled the old dressing away from the wound, trying not to open it up, as it pulled on his skin. "You're right, it's a bit sore today."

"You need to get that looked at by a doctor." Elisa was insistent. She took great care to put the new dressing on and made him promise to get medical care on the way to Plymouth. They finished packing their things and paid their bill, having decided to get breakfast somewhere on the way. Both were keen to put more distance between them and yesterday's events, although neither said it.

Daniel suggested that Elisa drive, since his arm was uncomfortable, and as she drove out of the car park he took out his phone to find directions to Plymouth.

"Do you know the way?" he asked.

"I'm sure I need to get to the A420, but not sure how." She continued down Fox Lane in the same direction they'd travelled yesterday before finding the pub. The road was increasingly rural, surrounded by farms and fields. Daniel directed her through the village of Wootton. They almost missed their turn-off, in the village's confusing streets, but a short while later they made it through, following the signs for Swindon and Bristol.

On the open road, Elisa's thoughts started to turn to their narrow escape yesterday. If the pale man had caught up with them, he probably wouldn't have even needed to shoot. He could have simply killed them with the big SUV. Each time she saw a big, dark-coloured vehicle a knot formed in her stomach.

47

"We should find a doctor and get your arm checked. I'm worried about it."

Daniel wasn't sure he needed it, but Elisa seemed quite determined. He searched on his phone, and located a medical practice in Faringdon, only ten minutes away. They might get some breakfast there as well. He gave her directions, and they took a right turn at the next roundabout, soon finding themselves in a quiet, built-up area.

The medical practice was happy to fit him in, and after he'd explained he was just visiting the UK and had accepted their fee, they sat in the waiting room together. The receptionist heard Elisa's subtle Australian accent and assumed they were a couple 'on holiday from the antipodes'.

"How about I get some food. I think I saw a bakery just down the road," Elisa offered.

"Great idea. I'm keen to get to Plymouth and find out more."

A few minutes later Elisa returned with two paper bags, one with a filled baguette protruding from the top. "It's not quite the breakfast I'd have chosen in better circumstances, but it'll do," she said, handing a bag to Daniel.

The receptionist said it might be a twenty-minute wait, so they split the baguette and started eating, hoping nobody would mind. Daniel was called in a few minutes later.

Elisa finished her portion of the baguette as she waited, occasionally glancing out the window. She knew it was unlikely the pale man would find them, but she was anxious nonetheless. She smiled at the receptionist, who had been watching her as she finished eating.

Daniel returned and went to pay, and Elisa joined him.

"It's infected," Daniel said. "Not too badly, but I need to get a prescription filled and buy some extra dressings. Need to change it every day, the doctor said."

"There's a pharmacy next door," the receptionist suggested.

"Thanks." They turned and went outside, towards the neighbouring pharmacy.

"She also said it's lucky I came in today. Another day or two and I might have needed a hospital. So thanks for insisting." He nearly said 'thanks for caring about me', but decided it might sound trite.

While they waited for his antibiotics, he finished his baguette. Before long, they were back on the road and driving towards Swindon, Elisa still in the driver's seat.

Twenty minutes after that, Elisa navigated a couple of roundabouts which took them south to the motorway. Memories of yesterday's harrowing chase filled her head. "Talk to me."

"Ah ... what do you mean?"

"Just talk to me," she repeated. "I keep thinking about that pale man."

Daniel paused for a moment. "Did I tell you about my sister?"

"No. I've often wondered what it would have been like to have a sister. Or brother."

"Katie. She lives in Sydney. We're nine years apart. We used to get along well when she was small, but we kind of drifted apart. I mean, we talk at Christmas and birthdays usually, but I often miss her."

"What happened?"

"I'm not really sure. It was a slow, drifting thing. She ... we had quite different perspectives on life. When we were growing up, I had the happy years and she didn't. My dad died when I was twelve and she was only three. Mum didn't cope for a long time, so there were a lot of nannies and helpers. We used to play when I got home from school. I'd moved out to go to university before she was even a teenager, and I saw a lot less of her. By the time she hit her mid-teens, she had a group of friends I didn't like. And I was working by then so had my own life. Now I look back on it and I think I was a bit selfish."

"Why do you say that?" Elisa asked.

"Well, I think she was a bit ... lost. But I had my own life to get on with and never talked to her about it."

"I imagine it must have been hard to grow up without a father," Elisa said. "You knew your dad, but she never did. I'm sure that's hard for a little girl. For any child."

Daniel remembered the pain he'd felt when he was twelve.

"I wonder if Katie might have seen you as a kind of father figure. Her big brother. Her protector. Maybe that's what she was feeling, and then suddenly you weren't there any more when she was still a child," Elisa said.

"I've never thought about it like that. That's very insightful," he replied. "Now I feel bad."

"Well you shouldn't," she admonished. "I used to blame my parents for dragging me across the world when I was fourteen. But it wasn't just my dad taking a promotion, it was also my mother. She wanted to be closer to her parents as they got older," Elisa explained. "I'm sure you were just doing what was right for you, and there's nothing wrong with that. Ironically, my parents went back to Sydney when Dad retired."

"But you didn't go back with them?"

"No, by then I'd finished my degree and had been lucky enough to get a job at Oxford, doing what I love. I was lonely at first, but Oxford's a good place to work and not too bad a place to live. Except for the weather!" She grinned at him. "Do you visit her?"

"Katie? No. I know it's only three hours, but neither of us has ever got around to it. How about you and your parents?"

"I video call them most weekends. They're enjoying retirement, and occasionally they ask me if I'm thinking about coming home," she said.

"And are you?" he asked.

"I don't know. Sometimes. I miss the hot summers, although I suspect I've probably gone a bit soft. Forty degrees seems a bit too much to cope with now!"

48

Soon they reached the coast, both feeling buoyed by the normality of their conversation. Elisa pulled off the motorway into a service stop twenty minutes outside Bristol. "I need to stretch my legs."

"I need coffee," Daniel responded.

"Good idea. I'm not sure we'll find anything decent here, though."

In spite of her lack of optimism, it didn't take them long to find drinkable coffee. They both ordered an extra shot.

"Would you like me to drive?"

"How's your arm feeling."

"Don't worry, it's okay."

They were more than halfway, and as Daniel drove they talked about family, about favourite books, movies, their best and worst holidays, and all manner of things. The drive down to Exeter seemed to go much more quickly, and there they joined the Devon Expressway. The brief silences were comfortable, and they were both looking forward to finding out more about the hydrographic survey anomaly.

The traffic thickened as they took the Plymouth exit and made their way to the university. Elisa checked her phone to give Daniel directions and said they should be there in about fifteen minutes. She texted Willow to arrange to meet, and ask whether there was anywhere nearby to park. Willow directed her to a council parking lot that was only a short walk, and gave directions to her building in the School of Biological and Marine Sciences.

They pulled into a car park and climbed out to stretch their legs. It had turned out to be a nice day, with the sun poking through the high cloud. Daniel paid for four hours, taking a guess, and returned to the car. Elisa was smiling at him, which warmed him more than the November sun.

"Can I put your papers into the backpack?" he asked. He already had his notes and laptop packed. During the last part of the journey, they had agreed they would share what they knew, just leaving out their suspicions about weapon development.

"Thanks. Good idea."

They followed Willow's directions into the university campus and located her building. Elisa was about to text her again, when a girl of about twenty-one, with short fair hair and a hint of sunburn, approached them.

"Elisa?"

"Yes. This is Daniel."

"Willow Peters," said the girl as they all shook hands. "Thank you so much for coming all this way. This is the most exciting thing that's happened since I started taking this course!" she said enthusiastically.

"Well, it's our pleasure," Daniel said. "I think we can probably help each other."

"I've booked a meeting room for us to talk, but first can I show you the hydrography?" Willow asked.

"That would be great," Elisa replied.

They followed her into a lift. Out of the lift and down the hallway, they entered a room where several people were working at large screens, most looking at complex and surprisingly brightly coloured images. Willow took them to a free table, the one she'd been working at, picked up a water bottle and drank from it. "Sorry. Forgot to ask, did you want a drink?" Willow said, pointing out the door to the water cooler and paper cups they'd passed in the corridor.

"No," Elisa and Daniel both answered.

Willow clicked the mouse and brought the screen to life. A few clicks later, she'd loaded a file called 'David's Anomaly'. A rainbow-coloured image appeared, much like the others around the room. Not *entirely* like the others, though.

"This is best view of the area. You're looking at the sea floor, depth of two thousand nine hundred and seventy metres. It's high-resolution bathymetry data, collected with our ROV and multibeam echo sounders. Sorry, that's a bit high tech. Basically, I'm saying this data is dense and pretty reliable," Willow explained. "The colours are there just to give you a sense of perspective; they represent different depths. But you can see *this* image is special, can't you?" She looked up at Daniel and Elisa. Before either could answer her, she gestured to the two screens on the table just in front.

"Yes, I can see the difference," Daniel said. "All those straight lines on this one. Can't be natural."

"Right! It's just amazing." Willow's effusiveness was more than a little contagious.

A young man a few tables down came over to them. He was a little older, late twenties maybe. "Don't get too excited. This is just first pass data, and there are a few possible interpretations."

"This is Owen. He was on the survey ship, too," Willow said, and they shook hands. "And we don't agree," she added pointedly. "We've been debating this for a few days now, and the one thing we do agree on is that a proper survey should be done."

"It does look very artificial," Elisa observed to Owen.

"Yes, true. My first thought was that it could be wreckage, debris from a naval battle or suchlike," Owen said. "The basic problem I have with it, to be honest, is that as an archaeologist I know there can't be ruins down there. It's the middle of the Atlantic and it's three kilometres deep!" He was quite emphatic. "Willow is right, though. It does *look* like ruins," he conceded.

"I think we have a story to tell you then," said Elisa enthusiastically, sounding more like her old self.

"Okay, let's go. I've got the room down the hall," Willow said, getting out of her seat.

Daniel, Elisa and Owen all followed down the hall, into a smaller room with a table and six chairs, overlooking part of Plymouth and across to Drake Island in the harbour.

"Daniel, would you like to start? You found the first piece of this puzzle," Elisa said.

"Sure. *The Doomsday Tablet.* The one that started it all." Daniel went on to explain about finding his great-grandfather's notes, and the tablet, allegedly dredged up from the Mid-Atlantic, while laying the first transatlantic telegraph cable in the eighteen hundreds. Close to where 'David's Anomaly' was discovered. He explained that the language was previously unknown, but seemed to have links to Sanskrit, as well as Icelandic and the Baltic languages.

"My great-grandfather was a professor of archaeology at Oxford between the wars, and it seems he was a reserved and cautious man. He kept his research to himself, and I think it became a bit of an obsession after he retired," Daniel said. "Anyway, he carried on translating it and formed a view that it described a civilisation destroying itself, with its own technology." He could see he was losing Owen. "No, I didn't believe it either," he added for Owen's benefit. "But I went to Oxford to find out more about his work, and from there ... well, it got more interesting." He gestured to Elisa to continue the story.

"Just before I met Daniel, I received an email from the archaeology department here letting us know about what you seem to have discovered out there. It's a bit of a long story, but the head of archaeology here remembered that a former professor at St Dunstan's had been researching a strange tablet from the Mid-Atlantic."

"Your great-grandfather?" said Willow, looking slightly bewildered.

"That's what I thought," said Daniel, "but no." He glanced over at Elisa for her to continue. "Sorry, carry on."

"It was Professor Gillard. Your archaeology department head

apparently knew him. Gillard had started a line of enquiry that sounded like a search for Atlantis so was quickly persuaded to stop. But the HoD said he was a good man. So I went in search of Professor Gillard's work, and found it in our archive.

"In the box, there was another artefact. A tablet like the first one. It was also reported to have come from the Mid-Atlantic, but provenance is not strong. There were some notes about its origin and the professor's attempts at translation. He didn't want to lose his job, though, so he stopped," Elisa said. "He was also forming a view that it was some sort of religious doomsday story, rather than a recording of events."

"Wow, this is amazing," Willow enthused. "This is really going to help us get a proper survey commissioned!"

"Well, there's more ..." Elisa continued. "I could see how work on the two tablets had stopped; there were different reasons for each, but I think it's generally true, or at least it's generally *been* true, that no serious academic wants to risk his career by claiming he's discovered Atlantis." She paused and collected her thoughts. "So I started thinking if there *was* something out there, why on earth would the *only* two relics be at *Oxford?* We're not even anywhere near the coast. Surely there must be others, maybe forgotten, maybe miscategorised ..." She was going to add 'maybe even suppressed' but thought better of it. "... sitting in other institutions."

Daniel went out for some water.

"So I started to ring people I knew, in places with an Atlantic coast. Halifax, Boston, New York, France, Spain and Portugal. And I got lucky. There was another one in Lisbon!"

Daniel returned with two cups of water and handed one to Elisa.

"We went to Lisbon and saw the tablet they had. It was a little bit different, supposedly coming from a little further north, nearer to Iceland, though still Mid-Atlantic. It, too, had the same language on it," Elisa's enthusiasm was starting to engage Owen a bit more.

"When we started translating," she continued, "it was a little bit different. It seemed to tell a story more about the catastrophic end of a city. Or a whole island. We think it was describing seismic or volcanic events, possibly tsunamis, and certainly mass destruction."

"So now there are three artefacts, all with different provenance that suggests the Mid-Atlantic, and they all indicate the destruction of a civilisation," Daniel summarised. "And then there's the map."

49

O wen and Willow were both staring at Daniel.

"Yes, the Zeno map." He paused again for effect and smiled at Elisa, who was now enjoying herself.

Owen and Willow waited for an explanation.

Daniel opened his backpack and took out his laptop. He opened it and located the files he'd saved, selecting the image he wanted. "This map is from 1380, drawn by Nicolo Zeno," he explained. "It's a slightly unorthodox projection, but you'll get your bearings."

Willow grabbed a blank sheet of notepaper and a pencil and drew lines of longitude and latitude. She then marked out Greenland, Great Britain, Iceland and the eastern edge of Nova Scotia. Daniel, Elisa and Owen watched patiently as her rendition came together. She was quite good at it.

"Okay," Willow said, "that seems to make sense. Now, what is Frisland?"

"Exactly," said Elisa. "What *is* Frisland?"

"I'll be back in a minute," Willow said, leaping up and rushing back to the other room. Owen was having a closer look at the Zeno map on Daniel's screen.

"Let's compare." Willow had brought back a printed copy of the hydrographic survey, with overlaid lines of longitude and latitude. She carefully plotted the location of their find onto her sketch of the Zeno map. The unexplained lines and shapes sat directly on top of southern central Frisland. "Oh ... my ..." She looked at the drawing, open-mouthed.

Owen looked unimpressed, as he studied something on his phone. "That Zeno map has been debunked, you know," he said flatly.

"Yes, we know," said Elisa. "There are errors in it. But mostly, it's debunked because there's no island anywhere near where Zeno's Frisland sits. Our tablets tend to support a different view, though. So does your survey."

"We've had this argument before, Owen and I," said Willow. "Have you heard of Yonaguni?"

Elisa said 'yes' at the same time Daniel said 'no'.

"It's submerged ancient ruins, off the coast of Japan."

"Or it isn't," Owen interjected. "It could just as easily be natural geological features."

"My point exactly. Our disciplines do not agree."

"But this anomaly," Owen said, pointing at the hydrographic image, "is three thousand metres below sea level. Yonaguni isn't even a twentieth of that."

"We have a friend, a geophysicist, who thinks it's possible Frisland has been subsiding for thousands of years, as the Mid-Atlantic Ridge grows," Elisa said.

Owen stroked his chin, and nodded slowly.

"There's another image worth taking a look at," Daniel said, looking to head off an argument. He started to search for a particular file. "Do you remember I said the first tablet was supposedly found on a voyage laying the Atlantic telegraph cable?" he asked. Willow nodded. "The story is slightly more involved. Bear with me for a minute."

He paused while bringing up an image of a map showing the location of the first transatlantic telegraph cable. "My great-grandfather, Professor Foxton, recorded in his notes that his wife's grandfather, a man named

Henry Hobbs, was on the first telegraph cable voyage. Foxton wrote that apparently Hobbs had told stories of finding the stone tablet when they'd hauled in a tangled cable, 'right in the middle of the Atlantic, a thousand miles from anywhere'. Hobbs had souvenired it, and that's how Foxton came to have it." Daniel paused while that sank in.

"That provenance is easily argued against, but for me it rings true," he continued. "Take a look at where the original telegraph cable sits on your drawing," he said to Willow, turning the screen towards her.

Willow put pen to paper. "Incredible," she said. "That's astonishing."

She had carefully drawn the arc of the first cable onto her printout. It cut right through the area of Frisland that appeared to be some sort of city or port.

"It's not proof," Elisa acknowledged. "But with each piece we've uncovered, it's become more and more convincing."

It was now close to mid-afternoon. Owen still hadn't agreed, but he was more interested. The conversation turned to the connection between their colleges, and Willow suggested they might want to meet the head of the archaeology department, Dr Frye, who had known Professor Gillard.

"That'd be great," Elisa said, and Willow disappeared to find contact details.

"It's a great story," Owen agreed, "but what it really needs is either a proven Mid-Atlantic artefact, or an original map, *with provenance.* One that can be confirmed as the medieval map's source, and also shows the same *non-existent* island."

"You're probably right," Elisa said, looking for a way through Owen's scepticism. "Just a few days ago, we didn't believe it either, even though our evidence is mounting. As an archaeologist, my training also says it can't be true."

"And as a historian, it's the same for me," added Daniel. "But the facts are hard to ignore."

Willow returned. "I've spoken with Dr Frye, and she says she'd be delighted to see visitors from St Dunstan Hall. She's actually free now, if you like."

"Perfect, where do we find her?" Daniel asked.

"It's not far," Willow said. "I'll take you."

They had thanked Owen and said goodbye, and followed Willow back to the lift and out the front door. Unlike much of Oxford, there were many new buildings and modern, well-designed pathways and gardens. The whole effect was probably enhanced by the weather, too; it was now a lovely sunny afternoon.

They reached the archaeological department, and Dr Frye's office on the fourth floor. As they approached, Willow asked if they were free for dinner. She said some of her fellow students from the survey voyage would love to hear their story. Willow knocked when they reached Dr Frye's office.

Almost immediately a woman's voice said, "Come!"

"I'll leave you to it," Willow said. "I'll text you," she called.

Daniel and Elisa entered the office to find Dr Frye walking around her desk to greet them. She was a small woman in her sixties, with wispy grey hair, and small round tortoiseshell glasses.

"Welcome, welcome," the doctor said, in a robust but cordial voice. "You're from St Dunstan's, Ms Peters told me. What brings you to Plymouth?"

"Hello, doctor. Yes, I'm from St Dunstan's," Elisa said as they shook hands. "This is Daniel Reade, a historian from New Zealand," she added, not quite sure how to introduce him.

"Doctor, it's a pleasure to meet you," Daniel said, as Dr Frye shook his hand more vigorously than he expected. Was he now just a visiting historian? His heart sank a little as he sat on the sofa next to Elisa. The brass nameplate on the desk said 'Dr Penelope Frye – Head of Archaeology'.

"I remember Ed," said Dr Frye, evidently not having too much need for preamble. "Did you know him? He was a lovely chap."

"No. I'm afraid he died well before my time at St Dunstan's," Elisa said.

"I didn't even know of his work until your department alerted me to it this week."

"That was my idea," Dr Frye said cheerfully. "I always wondered what happened to his work, and he was a good friend. We helped each other out, you know." Dr Frye paused to put the kettle on. "Tea?"

"Yes, thank you," Elisa said. "Black, no sugar."

"Same for me," added Daniel.

"Yes. He was my professor when I took my first degree. I was accused of plagiarism by a fellow student, an over-privileged, nasty piece of work," she said with distaste. "Completely unfounded allegation, of course, and Ed supported me. I wasn't from a rich family so wouldn't have stood a chance otherwise. I never forgot it. We reconnected after I took a tenured post here." Dr Frye paused to pour the tea. "I'm sorry there are no biscuits. Type one diabetes. If I had any biscuits, I'm afraid I'd eat them," she laughed.

"When he had that trouble with the Atlantic tablet, I finally got to return the favour. He nearly lost his job, you know. I thought it was most unfair; all he was doing was researching a *real* artefact!

"We talked quite a bit during that period. I think he was quite lonely, poor man. He had gone down a bit of a rabbit hole too," Dr Frye said as she sipped her tea. Elisa prompted her to go on.

"He'd started to search for old maps that could help support a theory of an Atlantic civilisation. A risky business. He'd found a few maps from the sixteen hundreds that showed Atlantic land masses, but there were so many inaccuracies in them I don't think anyone took any of them seriously."

"A friend referred us to the Zeno map," Elisa acknowledged.

"Yes, that's one of them. I know it. Miss Peters told me you're exploring Ed's work, based on new evidence. Tell me, what did you make of Ed's work on the Guillaume de Machaut manuscript?"

"I've never heard of that," Elisa said, her eyes opening wider.

50

Angry determination had now morphed into a cold, inexorable force that dominated Rigo's thoughts. Sheer dumb luck had been with Reade and Mansfield yesterday as they had managed to evade him. He stopped on the side of the road as he realised he had no way of knowing which exit they'd taken at either of the last two roundabouts.

He sat at the wheel, brooding about his next move, acutely aware he needed to have something to report to Zapas. He looked forward to finding the pair and making them suffer. A picture formed in his mind; a bullet to incapacitate Reade and the garrotte for Mansfield, slowly, while Reade watched helplessly. As he sat, he fleetingly reflected that yesterday's anger seemed to have turned into vehement hatred, and it was the most emotion he had felt in many years. It made him feel stronger.

But without knowing their next destination, all he could do was search their homes, so he'd returned to Oxford first. Mansfield's flat had been easy to search; it was small and minimally furnished. There was nothing of use, nothing relating to the stones, nothing to indicate their next move.

As dusk approached, Rigo decided to stay in Oxford and drive down to Chidwick the next morning. Perhaps there would be news of them from the organisation's security people or their extensive network. He had decided, if Zapas called, his report would simply be that he had obtained the new tablet and despatched it yesterday, as instructed, then searched the woman's home. That now he needed information, and that surely they would turn up at another institution where Zapas had an informant? As for his explanation for killing the porter, that still needed work.

This morning, he had driven down to the Chidwick house and parked his SUV in the same heavily wooded place as last time. The village had been as quiet as the previous night, and he encountered no one on the forest path to Reade's house. This time, at least, the path had been neither muddy nor slippery.

He reached the back door, disappointed the kerosene can had been removed. He was tempted to burn the house just to show Reade that he, Anton Rigo, could do whatever he wanted. He put his gloves on, picked the old lock easily and quietly entered the house. He started upstairs in the main bedroom. His primary objective had become to find out where the pair might be headed. He knew Zapas wanted their notes first and foremost, but Rigo wanted *them*. They were unfinished business.

He searched through Reade's suitcase and checked shelves, drawers and tables, all to no avail. He also searched for a safe or hiding place, since Daniel had led him upstairs to find the papers, after he had aimed his pistol at the woman. Her fear had delighted Rigo, and he savoured the moment again. "Your time will come," he whispered to himself, the predatorial half-smile returning to his pale face, as he searched the small rooms off the master bedroom.

The bedrooms at the top of the landing were next, starting with the one Reade seemed to have been leading him to. It looked more promising, being furnished as a study. He started with the desk, removing all the drawers and thoroughly checking its construction for hidden compartments. Then the bookshelves, carefully tracking the dust on the books and the front edge of the shelves, looking for disturbance. Nothing. The fireplace did not seem to have been used for some time, and the chimney yielded nothing other than a blackening of his gloves, which he wiped off on the curtains.

He then searched the wood panelling for a hidden wall safe or compartment. He carefully tapped and clawed at the panels and joints looking for any unexpected movement. Still nothing. He lifted the rug and checked the bookshelf again for structural anomalies that could indicate a hiding place.

Satisfied the room contained nothing useful, the smaller bedroom next door took only minutes to search, being almost empty. Then he went downstairs to check the dining room and small bedroom. Again, nothing. By now he was certain he was wasting his time, but he also knew that if he was to burn the house, he needed to have exhausted all possibilities.

51

Doctor Frye looked at Elisa in surprise.

"The Guillaume de Machaut manuscript. He was a fourteenth-century chronicler and member of King John of Bohemia's court," the archaeology head explained, still looking for any recognition in Elisa's face. But there was none.

"I went through the boxes in our storage, and I don't believe there was anything about him. There was nothing about any ancient maps either," Elisa said.

"Pity, but I can't say I'm overly surprised. That was the stuff that had really set the head of your college off. 'Totally spurious nonsense', the man had said at the time. Ed wouldn't have left it at the hall. He might have destroyed it."

"Can you tell us any more about it?" Elisa was excited.

"Oh yes. Machaut was somehow involved with the king's extensive travels and was rumoured to have a 'secret knowledge' of the seas. Ed wrote to me about it. I'm sure I still have the letter," Dr Frye said, surprising both of them by suddenly standing up and walking over to the large filing cabinet in the corner. She pulled a brown folder out of one of the drawers and handed it to Elisa.

"I'm not sure why I've kept this. Posterity perhaps. It probably belongs with his work. Maybe one day he'll be proved right!" she smiled, but it seemed clear she didn't think that day was likely to come soon.

Elisa opened the file and saw a copy of an old encyclopaedia entry on the life of Guillaume de Machaut, poet, composer and chronicler in the Bohemian court. It confirmed Machaut was widely travelled and had an uncanny navigational knowledge and skill. There was also a letter from Professor Gillard to Dr Frye. Elisa unfolded it and looked over at Dr Frye.

"Oh go ahead, it's not personal," the doctor said.

It was written in a neat hand, with the occasional small ink blot.

My dearest Penny,

Since our last conversation, I have discovered an exciting manuscript. Written in 1375, two years before the death of its author, Guillaume de Machaut of the court of King John of Bohemia. It indicates Machaut had access to the ancient source of some of the most unusual and unexplained medieval maps. His manuscript describes a 'special scroll' that depicts the 'real ocean' [Atlantic] in great detail!

This may be the evidence I need! If it supports the Zeno brothers and the others, then I may have proof! With some digging I have traced it through records of priceless artefacts looted by the Nazis. It was taken from Prague in 1943 then sold in Vienna on the black market near the end of the war. The records I've found indicate it's currently in the Austrian National Library in Vienna! I intend to travel there at the earliest opportunity to see it for myself.

I am forever indebted to you for supporting me and believing in my work during these recent difficult times, and I look forward very much to being vindicated and celebrating that success with you, my dear friend.

Yours most sincerely,

Edgar

Elisa was holding Daniel's hand tightly as she read it. Her excitement was contagious; Daniel could feel it too.

"That was two weeks before he dropped the whole thing," Dr Frye said, interrupting their thoughts. "I think he must have started to arrange his travel, or possibly seek university funding for it, and had the whole idea stepped on quite firmly."

Elisa had let go of Daniel's hand, and started to slide the letter carefully back in the folder.

"I have to tell you, I was less excited by this than Ed clearly was. I've encountered a lot of historical curiosities purporting to be a lot more than they actually are. Particularly medieval ones. It was usually in the interests of the author or owner, Machaut in this case, to talk up the air of mystique around themselves." Elisa started to hand the folder back to Dr Frye. "No, please keep it. It should be with his work, especially if he hasn't kept any record of it at St Dunstan's. God knows, they can't do anything to him now!" Dr Frye stood up to collect teacups, and Elisa and Daniel took their cue.

"Thank you so much, doctor, that was really helpful. We're another step closer to piecing this all together," Elisa said, shaking the doctor's hand.

"Thank you, Dr Frye," Daniel added. "It was great to meet you. And thanks for these papers," he added, as Elisa handed him the brown folder to put into the backpack. He shook hands with the doctor on the way out.

As the lift doors closed, Elisa was the first to say it. "I want to see that manuscript." She grabbed Daniel's arm. "If we're lucky, this could confirm Frisland was a *real* place."

"I was thinking exactly that. We could fly to Vienna tomorrow morning. It's probably not as long as the drive to Heathrow! But first we'll need to find somewhere to stay tonight," he added. He thought he saw her face change slightly, but she looked away to retrieve a campus map from her pocket.

"First we'll need to find our way out of here and back to the car," she said, looking at the map.

They wound their way between buildings and through open areas back to Drake Circus, and then down a lane to the car park. Elisa started searching for a hotel and quickly found one close by that advertised off-street parking.

Daniel was about to climb out of the car and get their bags, when Elisa put her arm on his. "Daniel, I ... I hope you'll understand, but I need ... some time to think." She looked into his eyes. "This is all happening too fast. I'm just overwhelmed. I need a little bit of space. I need to book my own room tonight." She was gazing intently at him, and he couldn't tell whether there was sadness or confusion or something else in her eyes. "Please understand," she implored.

He was looking into her eyes thinking right now he would do whatever she asked of him, but he was feeling more hurt than he wanted to admit. It took him a few seconds to answer her. "I think I understand," he said, not understanding much. "I won't put any pressure on you. I know it's been an intense few days. In lots of ways." He tried to smile reassuringly.

52

The silence was broken by the ping of a message on Elisa's phone. "It's Willow," she said. "She and a couple of friends will meet us for dinner. She's suggested the White Horse at seven."

Daniel looked it up. They were both glad to have the brief distraction. "It's just a block away from here," he said. "Sounds fine." He got out of the car and retrieved their bags from the back.

"Please understand," Elisa said to him again, in a little voice. She was looking into his eyes, waiting.

"Okay," he said eventually.

As they walked into reception, she discreetly wiped her moistened eyes. They were able to get adjoining rooms on the first floor.

"Shall we meet downstairs in an hour?" Daniel asked. It was five forty-five.

"Yes." Elisa kissed him on the cheek and went into her room.

Daniel felt confused. Had he done something wrong? It had all happened so fast, but from his point of view it was wonderful. He hadn't felt this way about anyone in a long time. Should he have told her that? Was it too soon, or wasn't it?

He dropped his backpack on his bed. *She just needs some space,* he reasoned. At least she didn't say 'can we just be friends?' or 'it's not you, but ...' Tomorrow they would go to Vienna together. There was plenty of time. Then he had a sudden alarming thought. *Do you still have your passport?* he texted her.

No response for a few minutes, and then his phone buzzed. *Yes! Luckily I'd forgotten to unpack it yesterday. You?*

Yes. See you at 6.45.

Daniel put a jersey on and went down to reception just after half past six. The last half hour seemed to pass very slowly. He hoped there would be time to buy a proper overnight bag for their trip tomorrow.

Elisa came down the stairs to join him, wearing a cream silk blouse under her tailored navy jacket, the cashmere scarf tied around her neck.

She looks beautiful, as ever. As he'd got to know her, she just seemed more alluring each day.

They went outside into a cool but calm evening. They strolled to the White Horse, and arrived a few minutes early. As they went in, they saw Willow waving to them from a table in the corner. It was a noisy student pub but not too crowded. It was warm inside so they took off their jackets and draped them over the backs of their chairs. She introduced her friends. A girl with long blonde hair tied at the back was the first to stand up.

"This is Marie, she's studying geology. Hasan and David are doing hydrography with me." A young man with black hair and a full beard extended his hand, followed by a tall, ginger-haired colleague. After the handshaking, and Daniel and Elisa introducing themselves as they all sat, a girl with a half-shaved head came up to take their drinks order.

"Thanks so much for meeting us," Willow said. She told the two boys what she and Owen had showed Daniel and Elisa that afternoon. Drinks arrived, and she asked Elisa to recount their story. Over the next few hours they ate, enjoyed a couple more drinks, and all talked enthusiastically about where this might be heading. Elisa told them about the letter Dr Frye had given them, and that they planned to go and find the manuscript tomorrow.

At one point, as Elisa talked about the Lisbon tablet, a look passed between her and Daniel that Willow caught. "What's wrong?" she asked.

"Well, we don't know why, but somebody wants the tablets. In fact, we think they may already have them all. We didn't want to worry you, but things have happened ..." Elisa explained about Cláudia being attacked, and Mr Hearne, and the tablets being stolen. She left out the incident at Daniel's house.

"But what about the first one, your great-grandfather's?" Willow asked Daniel.

"That's gone too, as far as we know. It was a long time ago, and could be just a coincidence, but it disappeared from his house during World War Two. He was murdered in that burglary." The Plymouth students were silent.

The girl returned to take coffee and tea orders, and Daniel asked about the next steps for the hydrographic survey of the area they'd discovered. Willow said she had already talked with her supervisor about making the case for a detailed survey, and that the information Daniel and Elisa had supplied had been particularly helpful. She said it was mostly the data that had persuaded the supervisor to go into bat for them. Willow said Dr Frye was supportive. They were hoping the work could be done as part of the 'big survey', a joint transatlantic venture between the University of Plymouth and the United States National Oceanic and Atmospheric Administration. They were lobbying the NOAA relentlessly, they said.

"Hopefully we'll get under way within the next two weeks, only just before the weather turns too bad," David said.

They talked more about the upcoming survey, confident there was a strong enough case to study their site in detail, and 'how great would it be to find something amazing in our final year'. They said their goodbyes, Willow wishing Daniel and Elisa good luck with the manuscript, and Daniel and Elisa hoping the survey would be approved. It had been an enjoyable night of lively conversation, Daniel reflected, although Elisa had been more reserved than usual.

As they strolled back to their hotel, Daniel reached for Elisa's hand and she took his. It was only half past ten, but they were both feeling the effects of the last few days. Wearily, they climbed the stairs to their rooms.

"Breakfast at seven-thirty?" Daniel suggested.

"Fine with me. Good night." Elisa kissed his cheek.

"Good night."

Elisa sat on her bed and put her hands to her face. *What am I doing?* Her feelings for Daniel were real, but she had never forgotten how she'd felt after Will had ... well, *betrayed* her. That was probably why there had been no one since. There had been opportunity, but a casual fling was not for her. And there was Mark. He asked her out a few times, but she saw him more as a friend. He'd moved on and they *were* friends. She told her mother that perhaps she just wasn't good at relationships, and her mother said 'don't worry, you just haven't met the right man yet'.

As she got herself ready for bed, her mind kept turning it over. Was she getting ahead of herself? She thought about last night. Spontaneous. Wonderful. Daniel was ... well, the spark between them had been undeniable. Unavoidable. It had not been that way with Will. Over some weeks, he'd called and texted her many times, bought her flowers. He was persistent. She'd felt flattered, he seemed nice, and she gave in. But this was different. It felt like the pieces of her usually well-ordered life had been thrown up in the air, and she wasn't in control of where they landed.

She climbed into the cold bed, and as she lay there she resolved that they just had to get through this – whatever this mystery was – and then she would be able to see things more clearly. She tried to put the thoughts out of her mind, but images of the pale man soon replaced them. How long would it be before he found them again? She felt overwhelmed.

She tried to distract her busy mind with the mystery of the ancient technology. How could they convince the authorities there was real danger? *Daniel's right,* she supposed; when looked at in the cold light of day, it sounded so implausible. But now they had further provenance of an actual Mid-Atlantic civilisation, thanks to Willow and friends. *Will that help?* They needed something more concrete, more compelling. If only there was something in the tablets that described the technology in more detail. Or described its power source. Something that made the message more than a 'doomsday warning'. Wasn't that what DI George had said, as he linked the idea immediately to a religious cult?

Maybe the Machaut manuscript would give them enough *evidence* to convince the sceptical DI George.

Those thoughts eventually gave way to a fitful sleep.

53

José Zapas sat quietly in the upstairs living room overlooking the gardens. He could still picture Josef in this room on the last day of his life. The day José took control of his destiny. That memory appeased him a little. In fifteen minutes, his car would be waiting to take him to a televised press conference and debate with his rival, the current president. Zapas was not particularly worried about it, since, according to the polls, he was now the front runner. Even so, he wanted to ensure he gave the impression of complete calm and control, and that had been difficult this morning.

Yesterday, the third tablet arrived from Oxford, sent by Rigo, who had failed again to get the translation notes from Mansfield and Reade. He had been furious with Rigo, and forcefully instructed him to get his job done. To make matters worse, Zapas's academics had just told him they could not get any new data from the latest tablet. It was, in fact, less informative than the first one. The scant detail from Lisbon had been more helpful. Días kept reminding him that they badly needed some information about the technology's power source. There was nothing in the Lisbon translation that gave any sense as to how to scale up the device, and Días believed it could destroy itself well before any effects like those described in the tablets became evident.

Rigo reported that he'd thoroughly searched the residences of Reade and Mansfield, but their notes were not there. Nor did he know where the pair were. He assumed they had everything in their possession, and must have been following a new lead. Neither did he know what that lead was. Zapas's own organisation had no new leads either. Their network of contacts in academia was thin and had not been active for some time.

Rigo said it was now personal. He sounded angry, which would lead to more mistakes. Zapas had no tolerance for carelessness, but he had no other operatives he could quickly deploy. Pulling Rigo back in would leave him with no one in the United Kingdom, since Rigo had inconveniently killed their informant at St Dunstan's. Zapas's rage had boiled when Rigo made a weak excuse about the man being a risk, and therefore a 'loose end'. Almost *all* of the organisation's informants were risks, given they were being blackmailed into compliance.

Rigo had been one of the best, but he was starting to lose his edge, and mistakes were unacceptable. *I will have to replace him soon*, Zapas thought. Of course, when he did replace him, the successor's first task would be to kill Rigo. He simply knew too much; he could be connected to the organisation.

But for now, Zapas decided to hold back because Rigo was still his best chance to get Reade and Mansfield's notes. *And the woman herself.* She might lead him to more information about the technology and its power source; something that had eluded his father, as well as Días. The only downside was that between the Mansfield woman and Plymouth University's discovery in the Atlantic, the existence of the ancient technology might be exposed. An acceptable risk for now, he decided, so Rigo remained useful.

Zapas stepped out onto the balcony and surveyed his gardens. The press conference would go well. There would be a violent protest against the president outside the television studio. José Zapas would be appalled by the ill-feeling and violence that follows this man around. He had rehearsed his lines already. He further calmed himself by thinking about his new life as President of Brazil. *I wonder what the old man would make of that?* Josef had always wanted wealth and power, but he also liked the shadows. Not José. He could live in the Palácio da Alvorada in Brasilia, or he could move the capital to São Paulo and have a new presidential palace built. *Why not? The country will soon be mine.*

54

The alarm went off at six-thirty, and Daniel awoke feeling tired. He'd lain in bed last night thinking Elisa seemed to have decided their night together was a mistake. Just thrown together by circumstance and fear. He'd said he trusted her, and it was true; he trusted her to be honest and open with him. But he knew that didn't mean things would turn out the way he wanted. He trusted that there was a depth to her, an integrity – one of the things that drew him to her.

He'd eventually drifted into sleep but had woken during the night thinking about where this new development, the manuscript, might lead them. He wondered whether they would find something that would be enough to convince the police or someone in authority that lives, possibly many lives, were in danger. As he tossed and turned, he'd boiled it down to a simple fact: they needed to know more.

In the cold morning light, he sat on the edge of the bed and shook the thoughts from his head. A hot shower helped a little. He went downstairs to breakfast. Elisa hadn't arrived yet, so he chose a table and made himself a coffee.

Elisa walked into the small restaurant looking lost. Daniel gave her a wave and she joined him.

"Hi," she said.

"Hi. How did you sleep?

"Not well. I've been thinking about how we get the attention of the police. We need to find something more concrete, don't we?"

"Yes. I've worried about that, too. No real answers, I'm afraid, but we got one more piece of the puzzle yesterday, the survey data. The next might be the manuscript. We need to see it."

"Yes, we do," Elisa said emphatically.

As they ate, they worked out how long it would take to drive to Heathrow, and booked a flight to Vienna for early afternoon.

In her room, Elisa quickly packed, shaking her head at the inadequate supply of fresh clothing she had left. She checked her face in the bathroom mirror, wishing she didn't look so tired. A knock on her door startled her. She nervously peered through the spyhole. Daniel.

"Hi," she said. "I'm not quite ready."

"Sorry. Not rushing you." He showed her the plastic bag with his replacement dressing and antiseptic.

"Oh. Of course, sorry." She stepped back from the door and he came in, taking off his shirt.

"Thanks. Sorry to have to ask, but I can't do it with one hand."

"I don't mind." She took the antiseptic and gently applied it with a tissue.

He winced as it stung the still-reddened wound, muscles flexing as he did so. She looked at him with concern in her eyes.

"It's okay," he said, as she started to gingerly apply the fresh dressing. She was standing so close he had to resist kissing her.

He put the medical supplies into his backpack, put his shirt back on and jacket over the top, as she finished putting the last of her things into her bag, and checked her face in the mirror.

"You look gorgeous," he said.

No I don't, she thought, but it was sweet of him to say it.

They went down to reception and checked out.

The drive out of Plymouth in peak traffic wasn't too bad, and they soon reached the expressway. While Daniel drove, Elisa found contact details for the Austrian National Library in Vienna, and called them, pleased to have something to do. After a brief explanation, she was put through to the State Hall, where the manuscript was supposedly housed. An assistant librarian, Anna Holger, had been able to confirm that the State Hall did indeed have the Guillaume de Machaut manuscript in their catalogue. If Elisa could call back in an hour, she should have located it and would be able to advise whether Elisa would be able to view it. Anna had explained that some of the older texts were not permitted to be handled, but she would be happy to at least meet with them.

"If they can't find it, is it still worth going?" Daniel asked.

"I hope so. I'm sure we can at least talk to her and find out more about Machaut. We have no other leads to follow," Elisa said, feeling flat. "At least we will be further away from that man."

An hour later, Elisa called Anna again, who confirmed she had retrieved the manuscript, and limited access would be possible. Anna asked if there would be an official request from Oxford, as that would help with the formalities and the library's processes. Elisa agreed to try and arrange it, and Anna asked her if a transcript and translation would be helpful.

"That would be absolutely brilliant!" Elisa said, adding that they should be able to get there before five o'clock.

Anna said the library was open until six, and she would be there until closing. They exchanged email addresses, and Anna said she would send details of where to address the official request from St Dunstan's.

Elisa then phoned Alan, knowing she would owe him another favour, to ask if he could write the request, and print it on St Dunstan's letterhead to scan to Anna. He was happy to oblige, and several texts and half an hour later, it was done.

"All arranged." Elisa relaxed a little and closed her eyes.

"Great," Daniel replied, squeezing her hand.

They decided not to stop anywhere along the way, and arrived at the airport just over two hours ahead of their flight time. After returning Daniel's Citroën to car rentals, they checked in and were now waiting in the busy terminal, grimacing while drinking airport coffee and eating airport sandwiches. They were both feeling tired and, with nowhere comfortable to sit, and were relieved when the boarding call came. The flight was two hours and fifteen minutes. They worked out that, allowing for a ride into the city, they should be able to check in to the hotel and then walk to the library well before closing.

They stowed their bags in the overhead locker and sat.

Elisa shivered. "Is it cold in here, or is that just me?" she asked.

"No, it's cold." Daniel took a blanket from the overhead locker and passed it to her. They both sat back and Elisa spread the blanket, offering some to Daniel. Twenty minutes into the flight, Elisa was asleep, her head nestled next to Daniel's, and five minutes after that he, too, was asleep.

Daniel woke up some time later to find he'd been sleeping with his arm around her and she'd snuggled up close. Soon after that, a flight attendant announced they would shortly be commencing their descent into Vienna.

"Mmm," Elisa murmured as she woke up, giving Daniel a smile that gave him some hope that maybe she hadn't yet consigned him to the 'regrets' category. For a minute he just held her, savouring the moment, until she had to move when the crew wanted to ensure their seat belts were fastened.

55

Outside the Vienna International Airport terminal, the air was chilly. They quickly found a ride. It was raining softly in the afternoon twilight as they made their way into the city. The hotel was apparently a five-minute walk from the library, and was in a delightful old part of the central city. Conveniently, it was right across the street from a bank cash machine, since they'd realised they had no euros.

Elisa took their bags into the hotel lobby, while Daniel ran across the street to the ATM. They checked in, surprising the girl at the reception desk when Daniel requested two rooms. He'd decided not only would he respect Elisa's wishes, but he would make sure it wasn't awkward or embarrassing for her. After they had been given their room cards and the usual breakfast and Wi-Fi information, Daniel went over to the concierge desk to ask for an umbrella, which, thankfully, the man was able to supply.

They took the lift up to their floor, and Daniel left Elisa at her room. His was the next one along the corridor. He unpacked a few things and went back down to the lobby, wishing he'd packed a warm coat. Elisa arrived a few minutes later. She had checked her phone and confirmed that all the connections had been made; the library had the official letter, and Anna was looking forward to meeting with them.

It might have been a delightful walk were it not for the fact that the rain had turned to sleet as the temperature dropped near zero. They huddled under the umbrella as they navigated past the famous Café Mozart, and along Augustinerstraße to Josefsplatz. Kaiser Josef II, on horseback, was poised to charge away from the State Hall of the National Library of Austria.

As they entered the National Library, the temperature rose some twenty degrees, and they were able to start thawing out. Elisa texted Anna to announce their arrival. The building was stunning. Even the ceilings were extraordinary. They were still taking it all in when a tall young woman approached them.

"Elisa Mansfield?" she enquired tentatively.

Daniel and Elisa introduced themselves and shook hands.

"Did you find somewhere to hang your coats already?" Anna asked. Nearly everyone they had passed on their short walk had been wearing an overcoat. A few had stared at Daniel and Elisa in their jackets only, with their hotel umbrella, no doubt assuming they were ill-equipped tourists.

"I'm afraid we didn't bring coats," Daniel said. "We packed in a rush."

"You must be freezing," Anna observed.

"Yes," Elisa said, her shivering having stopped only just enough to speak.

"Please come through." Anna ushered them through the grand hall and into an astonishing reading room. It was more of a hall than a room, with beautifully carved bookshelves lining the walls, punctuated by tall windows with deep sills. There were gold-leafed sculptures and figures, and a long, thick red carpet ran down the centre of the parquet floor. Its most striking feature was the muralled ceiling, a stunningly beautiful medieval masterpiece.

"Would you like to see the manuscript?" Anna brought them back to the present.

"Yes, very much, please."

Anna invited them to sit down at one of the tables, and she disappeared through the door. Daniel and Elisa were both still awestruck by the reading room, when Anna returned with a large, but unexpectedly slim ancient tome. There were some papers resting on top of it, and two pairs of white cotton gloves. She placed the manuscript in front of Elisa.

"You are welcome to open it and turn the pages, but please be careful, and you'll need to wear these gloves. We don't always require them, but you'll see inside that there are a lot of illustrations, and there is some gold and other metallic leaf, so it is for the best."

Elisa acknowledged her instructions.

"Also," Anna went on, "please turn the pages slowly, and as few times as possible."

"Of course," Elisa agreed. "Thank you so much for arranging this."

"It is no problem," Anna said. "Photography is not usually permitted, especially with flash, but since you are officially here from Oxford University, we won't enforce that rule. Just please be discreet if others come into the room. It will give them the wrong idea." Anna left them alone in the majestic room.

"It's thinner than I expected," Elisa said, as she took a photo of the leather-clad wooden cover. She opened it to find that it consisted of only eight leaves, sixteen pages, of thick, yellowed parchment. Each page contained elaborate illustrations, and the first paragraph commenced with a large, very decorative but faded red capital letter. It was written in Latin, in decorative, difficult-to-decipher calligraphy that took both Elisa and Daniel some time to start making out.

Anna had also left them with the four A4 printed pages. The first two were the untranslated Latin text, and the second two were the English translation, completed by academics at the National Library, according to the footnote. Elisa carefully took photos of each page and both covers, ensuring the illustrations were captured in the right light, since these were not included on the A4 pages. The illustrations contained various beasts, men working, something that appeared to be map-making, an odd-looking ship, and assorted religious imagery.

"We're not going to make much progress here tonight, I don't think," Elisa said.

"No, but there's a lot to take in. I wonder if they have anything else on Machaut," Daniel replied.

They had both read the A4 translation, and, while it was clear Machaut claimed a 'special knowledge of the seas', there was no apparent clue as to what he meant. That reference, or the reference to the 'real ocean' may have been what attracted Gillard's attention, but that could simply have been emotive or poetic language harking back to the days of the ancient Greeks.

"Maybe. Let's ask Anna. You're right, though, there's a lot to take in here. The illustrations, for instance; there's always some meaning behind them, yet the translators don't appear to have considered them."

"I'm sure the translators have done a good job, but interpreting something like this has to be done in its full context," Daniel said.

"How do you mean?" Elisa asked.

"It's not just about literally translating the words. *Everything* is important. The illustrations, the traditions and norms of the time, the context of King John's court and whatever he was seeking from his voyages. These would have influenced *how and why* Machaut wrote, not just what."

It was a quarter to six when Anna returned. "Hallo, I hope this has been useful."

"Yes, very much," Elisa said. "Do you know much about this work?"

"Not a great deal. It has not been seen as important. It is … fanciful. Guillaume de Machaut was known more as a poet and composer than as a reliable chronicler."

"Do you have any more of his works?" Daniel asked.

"No, I'm afraid not. I do know there is a Guillaume de Machaut museum in Prague. Well, it is privately run, perhaps more of a tourist attraction, but I have seen it myself. They have other writings, and some of his collection."

"His collection?" Elisa asked, her eyes widening.

56

R igo had been sitting in his flat, brooding over his inability to find Reade and Mansfield. There was nothing he could do without a new lead, or a stroke of luck. His powerlessness made him more angry. He needed to regain control. He was certain they would not return to Oxford or either of their homes. They could have gone to ground virtually anywhere. The direction they had been driving could even have taken them to Heathrow or Gatwick. He knew also that Zapas would still expect him to get results, regardless of the circumstances.

Driving to airports to look for the vehicle seemed pointless, as he already knew it was a rental, so it could have easily been returned and re-rented by now. Rigo was edgy and impatient. Usually he was focused singularly on his work. Emotionless, detached, coldly professional. Surroundings did not matter; they were nothing more than irrelevant background. He looked around his flat – plain walls, sparse furnishings, takeaway food cartons on the tiny kitchen bench. He did not understand why today these things angered him. He needed something to do. A lead, something to take him to Mansfield and Reade. They were the reason he was stuck in this lifeless place, itching to end the assignment by closing the book on the pair and their notes with a vehemently satisfying finale.

241

His reverie was interrupted by his phone. "Yes?"

"Reade and Mansfield are in Vienna. Our associate at the Vienna National Library has alerted us that St Dunstan Hall have requested access to a manuscript they hold," Zapas's security head explained to Rigo. "You are to travel there immediately and find out more about this manuscript, and obtain it."

"I will need more information," Rigo said.

"You will receive a copy of the letter sent on their behalf. All the details you should need are there."

"Where are they staying?"

"We don't have that information yet. And he wants the woman, alive." The security head ended the call.

Alive. That would be more difficult.

Anton Rigo was on his way to Heathrow within ten minutes. He expected to arrive in Vienna late that night. A sense of anticipation for his unfinished business brought a humourless smile to his pale face. *If Zapas wants a plaything, there's no reason why I can't enjoy myself first.* He fingered the wire of his necklace.

* * *

SÃO PAULO, BRAZIL

Zapas entered the lab in a dangerous temper. Días knew all too well just how impatient he could be, but since the news about the ruins in the Atlantic, he had been even more unreasonable than usual. Días had braced himself and done his best to prepare for it by working up possible ideas for the demonstration of the technology. He knew Zapas was itching to wield his new power.

"I want the weapon ready for testing by tomorrow," Zapas demanded.

"We are close, but I can't work miracles. I need another day," Días countered boldly.

Zapas marched up to Días and stood within centimetres of the man's sallow face. "Tell me, Dr Días, if I give you another day, how would *you* deploy my weapon?" Zapas demanded, with menacing force.

Días stepped back, involuntarily. "The effect it has on rock and stone is the most promising," Días started nervously. "It could be used to collapse buildings or possibly even whole city blocks. It could deform railway tracks and supports, derailing trains; it could create large sinkholes."

"Not enough. I want a decisive demonstration of its power. Think big, doctor," Zapas pushed.

"It could cause landslides," Días ventured, thinking quickly. "Even trigger an earthquake, if deployed in the right place."

"Yes. That's better." Zapas backed off just a little. "Tell me how you would do that."

Días was nervous now. Zapas was enjoying pushing him. Días reached for his cigarettes, but the glare Zapas gave him stopped him in his tracks.

"Well, doctor?" Zapas stepped up close to his face again.

"It can soften rock. We proved that. If we can align it along a fault line, we might be able to trigger the fault to rupture. The soft rock would act like a lubricant. We just need the right fault, with enough strain built up over years," Días said.

A faint smile began to cross Zapas's face. "Yes," he said. He looked pleased with himself, Días thought, perhaps like a teacher satisfied that his pupil had learned his lesson. No, a dictator satisfied that the people had bowed down. "That is what you will do, doctor. The power stored within the earth is the power you've been wasting years searching for." Zapas's contempt was palpable. "California will be your target. Choose where you can do the most damage. You have one hour."

Zapas left the laboratory satisfied. Not only a decisive display of his power, it would be a significant blow to the United States economy, California being one of the wealthiest states. He directed his security head to send a message to Rigo: that he was to get ready for immediate travel, and his next destination would be advised soon.

After a brief discussion with his technicians and some web searching, Días decided the southern San Andreas fault would be an ideal target.

That part of the fault had not had a major event in three hundred years. They settled on a location near an international airport to which equipment could easily be freighted, and Días informed Zapas.

A short while later, the senior security man arrived to let them know the equipment would be collected tomorrow afternoon, for freight to the United States via one of the Zapas companies. The men would be issued with the necessary passports, US visas and air tickets. They were to have everything ready by early afternoon, and arrangements were being made for the precise location of the demonstration.

In his media room upstairs, José Zapas was pleased with the choice of demonstration site. *This will be perfect*, he thought. Upwards of twenty million people might be affected, and it seemed likely many thousands would be killed. The power Zapas felt in his veins exhilarated him.

Future President Zapas started to rehearse the impassioned speech he would give, expressing his heartfelt sympathy for the people of California after the tragedy.

57

VIENNA, AUSTRIA

"Yes, his collection is in the little tourist museum," Anna said. "Guillaume de Machaut collected items of 'memorabilia', I think you would say, from his life and travels. Curiosities mostly, but there are some other writings. It's set up in a house he was said to have lived in, but of course no one knows that for sure. I can give you its details and location. I saw it last year. On holiday."

"That would be very helpful, thank you," Daniel said.

Anna wrote down the details and wished them all the best in their search. They left the reading room, taking one last look at its grandeur, and walked through to the main entrance of the State Hall. Daniel mused that under better circumstances it would be nice to spend more time here in this wonderful library. In this historic city, sometime in the future. The museums of Vienna were also famous, and he wished they had more time. Maybe one day.

Outside it was now fully dark, but the sleet seemed to have given way to light snow, which they agreed was an improvement.

"Are you ready to freeze again?" Daniel asked.

"Ready," she replied, not really meaning it.

Elisa took Daniel's arm, and he held the umbrella over her as they hurried back the way they had come, resolving on the way that they needed to get new bags and pack properly. They arrived at their hotel in under ten minutes, slowed only by a little snow underfoot, which made the paths slippery. They were relieved to step in out of the cold.

"Can we transfer my photos onto your laptop?" Elisa asked, shivering, as soon as they were inside the lobby. Clearly, she was keen to see what they had!

"Sure." He looked around. "If you want to grab us a space with a table, I'll go up and get my laptop. Let's talk about Prague, too. It's only an hour or two from here, I believe." He pulled the pages Anna had given them out of his jacket pocket and handed them to Elisa before he left.

Daniel returned to find Elisa sitting on a sofa beside a small table in a quiet corner. She was engrossed in the papers and didn't look up until he was practically standing beside her. He put his laptop on the table and sat down on the armchair, pulling it in closer.

"Okay," Elisa said. "Let's transfer those photos onto a bigger screen."

As she started studying the images, Daniel picked up the Latin transcript and its translation and laid them side by side on the table. He'd started to compare them, when Elisa looked up.

"You read Latin?" she enquired.

"Occupational hazard for a historian," he said. "I got sick of having to get old documents translated, so I spent a year learning it."

"I'm impressed," she said. "You're a man of hidden talents."

Daniel smiled and went back work. It was fairly slow going. True, he'd learned Latin, but he hadn't had a great deal of practice using it, and he had to check the occasional word on his phone. "There's not much here other than the usual medieval guff."

The quizzical expression on her face prompted him to explain further.

"Probably not the most eloquent description of a historical document I've ever used, but I'm looking for something that stands out. Something that might help us. So far, nothing," he said.

"I suppose it'll take time," Elisa acknowledged.

A solidly built man with a short, military-style haircut came towards them, staring at Elisa. She shivered, as Daniel looked up, her nerves clearly still unsettled. The man nodded to them and walked on.

"It's okay," Daniel said, as they both paused and took a deep breath.

The hotel lobby was now busier than before, which was at once both comforting and threatening. He was glad Elisa had chosen a corner table, and pulled his chair around further so they could both have their backs to the wall and a clear view.

"Do you want to go to one of our rooms to continue?" Daniel asked.

"Oh, it's all right. I'm sure we'll be fine here. And this manuscript has nothing directly to do with the tablets," Elisa rationalised.

"Okay." Daniel was unconvinced, but they were certainly far from the danger in the UK. He looked down back at their work. "There are a lot of references to travels within Europe, but nothing yet that specifically suggests the Atlantic. And references to the illustrations, too. Again, usual stuff. Mystical beasts, a ship of lights, farming ... It's a bit random," Daniel explained.

"What would a ship of lights be?" Elisa asked.

"Well, I'd say *navis luminare* in Latin, but what it means might depend on the case ... Latin translation can be finicky. Just looking for it now." Daniel scanned the transcript. "That's odd. I've got *navis illustratio*. That's not ship of lights, but it could be 'ship of illumination'.

"Isn't that 'lights'?" Elisa asked.

"No. It's more like 'ship of enlightenment'," Daniel said. "Still doesn't help us, though."

"Come and look at the illustration. Maybe that will help," Elisa suggested.

Daniel moved onto the sofa next to her and leaned in. He breathed in her perfume as she enlarged the image on the screen. '*Navis Illustratio*' was indeed the caption of the elaborate illustration of the ship.

"That's slightly odd," Daniel said. "This is the thirteen seventies. I'd have expected a drawing of a Viking longship or knarr, or perhaps an oared ship like a galley, but this doesn't resemble any of those to me."

"What could that mean?"

"I don't know. It's quite ornate, too. Does it look out of proportion to you?"

"Yes, maybe. What am I looking for?"

"The carving at the front. On a Viking ship, that would be half a metre high, but on this ship, if it's to scale, that would be at least two metres high, or even three. That's a lot of wood; a lot of unnecessary extra weight at the front of a ship," Daniel suggested. "It's way out of proportion."

"Maybe it's just not a good illustration," she offered.

"But the detail in the rest of the manuscript, the precise calligraphy, the drawings in the book itself, all seem very well done to me."

"All right. Let's check the others," Elisa said, scrolling through the images. There were men working on a farm, a man drawing a map with what appeared to be a small scroll in front of it, and illustrations of animals. Elisa enlarged the image of one of the animal pictures, and neither could see anything out of the ordinary. She scrolled on to the next image and did the same. "These are buffalo, I think," she said.

"Yes, I think so. Native to Africa and Asia. I'd expect those in a medieval manuscript like this," Daniel responded.

"I don't think they look the same as the buffalo in the previous image. And why would there be *two* illustrations of buffalo?" She scrolled back, and sure enough, on enlargement, Daniel could see they weren't the same.

"Are these a different type of buffalo? It looks like there's a hump at the shoulders," Elisa said.

"Oh ... Now that's very odd. Those aren't buffalo. They're *bison*," Daniel said.

"How is that odd?"

"Bison are native to *North America*, and that, supposedly wasn't discovered until a hundred and seventeen years after this was drawn!" Daniel exclaimed.

Elisa moved forward to study the image. "Look at that," she said, pointing at the screen. "I thought it was vegetation in the background, but now I think it's *antlers*, on that buffalo, or bison."

Daniel leaned in closer, her hair touching his face. "That could be a *moose!* We could be looking at a scene from eastern *Canada!*" Daniel exclaimed, unable to hide his enthusiasm. "This is amazing."

"It's hard to believe no one's noticed this before."

"I think it's likely that apart from the fact Machaut wasn't an important figure in history, we're now looking from a *very specific* viewpoint. Would we have spotted those bison and moose otherwise? Most people would just see buffalo."

"You're probably right. I guess Professor Gillard only found it because he was looking for specific things like 'secret knowledge of the seas'," Elisa replied. "And of course this work was deemed to be 'fanciful medieval ramblings', remember?" Elisa added. "It just wasn't seen as important. Machaut wasn't seen as important. Let's keep looking."

"After dinner?"

"Good idea."

58

Standing on the platform, Daniel and Elisa waited to board the ÖBB Railjet to Prague. Cleaning and maintenance staff had almost completed their duties, as passengers waited in the new central station complex. It was as much a modern railway station as it was an upmarket shopping mall. Daniel had purchased a suitcase large enough to fit his backpack inside, offering Elisa some space if she needed it. 'I'll see if I can pick up some things in Prague,' she'd said.

The previous night, they dined in the hotel restaurant in the old cellar. Briefly, they'd been able to forget about the pale man who wanted to kill them. 'Maybe we'll come back sometime and be able to enjoy this,' Daniel had said, but a look of melancholy briefly crossed Elisa's face and he changed the subject, suggesting they travel to Prague by train.

A quick search revealed the train would be about four hours; not much different to flying when allowing for rides to and from airports and waiting time. Fortuitously, as they checked the map, they'd discovered the Machaut museum was less than a kilometre from the Prague central railway station. Having a plan, and keeping busy, kept their minds off the threat of their pursuer. It had been four days since he'd tried to kill them in Chidwick, and those four days had been a roller coaster.

The day before their attack they had been in Lisbon, just a few hundred metres from where Cláudia had been brutally assaulted and the Lisbon stone taken. Since then, there had been the murder of Mr Hearne and theft of the last tablet, the terrifying car chase out of Oxford; all the work of the same man, they were sure. Then Plymouth, Willow and their amazing find, the discovery of the manuscript and spur-of-the-moment trip to Vienna. And now Prague.

'I'm shattered,' Elisa had said, as she gave Daniel a quick hug outside her room door, whispering 'thank you' into his ear, lifting his spirits a little.

They boarded the train and located their seats, Daniel stowing his case underneath and Elisa's bag overhead. He took his seat next to Elisa and they sat in silence as the train pulled out of Vienna. There was an overhead monitor just a few rows ahead of them, showing a newsfeed intermingled with advertising for ÖBB's services. As the train emerged from underground into the morning's dull light, they watched the landscape start to rush by as the train worked its way up to speed. Elisa sighed, gently resting her head.

The coffee and breakfast on board were good, but the last four days' events still weighed heavily on them, and they both found it difficult to relax.

"Let's get back to the manuscript," Elisa suggested, keen to have something to do.

"Good idea." Daniel spread the notes out on their generous tray tables. "I'm going to have a look for that reference to the 'real ocean'. I saw it in the translation last night, but I want to see where, exactly, it is in the manuscript."

"Why? Is there something we've missed?" Elisa asked.

"The text says *amidst the real ocean*. It just seems odd. It might help to see any illustrations nearby." Daniel went through the photos until he saw the one that was the most promising. The embellished calligraphy was hard to make out, but he found the reference, just underneath the illustration they spotted last night with bison and, maybe, moose.

"I think this is indicating these creatures are 'amidst the Atlantic Ocean'. In the *middle* of the ocean. That seems like another confirmation to me." Daniel pointed out the placement to Elisa, who nodded her head.

"How about the map-maker's drawing?" Elisa asked.

Daniel located the right image, and they both leaned forward to take a look. "I don't know what would be usual or unusual for an illustration like this," he said.

"Neither do I. Could he be copying from one to the other?"

"Could be. Copying from the scroll onto the parchment?" he guessed. "It's pretty hard to make out. The map he's copying to – the rectangular one – that looks different to the other one on the scroll." *It does look different.* And then it dawned on him. "It's a different projection. Do you know much about map projections?"

"Mercator? Didn't he devise the projection we're familiar with today?" Elisa asked.

"That's right. In the fifteen hundreds. There were many different varieties before then. Maps were often just drawn flat, using the map-maker's location as the reference point. But here, we seem to have this guy copying from what might be a circular projection. It's an older map style with all lines radiating out from a central point, often the map-maker's home. He might be making a portolan, a navigation chart."

"How sure are you? I can't tell much difference," Elisa said.

"Yes, it's hard to tell, but look at the map on that scroll. It seems to me there's a central point, and all the lines radiate out from it. That's how a polar projection map looks. The illustration isn't detailed enough to confirm it, but I think I can see there's no land mass at the central point." Daniel paused to make sure Elisa was keeping up. "If I'm right, that's a good sign, because it means it's not drawn from the map-maker's home, or his king's capital, or similar."

"Okay, I'm with you," Elisa said. "So it looks like the map-maker is drawing a navigation chart from an older map source produced by someone who used an ancient map-making technique."

"Well, yes. I think it does," Daniel replied. "And I think I've had enough coffee," he added, heading to the bathroom at the front of their car.

He returned a few moments later and saw that something was terribly wrong. Elisa's eyes were wide and her face ashen. He rushed back to her.

"What happened?"

"Anna. It must be her." Daniel turned to look at the newsfeed. The English subtitle told him all he needed to know. *'Breaking news: A young woman was brutally murdered this morning at the Austrian National Library.'*

Elisa gripped Daniel's hand as they both read the scrolling subtitle: *'A young librarian was found beaten and murdered in an unprovoked attack at the State Hall of the National Library in Vienna early this morning. The motive is not known; however, library staff have confirmed that a medieval manuscript is also missing.'*

"We shouldn't have gone there," she said in despair.

"There was no way of knowing. We can't blame ourselves."

"But if we hadn't gone there ..." she lamented. "But how did he know? We seem to be just one step ahead of him."

"We can't be sure it's the same man."

"Who else?"

*　*　*

"They are en route to Prague. There might be other relics of interest. My flight is boarding in ten minutes."

Silence.

Rigo waited a few more seconds before Zapas responded with a curse.

"Puta que o pariu! I *will not* have my technology exposed." Zapas spat the words out. "Go there, get me these relics or destroy them! And kill Reade and Mansfield this time."

Rigo was pleased with the change in plan.

Zapas cut the call off angrily. This was not what he had been planning for the woman; he had been savouring the thought of interrogating her.

But the risk of exposure now outweighed her usefulness. And the ability to trigger an earthquake meant the weapon was now ready.

59

They sat in a desolate silence for a few moments, until the penny dropped, for Elisa first. "He'll know we're going to Prague. Anna wasn't just struck once from behind like Cláudia, she was beaten before he killed her. He *interrogated* her."

As she said it, Daniel knew she was right. "Did the news story say when it happened?" he asked.

"Not that I saw." Elisa took her phone out. "The Vienna National Library opened at ten o'clock." She looked at her watch. Nearly an hour ago. Another search on her phone. "Flight time to Prague is about fifty-five minutes. And he could be at the airport *now*."

"He must have been at the library for at least twenty minutes, probably more like half an hour." Daniel thought for a moment. "He'd have had to find Anna, take her somewhere to question her without being seen then force her to retrieve the manuscript. But yes, he might be arriving at Vienna airport now."

"Let's say he boards a flight, say, within half an hour, he *could* arrive in Prague ten or fifteen minutes after us. How far is Prague airport from the old city?"

"Twenty-two minutes, according to the phone map," Elisa replied. "I guess we could safely add another ten to fifteen minutes before he gets through the terminal."

"Okay, then by my reckoning he could conceivably get to the museum as early as one o'clock."

"How far is the museum from the station again?"

"Less than a kilometre," Daniel remembered, quickly checking his phone. "A ten-minute walk, it says. We could put our bags in a locker at the station and run," he suggested.

Elisa was glad she was not wearing her boots.

"We'll be arriving in about an hour," Daniel said, thinking perhaps the train wasn't such a good idea. The top of the screen indicated they were travelling at 220 kilometres an hour. It didn't seem fast enough.

Sixty minutes later, the train pulled into Prague main station. They raced out onto the concourse, quickly finding an empty luggage locker. Thankfully there was an attendant who helped them get the necessary coins, and within minutes they'd stored Daniel's new suitcase and Elisa's bag in a large locker. Daniel shouldered his backpack, and with mobile phones in hand, they hurried out of the station, following the directions. The weather in Prague was at least an improvement on Vienna. The sun was almost penetrating the thin grey cloud overhead, and it must have been close to ten degrees.

Exiting the station, they ran under the road and through the gardens to Opletalova. Elisa almost tripped as they navigated the pathways, and Daniel reached for her hand. They quickly made their way through the narrow city streets, jogging hand in hand, and soon reached the outdoor cafés of Wenceslas Square.

"Now where?" Daniel said as they both checked their phones again.

"Over there," Elisa said, pointing to a street sign across the road.

Another hundred metres and they were on narrow cobblestone streets, in a part of the old town that didn't look like the kind of place a museum would be located in.

"Is this right?" Elisa asked, urgency in her voice. She rechecked the address on the map, but apparently they were in the right area. There were a few people sitting on the window ledges of the old buildings, outside trinket shops and other tourist traps. They were looking at Daniel and Elisa; nobody else was running here.

"There," said Elisa, pointing just up ahead. An old sign outside a shopfront said 'Guillaume de Machaut Museum'.

"Twelve-twenty," Daniel said.

They ran up triumphantly to find it was locked. The sign on the door was in Czech, but they could read the number '5'. Elisa pointed her phone camera at the sign and got the translation: 'Back in 5 minutes.'

Minutes later, a young man approached, carrying a paper bag with an overstuffed baguette poking out of it. "Hallo," he said.

"Hello. Are you opening now?" Elisa asked, still a bit breathless from their run.

"Yes. Please come in," he said in English. "My name is Tomás. Would you like to tour the museum?"

Elisa thought the term 'museum' was used quite generously. The place was clearly a tourist trap. It was quite small and appeared to have a limited collection of curiosities dotted on shelves and tables around the walls. A narrow timber staircase promised more trinkets upstairs, but they were not particularly hopeful.

"Yes, please," Daniel said.

"You are quite lucky. It is a very quiet time of year, and we don't open every day. It will be one hundred and twenty koruna each, please."

Elisa looked at Daniel, surprised.

"Do you take euros? We don't have any Czech currency. Sorry," Daniel said.

Tomás looked at them both and after a few seconds replied, "Of course. It will be ten euros each, please."

That seemed high to Daniel, but he had no idea how much one hundred and twenty koruna would be in euros. Nonetheless, he paid and Tomás pocketed the cash, opening a narrow door behind the counter revealing another staircase and boxes filled with brochures. He took two amateurish-looking coloured leaflets out of the box on top and handed them one each.

They thanked him and quickly scanned the ground floor, looking at the various papers and memorabilia. Some of it appeared to relate to the court of King John of Bohemia, but there was little of any real interest or historical value. Tomás sat on a stool in a small room at the back, quietly eating his baguette and paying them no interest whatsoever. Elisa opened her brochure and suddenly squeezed Daniel's arm.

"Look at this!" she whispered urgently.

Daniel saw a picture of the illustrated ship. Or at least one that looked very much like it. "Of course, the illustration in the manuscript is of a *model* ship! It must be here!"

60

"Let's try upstairs." They climbed the narrow staircase. At the top was another similar-sized room, dimly lit by the natural light entering the tiny front window. The room contained a few more trinkets and some pictures on the walls, allegedly of Machaut himself, and also Machaut with King John. And on a bookshelf against the far wall, there it was! A timber model of an odd-looking ship. It resembled a Viking longship, which would be correct for its alleged age, but it was out of proportion, and had a large, central wooden structure that Daniel could not explain.

He checked his phone. 12.30.

Elisa found a light switch near the top of the stairs, and the old light bulb came to life. The ship was clearly old, the pieces of wood obviously hand cut and carved, and some of the mortise and tenon joints had loosened with age. Some of these had been clumsily glued together, decades or centuries ago, judging by the brittle, yellowed glue residue. The central wooden structure served absolutely no purpose, as far as Daniel could tell. It looked like a medieval child's toy, and had it not been in one of the illustrations in Machaut's manuscript, they would have taken little or no notice of it.

"It doesn't look like a 'ship of enlightenment'," Elisa observed.

"No. It looks like a toy. But why go to the trouble of drawing it in the manuscript?"

"There must be something significant about it."

Daniel picked it up, tapped the bottom, then the sides and the central section. The central structure made a different sound. "Hollow. It could be a puzzle box." A childlike excitement showed on his face. "You know, the kind of puzzle that only opens when you find the secret lock. Popular child's toy in the Middle Ages. They were used to hide jewellery and other valuables, too."

"Can you open it?" Elisa said, picking up on Daniel's excitement.

"With a hammer, sure. Otherwise I'll need to figure out the secret key." Daniel picked up the ship and gently shook it. There was no sound. Nothing that suggested there was anything concealed inside it. Undeterred, he placed it on a table nearer to the light so they could see it more easily, examining every visible joint for a moving part. He was applying a gentle pressure to the rear panel of the box, but it wouldn't budge. It was one of the places where some ancient glue had been applied. "Do you have a nail file? Or something?" he asked.

Elisa quickly retrieved a half-size nail file from her handbag and handed it to Daniel. "Are you sure you should be doing this?" she asked quietly.

"No." He used the file to pry the brittle glue out of the tiny mortise. After a little effort, the glue cracked into fragments and fell onto the floor. The rear panel of the box moved a little, covering the mortise. Daniel tried the same technique on the other end of the box structure, and it, too, moved. He handed the file back to Elisa. As he pushed both the front and rear panels so they moved towards each other, they heard a small click.

"What are you doing?" Tomás had appeared at the top of the stairs behind them. Elisa's quick intake of breath startled Daniel as much as the young man's question.

"You cannot do that," he said, reaching for the ship. The front panel slid out of its moorings and fell on the floor. They all looked inside the box and saw an old piece of thick cloth. Tomás was as curious as they were.

He watched as Daniel carefully removed the cloth, revealing a metallic object, gleaming like gold.

"You cannot take that," Tomás said.

"We know. We don't want to take it. We just want to look at it," Elisa said earnestly to him. Whether it was his curiosity, her charm, or the fact that he felt guilty for overcharging them, he relented enough to let them unwrap the object.

"I should call my father," he said, but he stayed where he was, watching intently.

"If this is what I think it is, you might need to call the Prague museum, too," Daniel replied.

He carefully unwrapped the piece of gold, and the cloth wrapping partly disintegrated into dust. It was clearly ancient. The object looked like it was made of gold, although it was possibly slightly more pink in colour and had a sheen to it that didn't quite resemble pure gold. It was a tightly rolled scroll, about twenty-eight centimetres long and almost five centimetres in diameter.

"You're the archaeologist," Daniel said to Elisa. "Do you think we can unroll it?" She looked at her watch nervously, wondering what they should say to Tomás about the danger they might all be in.

"Yes, very slowly." Elisa glanced at the young man, and he nodded, his curiosity clearly outweighing his caution.

Elisa carefully put one hand on the top of the scroll and gently picked at the rolled-up edge until there was enough of a gap to get her fingers between. Daniel then held the top of the scroll as Elisa slowly started to unroll it. It was surprisingly firm, and it seemed that their assumption it was gold, or a similarly soft gold alloy, might be wrong. As they worked, Tomás made his phone call.

With the right balance of effort and patience, they managed to fully unroll the ancient scroll. It was impossible to tell what it was made from. It was definitely harder than any gold, but it hadn't tarnished as they would have expected from any form of bronze, brass or other copper alloy. The interior surface had a lustre to it that was neither brass, nor bronze nor gold. But its most striking feature was what was etched on it.

Tomás was looking over their shoulders, open mouthed. "What is it?" he asked.

They were all staring at it. Around the edges was some etched text in the same ancient language as the tablets. There were illustrations of animals on each side, similar to the illustrations in Machaut's manuscript. But the etching that took up the entire middle section was what had surprised them all.

"It's an ancient map. This could make history. Or rewrite it," Daniel said.

"It's hard to make out," said Elisa. "It doesn't look like the maps of today."

Lines radiated out from the central point, which appeared to be in the middle of the ocean. There were vaguely familiar land masses but they didn't seem to be in the right places.

"No. It looks like the polar projection I mentioned, which would mean the centre point is probably the North Pole. The true North Pole, I think, not magnetic north," Daniel said.

"Let's get some photos," Elisa said. "While we still have the opportunity." She checked her watch again. 12.45. She took photos from several angles, both with and without flash, hoping to ensure they had captured every detail. Daniel took a few shots also, as a backup.

At that moment, an older man came in and spoke aggressively in Czech to Tomás. He then strode over to Daniel and Elisa and pushed Elisa out of the way, saying something to her in his language.

"Don't touch her." Daniel stepped in and stared the man down.

"He says it's not yours," Tomás translated, as the older man took a step back, looking belligerent.

"We know that. Tell him to calm down," Daniel said.

Tomás said something to his father, who raised his hand aggressively to his son. Next to his father, Tomás looked more like a boy, as he acquiesced.

Again Daniel stepped towards the man, ready to challenge him.

"This is a valuable scroll. You should talk to the national museum, or library," Elisa said to both men.

They had a brief exchange in their language.

"He wants to know what it is worth," the boy explained nervously.

"I don't know. But it could be thousands of years old," Elisa explained. "It needs to be examined by experts."

"How did you know it was here?" the boy asked, with a look that Elisa read as genuine curiosity.

"We didn't. We were following a hunch based on a manuscript written by Guillaume de Machaut that's in the Austrian National Library in Vienna," Elisa explained.

The older man spoke to Tomás aggressively. The boy took the scroll and slipped it into his pocket, silently walking to the back of the room. Elisa heard him climb down some unseen stairs.

"Go!" the father said bellicosely to Daniel and Elisa.

They turned as they heard rapid footsteps on the stairs they'd climbed a few minutes earlier. A pale face appeared on the landing, with a smile that was anything but appealing.

61

On the ground floor of the Zapas mansion, a relatively austere level below the grand entrance and reception rooms, Lucas Santos had just left the security officers' dormitory and recreation room. He was on a break, and, with Zapas out, it was quieter than usual. Everybody was more relaxed. He'd decided now was the safest time to retrieve his special device from its hiding place in the staff locker room. He'd chosen that because it was in the far corner of the ground floor, and with the concrete corridor, it was possible to hear anyone coming from some distance away.

He turned on the device and it came to life almost immediately, although with a 'low battery' warning. *Dammit.* Charging it was his highest-risk activity. He would have to do that late tonight. He pocketed the device and crossed the hallway to the toilets. All the rooms had surveillance cameras, but he knew from the control room's monitor array that the camera did not see down behind the doors. Sitting in his locked cubicle, he keyed in his twelve-digit PIN. Lucas had just learned there was to be another test. His boss had been making arrangements to send equipment to southern California.

He silently typed his brief report: TEST ARRANGED. DEVICE SHIPS TO PALM SPRINGS TODAY. He sat and waited, expecting a quick response.

Lucas had spent the best part of the past eighteen months infiltrating the Zapas security organisation. He had earned enough trust that he'd worked at the mansion, for the security head, for the last four months. He'd been assigned his mission when his masters learned the organisation was developing new weapon technology. At first, they did not know any more than the information being carefully spread on the Dark Web, that there would be a 'world-changing weapon' soon to be demonstrated. It would be made available to the highest bidder. His mission was to find out what the weapon was and, more importantly, where and how it was to be demonstrated and subsequently sold. He expected a quick answer because he had named a location in the US. He could already feel the release of adrenaline in his body. His expectations were soon met.

TEST SITE DETAILS NEEDED. CODE RED.

Lucas had not seen a 'code red' before. It meant he was to get the details *at all costs*, including risking breaking his cover, and potentially dying in the attempt. He did not know for sure but suspected he was his masters' last hope; he was aware the lead agent, the man who had been on the council of eight, had been executed by Zapas. At least he'd been able to deduce that from the disposal of the body of his driver a few days ago.

Lucas turned off the device and pocketed it, flushed the toilet for effect, and left the cubicle, crossing the hallway back to the locker room. He slid it back into its hiding place under the security chief's locker as he heard approaching footsteps.

"Luca," the other man grunted as he entered, noisily throwing a pair of trainers in his locker. All the men called him Luca. He didn't bother to correct them.

"João," he replied, giving the man a nod. Both men went out, and João returned to the rec room.

The information his masters wanted was most likely in the lab, which he knew was on the level below, and to which he did not have access. But it was possible there might be something in the security control room. Lucas decided that was his best bet, but it would be dangerous.

He went to the control room, hoping he would be lucky and it would be near empty, as many of the men were still at lunch. He swiped his access card and entered. There was only one man inside, the AV security technician, sitting before a bank of monitors showing various views of the Zapas estate.

"Have you seen my magazine?" he improvised. "I must have left it here earlier."

"No," said the tech, not looking up. Lucas started to rummage through papers on the central bench, hoping the man wouldn't take too much notice.

After a minute or so he found something useful in the security chief's tray. 'Meet van sunrise vista chino Palm Springs map to site'. *This must be it.* But there was no map with it.

"What are you doing?" The tech was looking directly at Lucas who had his hand on the papers in the chief's tray. He was about to press the alert button on his panel when Lucas swung around and struck him hard. The tech dropped to the ground and Lucas struck him again on the back of his skull. He ran for the door, hoping the man would stay down long enough for him to get out. The prospect of being caught was terrifying, and Lucas felt the surge of energy the fear triggered. It wasn't that Zapas would kill him; in this line of work, the risk of death was ever-present. No, it was what Zapas would do *before* he killed him, to get the information he wanted.

He quickly exited the room and tried to look calm as he walked to the lift to the underground area. He knew he would never make it out of the estate through the main entrance, so he had to get through to the tunnel. He got into the lift and pressed the basement button. The descent seemed to take a long time, but eventually the lift stopped and the door opened. There was no one waiting for him. He swiped his card and the double security doors to the bunker car park opened. The car park was also empty, and he ran across to the tunnel door. A swipe of his card opened the door, and he started to sprint to the other end.

He was almost there when an alarm sounded, echoing loudly through the whole facility.

62

The museum's proprietor stepped towards the pale intruder and was about to tell him to leave, when Rigo lashed out at lightning speed, striking a vicious blow to the man's throat. Elisa gasped in horror as they heard the crack of the man's larynx being crushed. He dropped to the floor holding his neck, flailing as he tried to breathe.

"Mr Reade and Ms Mansfield," Rigo said, his tone as menacing as it was calm. "How nice to see you again."

Daniel noticed he had no gun this time. He appeared to be carrying no weapons at all; possibly a consequence of his hurried flight from Vienna.

"I'll take your backpack," he said to Daniel.

As Daniel started to take off the backpack, he remembered the hidden stairs the boy had used earlier. *Can we get to those ahead of this killer?*

Daniel picked up the wooden ship from the table and threw it at the pale man, missing his head by the tiniest margin. While Rigo was momentarily distracted, Daniel grabbed the small table and, holding it by its top, he thrust the base into his stomach. As the pale man stumbled back, Daniel grabbed Elisa's hand and the backpack and ran to the back stairs. He dropped the backpack down the stairs, grimacing at the sound it made when it hit the landing, and tried to get Elisa around ahead of him and down the stairs first.

Rigo was quick to recover, and upon them in seconds. He struck Daniel heavily with a closed fist on the side of his head and grabbed Elisa, pulling at the large pendant around his neck. Daniel hit his head as he fell into the wall behind the stairs and stumbled down the first flight to the landing. Elisa watched Daniel slump against the wall as she felt something slip over her head. She got two fingers under the wire garrotte, but the pale man was powerful and soon wrenched her hand out as the wire tightened.

Daniel shook his head groggily as he heard Elisa's scream being quickly stifled. He looked up to see the pale man twisting something behind Elisa's head, as her eyes bulged in sheer terror. Daniel leapt back up the stairs and got his hands around the man's throat. Rigo hit him in the face with his free hand but held on to the garrotte. Daniel kept squeezing as hard as he could until Rigo released Elisa.

She was able to loosen the garrotte enough to breathe, but not enough to remove it. She could feel blood running down her neck from where the wire had cut into her skin. With both hands free, Rigo was able to strike Daniel with such power that he fell back against the wall, momentarily stunned. The man was a force to be reckoned with. He reached again for the garrotte and started to twist the heavy pendant to tighten it around Elisa's neck. The top of the balustrade was still between Daniel and Rigo, as Daniel recovered enough to launch himself at their attacker. The abject terror on Elisa's face as she struggled for air gave Daniel superhuman strength. As Rigo watched Elisa suffocate, his pleasure distracted him.

Daniel was able to get his arm around the pale man's neck in a grip of iron. He was not going to watch Elisa die. Eventually, Rigo let go of the garrotte as Daniel held on with every bit of force he could muster. Elisa clawed at the wire but could not release it. The panicked look on her face almost caused Daniel to let go of their assailant. She looked desperately around the room and saw a rusty metal object on a shelf near the back stairs.

Elisa leapt over and picked up the iron object and hit Rigo over the head as hard as she could. The blow made a sickening sound, and he dropped to the floor, almost dragging Daniel down with him. Daniel freed his hand and saw Elisa was still clutching at the garrotte wildly, her lips now blue and eyes bulging. She was about to lose consciousness. Daniel frantically unwound the garrotte and pulled it from the bleeding wound. He put his arms around her as her legs gave way.

"Elisa!" He held her firmly, looking at her face, straining to hear whether she was breathing. "Elisa!"

I'm losing her. He was stricken.

She gasped for air and slowly opened her eyes. He held her tightly, searching her face to know she was going to be all right. She coughed and winced with pain. She tried to speak. "Let's get ..." she started, but was unable to continue.

Daniel understood what she meant and helped her to the stairs. As he did so, a dull light appeared on the floor, half underneath their prone assailant. A mobile phone, presumably fallen from his pocket. On the screen was a message – just three words: *desert hot springs.*

Daniel put his arm firmly around Elisa and helped her down the stairs, grabbing his backpack on the way. Still with his arm around her, they quickly left the cobbled laneway and walked around the corner to a busier area with traffic. Elisa coughed repeatedly, wincing each time. People were staring at them, at the blood on Elisa's blouse, her ashen face and red eyes. Daniel looked only marginally better. Elisa was still unable to speak but pulled out her phone and showed Daniel the ride-sharing app and he nodded. He wanted to get as far away from here as they could.

"Our bags?" he asked.

She nodded, booking a ride to the station. Across the street, a stand outside a store carried brightly coloured hand-painted hats and silk scarves, blowing gently in the breeze. Elisa pulled Daniel over by the hand and chose one with lots of reds in a busy design. He understood and went in to pay for it. He was lucky the shop accepted euros. As he returned, their ride arrived and Elisa quickly tied the scarf around her neck, concealing most of the injury and blood.

The drive to the station took longer than their earlier walk. The driver spoke very good English and asked them where they were staying. Trying to appear calm, Daniel asked him for a hotel recommendation.

"Old town?" he asked.

"No!" they both said quickly.

Daniel added that they were looking for something closer to the airport. The driver gave him a recommendation, which he noted on his phone. At Prague central station they located their luggage locker, having to get their bearings first and recheck the slip of paper the machine had spat out when they'd arrived. Back outside, they booked another ride to the hotel. Less than half an hour later, they had checked in. It was connected to a shopping complex, so after escorting Elisa up to their room and leaving the bags, he went to find a pharmacy.

63

Rigo turned his head slowly to one side, immediately feeling a sharp pain as his head wound made contact with the balustrading. He touched the wound and felt dried blood in his cropped hair. He saw his phone on the floor and picked it up. He'd been out for only ten minutes. There was a new message. At first, he did not understand what it meant, but then he remembered the previous message about where he was to fly next, and it made sense.

He stood slowly, briefly unsteady on his feet, and went over to the man lying prone on the floor near the front stairs. He kicked him and then listened for breathing. Nothing. He was dead. Rigo checked his pockets, removing his wallet. Surveying the rest of the room, there was ample evidence of the fight, and blood in various places, including his own. He climbed down the stairs and locked the front door, flipping the open/closed signed around.

Next, he went to the staff area at the back, looking for bleach or something else useful. All he could find was a spray wax polish and a bottle of cleaning spirit. He took the spirit. In the absence of bleach, which he knew would destroy blood DNA evidence, he liberally poured the spirit on the upstairs furniture, timber floor, bookshelves and staircase. He took a cigarette lighter he'd recovered from the dead man's pocket and set the place on fire. The spirit was much less volatile than petrol, so he had plenty of time to escape.

He climbed down the back stairs and out through the little shop's back door into the empty street. Around the corner and off the cobblestones he found a souvenir store and purchased a cloth cap to cover his head wound. People in the store quietly stepped out of his way and did not make eye contact, the anger within him visible and barely controlled.

He had not had time to obtain a handgun since arriving in Prague, but he had managed to dispatch the manuscript to São Paulo, via the organisation's contact at the National Library in Vienna. Zapas would, at least, be receiving something to keep him appeased for now, Rigo hoped. He was fuming that he would have to leave Reade and Mansfield alone for now.

He flagged down a taxi and headed to the airport, not looking forward to the long flight to the United States and the inevitable long wait he would have at the airport before it.

* * *

Daniel returned to the hotel room to find Elisa sitting at the desk writing notes on a pad. "How do you feel?" he asked, trying to read an answer in her eyes.

"Every bit as good as I look." She winced as she spoke, her voice strained and hoarse. Her face was still pale, her eyes red, and he could see the dried blood on her blouse under the new scarf. He wanted to know if she needed medical attention for her neck, but she seemed intent on the notes she'd been working on. "Hmm," was all he said, as he looked down at her notes.

- Ancient technology. Acoustic weapon. Doomsday tablet.
- Cláudia and the stolen tablet.
- Brazil nightclub incident.

- Chidwick attack. Looking for our notes specifically.
- Mr Hearne and the stolen tablet.
- Hydrographic survey confirms Mid-Atlantic ruins.
- Lisbon, Machaut manuscript and Anna's murder.
- Prague, the scroll and our attempted murder again. Same man.
- Phone message: 'desert hot springs'?

"What do you think *'desert hot springs'* could mean?" Daniel asked. "Don't answer if it hurts too much."

"I have no idea. A place, perhaps?" Elisa whispered slowly. "But how many hot springs in a desert might there be? Thousands?"

"I hope we have enough here to get DI George's attention this time. What do you think?" Daniel asked.

"Maybe enough. That's why I wrote this down," she rasped.

"Do you still have his number?" he asked. She nodded, as she rummaged through her bag for his card. "But let's see about your neck first," Daniel said, tipping the contents of his pharmacy bag onto the desk.

Elisa started to remove the scarf, but it had adhered to the neck wound as the blood had dried. Daniel took a small towel from the bathroom, moistened it and lightly dabbed the wound until the scarf fell away. He could see where the garotte had cut into her skin at her throat but the rest of the injury was a nasty red line rather than broken skin.

"I don't think he was able to get that thing as tight as he wanted to," Elisa whispered. "Thanks to you."

"This might sting a bit," Daniel warned as he gently applied antiseptic.

Elisa could see the concern and tenderness in his eyes as he carefully ministered to her. Tears started to roll down her face, and Daniel gently dabbed those too.

"We're okay." He put his arms around her and felt her shaking. "He doesn't know where we are."

For a few minutes they held each other, Elisa still in the chair and

Daniel kneeling on the floor, as Elisa let the emotion out. Daniel released her when he felt her sobbing stop.

"I'm not usually ..." she started.

"You might be the strongest woman I know," Daniel said. "You probably saved both our lives in Chidwick. Don't forget that." His eyes held hers, and to Daniel it felt as though they were drawing strength from each other. "Now let's get this work finished," he said firmly.

He found an adhesive bandage of almost the right size and applied it, and then put the bloody scarf in water in the bathroom sink to wash out the blood, assuming she would want to use it again. By the time he'd returned, she had removed her blouse and was looking at her neck in the mirror.

"Nice work," she said, without enthusiasm.

Daniel took the moist towel to her and softly wiped the remaining blood from her throat and chest, kissing the red line on either side of her neck.

64

Lucas had fervently hoped he would make the tunnel door before they knew he was on the run. He had to hope they hadn't yet disabled his access card or locked down all the doors. He swiped his card anyway and was hugely relieved when the door started to rise. But within seconds it stopped, so he dived under it, just squeezing through the forty-centimetre gap as it started to come down again. He knew he was in the lower garage assigned to the penthouse suite, so there were another two doors to get through to freedom, but he'd scouted the area months ago and also knew there was an air vent that connected the parking garages to the gardens.

He ran across the floor to the vent, opened the grate, climbed in and closed it again as best he could from within. It was a narrow space, and he couldn't quite get the grate perfectly back in place. Using his training shoes for grip, he climbed the narrow metal duct. It was extremely hard work, and the taut muscles in his legs were bulging and aching excruciatingly, but adrenaline kept him going.

At least there is no camera in this section, fearing that Zapas's men would soon come through the tunnel. As he reached the next level, his fear was answered by men's shouts below. He was now in the upper level underground car park, so he could jump out here and try the stairs or continue climbing the ducting. He hadn't climbed this section of duct before, as he knew CCTV covered this level. He would have been detected by the camera had he attempted to open the grate. He'd only checked access from the garden outside.

Lucas quickly decided to stay in the air vent and keep climbing, and as he reached the grate to the garden he heard the men shout that he was in the duct. They must have spotted the loose grate below. As he reached for the top grate, he was horrified to see it now had a new padlock on it. *No way out.*

He decided it would be best to fight to the death with the security men. That would be preferable than being caught alive and handed to Zapas. But Lucas wasn't a man to give up easily, so he got into position, bracing himself against the back of the duct, and kicked wildly at the grate. To his great relief, the screws holding the grate in place opposite the padlock started to give way. He knew he was making too much noise, but he also knew he was going to die if he didn't get free quickly.

Another kick and the grate came loose. He tumbled out into the apartment building's garden and ran to the two-metre high garden wall. He launched his body at the wall and managed to pull himself up and over, landing heavily on the ground on the other side, legs aching. He was now outside of Zapas's property, but not yet out of his reach. He could hear men shouting from the garden. He ran to the other side of the yard he'd just landed in and ducked down the side of the large house, hoping no one challenged him. He climbed the fence swiftly and ran through the next yard.

Lucas knew where he was headed; one more fence and he would be in a service laneway that would take him to the main road and small shopping area, where he hoped he would be safer. He leapt up to climb the final fence and landed in the lane. Shouts in the distance told him he was not safe yet. He threw his mobile phone as far as he could across the yard of a house just off the laneway and then ran in the opposite direction and reached the back of the shops. If they were tracking his phone, he hoped that might buy him some time. He knew the phone was monitored so he couldn't use it anyway.

He burst through the first open door he came to and found himself in the back of a café. The kitchen was to his left and toilets to his right. That was a stroke of luck, as the customers would just assume he'd used the toilet, rather than being a fugitive. He tried to look calm as he went out through the café's front door. Two doors down was the small phone repair shop he'd noted earlier, and he ducked inside.

He calmed himself and bought a SIM card with cash, along with a cheap disposable phone, one of the cheapest mobiles the store had. The set-up took a couple of minutes, during which Lucas watched the door from behind a stand carrying phone accessories, trying to look inconspicuous as he did so. The man handed him the phone and its packaging separately, and Lucas quickly texted a United States number. '*meet van sunrise vista chino Palm Springs map to site. LS*'. He left the shop and went into the nearby department store, throwing the phone's packaging in a rubbish bin as he walked.

He bought a pair of jeans and a light-coloured jacket – anything that looked unlike his current clothing – and put his old clothes in a rubbish bin behind the counter. His new phone vibrated in his pocket.

Can you talk? the message read.

Yes. A moment later the phone rang.

"Nothing more?" a male voice asked.

"That's all there was," Lucas said in fluent English. "The note said '*map from Palm Springs*', but there was no map. '*Meet van sunrise vista chino*' seemed like a good lead."

"Sunrise Vista Chino is a place. In Palm Springs. It's not a meeting at sunrise."

"Dammit. I can't get any more. I'm compromised and barely made it out. You need to get me out of São Paulo."

Lucas gave the caller details of where he was and was told there would be a car within the hour. He decided to stay in the store pretending to browse, assuming he would be safer inside than out on the street.

65

"I hope you don't mind that I just booked us one room. I didn't think about it," Daniel apologised. "I can go and book another."

"No. I don't want to be alone."

"I don't either."

"We should ring DI George," she said. "He might listen now."

Daniel took the business card from the desk and called. He was surprised when the phone answered almost immediately. After a brief introduction, the DI remembered Daniel, as well as yesterday's events. Daniel put the phone on speaker.

"We're not sure who to talk to, but there have been further developments, and we now think lives might be in danger," Daniel said. "Lives other than ours," he added.

"Go on," said George.

At least he sounds interested. Daniel went on to explain the chronology of events since Mr Hearne's murder, initially leaving out 'ancient technology', 'acoustic weapon' and 'doomsday tablet'. When he got to the Lisbon attack, the DI stopped him, asking if he was suggesting the same crazed man was following them around Europe. He sounded sceptical.

"We know he was. He followed us from Lisbon to Prague and tried to kill us there, too. We were face to face. There was no doubt it was the same guy. The pale man who knew our names and wanted our notes." Daniel paused for that to land with the detective.

"And now you think other lives are in danger?"

"Yes." Daniel explained their ancient technology theory, the three related tablets from UK and Portugal that supported the theory, the hydrographic survey results – firm, well, *firming* proof of a destroyed ancient civilisation, the manuscript, and the Brazil nightclub incident being linked to a new acoustic weapon technology.

"It sounds far-fetched to me," DI George said blandly.

"We know it does. But there's no doubt that this man who's trying to kill us is the link to all three tablets. And he's very real," Daniel declared vehemently. "The only reason we can think of as to why he wants the tablets and our notes is that they are still developing their weapon. There was a message on his phone I saw as we escaped. It said 'desert hot springs'. It must have something to do with the next attack."

"Desert hot springs? What does that mean?" the DI asked.

"We don't know yet." Daniel shook his head. He knew wasn't getting through.

"And you're in Prague now, you say. What would you suggest I do, Mr Reade?"

Daniel realised this wasn't going anywhere. Even if DI George wanted to help, it wasn't an unreasonable question. What could he do?

The detective inspector ended the call by suggesting that when they return to the UK, they might provide a more detailed description of the pale man, as a prime suspect in the Oxford murder.

"At least he's recognised Mr Hearne's murder was likely the work of the same man. That's some progress, I suppose."

"Yes, I guess so," Elisa rasped. "And what *does* 'desert hot springs' mean?"

Daniel opened his backpack and retrieved the laptop. The screen was not quite sitting properly, no doubt a consequence of being dropped onto the landing in the little museum shop. Still, it started up as normal, and warned him of a low battery. He pulled out the charger and European adapter and plugged it in. A quick search for 'desert hot springs' revealed that, among other possibilities, it could refer to a town in southern California of that name. They checked the map and discovered it was just twelve miles from Palm Springs. Looking at the map, Elisa remembered something Avery had said.

"Can you see where it sits in relation to the San Andreas fault?" she asked. He searched again, and they could see that the town of Desert Hot Springs sits more or less *on top of* the San Andreas.

"Do you remember what Professor Compton said? That this technology could trigger an earthquake. And that might have been how their cataclysm occurred."

"Yes, I remember."

"But now what?" she asked.

Daniel shook his head and they both sat on the bed, feeling deflated. "And where to next?"

They had no answers. Just to have something to do, Elisa picked up her overnight bag and opened it, frowning. "I don't have any clean clothing left. Are there good stores in this complex? I don't want to go outside."

"Yes, quite a few."

"Will you come with me?" she asked in a small voice.

"Of course I will."

She retrieved a T-shirt, fleecy top and a scarf from her bag and dressed, gingerly tying the scarf around her neck. "How do I look?"

"Stunning. For a girl almost garrotted this afternoon."

Elisa managed a weak smile. They left the room and took the elevator down to the lobby.

Both were still shaky from the attack. In the shopping complex they couldn't help themselves from scanning the corridors and stores for the pale man, not knowing whether he had survived. Neither wanted to spend too much time in the open, so their shopping was targeted and fast. Even so, after a short while, just having something mundane to do became a much-needed therapeutic experience.

Before dusk they returned to the room with a new mid-sized suitcase for Elisa and a few essentials. She repacked and decided, not without some regret, to discard her overnight bag.

"I'm shattered," she sighed.

"Hmm. Me too." Daniel slumped onto a chair. He was physically drained, but his mind was active. Briefly stepping out of the adrenaline-fuelled havoc of the afternoon had helped bring some perspective back. They both knew what they had to do. And neither was prepared to turn their backs and run.

Elisa mustered her remaining energy, turned back to Daniel's laptop and entered his password. Within a few minutes, she found what she was looking for.

66

"A few sources here say the last rupture of the southern San Andreas fault was three hundred years ago. If that's correct, there's some serious energy pent up in it," she said grimly. "Apparently a quake greater than magnitude eight is possible."

"That's massive. A quake of that size hit Wellington in 1855 and lifted some of the coastline by six metres. I remember learning about it. Most of the current CBD and shopping area used to be under the sea," Daniel explained. "Apparently the water in Wellington Harbour sloshed back and forth for days, damaging buildings on both sides. I remember one story that, even a few days later, people hundreds of kilometres away could feel a vibration when sitting or leaning on walls. And the epicentre was about fifty kilometres from the city."

"That vibration thing, does that remind you of Avery's thoughts about resonance?"

"Yes, it does," Daniel replied. "And now that I recall the story, the ongoing effects and damage caused remind me of the warning on the doomsday tablet. That whatever it was 'consumed itself and all around it'. Did the ancients set off some kind of chain reaction, like tsunamis and days of quakes and aftershocks that usually follow a big one?"

Elisa sighed. "This is too depressing. Should we go back to the images of the scroll? We may never see it again, but at least we have photos."

"Shall we order some dinner first?" Daniel asked, realising they'd had no lunch.

"All right, but I'm not hungry. Maybe a sandwich?" Elisa said.

Daniel found the room service menu and phoned in an order. While they waited, they sat together to go through the photos they'd transferred from their phones. The scroll was a truly incredible find, and both were soon absorbed in it.

"Look at the detail. It seems remarkably accurate to me," Daniel said. He worked his way around the map. "You can see Canada, and Hudson Bay, then ..." he paused briefly, "... there's Alaska and Siberia, but no Bering Strait. They're joined together. Remarkable!"

"And here, further around, here's Scandinavia. And the British Isles – no, wait, they're joined to the European mainland. There's no English Channel either! And Ireland is partly joined to Britain. They also look out of proportion to me. Larger maybe. This is just amazing."

"There it is!" Elisa said, pointing to a large island to the south of the Denmark Strait, the sea between Greenland and Iceland, smack in the middle of the Atlantic and directly between Nova Scotia and Ireland.

"Frisland. Our lost island!"

"There can't be any doubt this is Machaut's ancient source, but where's it from?" Elisa asked.

"I suppose the clue to that might be in the text. It's clearly related to the tablets inasmuch as it appears to be in the same unknown language."

"I hope the young man got away safely with it."

"Perhaps if we stay here we might be able to find him," Daniel offered.

"What if he thinks we killed his father, or set the fire?" Elisa responded. "Or what if we lead that pale man to him?"

"Yes, you're right. But it needs to be *studied*."

"Absolutely. Those anomalies, like Siberia and Alaska being joined, maybe they can help date it," Elisa pointed out.

"The material it's made from might help do that, too. Do you remember the look and the feel of it?" he asked.

"Yes. It wasn't like anything I've seen before."

"Have you heard of orichalcum? It's in Plato's Atlantis story."

"No. What is it?"

"Nobody knows for sure. In Plato's description, he said the outer citadel wall of Atlantis *flashed with the red light of orichalcum*. His Atlanteans revered it. It's been described as a copper-based alloy similar to brass or bronze, or possibly containing other mineral substances, such as zinc oxide. But if it was a highly prized precious metal alloy, then a form of rose gold makes more sense to me. Plus it had a strange gleam to it, don't you think? Like there was carbon or an oxide of some sort fused in."

There was a loud knock at the door, making Elisa jump. "Room service." A muffled voice through the door.

Daniel looked through the viewer to see a young man with a trolley. He wheeled dinner in as Elisa cleared the table. Daniel had forgotten to order something to drink, but Elisa said not to worry, water would be fine. He wished them bon appétit as he left.

Daniel uncovered his meal to find that the Wiener schnitzel filled the entire plate. There was a slice of lemon sitting on top. A second, smaller covered plate had fries and coleslaw. Elisa's dinner was a chicken-and-salad sandwich on a German-style rye bread.

She had to take small bites because of the neck wound, and clearly had some trouble swallowing, but she made short work of the first half of the sandwich. "I'm hungrier than I thought," she said, eyeing Daniel's fries.

"Go on. You know you want to," he replied with a smile, handing her his fork. She skewered some fries. Another little bit of normality that made Daniel feel more positive. She passed the fork back, and he cut some of the schnitzel for her, placing it next to the other half of her sandwich. While she ate, he fetched a couple of glasses and poured them both some water. He grabbed the remote on the way back and switched on the television, found a news channel and turned the sound down.

And so it went, they shared the food on the table, enjoying the brief moment of respite, until a news item caught Elisa's eye. A headline banner in English at the bottom of the screen. *Man killed in arson attack in Prague tourist museum.* She turned the sound back on but it was in Czech. A quick search on the laptop provided the details. They read together:

> *Police are investigating an arson attack on a small privately run tourist museum in Prague's old town. The proprietor was killed, and police have confirmed that he also had injuries inconsistent with the fire.*
>
> *The proprietor's son, a student who also worked in the museum, told reporters he had returned to the store after visiting some local dealers of antiquities, to find the shop's upper floor engulfed in flames. The boy was shocked but unharmed. Police are searching for a couple who visited the museum immediately before the fire, to assist with their enquiries.*

67

The estate security head nervously alerted Zapas that there had been an incident – one of the security men had been caught rifling through papers in the control room.

"I will be back in thirty minutes. Keep him locked up and make sure he can't contact anyone," Zapas barked.

"Sir, unfortunately he has escaped," the man said. Zapas cursed viciously into the phone. "We've got his mobile phone, dropped while he was escaping, so we know he didn't contact anyone."

"Get out and find him. I want him back in a cell when I get here. Don't fail me." Zapas swore again and cut the call. He intended to question him personally, and he would get all the information he wanted, no matter what lengths he had to go to. It would also serve as an example to the others, when they disposed of whatever was left of the man.

Even before the call, Zapas was angry that Rigo had again failed to deal with Mansfield and Reade. He'd made the excuse that he needed better intel. Zapas had exploded at him for blaming the organisation for his own failure. He hated excuses.

Rigo had, at least, obtained the manuscript, and although it did not sound promising, it should arrive in São Paulo by tomorrow morning.

After he followed the new Prague lead, also not a promising one, Zapas had directed him to go to the test site. Días and his small group had already left for Palm Springs. They would be arriving early the next morning. The equipment had been freighted via Mexico but should still arrive before the men. Rigo would likely arrive later in the day. There he could keep the technicians in line and ensure they felt the pressure of urgent delivery.

And if he didn't survive the demonstration, no matter. Zapas was already looking for his replacement.

Lucas Santos had spent the last twenty minutes trying on clothing, taking his time browsing and selecting, while trying to keep out of sight of the store's front windows, and then taking even longer in the changing rooms. He was sure store security would have noticed him but confident his behaviour was reasonable enough not to attract any undue attention.

He had just returned from his second trip to the changing rooms with several shirts, when his luck ran out. As he went back to the rack he'd selected them from, one of his co-workers saw him.

"Hey, Luca!" the man said, waving at him. "You too, huh." The man was shopping. Lucas couldn't recall seeing him today, so it might be his day off. Or a long break. Either way, Lucas knew he was going to have to incapacitate the man, or kill him. His ride to safety was probably still more than half an hour away.

"Hey, Cris." Lucas weighed up his next move. If the man was on a day off, maybe he could let him live, leave the store and take his chances finding a new rendezvous location. It was feasible.

"Day off?" Lucas asked.

"No. Start my shift in fifteen minutes," Cristiano said.

Dammit, I'll have to kill him after all. As he was formulating his plan, one of the estate security detail entered the store, gun in hand. Cristiano followed Lucas's eyes to the man, and a look of surprise flashed onto his face.

"What the fuck?"

Lucas grabbed Cristiano around the neck and made out he had a gun pointed at the man's back. "Don't move, or I'll shoot a hole in your spine," Lucas shouted. Another armed man marched into the store. The pair approached Lucas and his apparent hostage.

"Let him go, Luca. We need to talk." The man smiled as he said it. He knew what *'talk'* meant, when it came to informants or spies. The store staff had disappeared completely, like mice into cracks and crevices. His only chance now was that the police would arrive before he was killed. But the two security men kept coming, and Lucas knew he now had no choice. Neither he nor Cristiano had weapons. He waited as long as he could, until the men were just four or five metres away, then made his move.

At lightning speed, Lucas shoved Cristiano at the nearest one then charged at the other, a hothead named Diego. He made it halfway to the man. Diego's first shot whistled past his ear, but the second stopped him in his tracks. Cristiano watched in shock as a small red spot appeared on Lucas's forehead, at the same time as the crisp white shirts on the clothing rack behind his friend were spattered with blood and brain matter.

68

"Well, that might get DI George's attention," Elisa said, not without irony, as she pointed at the article on the screen. "And we're famous."

"Yes." Daniel raised his eyebrows at her attempt to make light of the situation, worrying about how close to the edge she might be. He wasn't far away himself.

"I guess he'll be more inclined to believe this really happened. Maybe we should have flown out this afternoon," he added.

"But where to?" Elisa asked, yawning.

Where to indeed? Daniel wondered, as Elisa stood and went over to her newly packed suitcase.

"I think I need some sleep. But first, a shower," she said, disappearing into the bathroom with her toilet bag and some fresh new clothing, leaving Daniel to wonder about sleeping arrangements. Neither had given that a second thought.

She emerged from the bathroom and Daniel took her place. By the time he returned, she was asleep. He closed the curtains, turned out the lights and climbed in next to her. He marvelled that it had been barely a week since he'd found Foxton's notes and met Elisa. Over the past few days, any sense of normal life had vanished, and it felt like he'd known Elisa forever. She had her back to him, and he nestled in close, gently putting his injured arm around her. He was rewarded with a soft, sleepy sigh.

"Mmm."

Daniel awoke feeling cold and reached out for Elisa to find her gone. He opened his eyes, suddenly needing to know where she was. The light of Elisa's phone screen gave the answer. She was sitting at the desk reading something. The clock on the bedside table said 4.25.

"Hey," he said quietly.

"Sorry. Couldn't sleep," Elisa whispered. "I checked my phone and there was a text from Avery. He said he sent an email yesterday and hadn't heard back so wanted to know that we're all right. I've texted him, but I couldn't help wondering what he'd emailed."

"Aren't you cold?" She was sitting in her T-shirt and underwear.

"Yes."

Daniel climbed out of bed and put his arms around her.

"You should read this," she told him. She turned the phone on its side and they read it together.

"It's quite long," she warned him. "Avery writes emails rather formally."

My dear Elisa,

I've been ruminating over our last conversation, and I've come up with another possibility, I'm afraid. Let me give you some background first.

There are theories that large asteroids, comets or suchlike have come close enough in the distant past that their gravity has pulled on our planet's soft mantle to raise mountain ranges, such as the Himalayas. Or, for that matter, the Mid-Atlantic Ridge. This displacement would, of course, cause other parts of the crust to sink as the supporting mantle underneath was pulled away.

It's just a theory, and it is not widely accepted, but as a physicist I believe it certainly makes sense. The science of it is sound. The point is that a notable change in the mantle would have inevitable effects upon the crust. Daniel will have heard of liquefaction, it was one of prominent effects of the Christchurch earthquakes. This is when waterlogged solid ground suddenly becomes liquid, usually during an earthquake. This liquid, under the pressure of just a few metres of earth, spouts out from the ground, and the ground surface can suddenly sink.

My alternate theory is this: Earth's mantle is under immense weight and pressure, hundreds of thousands of times greater than atmospheric pressure, and it has a malleable consistency. In my view, if something changed the consistency of the mantle to suddenly become more malleable, let's say more like oil than treacle, then the most likely effect would be an immediate and immensely powerful volcanic eruption.

Furthermore, in this case, the vent through which it ejects, the Mid-Atlantic rift, is very, very large. The mantle could have erupted out extremely quickly. I think it is theoretically possible Frisland could have sunk into a deep void in a day and a night. This would obviously cause quite extreme earthquakes, volcanic eruptions, tsunamis, much as Plato wrote.

I believe that if the technology that may have caused this is rediscovered, then we are headed into very troubling times indeed.

Please do let me know how your quest is progressing, and please be very careful!

Yours,
Avery

"So Plato might have been right!" Elisa exclaimed. "They created their own apocalypse, and it *could* have happened within just a few days."

"And whoever is behind all of this may be about to unleash this weapon on a fault line overdue for a massive quake," Daniel added, ominously.

"They probably don't have any idea of the danger. The risk of a cataclysmic chain reaction." Elisa was holding Daniel's hands.

"Or don't care." It was a sobering thought.

"We *have* to find a way to get someone's attention. There could be thousands of lives at stake," Elisa said, desperation in her voice.

"I'll try DI George again first thing in the morning. If he can't or won't help, maybe he can give us a number or a name in intelligence. We should have enough information now to get *someone* worried!"

"I hope you're right," Elisa said, shivering involuntarily as she rubbed her neck.

"How's your neck feeling?"

"Sore, but it seems all right."

She sounds a bit better.

"We're an hour ahead here so can't call George for a few hours yet. Come back to bed," he said, reaching for her hand. "It's cold in here and we can't do anything more now."

Elisa looked up at him and winced as the dressing on her throat pulled at her skin. They climbed back into bed, and she kissed Daniel. "Thank you for caring for me today," she whispered.

"You don't need ..."

Elisa placed her finger on his lips. "Yes I do."

69

Días and Francisco were tired after the long flight. They had been travelling for sixteen hours, having stopped in Dallas for two hours on the way. The flights had been uneventful, and they had passed through customs and border control with no issues. The border control officer had wished them a pleasant and successful stay in the United States.

After trying several rental companies at Palm Springs International Airport, they had been able to rent a suitable white van, as they'd been instructed. They would meet Felipe and Carlos later in the morning so went directly to the freight terminal. The map was not as clear as it could have been, and Francisco had missed a couple of turns simply by being in the wrong lane, the traffic unwilling to let him cut in.

"Be patient." Días was clearly getting annoyed with him. "We can't have a traffic accident. Just go around again."

Francisco cursed as he performed an illegal U-turn to get back to the turn-off. He stopped at the red light, and for a moment was mystified when the driver behind started honking his horn.

"You can turn right on a red in this country," Días told him.

"*Que loucura,*" Francisco grunted, shaking his head as he drove through the red light.

They located the correct freight terminal office and, after an exchange of papers, they were able to collect the carefully packed 'scientific equipment'. There had been nothing in the boxes that had alarmed airport security, nothing remotely resembling any known weapons. The storeman at the terminal helped them load the boxes into the van, and soon they were back on the road.

The designated meeting place was a shopping complex in Sunrise Vista Chino, on the northern edge of Palm Springs. The weather was clear and already pleasantly warm. The radio announcer had said the maximum expected today was seventy-eight degrees, which Francisco worked out was about twenty-six degrees Celsius. Compared to the heat and humidity of São Paulo, this was mild. They pulled into a car park that wasn't too close to the pedestrian walkway and climbed into the back of the van to change into their maintenance clothing.

Días sent Francisco into the shopping centre to buy some food and drinks and sat in the front passenger seat, leaning back with his eyes closed. Nobody passing by thought he was anything other than a maintenance worker. Francisco returned and they ate and drank.

* * *

Carlos and Felipe had arrived at Palm Springs International an hour later than their colleagues. They had flown in from Mexico City on Mexican passports supplied by the organisation. Their flight was also uneventful, but they were delayed at US border control. Their passports and visas were not challenged, but Mexicans were currently getting a great deal of attention at the border. While they were being questioned in some detail about their intentions, they had become slightly nervous, which had caused the authorities to delay them longer and conduct a full search. Eventually, they had been cleared to cross and took a taxi to the shopping mall in Sunrise Vista Chino. They were still cursing the organisation for choosing Mexican passports, rather than Argentinian or any number of other countries, when they found Días and Francisco.

When Carlos and Felipe arrived, Días texted a contact he'd been given by the security head at the Zapas estate, and the four men sat in the van waiting. Twenty minutes later, a man wearing a telecommunications company uniform arrived, verified their identities and opened his tool case to reveal their new documentation. He supplied them with green cards and company IDs that said they were telecommunications maintenance men. All had new Mexican names to remember. The man also produced a pair of magnetic decals for the van carrying a local telecommunications maintenance company logo. Their contact had then demanded the passports they'd travelled on and all travel documents, saying it was 'for security of the operation, in case the van was searched'. Their passports would be returned after the demonstration.

He also gave them a map of the exact location for the demonstration, but there was a problem.

"You were supposed to be arriving tomorrow," the local man explained. "You can't access the site until tonight. You'll have to start preparing the equipment at your accommodation and transport it later."

"Have you reported that back?" Días asked. He expected an explosive reaction when he told Zapas later.

"No. That's your problem." The man gave Francisco the address of the house in Desert Hot Springs as Días cursed. They could assemble the equipment but couldn't even test it without connection to high current three-phase power in the electricity grid. The demonstration site had been chosen because high tension lines passed right by, and because it was supposed to be unoccupied but not disused, so a maintenance van would not appear out of place. The operation was developing a bad taste. Días braced himself for the call to Zapas and punched the number into his phone.

"There's a problem," Días said, getting straight to the point. "We can't access the demonstration site until tonight at the earliest. It was chosen because it's a perfect location *tomorrow, Saturday*. Not today." Silence. "We will assemble almost everything, as planned, but I can't promise there won't be a delay tomorrow," Días finished bravely.

Zapas was silent for another fifteen seconds.

"Very well. Make sure it is ready as soon as possible. Rigo will be joining you tonight. Make sure you don't displease him." Días swallowed hard as Zapas cut the connection. He knew Rigo had been Zapas's enforcer and clean-up man for many years. Días was afraid of Rigo. He rubbed his tired eyes and lit another cigarette, smoking it all the way down to the butt before he said anything to the others.

"Rigo is coming tonight," he said as they drove to Desert Hot Springs. "We need to get everything as ready as we can, and Rigo can check the demonstration site. He will let us know when we can start to deploy."

None of the others responded. All the technicians were afraid of Rigo.

70

The pale dawn light pierced the gaps between the curtains, waking Daniel first. He slowly lifted his head to see the clock behind Elisa. Almost seven. They were still entangled, more or less as they were when they'd drifted back to sleep almost three hours earlier.

Sensing his movement, Elisa slowly opened her eyes to see Daniel's face just inches from hers. "Good morning," she said.

"Mm."

"We have work to do," she said, making no attempt to move.

"You'll have to let go then."

"Hmm." With a wistful smile, Elisa climbed out of bed. After a quick selection of clothing from her new suitcase, she went into the bathroom and turned on the shower.

Daniel got out of bed and rummaged through his case for clothing, as well as his medical supplies from Faringdon. He peeled off the arm dressing to find it healing reasonably well, the red swelling almost gone. He swallowed his antibiotics, wondering whether he should save the rest for Elisa, not knowing when they could next get medical attention.

Elisa soon emerged from the bathroom almost dressed, with the sticking plaster partly removed from her neck.

"I'm sorry, would you mind?" she asked, pointing to the dressing. "It's pulling on the cut, and I can't easily see what I'm doing."

"Sure." Daniel gently removed the plaster, wiped the wound with antiseptic and applied a fresh dressing. He felt the intimacy of the moment between them acutely, at the same time as the stark reminder of the physical danger they were in. "You can return the favour when I've showered."

A quarter of an hour later, both were fully dressed and ready to face the day, with Daniel's arm dressing also replaced.

"Seven o'clock in the UK. Let's try DI George again," he said, picking up the detective's business card as he planned his strategy.

The DI answered on the third ring. "George."

Daniel put his phone on speaker. "Good morning, detective inspector, this is Daniel Reade again."

"Mr Reade. Are you back home already?"

"No. But there are new developments we think need to be ... considered," Daniel said, deciding that 'need to be taken seriously' might not elicit the help they needed.

"All right." The DI waited.

"We've received advice from a professor of geophysics at Oxford that the technology being developed has the potential to cause *mass destruction*, not just a localised event like the nightclub attack."

"Mr Reade, this is ..."

"Please, detective inspector, there's more," Daniel cut in, conscious of trying to get his attention before he was dismissed. "We've also worked out what 'Desert Hot Springs' means. It's a place in southern California sitting directly on top of the San Andreas fault, in a fairly heavily populated area." It seemed the DI was listening.

"We believe thousands of lives are in danger, and if that's where our attacker has gone, the danger must be imminent." Daniel paused, hoping his message had landed.

"Mr Reade, I'm an Oxford detective. What would you have me do?"

"Look, I know it's well outside of your jurisdiction, but I was hoping you could try to connect us up with someone in intelligence or defence. You have to admit, at the very least, it's extremely worrying."

"I'm a simple British policeman, Mr Reade. This is the kind of movie plot stuff that gets the Americans excited. I don't have any *contacts in intelligence,*" the detective said, his manner sardonic.

"If we're right, this organisation is operating, or at least *has* operated, in the UK. There might be a domestic threat." Daniel realised he was now clutching at straws.

"Unless I'm mistaken, there's no evidence of that. We have a break-in at your house, an unexplained death and *possible* theft in Oxford, with no real evidence to link them. As I said yesterday, when you return to Oxford, I'll be happy to take your statement and description of the alleged assailant for our investigation. Goodbye, Mr Reade."

Click.

Elisa had her head in her hands. "This is *so* frustrating! Why won't he listen?"

"Simple British policeman, he said. This is above his pay grade," Daniel replied solemnly. "Maybe we can try and talk to someone in defence or intelligence ourselves?"

"But as you said, there's no evidence there's any kind of domestic threat to get their attention. And we're in central Europe; how credible will we be?" Elisa said.

"Can we get a sense of the scale of the potential disaster? If we're going get the authorities involved, they'll need to believe we're a credible source."

"How would we do that?" Elisa asked irritably. "I'm sorry. I don't mean to take it out on you, it's just so frustrating!"

"I know. And I don't know the answer, but let's look at the map as a start."

Having agreed a magnitude 8 quake would serve as a benchmark, they soon learned that the 1906 quake near San Francisco had caused severe shaking for hundreds of miles along the fault line.

"It looks like we should include greater Los Angeles, right through to the whole San Diego area, in the damage zone, maybe even extending into

Mexico," Daniel said, as Elisa searched on her phone.

"So that looks like a population of up to thirty million people! The immediate area, say all around Palm Springs, where there would be extremely violent shaking, is roughly half a million people." She was appalled. "And what if this weapon triggers some sort of chain reaction?"

"But how? All we have is speculation," Daniel replied.

"Hmm. Let's go back to the translations and look again," Elisa suggested. "Maybe we missed something." Or maybe we know *more* now, so we might see something new."

"Okay, it's worth a try," Daniel replied.

"One thing that's been worrying me," Elisa went on, "is why would these advanced ancient people have gone to such trouble to chisel messages into stone tablets to last for millennia? If they were advanced enough to invent acoustic technology that we still haven't figured out in the twenty-first century, surely they invented a more practical recording medium than stone?"

"Maybe they wanted to ensure the message would survive a future cataclysm. Transcend their technology, to be passed on to distant future generations," Daniel suggested.

"Yes, that's plausible," she replied. "I suppose they might have had factions or protestors against the development, or 'weaponising', of their acoustic technology, just like we would today. Their society's own version of doomsday prophets, crafting enduring warnings."

"Well it seems they were right," Daniel observed.

"True. And stone was their medium. These people seemed to have developed technology that could manipulate, mould or even move or levitate massive stone blocks, simply using sound. It's remarkable and far-fetched at the same time, but there seems to be a lot of evidence to support that theory. Use of stone was probably part of everyday life. Why not use it as the medium of choice for long-lasting records? It's still good for that today."

"Yes, that's true. It's interesting that the only tablets we've found seem to relate to their civilisation's destruction. Maybe they were all made by survivors of whatever happened. Or maybe they were made during unrest that must have led up to the catastrophe and were taken on ships by those escaping the wars, revolution or whatever it was," Daniel ventured.

"That's a lot of maybes," Elisa said.

"I know. Just speculation." Daniel stood up to stretch his legs. As he left, Elisa reached for her translation notes, as well as the copies of Daniel's great-grandfather's notes. She had a nagging doubt. *Are we missing something important?*

The phrases in Foxton's notes included 'instrument of destruction' and 'consuming itself and all around it'. Their retranslation of the Gillard tablet had 'song of the waves' [or 'sound waves'], 'resounding harmony'. The Lisbon tablet repeated some of the same phrases but also added 'song in increasing harmony [or 'sound resonance intensifies]', 'mother[land?] trembling and turning to water', 'voices [sounds] of doom shrieking louder'.

"I think you're right," Elisa said as Daniel sat down. "Look at these translated phrases. There's a clear theme here about resonating sound intensifying. That was what caused the disaster." She paused to collect her thoughts. "Do you remember Avery talking about Pythagoras's 'music of the spheres'? The natural resonant frequency of the planets, and how NASA research has recently confirmed there *are* frequencies at which planets resonate. The sound, or song, of a planet."

"Yes, I do," Daniel said.

"What if this technology has a way of tapping into it? A way of using earth's natural resonance and energy *as a power source.*"

"So it wouldn't necessarily need a 'power grid' as we know it," Daniel said, his enthusiasm rising. "There are a lot of theories about ancient planetary power grids, natural energy sites like Stonehenge, the site of the pyramids et cetera. Could there be something to them?"

"Maybe," Elisa agreed. "But there's something else. That resonance. What was the weapon resonating *with*?"

"Hmm. Remember the story of the 1855 Wellington quake; people feeling *vibration* days later. Do you know what seismologists said about the

1960 Chilean earthquake?" Daniel asked. Elisa waited for him to continue.

"That's the largest ever recorded, a magnitude 9.5. They said the whole earth 'rang like a bell' for days afterwards!" Daniel said, answering his own question. "The whole planet *resonated* for days. That event was almost global in its reach, tsunamis all around the pacific, felt by half the world and recorded by seismologists in Europe."

Elisa nodded and went back to her notes. "Look at these phrases again. What do they suggest to you?"

"That something went wrong. They started something they couldn't stop. A *chain reaction* when their technology locked in with the earth's natural resonance."

"Yes! That's what I think it's telling us. Once this weapon is started, it's possible it can't be stopped until 'it consumes itself' in a cataclysm, like the one that sank Frisland nearly three kilometres into the Atlantic!" Elisa said, her face contorting in horror.

"So who do we tell?"

"DI George said this is the kind of thing that 'gets the Americans excited'. What about the FBI?"

71

A half hour later, they were sitting on the hotel bed feeling despondent. Elisa had quickly located a phone number for the Federal Bureau of Investigation in Palm Springs, but Daniel had spent the best part of twenty minutes trying to get someone to listen, without success. 'Do you have any evidence?'; 'this would be a good sci-fi movie'; 'have you taken any drugs, sir?'; 'have you sought psychiatric help?'; '*where did you say you are calling from, sir?*'; 'it's a criminal offence to mislead law enforcement in this country ...' They heard it all.

"We'd have to go there to convince them," Elisa said, defeated. They sat in silence for a moment.

"We could," Daniel said.

"We could what?" Elisa asked.

"We could go there."

They both sat in silence, staring at each other, as the idea sank in. They would likely be flying into great danger. They might have to face the pale man again, who had almost killed them twice. And there was no guarantee the US authorities would listen to them. *But we can't just walk away and let this happen.*

"I want to talk to Avery again. Let's test this theory with a geophysicist," Elisa said, reaching for her phone. She dialled his number but it rang out. "Dammit. He's not there," she said, her impatience visible.

"Try again. You never know," Daniel said remembering Professor Compton didn't always carry his phone around. Elisa hit redial and was soon rewarded with a cheerful greeting.

"Elisa my dear, how lovely to hear from you!" She put the phone on speaker for Daniel.

"Avery, hi, I'm sorry to call so early, but I have to run an idea past you. One that Daniel and I are quite worried about."

"Certainly. Do you want to pop in to see me?"

"We're in Prague now."

"My, you do get around! How can I help?"

"We now have a lead that indicates the acoustic weapon might be used to rupture the southern San Andreas fault. From a place called Desert Hot Springs, almost right on top of the fault. We understand it's been three hundred years since the last major earthquake there.

"We've also been through our translation notes and have a theory that the cataclysm the ancients unleashed may have been caused by their weapon locking into the earth's natural resonance, '*until it consumed itself and all around it*', as the tablets say."

"Hmm," said Avery.

Elisa could imagine him stroking his chin. "So, our first question is whether this sounds feasible to you?"

"Hmm. It is a very troubling thought, but yes, I think it is definitely feasible. There's ample evidence that acoustic resonance can cause quite spectacular effects."

"So if that actually happened, a kind of chain reaction that couldn't be stopped until it had fully run its course, what kind of effects would we be looking at?"

"Oh dear. Well, it's hard to predict, of course, but the possible extent could include the whole fault line system and surrounding area."

"The *whole* San Andreas?" Elisa interjected.

"Possibly well beyond. The whole *system*. All along the North American west coast, the Pacific plate and another small plate are subducting under the North American Plate. Basically, it means some areas of the coast from California to Washington, and into south-west Canada, will one day be under the sea.

"A significant rupture of that North American tectonic plate boundary could carve part of the US coast off as an island, or simply submerge part of it. It's a frightening idea. At its most extreme, while not necessarily the likeliest scenario, I'm afraid I could imagine mass destruction of coastal cities from northern Mexico to southern Canada, and of course the terrifying related effects." Avery paused for breath.

"Such as tsunamis?" Elisa asked.

"Yes. Of unprecedented scale. At least, a scale unprecedented in recorded history. It's possible there could be tsumanis that inundate Hawaii, Japan, New Zealand, most, if not all Pacific islands. Conceivably, even parts of Southeast Asia and Australia. It would also likely inundate low-lying areas inland in the United States."

"That could make the 2004 Indian Ocean tsunami pale in comparison," Daniel said.

"I'm afraid so. If the technology starts a resonant chain reaction, the planet could ring for days, with far-reaching effects. It could be a global cataclysm."

"That's appallingly sobering. Thank you, Avery."

"Please let me know how you get on, my dear, and be careful!" Avery implored, now sounding quite worried.

72

Rigo had arrived at Palm Springs International an hour ago. Customs had been no problem, and he'd rented a Toyota that he expected would be commonplace in California. It was evening, well after the time most Americans ate their dinner, and the roads were quiet. He had driven to the meeting place, met his contact and duly been supplied with his usual weapons of choice – a hunting knife and a Glock 9 mm pistol.

Rigo's contact had confirmed the technicians had arrived and had given him the address of their accommodation, as well as the site for the operation. He drove the ten miles out to the planned site, a preschool, expecting it to be quiet, vacant and dark. As he drove up, he could see a few cars parked outside and lights on in the building. It was supposed to be clear, but it was obvious something was happening there. Possibly a meeting of some kind. They would have to change plans.

In the dusk twilight, he drove to the other address he'd been given to find a small, nondescript house in a quiet street. There was a white van parked outside. He parked his Toyota across the street, walked up to the front door and knocked impatiently.

Francisco opened the door and, seeing Rigo, he just stepped back silently to allow him inside.

"Where's Días?" Rigo asked tersely.

Francisco nodded towards the back of the house then followed Rigo down the hallway.

The other three men were in the kitchen and dining area, with equipment spread across the floor.

Días was supervising the assembly, and in spite of the mild temperature, he was sweating. He put his cigarette on the edge of a half-full ashtray. "We'll be ready to transport within the next hour," he said to Rigo. "Have you checked the site yet?"

"Yes. We'll move the equipment early tomorrow. There were cars at the site. A meeting perhaps," Rigo said, impassively.

"But we'll need time to set it up and align it properly. Tapping into the high-voltage power supply is not a trivial task," Días retorted, unable to hide his frustration.

"We will move the equipment early tomorrow," Rigo repeated. His tone made it clear that he was in control and they would do as he said. "There are houses nearby, and people will not expect to see telecom maintenance men working late on a Friday night. You will just need to work faster tomorrow. Now, where's the other equipment?"

"Still in the van."

"Good. Come with me," Rigo ordered.

Días glared at him but did not challenge him. He gave instructions to the other three men and followed Rigo back down the hallway, after collecting the van's keys from Francisco.

Rigo climbed into the driver's seat and put his hand out for the keys. They drove a few blocks to a low-rent storage facility at the back of a shopping centre. Rigo gave Días the code for the door and waited while Días climbed out and entered it. The door rolled open and Rigo backed the van into the small warehouse loading bay. The two men dragged the last crate out of the van and onto a dolly waiting nearby. They wheeled it the short distance to the locker where Rigo pulled out some keys and opened the door.

"It is ready to use?" Rigo asked.

"Yes. Set up for US wall voltage, as instructed. Point and shoot."

"Good." Rigo took one of the keys off the key ring and handed it to Días. "Backup. Remember the door code."

They drove back past the group of shops and cafés, and reached the house. As they went inside, the sound of the men laughing echoed down the hallway from the back. As soon as the men saw Rigo, the mood changed.

Francisco told them there wasn't much more they could do until morning. The next steps would be to complete the on-site assembly, run the high-voltage power from the overhead lines to the device's specialised power supply, then carefully align it to the fault line. Maybe two to three hours' work. Francisco also informed them he had ordered a pizza delivery, which, for Rigo, was the final straw with these undisciplined fools.

"Make sure the driver sees only one of you, and nothing else. If he sees anything, detain him and call me. I'll take care of him," Rigo snapped, with a look of contempt.

"And you," he added, looking darkly at Francisco.

Rigo then left to make his own arrangements, instructing them to be ready to move at 6.30 the next morning. Días and the men were relieved to see him leave.

73

"We have to go," Elisa said, and Daniel knew she was right. It seemed crazy at first, flying directly to the epicentre of potentially the worst disaster in recorded history, but there seemed to be no choice. It was possible there could be literally millions of lives at stake, right around the Pacific rim.

They hadn't forgotten the pale man either. Elisa had shuddered at the thought of being unable to breathe as the cold wire had cut into her neck and closed her airway. Daniel had seen the man's face as he tried to tighten the garrotte around her neck. He had *relished* it.

At their first encounter, Elisa had surprised the pale man with her self-defence skills, and at the second confrontation the man had been unarmed, other than the garrotte. They had been lucky, and it was unlikely they would be so lucky again. He was obviously an experienced and ruthless killer who enjoyed his work.

So it was with a resigned determination that they started looking for flights, in the process being reminded that without visas they would need travel authorisation from the US Government. Without that they would be unlikely to be able to board a US-bound flight.

"Agh, why won't they just listen to us!" Elisa shook her head angrily.

Her frustration was almost boiling over.

Daniel continued typing furiously. "I'm on the website; it says approval is usually immediate. We just have to fill these damn forms in."

With a bit of perseverance and as much patience as they could manage, they were able to obtain electronic travel authorisation through the US Government online portal within an hour, although by then their nerves were even more tattered.

With flights now arranged, they quickly packed and checked out of the hotel and arrived at Václav Havel Airport by late morning. Their flight was scheduled to depart just before two o'clock, with stopovers in Frankfurt and Dallas/Fort Worth. It was an eighteen-hour trip, but with Palm Springs nine hours behind Central Europe, they would arrive at eleven o'clock in the evening.

Now, after the rush to make all the arrangements and get to the airport quickly, the enormity of the challenge ahead started to take hold as they waited to board.

"Are we crazy?" Elisa asked.

"You were right. We have to do this. We have to find a way to get the attention of the US authorities before people die!"

Elisa took Daniel's hand and squeezed it. "I still can't believe that we're doing this. It's so surreal." They heard the boarding call for their flight and joined the queue with a resolute determination and their hearts in their mouths.

As they levelled out, heading west to Frankfurt, Elisa was restless. "Should we look at the scroll photos again?" she asked, keen for something, anything, to do.

"Good idea," Daniel replied, standing to retrieve his laptop and notebook from his backpack in the overhead locker.

"There's not that much text on it, but let's see what we can do," Elisa said. "It might just be descriptions of the flora and fauna, which may not all be translatable if there are animals unknown today. Although this," she pointed at the larger text at the top of the right-hand half of the image, "could be some sort of title."

She had lined up the notes from Chidwick on her tray table, where she'd written out the characters and their likely translations on one sheet and phrases and their probable meanings on another.

They managed to make slow progress over the next hour. If their assumptions were correct about the proximity of the drawings of animals to their corresponding land masses, they had identified descriptions of buffalo and rhinoceros on what is now the European mainland, and bison and moose in North America. That alone would be a ground-breaking revelation, assuming it could be proven that the scroll predated the discovery of the Americas in 1492.

"Can the scroll be dated?" Daniel asked.

"Not as far as I know," Elisa replied. "I've heard of a relatively new technology for dating some metals. It's called voltammetry, but I think it works by analysing the corrosion of metals, like copper. I don't think there are scientific techniques for dating non-corroding metallic objects like this one, unfortunately."

"Maybe the different sea levels give a clue."

"Maybe. But many would just put that down to map-making errors, like the old maps on Avery's wall."

"Yes, I suppose you're right. But we do seem to be gathering a lot of evidence indicating Plato's Atlantis was a real place."

"And academics who say that out loud don't do well," Elisa said, turning her attention to the text at the top of the scroll.

She scanned the photos to find the best image of that section then copied out the characters onto a new page. Then they both started to look for any already translated phrases that looked similar, with little success. It was, as always, slow and painstaking work, but they kept at it for another twenty minutes, until Elisa had an idea and pulled another sheet of rough notes out.

"Here," she said, pointing at a line of text. She'd written *'mother [earth?] trembling and turning to water [liquefaction?]'*. They both looked at the original characters above the translation and compared it to the scroll. There was a definite similarity.

"That looks like a different form of the same word," Daniel said. "Almost the same, but the last character has another stroke in it."

"Yes. I thought 'mother earth', but why not 'motherland', as in 'our homeland'? That word could be a form of 'our homeland'." She stared at the map, head tilted slightly to one side. "Could this be a map of an ancient *empire*?"

"Now that sort of talk really will get you fired."

A flight attendant offered them sandwiches and something to drink, which they gratefully accepted. They realised they hadn't eaten anything since yesterday. Nervous energy had been keeping them going.

"Okay. Let's say it's a map of an ancient empire. What do the anomalies in it tell us: the land bridge from Siberia to Alaska, or the British Isles being connected to the European mainland?" Daniel asked.

"Yes, those sea levels, as you said. You might be onto something there. I was doing some work near Dover three years back, and I remember a study that had just been updated. The initial theory was that the Dover Strait had been created by the failure of an ice-dam lake at the southern end of the North Sea about half a million years ago. A subsequent revision held that there might still have been a land bridge, until after the last supposed ice age ended. The land bridge's disappearance was linked to rising sea levels *within* the last 10,000 years."

"Okay. That timing fits well with our theory. I don't suppose that study mentioned the Bering Strait?" Daniel asked.

"No. I don't know much about that, I'm afraid," Elisa sighed, as the flight attendant returned to tell them to pack away the laptop and tray tables for landing.

74

The stopover in Frankfurt was mercifully brief, as both Elisa and Daniel were increasingly edgy. They knew they were flying into a potential disaster of biblical proportions and facing the prospect of having to convince sceptical authorities of an almost unbelievable threat.

They had boarded the aircraft for the long leg of the flight; eleven hours to Dallas. As soon as they were able, they resumed the study of the photos and notes. It was a relief having something productive to do, to take their minds off the terrifying reality of their situation.

While they had been in Frankfurt Airport, Daniel searched for information about a Bering Strait land bridge and found an article he'd saved about 'Beringia', the large area of land that had once joined Siberia and Alaska. He'd shown Elisa a helpful time-lapse map, courtesy of the United States National Oceanic and Atmospheric Administration, that showed what the land mass looked like in thousand-year intervals, starting at 21,000 years in the past. He'd taken screenshots of the views from fourteen to ten thousand years ago.

They now sat in front of the laptop looking at a snapshot of twelve thousand years ago, Elisa switching back and forth comparing it to the scroll image.

"That's amazing. It looks like an almost-perfect match," she said. She scrolled forward to the image two thousand years later, which showed the land bridge was fully submerged at around 8,000 BC. "It's another proof point." Her energy had started to return.

Daniel stopped and stared at her.

"What?" she asked, staring back quizzically.

"It's you. Your enthusiasm is back. And your curiosity is relentless. I love it."

She smiled and turned back to the screen. "Let's take a closer look at those illustrations."

They started with the animals on the scroll, the ones it seemed Machaut had copied into his manuscript. The first was the illustration closest to North America. On the scroll it was clearer and sharper than in the faded manuscript, but there were no material differences. It seemed clear the animals depicted were bison and moose.

They compared it with the image from the European side, and it was just as clear that the buffalo there were quite distinct from the bison. But as they looked more closely at the scroll's sharper image of the European side, there was something unusual about it.

"What is that?" Elisa asked.

Daniel stared at it. He hadn't noticed before that there was another animal on the scroll, drawn above the buffalo. "What the ... Could it be an elephant?" he said.

"Near *Scandinavia?*"

"Good point," Daniel agreed with a sheepish grin. "A woolly mammoth? Weren't they in Northern Europe?"

"Yes, I think so. Until about ten thousand years ago," Elisa said.

"How did we miss that in the manuscript?" Daniel asked, flicking back to the photos they'd taken. They could see the illustration Machaut had copied onto his manuscript had been damaged. There was something on the parchment that had obscured that particular corner of it. The medieval blemish was evidently so old it had looked like part of the parchment until they examined it more closely.

They continued scrutinising the images and their notes until the meal was served, without any further success. Frustration had started to wear them down, and they gave up. Daniel packed up their notes and stowed his backpack overhead, while Elisa finishing writing another summary list of the key points – everything they would try and explain to the FBI tomorrow. Completing the list helped her relax just a little, but she knew they were likely to have a difficult time getting their message understood, and she simply couldn't unwind.

After dinner, the cabin lights were dimmed. They watched a news programme, looking for any further reports about the incident in Prague, but there was nothing.

"I'm going to try and get some sleep," Daniel declared. He had the window seat, so he placed the pillow against the wall and closed his eyes.

"I don't think I can sleep," Elisa said. "My head is so full it almost hurts."

Daniel squeezed her hand. "We'll be okay tomorrow," he said. "I'm sure we'll manage to convince them," he added, as confidently as he could.

Elisa kissed his cheek. "I'm glad you're here."

They were lucky the aisle seat next to Elisa was vacant. She still felt too wired to sleep and tried to watch a movie but she couldn't concentrate. She was tired, but her mind wouldn't slow down. Her head was filled with alternating thoughts of their situation: the pale man, the danger the US west coast might be facing, and her feelings for Daniel. She closed her eyes and tried to relax and eventually managed to push the thoughts away.

A little later, as most of the passengers slept, the flight attendant walked down the aisle past the couple who had looked anxious when they boarded. He always kept an eye on the nervous ones; they were often more difficult. He was pleased to see they seemed to have relaxed, the man sleeping against the window and the woman now nestled against him. The flight attendant wondered what their story was, as he quietly draped a blanket over them. Maybe they were having relationship troubles. A romantic himself, he was pleased they looked peaceful and happier now, as they slept together.

75

"Palm Springs International serves a very large area. Greater Palm Springs alone is nearly half a million people. Needle in a haystack without more information." The FBI agent had already told his national security colleague there was no point in pursuing this lead until they had more. They had checked for any consignments from São Paulo, or anywhere else in Brazil, but today there had been none into Palm Springs.

Two hours earlier, the security man had arrived from Maryland, with a special clearance ID and a phone call from high up. The LA office chief had introduced him to the local agent with a cursory 'This is Johnson, NSA. Give him what he needs'. Johnson wore a blue sports jacket and tan slacks, setting him apart from the bureau's usual standard of dark suits. The only clue to his profession was his short military-style haircut.

"Yeah, I know," Johnson replied testily. With his inside agent now dead and no means of getting the additional information they needed, he was worried. It was likely there was a dangerous weapon somewhere in Southern California and he had no idea where, how or when it would be used.

"What, exactly, are we looking for?" the bureau man asked. At the moment, the resources Johnson required were limited to the bureau agent

316

he was using as liaison and general dogsbody. The FBI man was not pleased.

"We don't know exactly." Johnson had already determined what he would and would not share with the bureau. "It's some kind of acoustic transmission device, but we don't know what it looks like."

"This is a lot of fuss for a *transmission device*," the FBI man muttered. It was late in the evening and he wanted to get home to his family. His NSA colleague ignored him.

"You can let your Palm Springs office know I'll be flying down there first thing tomorrow morning. I'm going to need a team of four to six men."

PALM SPRINGS, CALIFORNIA

Daniel and Elisa had collected their bags and made their way out of Palm Springs International Airport and into a waiting taxi by eleven-fifteen. The late evening air was still warm. They had managed to get just a few hours of fitful sleep before landing at Dallas/Fort Worth. The last leg of the flight was crowded and uncomfortable. They were relieved when the flight had landed.

The hotel was a fifteen-minute drive from the airport. They were lucky there was a cash machine in the lobby, both having forgotten that a small supply of cash was always essential in the US. The cab driver wanted his fare in cash, and of course, a tip. Check-in had been quick and easy, and they'd refused the concierge's insistent offer to bring up their two suitcases.

"I just can't relax," Elisa said. "There's a knot in my stomach that won't go away."

Daniel felt the same way. They could sense that whatever was happening seemed to be reaching a crescendo. "We can do this," he said, putting his arms around her. Her emotions were ragged, and she could feel that his were, too. He hugged her close, his eyes holding hers, knowing they'd been thrown together by circumstances beyond their control, but also knowing he didn't want their being together to end. Slowly, lingeringly, he kissed her. She responded with a hunger that took his breath away.

"I need a shower," she said, pulling back slightly but still holding him. It had been a long day, and although she should be tired, she knew they were running on nervous energy.

"So do I," he replied, still reeling emotionally. "You can go first if you want."

She opened her suitcase, took out her toilet bag and went into the bathroom. She could still feel the warmth of Daniel's touch and his mouth on hers. As she stripped off her clothes, she took in the bathroom's generous proportions, and the two shower heads in the large, open shower.

"Ooh, it's a double ..." she called to Daniel playfully, turning on the water, smiling as she heard his approaching footsteps.

The next morning, they awoke with the alarm clock at six, having had a reasonably good six hours' sleep. By half past seven, they were ready to walk around to the FBI field office. According to the web, the office opened at eight-fifteen, so they had one more coffee in the lobby then headed off on foot.

"Did you know the hotel was so close to the FBI office?" Daniel asked, as they stepped out into the cool morning.

"No. Just good luck."

"Well it's good to know luck is finally with us!"

"Let's hope," Elisa said.

They walked into the field office and immediately realised this would be difficult. At the front counter Daniel started to explain that they had information about a potential attack, but any details they supplied were met with the same unmasked scepticism they'd experienced on the phone. Ultimately, when Elisa suggested a potential *terrorist* attack, like a recent one in São Paulo, they finally got some attention. Their details were taken down, and an agent met them and escorted them inside the security area and into a small room without windows.

After twenty minutes of questioning, the man had stopped taking notes.

"So, tell me again about this man who attacked you," the agent said, beginning to run out of patience. Elisa and Daniel took turns trying to explain, as factually as they could.

"And you said there was a message on his phone about Desert Hot Springs."

"Yes. That's all it said," Daniel told the man again.

"So what makes you think there's a terrorist attack being planned?"

"Look, we're adding up a lot of discrete pieces of evidence here, trying to build a picture. We know our attacker wanted our translation notes, basically everything about the ancient cataclysm. We know the stone tablets describe an acoustic weapon, and we're sure the attack in Brazil was an acoustic weapon. We have confirmation from an Oxford geophysicist that the technology could trigger a major earthquake, and we *think* Desert Hot Springs being on top of the San Andreas fault is significant."

"Please wait here," the man said, as he left the room.

"This isn't going very well," Daniel observed, feeling that the room was increasingly claustrophobic.

"I hope it doesn't take a major quake to get their attention." While they waited in the little room they went through Elisa's list again but didn't find anything they'd missed that might help.

Fifteen minutes later the man had not returned, and Daniel stood to see if he could find a glass of water. He turned the door handle to find they were locked in.

76

Días was annoyed. Rigo had arrived at the house at six o'clock that morning and started tersely issuing instructions to Días's team. They were already well prepared, and the unnecessary show of control had put the whole team on edge.

They arrived at the site at 6.40 and quickly got busy taking a three-phase high-voltage feed from the power grid. The preschool was near the edge of the town, and one of the reasons they'd chosen this particular site was because there was a suitable transformer at the foot of a telegraph pole just outside. Francisco had been able to open the locked cabinet without much effort, and they had run heavy-duty cables across to the van, which was parked at the school gate.

An hour later, Días made the final connections to his transformer and power supply inside the van. The next step was to assemble the rest of the weapon then carefully align it using GPS. They also had a detailed survey of the fault line, stored on Días's encrypted phone. That would give him the precise angle to incline the focus of the transducer. He was still concerned it would not produce the results Zapas was expecting. There was simply no way of knowing how long it might take to sufficiently soften the rock to release the centuries of stress in the fault line. Nor was it possible to know if the weapon had sufficient power to penetrate the rock deeply enough.

Zapas, as always, simply expected Días to make it work. He was not interested in whether or not it was a reasonable demand. Días knew there was a lot riding on this demonstration, *if* that was really all it was. He knew Zapas had big plans for the weapon. He also knew that Zapas had told the organisation's leaders it would be ready; that today they would trigger an earthquake in California. If the weapon was not successful, Zapas would lose face. Días momentarily wondered whether his employer had become as obsessed as his father had been.

Of more concern for Días was the simple fact that if the weapon did not do its job, Zapas had no need of it. Nor would he have any need for the laboratory team. Días had engineered his new power supply for maximum effect, knowing his life was at stake. He steeled himself and called Zapas. "The location is secure, and we'll be ready in three hours," he said, allowing himself a little extra time. "There is no way of knowing how long the effect will take."

"Yes, yes," Zapas barked impatiently. "Call me when you're ready to start."

Click.

While Días worked to finish the set-up, he wondered again how the ancients could have powered their device. He could not understand how the technology had the apparent devastating effect the tablets said it did. There must be something he'd missed, unless the ancient civilisation had managed to build a power grid like modern man's, which to Días seemed preposterous.

As the men laboured, a police car drove past, slowing to look at them. Felipe, who was on watch, kept up the pretence of working on the telecommunications box next to the high voltage cabinet. He saw the patrol car approach and was briefly worried, but the officer driving past simply waved at him cheerfully and continued past. Felipe waved back, hoping the man hadn't noticed how jumpy he felt, nor the cold sweat on his brow.

*   *   *

PALM SPRINGS, CALIFORNIA

The bureau field agent had talked to his chief and was about to go back to the crazy tourist couple, give them a stern warning and send them on their way. As he sat in the chief's office, another agent came in.

"Sir, I've got a national security guy here who needs to mobilise a small team to look for a potential terrorist threat in the area. Some sort of new high-tech device." A tall, fair-haired man followed the agent in.

"Jesus, could it be an *acoustic weapon?*" the field agent asked. The chief and the tall man stared at him, astonished for very different reasons.

"Where did you hear that?" the tall man asked assertively, cutting the chief off.

"I've got a couple of people here from England who say someone's planning an attack in Desert Hot Springs."

"Take me to them." The agent looked at his chief, who nodded.

Daniel stood as the agent entered the room. He was about to ask why they'd been locked in when a tall man in a sports jacket appeared.

He extended his hand. "Johnson," he said cordially. "I'm sorry you've been detained."
Daniel and Elisa introduced themselves and started again to explain the urgency of the situation. Johnson stopped them.

"We just have some dots to join up here. We won't be needing you any longer, thanks," He looked at the agent. "And turn that off, please," he added, nodding at the camera in the corner.

The agent left looking a little sullen, and the three of them sat at the table.

"So, tell me about Desert Hot Springs," said Johnson.

Daniel explained about Rigo, the attacks in Chidwick and Prague, and the phone message when they'd barely managed to escape. Johnson took a cursory look at the red line around Elisa's neck, nodding to himself. He glanced up at the camera to see that the red light had gone out.

"We've been tracking this organisation for a few years now. The pale man is a shadow. He's their top enforcer and killer but we've never been able to identify him. No one alive, other than you two, knows what he looks like." He paused as Daniel and Elisa realised the implications of that fact. "We know they have a weapon, and we know they're linked to the São Paulo nightclub incident because of their Dark Web presence. The weapon technology is for sale." Johnson paused briefly. "But what's the connection to you two?"

"The weapon itself, we think," Daniel said. "We've discovered three ancient tablets that describe the destruction of an unknown civilisation, through what appears to be the use of an advanced acoustic technology. They created a chain reaction that destroyed their entire island. The first of the tablets was translated by my great-grandfather, who was murdered when it was stolen during the Second World War. We think this organisation may have been developing and perfecting the technology for decades."

"Tell me more about that chain reaction," Johnson probed.

"Well, it's just a theory, but we've been trying to work out what happened," Elisa said. "Basically, the little evidence we have suggests the ancient civilisation had technology that allowed them to build astonishing structures with monolithic stones that even today's engineers can't build with. There's still evidence all around the world supporting *that* theory. The pyramids, for example, and others in the Middle East, South America, Britain, Europe and Asia." Daniel looked at Elisa.

"We think this technology used acoustics, *sound waves,* and tapped into the earth's natural energy," Elisa continued. "We also now think the technology was *weaponised.* When it was used on the planet itself, in this case in the geologically unstable Mid-Atlantic, it started an unstoppable *chain reaction.* A reaction so powerful it affected the earth's crust and sank their homeland thousands of metres beneath the ocean. The translated tablets said it didn't stop until it *completely consumed itself.*"

Johnson took a moment to digest what they had said, leaning back to stroke his chin.

"So, in other words, if this weapon is used in California, on the San Andreas fault, you think it could cause the same catastrophic devastation," Johnson summarised sombrely.

"Yes, that's the advice of Elisa's colleague, a geophysicist from Oxford," Daniel replied. "And it's what we think happened in the Atlantic nearly twelve thousand years ago." He took his laptop from the backpack and quickly pulled out the copy of the Zeno map. "Here."

Johnson took a moment to study the map. "That's just open sea now, right?" he said, pointing at Frisland.

"Right."

"Okay, let's go. I'm getting a team to Desert Hot Springs to find these people. I'd like you to come along. You might be able to help identify your assailant, as well as filling in some more blanks along the way." Johnson stood and ushered them out.

Daniel told Johnson where they were staying and he arranged to pick them up in fifteen minutes after they'd checked out. They raced back to the hotel, feeling buoyed at finally having found someone who listened, though neither relished the thought of meeting their pale attacker again. They packed in record time and checked out of their hotel to see a black Chevrolet Suburban seven-seater waiting outside. A man climbed out and helped load their suitcases into the cavernous luggage area.

"Jeff," he said, offering his hand.

Johnson explained that Jeff was on his team and had been 'working out logistics' this morning. Daniel and Elisa climbed into the back row, sitting together. Johnson and Jeff sat in the middle row, with a uniformed man driving. Suburbia soon yielded to a desert landscape with mountains in the distance. It was strikingly beautiful, but somewhat surreal after Europe and the United Kingdom's lush green winter wetness.

They were driving on the 'Gene Autry Trail', which seemed more like a two-lane highway than the name suggested, and ahead of them was a wall of mountains, some snow-capped and gleaming in the morning light.

"That's the fault line. Those mountains ahead. Desert Hot Springs is just at the foot," Johnson explained, then changed tack to bring them back to the reality of their situation. "I don't mean to alarm you, but it's surprising you survived your attacks. As far as we can tell, that man is a capable killer."

Daniel explained how Elisa had caught him by surprise in Chidwick and they'd been lucky; then in Prague, because he followed them by plane from Lisbon, he was unarmed except for the garrotte.

"Can you tell me what you know of the technology we're up against?" Johnson asked.

"I'm afraid we don't know much. The tablets don't describe it. Only its terrifying effects," Elisa said. "We know it uses sound waves in ways that we're only starting to discover now." She went on to outline the discussion they'd had with Avery about acoustic levitation using high-powered transducers.

"So, would I be right in assuming we could be looking for something that produces a lot of noise?"

"High-pressure sound waves, for sure, but it may not be audible. They may be above or below the frequency range of human ears," Elisa said.

A road sign indicated the town of Desert Hot Springs, and after a few sets of traffic lights, they passed a shopping complex.

"We've established a temporary command base just over there," Jeff said. "I've had local police checking out possible sites. No luck yet, but it's not a big town."

The driver pulled the Suburban into a parking space outside the community centre building Jeff had indicated.

77

Johnson led them into the building, which turned out to be a community meeting room and theatre with a small mezzanine floor, presumably for the projection equipment. It also had a basic kitchen area. There were tables and chairs spread around, and six uniformed men engaged in various conversations.

Daniel suggested to Elisa that they take one of the tables near the back, out of the way of the whiteboards and bigger tables the agents were using. They sat by the metal frame stairs leading up to the mezzanine, not exactly sure what their role was going to be. With luck, it would just be to identify their attacker if the police were able to round up suspects. Or perhaps that was just naïve.

Two police officers came in, and Johnson signalled them over. "What have you got?" he asked.

"Hard to be sure, but five possible sites. There's a maintenance van that's been parked at the country club since before dawn, and men working on something in the building, maybe the air conditioning. There's two Hispanic guys working on the electricity substation out near Riverside, and a crew digging a hole for some equipment at Hidden Springs. There's four guys in a road gang working out near the abandoned

326

concrete mill, and a telecommunications van working at a preschool on the northern edge of town."

"Would you normally see a road gang working on a Saturday morning?" Johnson asked.

"Sure, it's not unusual. Local city council has them on a six-day roster now. Same as the telephone company," the officer explained. "We drove past the crew at the preschool and they looked okay. Another Hispanic guy was working on the junction box or whatever and he waved back at me."

"Okay, let's go ask those workers what they're doing. Tell them it's a routine check because there's been recent robberies. And keep looking for other sites." Johnson instructed one of his men to get hold of the city's maintenance supervisor to find out what work was scheduled for today. "Just a minute," Johnson called the officer back, and asked Daniel to come over.

"Daniel could you please describe the pale man, in as much detail as you can remember, to the officer here?"

"Sure," Daniel said, as he recalled the details from the attack in Chidwick. As he explained, Elisa came over.

"Sorry to interrupt, but I'm going to get a coffee," Elisa said to Daniel. "You too?"

"Yes, that would be great," he said, looking slightly uncertainly at Johnson.

"It's just across the street," Johnson said. "We'll keep an eye."

"Okay." Daniel continued with his explanation.

* * *

Rigo was not a patient man. He wanted the demonstration finished, and he wanted to leave the US. There were always too many law enforcement officers, everywhere he went. The only upside was that he could get a gun almost anywhere. Días had finished the alignment of the transducer, and all that was left was the connection of the elaborate power supply to the rest of the equipment. Then they could call Zapas and tell him they were ready. Francisco and Carlos were finishing the work, and Felipe stayed outside on watch.

"Pack up the tools and equipment you don't need," Rigo ordered Días. "And make sure there's nothing here that can connect you back to São Paulo or the organisation."

Días reluctantly complied, taking some items from the glove compartment. He then packed a toolbox with some of the more specialised equipment. The two men drove back to the house and collected the last of the gear. Rigo searched every room, and every cupboard and storage space to ensure nothing had been left behind that could link them. Días smoked in the kitchen while Rigo finished.

When Rigo was satisfied, they climbed back into his car and drove to the downtown storage facility, parking outside the garage door. Días climbed out to enter the PIN code. The door rolled open and they unloaded the few things from the van, carrying it to the locker. They locked everything in, except for the few papers Rigo had picked up. He told Días to put those into an empty rubbish bin and burn them, watching as he did it.

Días's phone buzzed. "It's ready," he said, reading the message.

Rigo called Zapas and informed him. He put his phone back into his pocket after a brief exchange.

"Tell them to start," Rigo said, and Días texted the order. There was now nothing more to do but wait.

"I need coffee," Días complained. He expected a gruff response, but Rigo surprised him.

"Very well. I haven't eaten yet." They closed the outside door and parked in a back street behind some shops.

78

Elisa walked out of the community centre and crossed the wide street. There was a café almost directly opposite, just behind a parked truck. As she rounded the truck, two men exited the café. One of them looked at her and her blood ran cold. The cold, dark eyes set into the pale face of the man who had almost choked the life from her. She would never forget him. She saw the instant recognition in his eyes as he threw his cup aside and pulled his gun out. The other man saw what was happening, dropped his unlit cigarette and started to run. Elisa could feel her heart pounding, as she ducked back behind the truck. The man fired. She felt an awful searing pain and fell to the ground.

Daniel heard the shot and saw her fall. He cried out and raced outside. Johnson's men burst through the door on Daniel's heels. Rigo was approaching Elisa, his gun still in his hand, but when he saw the men running from the building across the street, he changed tack, bolting into an alley next to the café. He was through the alley before Johnson's men had crossed. Días was already gone.

Rigo ran out of the alley and past a few parked cars. In an instant he decided not to use his car; the men were close behind and they would, at the least, get his licence plate and be able to get the pseudonym he'd used.

It wouldn't get them far, but it would be further than he wanted. He leapt a fence and sprinted across the yard he'd landed in. A small dog barked and ran after him. He cursed the dog for the noise it made, but it did not catch him. He was over the next fence in seconds. As he crossed the second yard, he heard a thud, as someone landed in the first yard behind him. He could also hear footsteps in the street running alongside the back fences.

He quickly scanned the yard he was in and saw an opportunity. There was a covered woodpile against the wall of a garage that fitted neatly between the house and the side fence. He leapt up onto the woodpile as quietly as he could and climbed the wall to the garage roof. It was a tin roof, but his soft-soled shoes muffled the sound. He ran across the roof and jumped down onto the driveway of the house, realising where he was. He'd landed in the front yard of a house that was only two doors down from the café and shops, and through the shrubs he could see the building the men chasing him had emerged from.

He jumped the side fence onto another lawn, surprising a man who was washing his car in the driveway. He contemplated taking the car, but there wasn't time. The man was just standing and staring, holding a dripping sponge. Rigo ran around the front of the car and pushed through some low shrubs into the next house. This time there was nobody in the yard. He kept going the same way through three more houses, reaching one with an open car parking area. There was nobody around, so he quickly pulled his jacket off and stuffed it into a pile of rubbish at the back.

He was sweating and started to feel out of breath, feeling his age. He was tough and fit, but he was also almost fifty. He was on a corner, so if he ventured out the front he would be on the same street as the building the pursuers came from, but if he jumped over the side fence he would likely be closer to those chasing him. He didn't know how many were in pursuit, and he had no way of knowing whether they were now doing a house-to-house, or still running and hoping he would make a mistake.

Wearing a dark-grey, long-sleeved T-shirt, without his black leather jacket, he hoped he looked different enough to cross the street and find his escape. He made his decision and climbed the low side fence into the side street. He calmed himself, walked briskly to the corner and crossed the main road. Nobody followed. Nobody called out. Starting to feel the pressure easing, he jogged to the next side street, past four houses, and turned left. He was now two full blocks from where he'd shot Mansfield. He'd seen her drop, but, thanks to the idiot Días, he couldn't be sure he'd killed her. Rigo continued until he reached another small group of shops that included a second-hand clothing store.

Ten minutes later, he left the store wearing blue jeans, checked shirt and a trucker's cap. He took his other clothing around the back and pushed it deep into a rubbish skip that smelt of rotting meat. That was the moment at which he realised his key to the storage locker was in the jacket he'd hidden in the rubbish two blocks back. Was he losing his edge? That was a mistake he would not have made in his Stasi days. It was the sort of mistake that could get him caught or killed. He would have to hope the jacket would not be found until after this assignment was complete.

Two blocks away, Johnson's men called in to report that they'd lost him. They didn't have enough manpower for a full house-to-house search. All they could advise was the direction he had headed, and a couple of streets they were confident he was not on. Johnson took down their current location.

"Okay, start a house-to-house from where you lost him," Johnson said. "I'll send more men to meet you and spread it out." Johnson made a call then gave Jeff details of where the men searching had lost Rigo. "The new detail will be there in ten minutes."

As Jeff took off, the patrolling police officers came in to update Johnson on their progress.

"The city maintenance guy has confirmed the road gang and the hole diggers at Hidden Springs are legitimate, and the country club cleared their guys too. We're looking at the others, but the preschool seems to check out. There are three Mexicans working there and all their paperwork and IDs check out." The officer closed his notebook.

Without warning, glasses starting rattling in the kitchen area. Then they felt the jolt of an earthquake. Some cups fell from the shelf and smashed on the floor as the furniture rattled. Men were looking around, wondering if it would be bad enough to get under the tables. A few of the men from out of state were shaken, but the Californians were used to it. Less than a minute later it had passed. One of the men swept up the smashed crockery. A quick scan showed no other damage. Outside, a few people had come running out of nearby shops.

"The tourists usually do that," Johnson said to one of the men, nodding towards the people running into the street. "That's how some were killed in San Francisco in '89. They ran outside and were hit by falling glass and masonry." The other guy just shook his head.

79

Minutes earlier, Daniel had watched out the window as Elisa crossed the street. He saw her fall as he heard the gunshot. Instinct kicked in. He burst through the door and ran across the street, and was almost hit by a car. He didn't even notice the blaring horn, as the driver missed him by less than a metre. He saw Elisa on the ground behind the truck and the man in black running down a lane ahead. With his heart in his mouth, he reached Elisa to see her bleeding from a head injury, just lying on the road with her eyes closed. He thought she'd been shot in the head.

"Elisa!" he cried out in anguish. He stroked her face as he looked more closely at her head wound. It was not a bullet wound, it was a graze, possibly from the back of the truck. Her face was wet.

"Elisa!" His gut-wrenching fear eased a little as she started to open her eyes. He realised her face was wet with his tears. He hadn't even realised that he'd wept. She looked at Daniel and blinked, but her eyes couldn't quite focus immediately.

"Daniel," she sighed.

His hand was wet with blood, and he could see her left arm was bleeding heavily. There was a deep wound across her upper arm, front to back. He stroked her face and kissed her forehead.

"Elisa," he said again, this time more subdued. The graze on her head seemed to be a minor injury. He gently tucked a wisp of hair behind her left ear and examined her arm. Delicately pushing the short sleeve up to her shoulder, he could see it was bleeding profusely. One of Johnson's men had run over to them, and called for an ambulance. Daniel quickly took off his shirt and used a sleeve as a tourniquet at her shoulder. The other sleeve was all he had to bandage the wound.

"Your shirt doesn't match mine," Elisa whispered, with a hint of a weak smile. Her eyes were now beginning to focus properly and she saw the look of anguish on Daniel's face give way to a sigh of relief as he looked into her eyes.

"I thought you were ..." he said, barely managing to speak.

She put her hand to her head. "I don't know what happened. I saw him, and maybe I fainted. Maybe the shock of the bullet hitting me." She was a little dazed, but coming around.

"You hit your head. On this, I think." Daniel tapped the rear bumper of the truck.

Elisa reached out, grabbed his hand and started to pull herself into a sitting position. "Did they catch him?" she asked.

"I don't know. They were right behind him, so let's hope so. Do you think you can stand up?"

Elisa was sitting on the asphalt and Daniel kneeling in front of her, just behind the truck. Her hand was on his bare chest. He picked up her handbag from the road, and as he did so, the ground jolted violently, throwing him almost on top of Elisa. He knew what it was immediately, even before the rumbling sound registered with either of them. Earthquakes were commonplace in Wellington, but Elisa was initially confused, then a look of terror crossed her face. As the ground lurched, the truck in front of them rolled backwards. Daniel leapt up, grabbed Elisa under her arms and lifted her onto the pavement, out of the way of the rocking truck.

"Earthquake?" Her voice wavered, and she was clearly agitated.

"Yes." They sat there for thirty seconds until the shaking had subsided.

"About a five, five and a half, I'd say, and shallow," Daniel added.

"It could be starting. The chain reaction!" Elisa cried. "We might be too late!"

80

When the shaking stopped completely, both of them exhaled. Daniel could feel Elisa's heart racing as he held her close.

"I think I can stand up," Elisa said, putting her good arm around Daniel's shoulders.

He lifted her up, her bag slung over his arm, and as they started to walk to the community centre, the paramedics arrived. The man who had dialled 911 pointed them out, and Daniel helped her to the back of the ambulance. The senior paramedic, a woman who looked to be in her late thirties, took off the makeshift tourniquet.

"Good job," she said to Daniel. "That's as important as the wound itself." She took a closer look at Elisa's arm. "Bullet graze," she said.

"Yes," said Johnson's man, before either of them had a chance to answer. "We have men after the assailant right now," he added, flashing an ID at the paramedic.

"You're lucky. It grazed your upper arm, missing the bone completely. It's cut through the flesh from front to back and seared some skin on the way, but you'll make a full recovery. It'll be a good scar to show your kids."

"I don't ..." Elisa stopped as the woman cleaned the wound with something that made her wince. The paramedic dressed the bullet wound

336

firmly, and then checked her head.

"I think I hit my head on the way down," Elisa said.

"Oddly enough, that might have broken your fall a little. I'm going to give you a concussion test, but you're one lucky woman."

The junior paramedic asked Daniel if he'd been hurt, also noticing the almost-healed knife wound on his arm.

"I'm fine," Daniel said. He wanted to ask Johnson if they'd caught the man, or found the weapon, but there was no way he was leaving Elisa.

The paramedics completed their tasks, gave Elisa some pain relief and antibiotics, and explained the symptoms of concussion she should watch out for over the next forty-eight hours. "And no flying for forty-eight hours either," she said, noticing that their accents were not American.

Daniel and Elisa thanked them for their help and crossed over back to the community centre.

Elisa was still unsteady, and grateful for Daniel's arm that was firmly around her. As they reached the building, she noticed the goose pimples on his bare skin. "You're cold," she observed.

"I'm okay, don't worry."

"Our bags are in the SUV," she said.

"I'm not leaving you." Daniel was firm.

"You need a new shirt, and I'll be fine," she said.

He gave her a look that said 'no way'. Jeff overheard their conversation and volunteered to sit with her.

"Did you catch him?" Daniel asked as he headed outside to the Suburban.

"Not yet, I've got a dozen men out there now looking. We haven't recovered the weapon yet either," Jeff called.

As Daniel made his exit, a young police officer came in with a tray of coffees and donuts. He offered a cup to Elisa first, and she took one for Daniel, too. As the officer offered Johnson a cup, a thoughtful look crossed his face. "You know, those guys up at the preschool checked out fine, but it was a bit weird, now I think of it. Their engine wasn't running, and it was completely quiet, but the van was *vibrating*."

Johnson dropped his donut back into the box and grabbed the radio. Moments later, five men ran into the building and Johnson was briefing them as Daniel returned, sitting next to Elisa. She updated him as she slipped her hand inside his T-shirt, and back onto his stomach where it had been keeping him warm. He could see she was still visibly shaken and distressed.

They watched in silence, each comforted by the other's touch, as the men went out to one of the SUVs to retrieve weapons and assault gear from the lock-up in the back. The six men then climbed into two vehicles and raced off, leaving Daniel and Elisa with an armed uniform.

They heard a low, rumbling sound in the distance, rapidly approaching. Then glasses and crockery started rattling, and the shaking started. Elisa grabbed Daniel with both arms and he pushed her under the table, squeezing in next to her. As the building shook, car alarms starting sounding in the street. This one was bigger. Elisa clung to Daniel, not knowing what to expect, and biting back the scream in her throat. He tried to calm her, but *he* didn't know what to expect either. The drills he'd done at work had taught him what to do, but there was no way of knowing how bad this quake was going to be. The convulsing floor lurched suddenly, throwing them together, and their heads collided. The furniture rattled and shook, and somewhere outside they heard a window smash. Elisa cried out involuntarily, and gripped Daniel even more tightly.

Then, with a final jolt as the secondary wave hit, the quake stopped. There was another slight tremor a few seconds later, and after another ten seconds, Daniel helped Elisa up.

"How ... how do you get used to living with that?" she asked, her face now ashen.

Daniel held on to her. "Are you okay?" he asked, kissing the spot where his head had hit hers.

"I think so." Her unsteady voice told a different story.

"And you don't really get used to it. Not bigger ones like that, anyway.

After the big ones in Christchurch in 2010 and 2011, there were a lot of people who just couldn't live there any more. Thousands of aftershocks went on for more than a year, and some people were so on edge they had to move away. Some even went to Australia."

"Sorry I'm so jumpy. It's irrational and I don't like it," Elisa said.

"It's normal," Daniel reassured her. "And don't forget this situation is different. That last one was quite strong, felt like well over six to me, and we don't get many like that. My guess is it might have been more violent because we're right on top of the fault line. If it was triggered by the weapon, then I'd say it was quite shallow, too."

"I hate quakes," said the uniformed man, who had a southern drawl in his voice. He'd been standing in the kitchen area and had simply held on to the bench, not knowing what else to do.

"We get them a lot at home," Daniel said. "New Zealand. You're not from California?"

"Texas," he said proudly. "Nothing more than an occasional tremor there, and they're rare."

"You should get under a table if you can. It's often furniture and fit-out, like ceiling tiles and so on, that injure people," Daniel said, trying to be helpful.

"You two been through a bit," said the man, glancing from Elisa's head and neck, to her bandaged arm, to Daniel's wound.

"Yes," said Elisa, still holding on to Daniel. She was still unsettled.

81

Five blocks away, two of Johnson's men were still out searching for Rigo when the quake struck. They were scouting further out, while the others continued door-knocking nearer to where Elisa had been shot. They walked past a property with a large outbuilding, a sleep-out of some kind, and as the pavement jolted them forward and back, they watched as the metal roof of the outbuilding started to separate from the walls. The windows in the front of the stricken structure shattered as the frames buckled, and at that moment a man ran outside. He was wearing blue jeans and a checked shirt, with a trucker's cap pulled down low on his forehead. He had an unusually pale face, especially for a local. The younger of the two men ducked below the fence, as the other one waved his arm.

"Hey," the older man called out.

The pale man looked over at him, pulling a gun from under his shirt.

"Gun," the older agent whispered to his partner, as he ducked for cover behind the low brick fence. As the shaking subsided, a bullet struck the bricks and some chips of masonry landed on the older man, as he pulled out his weapon. Trucker's Cap fired again, and the older man shot back, signalling his partner, who was ten years his junior, to go through the yard next door. The young agent squatted down well below the top of the fence

340

and was able to quickly cover the ground to the shooter. The older man needed to signal his partner somehow as to where trucker cap was. He fired another round over the man's head.

Rigo took the bait, firing a shot back. The older agent knew he could have shot him dead, but their orders were to bring him in alive if possible. Johnson had been clear that he wanted to be able to question him. The young agent was in position now, just behind the fence, some five metres away from the shooter. *It would be so much easier just to take him out,* the older agent thought.

Nonetheless, the older man knew what he needed to do. He stood up, momentarily putting his head above the brick fence, and fired another shot, aiming just over the pale man's head, and just as Rigo shot back, the younger agent jumped the side fence and tackled him down.

The other agent jumped the front fence and raced to the two men who had hit the ground. A shot was fired, and Rigo wrestled his gun free from under the man he'd shot. He wasn't quite quick enough to pull the gun out. The older agent launched himself at the pale man, kicking him brutally in the face as he tried to shoot again. Before Rigo had a chance to recover, he'd been cuffed and disarmed, and lay face down, bleeding onto the lawn.

The older agent breathlessly called it in on his radio, as he checked his partner for signs of life. He asked for an ambulance, too, but he knew it was too late. He stood with his gun pointed at the pale man's head, daring him to try something, while he waited for backup and medical assistance.

As Johnson and his men drove to the preschool, they felt the second quake. At first, it just seemed like the driver had swerved to avoid an obstacle or animal, but soon they heard car alarms going off and saw people running out of their houses. Being in moving vehicles, they had no way of knowing whether this one was worse than the last, but the shaking seemed to go on for longer, and they could see the overhead power lines swaying drunkenly.

The men were undeterred. They would not be distracted from their mission; they all knew they were there to stop a new kind of weapon that could theoretically cause earthquakes. When they arrived at the scene, the white van was still parked next to the school gate. Both drivers parked their SUVs across the driveway, effectively blocking the van from moving. The man who had been standing outside near the control box had ducked inside the van. Johnson's team took their positions behind their vehicles and Johnson called to the van.

"Step out of the vehicle with your hands raised!" There was movement in the van, but nobody came out.

"Step out of the van with your hands in the air!" Johnson shouted again. A man's head briefly appeared from around the side of the van. He fired a shot, hitting one of the SUVs.

"You are outnumbered. Come out now!" Johnson tried one more time, not expecting success.

Francisco and Carlos were in the van, while Felipe defended their position. They both knew there was no real hope of escape. They had been on edge for the past sixty minutes in any case, since the first earthquake. The machine had been operating for hours, and the ground had started vibrating beneath them just before the patrol car had checked them out. Less than half an hour later, the first quake had struck, and minutes ago, the second had hit more violently. Días had not returned, and they wanted to stop the weapon. What if it killed them, too? Días and Zapas did not care. They weren't here. Rigo wasn't here. And now Felipe was shooting at federal agents.

Felipe fired another shot at the SUVs and hit one of the agents in the shoulder. Several men fired back, and using the covering shots, Jeff and another stormed the vehicle. As Felipe poked his head around to shoot, Jeff shot him. Blood erupted from his forehead, and he hit the ground hard, eyes open but not seeing.

Francisco and Carlos came out with their hands in the air and were quickly cuffed and put in the back of one of the SUVs. Johnson spoke to them while Jeff and the others checked out the strange machinery to try and determine how to stop it. There was a low hum coming from the van and from the transformer cabinet at the foot of the telegraph pole.

"Do you feel that?" Jeff asked, standing on the pavement next to the van.

"Yeah. The ground is vibrating. What the ..." They could not readily see how to turn the machine off but followed the cables that led inside the vehicle.

Johnson sat in the front passenger seat of the SUV with the two prisoners in the back. "Tell me how to stop that machine," he said.

"It could be too late," said one of them, with a heavily accented voice.

"Just tell me how!" Johnson yelled at the man's face, pointing his weapon at his chest.

"Just disconnect the power cables," the man said hurriedly. "The ones that are screwed on."

Johnson shouted instructions to Jeff, who picked up a wrench from the floor and went over to the cable terminals. He touched the wrench to the large nut in order to loosen it, and immediately felt like he'd been hit by a truck. Even with rubber-soled shoes on the carpeted floor, the high-current power supply of several hundred volts was enough to physically throw him across the van. He hit his head hard on the roof near the driver's seat and slumped over the seat.

As Jeff was thrown violently off the terminal, the wrench fell and touched the other terminal, shorting the power supply. Jeff's men had watched in horror as he was knocked unconscious. A huge spark leapt across the weapon, and the wrench was thrown free, smashing the windscreen, narrowly missing Jeff's limp body. There was a small explosion in the transformer cabinet, and the humming stopped.

As one of the men tended to Jeff, another retrieved the wrench, picked up the thick, insulated rubber gloves from the floor and unscrewed the terminals. Even though the power source was dead, the short having destroyed the transformer in the cabinet, he was extremely cautious. He took the cables carefully outside and placed them near the cabinet.

The man with Jeff was administering CPR and Jeff was beginning to come around. At the rear SUV, one of the men had done his best to stop the bleeding from his partner's shoulder.

They soon had the wounded man in the back of the ambulance that had just pulled up, while one paramedic checked Jeff. He was lucky, the paramedic said. If he'd had both hands on the terminals, the shock would have gone straight through his heart and probably killed him instantly. He'd taken a hard knock to his head but was going to be fine. The paramedics left with the man who had been shot.

Two patrol cars arrived, and the officers spoke with Johnson. He arranged for them to have Felipe's body removed and handed over the two cuffed prisoners to take them to the local police cells. Johnson gave instructions that under no circumstances were they to be allowed to leave Desert Hot Springs police custody; nor were they to be permitted to talk to anyone. Johnson's men had already searched them and removed their wallets, mobile phones and all papers. They would assess those later and would interrogate the men later as well. Johnson could tell they were nervous, and he was going to leave them to sweat for some time.

"Johnson!" Jeff called from the pavement near the van.

"Hey," Johnson said. "Glad you're okay."

"Electricity 101. Rookie mistake, boss, sorry."

"Forget it." Johnson was now standing next to Jeff on the concrete pavement.

"Feel that?" Jeff asked.

"The ground is *vibrating*. Shit, what does that mean?"

"I dunno," said Jeff, "but it can't be good. The power is disconnected. It still feels the same as it was *before* I got zapped."

82

Johnson and his men returned to the community centre at the same time as the others returned with Rigo, cuffed and bloodied with his broken nose. As they reached the building, Elisa recoiled as she saw him. Even in the plaid shirt and trucker cap, there was no mistaking him. He stared at her, his intent clear. Johnson looked over at Daniel and Elisa, and they both nodded, confirming he was the man. Johnson considered having him put in the police lock-up, but he didn't want him close to the other prisoners. And he wanted to question this one first. Johnson scanned the room and identified the metal stairs. There were strong steel brackets securing them to the wall. The only way out would be to cut through the cuffs ... or an arm.

Rigo was cuffed to one of the brackets, about a metre and a half up the wall, forcing him to remain standing. Rigo seemed unperturbed. For a man in federal custody, secured to a wall, and with a severely smashed nose, he seemed unnaturally calm. He looked again at Daniel and Elisa and moved his head so he could run a finger across his throat.

Rigo was barely controlling his anger. Before this assignment, he would never have been caught by two agents, no matter how good they were. It was the incident in the old house in Wiltshire, when the woman had

345

bested him on the stairs. He'd let his guard down. He needed to redeem himself, and the best place to start that redemption would be to finish the job. There would be an opportunity. They had to move him at some point. He would bide his time, and he would kill them both. The woman first, so the man could watch her die.

Daniel and Elisa had moved to the other side of the room, away from Rigo. Johnson left his group of men, having given instructions for two of them to go and supervise the removal of the van and its equipment to a federal facility. Others were directed to continue the hunt for the missing man, the one wearing glasses who'd run away before Rigo had shot Elisa.

"The weapon has been neutralised, but the ground at the scene is still vibrating. What do you make of that?" Johnson asked directly. It was clear he was worried. Elisa and Daniel both looked stricken.

"Oh my God. It's in the tablet," her horror now palpable. "*Increasing resonance.* The 'song of the earth' getting louder, the quakes intensifying until 'it consumes itself and all around it'. You need to evacuate this city, and maybe others!"

"Yeah. I was thinking you'd say that." He pulled his mobile out of his pocket and made a call, walking outside as it connected. He stepped back in briefly to ask Jeff to check with the police at the scene whether the ground was still vibrating. Daniel was still worried about Elisa. He knew a visceral fear of earthquakes was a real phenomenon and could affect even the most rational and logical person. He'd seen it for himself. In fact, he didn't see it as all that surprising. When the one thing that's always static and stable – the ground beneath one's feet – is suddenly moving dangerously and uncontrollably, the base 'fight, flight or freeze' reflex quickly takes control.

Elisa was holding it together and perfectly rational, but she wasn't leaving his side. Neither was he leaving her side. She needed his support, and he wasn't about to let her down. At least he was used to quakes. They watched as Johnson returned, a grim look on his face.

"Can't evacuate. My superiors have been talking to the city mayor. This town is used to quakes, and there's no logical reason to evacuate unless we tell people these are not natural quakes," Johnson explained.

"But that's crazy. Hundreds or even thousands of people could be killed. How do they justify that?" Daniel asked, annoyance apparent in his voice.

"They say there's no proof these quakes aren't natural. They also say that if we tell people they aren't natural, we'll cause mass panic, and people will die trying to flee the city. That last point is probably true."

As Johnson said it, Daniel knew they were right. He had another idea. "What about a gas leak, or something like that? Can't you use that as an excuse?"

"I thought about that, too. People here are smart. They know what happens in a quake. They know when there's a gas leak. There would be endless questions from media and citizens alike. And there's a mayoral election coming up in three months."

And there it is. Votes more important than lives. Maybe that was unfair, but Daniel was exasperated.

"I know," said Johnson, seeing Daniel's expression. "But I have my orders." Johnson could also see Elisa was looking a little frayed at the edges. "I'm going to get you two evacuated, though. You've done what we asked and been injured in the process. The least I can do is get you safely out of here," Johnson said. "We'll get you to a medical centre in Palm Springs."

Johnson was about to call a man over when the floor started shaking, this time in a deeper, rolling motion at first. Daniel quickly pulled Elisa under a table, and they heard cups hitting the floor and smashing. There was a sharp, violent jolt and a window cracked, fell out of its frame onto the pavement and shattered. Ceiling tiles fell and hit some of the tables. Daniel could see some of Johnson's men scramble under tables as the debris and dust fell. A cupboard door in the kitchen opened and glasses tumbled out to smash on the floor. Daniel knew this was a big quake. Elisa gripped him in abject terror, unable to speak.

Looking across the room, Daniel could see the mezzanine landing at the top of the stairs swaying. It had separated from the wall. The stairs were rocking wildly. Car alarms blared and the sounds of furniture and fittings crashing down were all around them. It had been at least a minute, and the shaking hadn't abated. Daniel had never experienced a quake this large. *This is very big, or very shallow, or both,* he thought. Another jolt and the metals stairs swayed and buckled a little.

Rigo had stood still under the stairs, thinking they would protect him, but now they were moving. Perhaps his opportunity would come sooner than he had hoped. He watched the men in the room. Some had crawled under tables, some were frozen on the spot and didn't know what to do. The mayhem and confusion was, at the least, going to be useful. He looked over at his primary targets. They were crouched under a table, and the woman was clinging pitifully to the man. This was more than the vulnerability he'd seen in England. This was pure, visceral fear. It was delicious.

The bracket around which his cuffed hands were secured had started to separate from the wall. He pulled hard, and the cuffs cut into his wrists. The bracket didn't come away completely, but it moved. The pain in his wrists spurred him on. He pulled hard again, and this time the bracket moved a little further, almost far enough. Soon, he knew, the shaking would have to stop, so he pulled hard one more time. Finally, the bracket moved far enough that he could slip the cuffs free. He stared at Elisa, a malevolent half-smile on his face. She was still pathetically paralysed with fear under the table.

As the shaking started to ease, while the men were either under tables or clinging to doorways and fittings, he leapt across to the kitchen. He grabbed a large knife from the bench and was halfway across the room in seconds.

Daniel had watched as Rigo worked on his cuffs. He could see him pulling relentlessly at the bracket he was secured to, and he could see the movement in the whole stair assembly. He called to one of Johnson's men that Rigo was nearly free, but in the mayhem and noise, he didn't hear. Daniel then watched as Rigo broke free of the bracket. He was holding Elisa, who was rigid and unable to move. He assumed Rigo would take the opportunity to run out of the building, either through the door or the hole in the front wall where the window had fallen out. He would be free again, and in the confusion may never be seen again. *Until he comes for us.*

Instead, he watched Rigo jump in the opposite direction, to the kitchen area, and grab a large knife with his still-cuffed hands. Daniel watched in horror as Rigo looked across at Elisa with a look of pure evil in his cold eyes. The man then flew across the room to Elisa, like a wild animal leaping at its prey.

Daniel pulled free of Elisa's grip and launched himself directly at Rigo from under the table. There was another jolt from the quake and a shrieking, tearing sound from above as a beam separated from the swaying stairs. Elisa watched, frozen to the floor, as the two men collided about two metres away from her. A guttural cry came from one of them, she couldn't tell which, as the ceiling beam crashed down, bringing a dozen ceiling tiles, dust and insulation with it. Both men went down under the debris. Elisa screamed and suddenly found her feet.

83

B razilian presidential candidate José Zapas had called the media to a press conference. It was early evening in São Paulo, and news of a large earthquake in southern California had reached Brazil. Reports gave its magnitude as 7.6, describing significant damage in Desert Hot Springs, neighbouring Palm Springs, and some areas as far north as Palmdale. It had been felt all the way up to San Francisco.

This was an excellent opportunity for media coverage that would aid his campaign, as video footage showed emergency services personnel pulling people from damaged buildings and relief supplies already being shipped in. The situation was grim, and Brazil would offer its help. Electricity and telecommunications had failed in some places. The city of Desert Hot Springs had declared a state of emergency, and gas mains had been shut off. Water supplies were also damaged, and drinking water warnings had been issued.

News reports said this quake was unusual in that it had been preceded by two smaller quakes, the first being magnitude 5.2, and the second magnitude 6.4. Seismologists said this pattern, a seemingly linear progression in magnitude, had not been recorded previously.

There was also a news report saying a geoscience institute in San

Bernardino had recorded a ringing or vibration in the earth's crust at Desert Hot Springs that had started around the time of the first quake and was still being detected. This had mystified seismologists and had no scientific precedent, they said.

Zapas could not have been happier. Even though he'd lost contact with the team in Desert Hot Springs hours earlier, he'd been watching the news intently. Now, the reports of major damage and injury, with an added bonus of scientists declaring this quake pattern 'highly unusual', meant he had what he wanted. A proven weapon, *and* something he could point to in the future if he wanted to threaten, rather than attack, another nation. That was the icing on the cake – the report of the unexplained 'ringing', which suggested the quakes were not natural. He could point to the weapon as the trigger.

As he brushed down his suit and ensured that he looked presidential, he fleetingly wondered if Rigo or any of his people had survived. Not that it mattered. It would be helpful for Días to return with either of the weapons, but Zapas had the detailed blueprints and there were plenty of engineers. He'd already decided Rigo was a dead man no matter what happened. He'd failed to kill the pair, or seize the woman.

Zapas stepped up to the podium to address his waiting audience.

"Ladies and gentlemen of the media," he began. "It is with a heavy heart that I offer my deepest condolences to the good people of California. This is a tragedy of terrible proportions, and I want you to know that Brazil will stand ready to assist.

"Tomorrow, if I am to believe the polls," Zapas said with his most engaging smile, "the citizens of Brazil will elect me as provisional president. It will be my humble honour and privilege to extend any help that Brazil can." Zapas put his hand on his heart, and his face took on a most serious and sombre expression. "Our hearts go out to you all. May God bless you."

Zapas's wife, rarely seen with him before the presidential campaign, stepped out to the podium and linked arms with the leading presidential candidate. It was a well-choreographed show, and the media loved it.

At almost the same time as the evening press conference, several Internet news organisations in São Paulo and Brasilia received a leaked story that linked one of the Zapas group of companies with the recent attack at Club Na Beira, where thirteen people had lost their lives, and some were still seriously injured and likely permanently deaf. These news organisations were not part of the Zapas empire.

84

Johnson ran over as the shaking stopped, gun in hand. He reached the pile of debris at the same time Elisa did. She was wailing and had tears streaming down her face, reaching in and pulling tiles off the men. Johnson dragged her back. He didn't know if either man was alive or dead, and Elisa could still be in danger. She was fighting him off, reaching in to try and find Daniel. Another man ran over, helping to clear off debris, while Johnson held on to Elisa. She could see Daniel's white T-shirt spattered with blood, and cried out.

Another agent came over. He had a minor head injury that was still bleeding, but he pitched in to help. Johnson had to hold on to Elisa, she was still trying to fight him to get to the debris. Her tears were leaving tracks in the dust on her cheeks. The others continued pulling out bits of broken ceiling, clearing enough that they could see the two men lying still on the ground. Elisa couldn't see whether either of them was seriously injured or not, but Daniel's shirt was heavily bloodstained. Elisa cried out in anguish again, as the men, with a superhuman effort, lifted the fallen beam. Daniel's body moved.

Johnson felt Elisa's sharp intake of breath.

"Daniel!" she screamed.

He started to move backwards, and they could see Rigo's head had been crushed. The two men carefully helped Daniel to crawl out.

Elisa could see the knife under him. *Is that blood on it?*

Daniel started to stand up. There was a lot of blood on his back, but as he got up, Elisa could see he didn't seem to have been stabbed, and there wasn't much blood on his front. He had some scratches on his face and arms, and his head was coated in white dust from the ceiling.

"Elisa," he said.

As Johnson loosened his grips on her arms, she pushed away and reached for Daniel. He stood there and held her tightly for several minutes, until her sobs and shuddering subsided.

Johnson and the men cleared the bulk of the wreckage and pulled Rigo's body away. Neither Daniel nor Elisa could find any words. Daniel touched her face gently, she kissed him and cried, and they just held on to each other.

An officer walked into the community centre, looking dishevelled and dirty, and out of breath. He surveyed at the damage in the room and wondered why they were still in the building.

"What's happened?" Johnson asked him, ignoring the look.

"The van's gone," the officer said, panting.

"**What?**" roared Johnson.

"The ground opened up. Right underneath it. We barely got out alive. My partner is securing the scene, but I thought I'd better get down here. Our radios have been patchy since the last quake ... It's like a big sinkhole opened right up and swallowed the van, the patrol car and a couple cars parked on the street." The officer was clearly shaken.

"This area isn't known for sinkholes. Not enough water. How deep?" Johnson asked.

"Deep. About sixty to seventy-five yards. And maybe a quarter-mile long. One of the school buildings is sitting on top of a big hole."

"Was the ground still vibrating when you left?"

"Yes, sir, it was."

"Now we've got a reason to evacuate. At least in that part of town."

Johnson ordered his men to help organise the evacuation of the houses along the fault line near the chasm that had just opened up.

Daniel squeezed Elisa's hand and turned to Johnson. "We need to know more about that vibration; is it steady or increasing? Do you think we could get someone with a seismometer here? Or maybe there's someone measuring this already, in Palm Springs, or somewhere close by?"

"Good idea," Johnson said, pulling his mobile out of his pocket. "Shit. No signal. I guess cell towers are down. Let's get out of this building. I don't want to be in here if there's another quake!"

Johnson signalled for them all to go outside. Elisa and Daniel first. As Daniel turned to the door, Elisa saw the blood on the back of his T-shirt. Rigo's blood.

"Your shirt," she said, "it's covered in that man's blood." Daniel took it off. He saw there was some blood on her forearms, too. No doubt the same blood. She paled a little more as she looked down at her arms.

"That's two shirts in one day. Dammit," he joked, trying to lighten the mood.

They all went out into the street. The car alarms had now been silenced and there were a lot of people around. They had come out of the buildings and some were looking for loved ones. There didn't appear to be a huge amount of damage, but there were a few smashed windows, and a lot of dust in the air. An ambulance siren wailed in the distance. The café across the street was empty and looked to be undamaged. Johnson made his way over to it and went inside. A minute later, he returned to the group.

"We can use the café. It looks okay." It was smaller and older than the community centre, a single-storey structure. Elisa would have preferred to stay outside, but first there was some cleaning up to do. She led Daniel inside the café and through to the bathrooms. She wet some paper towels and gently rinsed the smeared dry blood from his back and shoulders.

"Thank you," he whispered into her ear.

They both washed their hands and arms, and Daniel washed the remaining dust from his face. "I could use a shower," he added, brushing particles out of his hair.

"Look at us both!" she said, gazing in the mirror. Daniel's knife wound, her bandaged arm and neck, grazes and scratches on their heads and faces and Daniel's hands.

Daniel took a closer look at Elisa's arm bandage. "How's that feeling?" There was a spot of blood on the dressing, although it wasn't necessarily Elisa's.

"It hurts a bit, but I'm okay. I'm just glad you're all right," she said, tears starting to well up.

They went back into the café, seeing Johnson on the landline phone and men sitting at the tables. The owner was picking up some broken cups. He acknowledged them with a nod as they passed.

"Thanks so much," Elisa said.

Johnson finished his call and turned to join the men. Elisa and Daniel followed him.

"We'll have seismographic readings in the next ten or fifteen minutes hopefully," he said. "That was good thinking." He nodded to Daniel. "I'll get one of the men to run you to Palm Springs medical centre."

"Thanks, that would be good, but can we just wait until you get the seismograph report?" said Elisa. "I need to know what that vibration is doing."

Jeff was tapping away on his mobile phone, Johnson noticed.

"I thought cell towers were out?" Johnson said.

"Café's lucky. Their Wi-Fi is still working. Pete over there," Jeff nodded towards the proprietor "gave me the password." He spelt it out for the others.

Elisa and Daniel took out their phones and logged into the network. They quickly found news reports confirming the escalation of the magnitude of the earthquakes, and also read a report of the strange vibration or ringing showing up on seismographs in the region. Seismologists were starting to speculate about this new unexplained phenomenon. And reports said it was still there. The phone rang and Johnson took the call. Jeff had managed to connect with their field office in Palm Springs. He read a message from his phone: *Palm Springs say cell coverage should be back in twenty minutes. The cell towers aren't all down, it's a network overload problem.*

"Well, that's good news," Johnson said, ending his call. "The seismology news isn't as good. Apparently, the vibration was picked up half an hour or so before the first quake, and it's been slowly but steadily increasing in intensity since then."

Nobody said a word. They all knew this wasn't over yet.

85

Daniel and Elisa had taken their coffees outside and were sitting in the sun at one of the plastic tables on the pavement.

The late afternoon November sun here is still warm, Daniel thought, as he stepped out into it. He was still worried about Elisa's state of mind. She was clearly terrified of another quake but also afraid of her reaction to it and was beating herself up for it.

"Are you okay?" he asked, not knowing what else to do.

"I think so," came the uncertain reply.

Daniel left her for a moment to retrieve another T-shirt from his suitcase, as Johnson came outside.

"There's a car coming for you. We're finally going to get you out to Palm Springs. You should both get medical attention," he said.

Jeff stepped out to talk to Johnson.

Daniel overheard them talking about arranging a small crane truck to pull the van out of the deep chasm that had swallowed it. *Surely it would be a lot easier just to leave it down there? They could bulldoze some landfill into the fissure when the quakes stabilise. I guess they want to analyse that weapon.*

A familiar black Chevrolet Suburban pulled up, and the military uniformed driver got out to talk to Johnson for a few minutes. Then they

358

walked over to Daniel and Elisa.

"Tyler here will take you to a medical facility and then on to your accommodation. He'll stay with you until tomorrow morning. I'll come to see you for a debrief then. Looks like the cell phone network is back online, and you've got my number if you need it."

"Thanks," Elisa said, relieved they would be heading away from the epicentre of the quakes.

They put their bags in the back and climbed into the Suburban. As Tyler slowly drove down the main street they saw occasional damaged buildings and broken windows, some already being boarded up with sheets of plywood. There were a few damaged awnings and signs being taken down, and one building that had been mostly gutted by fire, with a fire truck still parked outside. There were people walking around applying orange 'DANGER' tape, sweeping up broken glass and picking up rubbish.

Near the edge of town, Tyler turned off the main street, Palm Drive, and onto Dillon, and as he eased the speed up to fifty-five miles per hour, Elisa noticed the power lines swaying on their left. Tyler hit the brakes as the car started to veer left and right.

"Another one," he said, as he tried to retain control.

Palm trees to the right of the car were swaying impossibly, and as Elisa looked out the windscreen she couldn't believe what she saw. The asphalt tore itself apart right in front of them! Tyler slammed on the brakes and they felt the anti-lock braking system guide the car to a quick stop, just on the edge of the gaping black hole that had opened up. It was at least ten metres wide, and she couldn't see the bottom. They could feel the car shaking as the quake continued. A pickup truck behind them locked up its brakes and skidded, hitting the back of the Suburban. Elisa screamed as it hit them, pushing them forward a few feet and almost into the abyss.

The pickup driver started to get out of his truck and Tyler opened his door yelling at the man to get back in and reverse his truck. Seeing Tyler's uniform, the pickup driver did as he was told. Immediately, Tyler quickly reversed the Suburban, jammed it back into drive and skidded around to face the other way. Elisa looked out of her window and saw that the chasm next to the car extended almost as far as she could see in the dusty air. She grabbed Daniel's arm with a look of unreasoning terror on her face. He held her as best he could with his seat belt on.

Tyler sped away, back to Palm Drive, and turned right. The earthquake had stopped, but the traffic-light posts were still moving unnaturally. A few cars were still parked on the side of the road, their drivers shaken, but many had pulled back into the light traffic. Tyler slowed as he approached the freeway overpass, seeing cars and pickups stopped in the middle of the road. As the road rose up to reach the overpass, the additional elevation gave them a view across to the right, to where the fissure had opened up. Although the air was thick with dust, they could see something that appeared to be a black open wound in the landscape, maybe half a mile away.

Elisa could see that the overpass ahead had partially collapsed onto the freeway below. She shuddered at the thought of them driving over the edge to their deaths below. Tyler quickly turned the vehicle around again. He took another detour, and along the way had to slow the vehicle right down again as they drove past high-voltage power line towers. Elisa's heart was in her mouth all the way through them, frightened another quake would either crush or electrocute them in the car. She gritted her teeth, but Daniel knew how afraid she was by the fierce grip she had on his hands.

Another half-mile along the road there were wind turbines, right by the side of the road. *One day we will laugh about this*, Daniel thought, as he pulled Elisa closer and told her to close her eyes. Tyler sped past them, and soon they reached another intersection, turning right towards Palm Springs. Tyler slowed the car as they approached the freeway overpass. The traffic had thickened considerably, and Daniel could see why. The freeway was already backed up to the intersection they had just reached now, the cars being unable to get through further up. There were two bulldozers navigating their way along the shoulder of the on-ramp, heading to the Palm Drive bridge.

Tyler worked his way around the on-ramp traffic and continued on into Palm Springs. They could see some dust rising from the direction of the snow-capped mountains to their right. Quake damage was visible here but didn't seem to be as bad as they'd seen in Desert Hot Springs. They drove another ten miles or so and reached a sign announcing the *Desert Regional Medical Center*. There were cars and people everywhere; it was chaotic.

Tyler parked illegally on a grass verge and put an official ID on the dash. He told Daniel and Elisa to wait in the vehicle, and ran inside. Elisa had calmed down, and Daniel kept reassuring her she wasn't pathetic or irrational or hopeless and all the other things she'd said about herself.

"Trust me," he said, "fear of earthquakes is really a thing. Thousands of people have it."

"I don't like it. I'm a very rational person," she said stubbornly.

"I know. And this doesn't change that."

Tyler returned with a piece of paper in his hand and a plastic bag he handed to Elisa. "It's going to be crazy here for a while, and there are some serious injuries coming in. They've given me those supplies. That will have to do for now," he said, as he carefully backed the SUV onto the road.

86

An hour later, they were parked outside a US Geological Survey building near central Palm Springs. They had done their best to treat their wounds, then Elisa had searched for somewhere they might get access to a seismograph, or some way of keeping track of the seismic activity. "I can't stop thinking about it," she said. The building seemed alive with activity.

"Do you think you can get us in?" Elisa asked Tyler. "I need to know what's going on with that vibration. The ringing. What if it's still intensifying?"

"There hasn't been a quake for over an hour," Daniel offered.

"That could just mean the next one will be even bigger. We could still be facing something cataclysmic." Daniel knew she was right.

They stepped out of the car into the cool evening air. Daniel helped Elisa put her jacket on over her injured arm. The latest reports they'd read said the last quake registered 7.6 and, just like the one before it, its epicentre was near Desert Hot Springs. It was shallow, causing violent localised shaking. There were also reports of fissures opening up in the ground around the town, collapsing the Gene Autry Trail overbridge at the freeway, crushing at least two vehicles and their occupants.

The front doors were locked and there was no intercom or bell, so Tyler went to knock on a window. Daniel and Elisa stood on the front steps, waiting. Across on the next block they could see a second-floor balcony, where a party was well under way. People were standing outside drinking and talking loudly. As Tyler returned, a bearded man of about forty opened the front door for them. Tyler explained they'd just come from Desert Hot Springs, and Daniel and Elisa were guests of the US Government.

"I hope you don't mind," Elisa explained urgently, "but we want to look at today's seismographic data."

"Sure, come on in," the man said. "My name's Dave, by the way." They all shook hands, as Dave showed them in. "There's a hell of a lot of data, as you'd expect," he said.

"We're not so much interested in the individual quake data, unless you've seen something unusual in that. We're more interested in the vibration that's been picked up since this morning," Elisa said.

"Well, it's been an interesting day, that's for sure," Dave said, raising his eyebrows. "Are you seismologists?"

"No. Academics interested in geophysics and other things," Daniel fudged slightly. "It's a long story," he added.

"The ringing, or vibration, has been just bizarre. It's like something is causing a resonance in the earth's crust, in the bedrock. It started this morning, and we've watched the intensity steadily increase since then," Dave explained enthusiastically.

"So it's still increasing?" Elisa gasped.

"Yes. It wavered some when the four big quakes hit and during the aftershocks."

"Aftershocks?"

"Yes, there have been hundreds of seismic events since this morning, but most of them small. I doubt you'd have felt many, even near the epicentre. And that's another surprising feature of the quakes today. They've all had almost the same epicentre, just north of Desert Hot Springs. Usually we would see events like these distributed out a lot more."

Dave showed the three of them into a crowded room with screens everywhere. "Sorry about the noise. We've had USGS people and others come in from everywhere today."

Most of the room's occupants ignored the newcomers as they followed Dave to one of the workstations. He explained the equipment and introduced some of his colleagues to them. There was a television mounted on the wall, showing news footage with the sound muted. Elisa saw an image of a distraught and bloodied woman being pulled from the wreck of a car. She was screaming and looking at what was left of the back end of her sedan. It had been almost completely crushed by the concrete bridge.

Elisa dragged her gaze away from the awful images on the screen and tried to focus her thoughts. "Is there any pattern in the vibration or resonance?" she asked, glancing at some of their data. A few people looked at her in surprise.

"Well, seismic events don't usually follow an *orderly pattern*," someone said from a nearby screen, "but it's definitely been increasing since this morning." The man realised he'd been condescending and explained further. "We've been looking for an explanation. Some sort of government testing, or even local mining; there are still active gold mines in this area. But we found nothing. Do *you* think there's something like that?"

"Not necessarily," Daniel said, "but it's highly unusual, right?"

"Yes, it sure is," the man replied.

Then the floor moved, and Elisa screamed.

It was a jolt that almost knocked them off their feet. Everyone in the room started to dive under the nearest workstation. Daniel pulled Elisa under the desk with Dave.

"This feels big," Dave observed casually. He noticed Elisa's terrified expression. "Don't worry. This building is one of the safest in Palm Springs. It's rated to withstand a very big shake." His words did not calm her. She clenched her jaw and tried to stop herself from screaming again.

The shaking went on for another two minutes and the seismologists started to call out numbers. 7.3, 7.5, 7.8. Then the lights went out, and Elisa shrieked in panic. Daniel held her tightly, and Dave's face revealed his concern. This *was* a big one. From under their desk they could see the light fittings swaying from side to side in the pale twilight, as some of the ceiling tiles fell to the floor.

"The generator should kick in now," Dave said, trying to reassure them. And maybe himself. There was a final shudder, and the quake subsided as the lights flickered back on. Daniel started to climb out and Dave stopped him.

"Just give it a minute. Let's make sure no more ceiling tiles are going to fall." They waited, as Dave had suggested, then Daniel helped Elisa up. The dust in the air danced in the electric light. Through the window, Daniel could see the street was still in darkness. They were running on backup generator power.

The scientists in the room debated the quake's magnitude as they went back to their computers to restart them. Some had to clear debris from their desks and shake dust out of their keyboards. The general consensus was that, assuming the epicentre was still just north of Desert Hot Springs, it was around 7.6. There would be serious damage and almost certainly injuries.

87

SÃO PAULO, BRAZIL

"It is completely outrageous!" José Zapas was at his best. His indignation seemed to rock the very fibre of his being. He waved his arms in outrage in front of the crowd of reporters standing outside his home. "These lies, these false allegations! Dirty tricks from the government because they're losing the election! Show me a shred of proof!" he demanded. He had rehearsed the careful balance of shock, outrage and disgust in his voice.

The story had broken on the morning of the first round of Brazil's presidential election. Several newspapers in São Paulo, Rio de Janeiro and Brasilia, as well as major online news sites, had published a story linking the Zapas business empire to the recent attack at Club Na Beira, where thirteen people had lost their lives, and some were still seriously injured and deaf. The story claimed that one of his companies had been developing a technology for an unnamed foreign government, and the company was alleged to have terrorist connections as well.

Outwardly, Zapas now had his emotions under control, but since he'd heard the report, he had been reeling. He'd explosively vilified his own security people and screamed into the telephone at his media executives. Antônia had left hastily, in fear of her life. Then, when he'd controlled

366

himself sufficiently, he had formulated the strategy for his response with his personal media advisors.

He had given his first press statement hours earlier, but now, in the early evening, it was clear he had lost a lot of ground and it was likely to be a close-run election. He would have to continue to fight on to the second round in three weeks. Zapas was incandescent with rage, and he still couldn't see where the leak could have come from. They hadn't even got all the details right; it was possible it might have been misinformation. *But planted by whom?* In spite of his statements to the media, he did not believe the current president would resort to tactics like that. The man just didn't have the backbone.

Either way, the damage had been done. If Rigo returned from the United States, he would have him hunt and kill the journalists who started this story. Or, better still, Rigo could beat the story's source from these parasites first.

Zapas was at least able to console himself that Días had made contact that morning. He had managed to get out of Desert Hot Springs with only minor injuries, and, more importantly as far as Zapas was concerned, he'd also got the backup weapon out. It was already carefully packed as freight and on its way to São Paulo. That was not something the organisation needed to know. For a fleeting moment, Zapas imagined using the test weapon on the news media.

88

Elisa tugged at Daniel's shirt. He turned to see that she was very pale and looked like she might pass out. "I need to be outside," she muttered.

Daniel helped her out of the room and through the front doors. Tyler followed. In the car park, metres from the nearest possible falling object, Elisa almost collapsed in Daniel's arms. Tyler looked at Daniel, silently mouthing 'is she okay?' Daniel nodded. They could hear sirens and alarms from every direction.

Elisa slowly composed herself as Daniel held her. They were both exhausted but running on adrenaline. He led Elisa to a low wall, and they sat, as a fire truck raced past, siren blaring. Beyond the car park, in the street, people had come out of a house or building. One of them was bleeding. Elisa could hear laughing and looked enquiringly at Daniel.

"Californians are used to earthquakes. They've had bigger events than that last one," Daniel said by way of explanation.

The front door of the USGS building opened, and Dave walked over.

"Are you okay?" he asked Elisa.

"Yes. Just a bit jumpy. Sorry."

"Don't be. That was a big one. Seismographs confirmed it was a 7.6."

Daniel saw the colour had started returning to her face.

"Before that one hit, I was going to ask you about your data," Elisa started, composing herself and recollecting her thoughts. "Are you able to plot the intensity of that ringing over a time series?"

Her question surprised Dave. "Well, yes, I guess so. We have all the data. But there have been literally hundreds of quakes today, and I'm not sure what that could tell us. Seismic events follow their own rules, not regular patterns."

"I'm mostly interested in the resonance," she said. "Maybe just the stronger quakes, too. Would that be, say, over 4.5?"

"Sure." Dave looked sceptical but also curious. "Shall we go back in?"

Daniel stood, but Elisa didn't move. Her face said 'I want to see this', but her legs didn't want to move.

"We could wait here," Daniel ventured.

"No, I have to see this." Elisa stood, gritted her teeth again and marched towards the entrance after Dave. She forced herself to go back inside, and back into the same room. The clock on the wall said 11.30. Hours had passed since they had first arrived.

Dave talked to a couple of people standing at his workstation, explaining what he wanted to do. They all had the same reaction he'd had. *Why? Quakes don't follow any known rules.*

He worked through the detailed information, taking out data points at fifteen-minute intervals, and put them into a table. Elisa watched over his shoulder until someone pushed a chair over to her. She sat and watched the man work, Daniel standing behind her. They both looked at the numbers, trying to make quick mental calculations.

"Oh my God, it's *still* increasing," she cried. "They stopped that ..." She caught herself just in time. She'd almost said 'weapon'.

"Yes. Nearly twelve hours ago," Daniel said quietly, knowing what she'd meant. Fortunately, no one else picked up on her words. They exchanged a look of dread. *Is this the 'unstoppable resonance'? Will it 'consume everything around it'?* Daniel could feel Elisa's fear in the pit of his own stomach, too. But there was something about the data that made him look again.

"Is there another pattern here? This data isn't quite linear," Daniel said. Elisa and Dave took a closer look.

"You're right," they both said.

"The gaps are getting slightly smaller," Elisa added. "The resonance is going to reach a peak."

Dave stared at her for a moment. "I think you're right," he said, incredulous. He worked furiously to finish the data plot then selected the time series from his table and opened a chart tool. They all stopped and stared at the screen.

"Well, I'll be damned," Dave said. "How the hell did you know that?"

"I didn't. It was a guess," she said. They were looking at an arc that curved steadily, becoming less steep. It seemed to be perfectly uniform.

"Have a look at this," Dave said, calling people around the screen.

Someone whistled. "That's amazing." Others muttered to themselves.

"It's still intensifying," somebody commented, repeating Elisa's fearful words. Small ripples appeared in the coffee cup on the desk.

"Another one," Dave said, as the shaking started.

People started diving under desks again, expecting the worst. Elisa cried out and grabbed Daniel. They ducked under a desk, and Daniel did his best to comfort her, although in truth he was just as scared.

Thankfully, the shaking subsided more quickly this time.

"Aftershock," Dave observed. "Doesn't necessarily change this pattern."

People emerged from under the workstations, checking that the computers were still working.

"Seismograph reads 6.4," someone called.

Many of the geoscience people in the room were scratching their heads. They were still amazed at the pattern Elisa had pointed them to.

"Earthquakes just don't do this," a young woman nearby said, to nobody in particular.

This time around, Elisa recovered her composure quickly. It was sheer determination, Daniel thought.

"Can you extrapolate that data series into the future? Say, the next three to four hours?" Elisa asked Dave.

"Sure, I guess so," he said, looking perplexed. Turning back to his screen, he found what he needed in the tools menu. Using the half-day's actual data as a guide, he plotted the next dozen quarter-hour intervals into the table, then selected the columns and rows he wanted and pasted them into a chart. He stared at the screen, open-mouthed, as Elisa pointed at the new arc.

"There's the apex!" she said. "That's when it peaks. What time is that?"

"Just before three tomorrow morning," Dave said. "*This* morning," he corrected himself, glancing at his watch. "But how could you know that?"

"Just maths. Looking at your numbers in the table."

"That's incredible. Are you a seismologist?" someone behind Dave asked.

"Archaeologist." The man just stared for a minute.

The others gathered around started to go back to their screens and try their own experiments with the data. The noise level in the room had dropped considerably as people concentrated on their work.

"This could change the way we understand earthquakes," Dave said.

The young woman at the next table came over with a grim expression on her face. "I've just plotted today's quakes, the ones over 4.5, like you said earlier, and extrapolated out the next few hours. They're not as uniform as the resonance, but there's definitely a pattern. I think we can expect a couple more large quakes over the next three hours. At least one greater than 7.6."

Elisa just stared at her, squeezing Daniel's hand hard.

"It's not much more than a guess," the woman explained. "There no scientific precedents for what I've just done, but since that resonance has such a distinct pattern, it sure seems plausible."

Dave seemed to be ready to argue with her, but checked himself. Some truly strange things had happened today.

"Are you able to print those charts out for me?" Elisa asked.

"Sure, okay." He pointed to a printer at the side of the room. "They should come out over there, if it's still working."

Elisa went to the printer, gently towing Daniel along behind her. The printer was in a quieter, unoccupied space.

"I hope we haven't said too much," she said discreetly into Daniel's ear.

"I don't think so. You've only pointed at the data they already had. Somebody somewhere else may already have figured this out," Daniel whispered back.

She picked up the printout and went back to Dave's workstation.

He had fine-tuned his chart. "The peak is at 2.52 am, to be more precise," he said, and Elisa shuddered.

So it's going to intensify for almost three more hours.

89

Tyler hurriedly followed Daniel and Elisa outside. He'd been standing behind the group gathered around Dave's workstation but had heard the discussion. *The peak is 2.52 am.* After her visible reaction to the last few quakes, Tyler understood why she had rushed back outside. He wasn't keen on being in that room, either, if a bigger quake struck, although his orders were to stay with them.

"I can go back in and check with Dave in about half an hour if you like," Daniel offered, as they stood together in the moonlight. He was as keen as Elisa to know whether their prediction would pan out.

"Yes please, that would be good," Elisa replied shakily. "I don't think I can go back inside for a while."

Tyler unlocked the SUV. "Let's wait in the car," he suggested. "You two look cold."

They climbed in, and Tyler reclined the front seat and relaxed. "I guess we're here for a little while," he said, closing his eyes. Elisa and Daniel arranged the back seats to make themselves more comfortable, and Daniel pulled Elisa to him.

"You've been amazing tonight," he said softly into her ear. She turned and kissed him in response. In spite of their fatigue, he could still feel the tension in her body.

"I've been a neurotic and emotional mess, actually."

"No, you haven't. Today we've had some of the biggest quakes I've ever felt, and we both nearly died. Like I said, you've been amazing." She sighed and lay her head on his chest, closing her eyes.

Daniel woke with a start. Elisa was asleep on him, and Tyler rhythmically snoring in the front seat. The street lights were still out, but it seemed quiet outside. It was 1.35, according to his phone. More than an hour since Dave had plotted the predictive data. *We need to know,* he thought. He tried to gently extricate himself without waking Elisa, but she woke immediately.

"What time is it?"

"After 1.30. I'm going in to check the data," he said. Elisa yawned, and moved to let him climb out.

As soon as he opened the door, Tyler was instantly alert. "What's up?"

"Just going to see if our prediction was right," Daniel replied, closing the door and walking to the building.

He had to tap on the window again.

Dave saw him, and dashed around to open the door. "I'm glad you're back. We've seen some totally amazing things today, but none more so than in the last hour!" Dave exclaimed. "That weird resonance, the vibration, has done exactly what we predicted. *Exactly.* We've just *predicted* seismic activity. First time ever!" He was exuberant. "Where's Elisa?"

"In the SUV. She's not used to quakes like Californians. And New Zealanders."

"I want to thank her. Both of you. This is going to change seismic science," Dave said. "Based on the data we now have, we plotted this out all the way until the ringing stops altogether. That's in about twelve hours, if it stays on the same trajectory. The next thing for us to do is figure out what the resonance *means.* And how it started."

"Maybe the first quake started it?" Daniel suggested. He hoped they didn't reach a conclusion that it was artificial. *The world is not ready to know that massive earthquakes can be triggered at will.*

"Well, there are hundreds, if not thousands, of seismologists thinking about that now," Dave explained. "It's crazy in there. We've had calls from all over the world. People are coming in from all over California, Arizona, Nevada, even Mexico. The data is astounding people everywhere."

"Well, thanks again, Dave, you've been really helpful," Daniel said, shaking his hand.

Dave handed Daniel a card with his number on it. "Feel free to call, any time, if you want to know anything more, and please thank Elisa for me. It was great to meet you both."

Daniel turned and left. As he walked through the front doors, he saw Elisa coming his way. She climbed the steps to meet him.

"I couldn't have got through today without you," she said, holding him tightly. "Thank you." She kissed him as he wrapped his arms around her. Then the shaking started. At first a sort of deep, rolling motion, followed by a sharp jolt. Fear was instantly back in Elisa's eyes, as she held on tight.

From where they stood on the steps, Daniel could see across the centre of the city in the moonlight. Something looked very wrong. He held on to Elisa, trying to comfort her, but he could not take his eyes off what he saw. About a kilometre away, a building seemed to disappear into the ground. Then another. Elisa noticed his eyes widening and turned to look. She gasped in terror and momentarily forgot the shaking underfoot.

A narrow dust cloud was rising as the earth swallowed buildings, carving a chasm that was headed directly for them. They saw the party on the next block. People on the balcony had turned to see what the noise was, and Elisa heard their screams as the chasm opened up underneath them. Neither could turn away, as they watched the building sink into the writhing earth.

Elisa screamed, and Tyler leapt out of the SUV, running towards them. Daniel pointed at the gaping trench rapidly approaching.

"Run!" Daniel shouted, dragging Elisa down the steps with him. They dashed past the SUV and into the street. Car alarms sounded all around them, as they raced along the road. Trees swayed overhead, occasionally forcing them to duck under moving branches. They sprinted past people emerging from houses, who just stared at them, dumbfounded. Daniel held on to Elisa's hand, not willing to let go of her. Tyler kept pace, though Daniel was sure the man could easily outrun them.

Daniel turned back to try and see what was happening and tripped on something, landing awkwardly. He cried out as he twisted his ankle before hitting the pavement. Tyler and Elisa stopped to help him up. They were less than a kilometre from the USGS, and to their left they could see the growing dust cloud.

"Can you go on?" Tyler asked, barely out of breath.

Daniel tried the ankle, but he could not put weight on it. Both Daniel and Elisa were gasping for air. They could go no further. They all looked back to the USGS building. The cloud of dust was close, but the shaking had stopped, and it hadn't quite reached the street the building stood on. They could hear the familiar sound of sirens in the distance.

Now what?

Elisa hugged Daniel and cried. She couldn't stop herself. The emotion just poured out of her. Daniel held on tightly as sobs racked her body. He could feel her warm tears running down his neck. He had no words. There was still another hour until the ringing peaked, and then another ten or eleven hours until it actually stopped. He wasn't sure he could withstand another ten hours of this, and he was certain Elisa's emotional state would not. They stood in the street, locked in their embrace for a full five minutes. Tyler sat on a fence at the edge of the pavement. None of them spoke.

90

PALM SPRINGS, CALIFORNIA

Tyler's phone broke the silence. He looked at it in surprise and took the call, mostly listening, and occasionally giving brief answers.

"How do we get out of here?" Elisa whispered to Daniel, while Tyler was on the phone.

"To be honest, I don't know," Daniel replied. "Maybe Johnson can help."

They overheard Tyler explain to the caller how the ground had opened up in central Palm Springs, and that the seismic data predicted a peak at 2.52 am, after which the vibration should slowly subside. He finished his call with a 'will do'.

"I'm surprised the phone network is still working," Tyler said. "That was Johnson. He wanted to know what we said to the seismology people. I told him you were careful. Sorry to have to say it, but he also asked me to remind you that the whole weapon thing is classified."

"We know. Did he say how things are in Desert Hot Springs?" Daniel asked.

"Not pretty. Only seventeen fatalities we know of so far, but hundreds injured. It will be the same here after that last one. Maybe worse. He said the ground opened up in a few more places and swallowed cars, roads and a couple small buildings. Nobody understands it. They don't get sinkholes around here." He shook his head. "I'm going to get the SUV. Back in ten minutes." Tyler sprinted back down the street in the direction of the dust cloud.

"I should call Dave," Daniel said. He took out the card and dialled the number. *No answer.*

Elisa shivered, as they worried and waited for Tyler to return.

It seemed like less than ten minutes when Tyler pulled up next to them. Elisa helped Daniel limp over and climb in.

"We tried calling Dave. Are they okay down there?" she asked.

"Yes. Dave said no one was hurt, luckily. All the lights are still on and they're all working like hell in there. From the front steps I could see the hole. It opened up all the way to about two hundred yards from them. Never seen the ground open up like that, until today. I hope I never see it again."

Elisa shuddered at the thought of the chasm tearing open and racing towards them, not for the first time today. Fear and anxiety were written all over her face.

"Johnson wants me to get you two out of here." Tyler could see relief on her face as he said it. "It's not going to be as easy as I'd hoped, though. The airport is closed; multiple runways have been damaged. We've got a two-hour drive to San Diego."

"Okay. At least that's in the opposite direction to the fault line," Daniel replied. He could feel relief coursing through Elisa. *Or maybe himself.*

They sat together in the back seat of the SUV as Tyler drove them out of Palm Springs and south-west towards San Diego. A little way out of the city, Tyler took another call from Johnson, answering with, "Got you on speaker, boss." The two men discussed, in circumspect language, plans for the next day, including retrieving the van and the acoustic weapon from the deep chasm in Desert Hot Springs. Apparently, the fissure had opened up further, and the van was now down a hundred and twenty metres. Tyler asked the question that was on Daniel's mind.

"Why not leave it there? Bury it permanently."

Johnson's response was a curt, "That's above my pay grade."

Johnson said there should be enough conflicting opinion of the seismic data to keep people guessing for years, and if there was any suggestion of a man-made cause, they would ensure there was a plausible scientific denial.

But that was not the most alarming part of their conversation. Johnson explained that he had gone back to the police lockup to question the two men captured at the scene, but that had proved impossible. "Well, that's the weird thing," he said. "I got to the police building a couple hours ago, and they were both dead inside their cell. No wounds or obvious cause of death. Just a little blood coming from their noses, mouths and ears."

91

A light dusting of snow had fallen overnight, unusual for mid-December. It was still cold, but the sky had cleared and the morning sun was quickly melting the remaining snow. Elisa and Daniel had decided to walk to the campus to meet Avery Compton. Avery had been keen to hear all about their adventure and had called Elisa a week earlier. She had promised him that when they got back from Chidwick, they would visit.

After their return from Palm Springs, there'd been a lot to do, but before any of it, they just stayed at Elisa's flat, mostly staying indoors, unwinding in each other's company. Elisa's bullet wound was almost healed. She could remember the first time Daniel changed the dressing for her. His touch was so gentle, and he'd had such a concerned and caring look on his face.

Elisa had contacted Cláudia. She'd made a full recovery and was relieved when Elisa told her the man who attacked her was dead. She'd said she still had copies of everything and would be happy to work with them. She also invited them to visit her in Lisbon.

Daniel had contacted the police in Prague and, after some difficulty, had managed to explain that they were the tourist couple police had been seeking following the Machaut museum fire. After ten minutes on the phone, Daniel had finally been connected to a senior officer who explained Interpol had been in touch, courtesy of the Americans, and the case was closed. Daniel asked about the boy, and he was told he had been located, but, no, Prague police could not give contact details for him.

After the first few days back in Oxford, they drove down to Chidwick. They spent a week there, walking around the village, enjoying home-cooked meals by a roaring fire, as well as the occasional pub dinner. It had been almost idyllic, just what they needed to recover, but there was also a purpose to it.

They worked to finish packing up the house and clearing out personal belongings so Daniel could sell it. It could have been a lonely task were it not for Elisa. He was a little torn about the house; after all, it had been in his family for five generations. In the end, he had decided he would sell, to give Katie her share.

Daniel phoned his mother and shared some of the highlights of the past few weeks. He told her he'd likely be busy in the UK for at least a few more weeks and wasn't sure when he would be home, and also that he'd met someone.

Elisa phoned her parents and repeated more or less the same things. Daniel left the room to make tea, to avoid Elisa's cheeky grin as she told her mother all about him. Elisa's mother realised she was in love, and said, "I knew you'd meet the right man, one day."

The question of 'where to next' was one they hadn't got to yet. Both of them knew there was a decision to make.

When the Chidwick house was more or less ready for sale, they drove back to Elisa's flat and contacted Avery. That was yesterday.

Today, they trudged through the melting snow on the university paths and into Avery's building. His door was closed, but when Elisa knocked, he opened it quickly.

"My dear Elisa! Daniel! Do come in, come in," he said. "It's cold in the hallway." He ushered them to the armchairs. "Wonderful to see you both! May I offer you some tea?"

"That would be perfect," Elisa said, pulling Daniel's hand towards the old maps on Avery's wall. "I love these old maps. And now we know so much more about them!"

Avery returned with a tray, complete with teapot, three cups and some jam-filled shortbreads. "That should keep us going while you tell me your story!" he said, with anticipation in his voice.

"All right!" Elisa began. "Let's pick it up from our last conversation." And they went on in turn, telling Avery all the details, starting with the attack at Daniel's house. The call from Plymouth, meeting Dr Frye and her connection with Professor Gillard, the link to Machaut, the manuscript. Avery had noticed the scar on Elisa's neck, tut-tutting as she explained.

He wanted all the details of the scroll, and they spent twenty minutes showing him the detailed photos of it.

"Astonishing," Avery said. "Simply astonishing."

Elisa told him that from their brief research, the scroll must date back to around twelve thousand years ago. Avery agreed the sea levels around the coasts, particularly the British Isles, and of course the Beringia land bridge, confirmed their assessment.

"What was it made from? It looks like copper in the photographs, but it's untarnished."

"We thought it looked a lot like rose gold, but not quite. And it was definitely harder than gold."

"Hmm. Orichalcum," Avery mused. "Plato wrote that the Atlanteans' precious metals were gold, silver and orichalcum, but no one knows for certain what orichalcum was.

"Oh, this is just remarkable! Do you realise that this map changes history?" Avery asked. "It's absolutely astounding."

"Yes, *theoretically*, but we don't know where it is!" Daniel said.

"Last time we saw it, it was in the hands of a frightened young man, and we don't know how to contact him," Elisa added.

"One of the archaeologists we met at Plymouth said the Zeno map had been debunked," Elisa said. "The scroll tends to prove that theory wrong, but the scroll wasn't in Italy in medieval times, it was in Prague. They're five hundred miles apart. What would the connection be, do you think?"

"Hard to say, my dear, but travelling five hundred miles in medieval times certainly wasn't unheard of. The Zeno brothers were from the Venetian Republic, a widely travelled people. Enrico Dandolo, the Doge of Venice in the twelfth century, even participated in the Crusades. He's buried in Istanbul. The Bohemian empire was a Catholic empire, so a connection can be reasonably assumed."

Avery poured them another cup of tea. Elisa told him about Desert Hot Springs. As a geophysicist, Avery wanted no details spared on the quakes and the strange vibration, the ringing, that seismographs had picked up, the fissures opening up to swallow cars and buildings.

"Elisa surprised the seismologists with their own data!" Daniel said. "They hadn't expected linear behaviour for the vibration and were surprised to see a regular pattern, after Elisa asked them to plot the intensity over time. They were able to predict the peak and when it would begin to decline. Very accurately, as it turned out."

"The vibration didn't stop when the weapon was stopped, it didn't even register a change," Elisa added, pulling out the seismic chart printouts she knew he'd want to see.

"That's very interesting," Avery said, stroking his chin. "It seems as though the machine had started a ringing with earth's own resonant frequency, as we theorised. The 'music of the spheres'. Perhaps it set up a chain reaction that started our planet ringing like a bell. Like the 1960 Chile earthquake."

"Yes! That's what we thought! We'll have to wait and see what the seismologists make of it, I guess," Elisa said. "Although Daniel contacted the USGS people after we got out of San Diego, and they confirmed the predicted quakes on that second chart *actually happened*, within just a few minutes of those predictions."

"Now that's truly amazing," Avery exclaimed. "That could change the world of seismology." His face took on a more serious expression. "Oh my. Imagine if the weapon hadn't been stopped." He paused as they all considered that. "The resonant vibration may have escalated into a full-scale catastrophe ... The fault could have opened up and swallowed the whole city, or the chasm ripped open all the way to the sea. It doesn't bear thinking about. It would be ... would be ..."

"Like Plato's description," Elisa finished.

"Ah yes, my dear. Like Plato's description, indeed. I think you have an insight into what may have happened to Frisland, eleven and a half thousand years ago."

"Well this time, thankfully, US authorities were able to stop it," said Daniel, wanting to lift the sombre mood. They had decided not to tell Avery, or anyone else, about the second weapon, the one that must have been used on the men in the police lockup. Nor about the man who obviously got away.

"That reminds me of something." Avery stood and searched through a pile of papers on the bookshelf. "Ah, here it is." He pulled out a newspaper and found the article he wanted, handing it to Daniel. "What do you make of that?"

It was brief account about the newly elected president of Brazil, a wealthy businessman who had won by a slim margin. A recent controversy had almost cost him the election. The paragraph Avery had underlined linked a military technology company, owned by the new president, to the unexplained terror attack on a São Paulo nightclub. The stories that had emerged from the patrons of the club all pointed to an unknown, powerful acoustic weapon which had killed or permanently deafened dozens of people. President-elect Zapas strenuously denied any involvement, but there were threads of doubt and the US Government had hinted at further investigation.

"So maybe another nation has this weapon technology after all," Elisa murmured. She was standing behind Daniel, reading over his shoulder.

"Each knows the other has it. Maybe that will be enough deterrent," Daniel replied. "We can only hope."

"Indeed," said Avery. "Whatever the case, you two very likely saved thousands of lives in California. Don't forget that."

Neatly changing the subject, Avery asked, "What will you do next?"

"We don't know yet. We've started putting our notes together, but ..."

She was thinking about the unspoken dilemma. *But, where is home?*

"Just *notes*?" The professor raised his eyebrows. "Elisa, you have a *book* to write. You and Daniel."

"Do you really think so?" Elisa asked as Daniel returned.

"Yes! If you can find that scroll, and if it can be dated, you'll have some proof that will be hard to refute. Even the metal it's made from will cause a stir. The bronze age, the first known manufacture of metallic alloys, didn't start until six or seven thousand years after the scroll must have been made. You have the detailed scans and photos of the tablets as well. But even if you don't have proof, you have an amazing adventure to write. You must write it!" Avery was ebullient.

They finished their tea and thanked Avery for his hospitality, and for his encouragement. Daniel shook his hand, and Elisa gave him an unexpected hug. As she did so, he spoke quietly to her.

"It's wonderful to see you so happy, my dear."

They left Avery and went outside to find the temperature had risen several degrees and the morning's snow was gone.

"Now what shall we do?" Daniel asked.

They called in to St Dunstan's, but none of her colleagues were there. The academic year had finished, and the whole university was quiet. Daniel led her into the large dining room and pointed out the gold-leaf name board. *John Foxton, Professor of Archaeology, 1917–1939.*

"Your ancestor," Elisa said. "The man who translated the tablet that started all of this."

"Do you know what I think we can do now?" Daniel asked, but continuing before she had a chance to reply. "I think we should try to track the boy from Prague down. We need to know."

"How?"

"I don't know yet, but I'll race you to find clues."

92

Daniel winked at her, extracting his phone to start searching. Elisa followed, with a quizzical expression on her face. Daniel started searching news articles for the fire and murder at the Machaut museum, and within five minutes had spotted an article that named the man killed in the fire, Petr Novotny. He continued looking but did not find a reference to the son's name in subsequent news stories. He'd just been referred to as next of kin.

Elisa, instead, had been looking for travel or editorial stories about the Prague Machaut museum and finally had seen a magazine story that described the little business, run by father and son, Petr and Tomás Novotny.

"You win," Daniel conceded with a grin. "Now what?"

"Hmm. Do you think we would find an English-speaking directory assistance in the Czech Republic?" Elisa started to search for one.

Daniel had another idea. He started to search social media sites for the name Tomas Novotny. There were a lot of Novotnys. Apparently a common Czech name, but eventually, when he got the accent right in the first name, he found a Tomás Novotny with a link to the Machaut museum, based in Prague.

"I'm not having any luck with directories," Elisa said.

"No problem. I've found him!" Daniel told Elisa how he'd done it, boldly claiming victory.

"Okay, Mr Winner, how will you get his number?" Elisa said playfully.

"Already messaged him."

"Oh ..."

"Come on, I'll buy lunch," Daniel said.

They left St Dunstan's and strolled to a nearby café Elisa knew well and had a light lunch. As they ate their toasted sandwiches, Tomás Novotny messaged Daniel back. Daniel had taken a chance, simply saying "Need to talk about the ship we broke in your museum. Please reply."

"Who are you?" was the response.

"What do you think I should say?" Daniel asked. "We need him to trust us."

"Try calling him. With the app. It might work," she suggested.

No answer.

"Damn. I'll message again." As Daniel started typing, his phone rang.

"Hello, Daniel speaking," he said, hoping it was the boy.

"Hallo ..." He didn't seem to know what to say.

"Hello, Tomás? This is Daniel Reade. Please listen. I was in the museum with my friend," he shrugged at Elisa, who was mouthing the word 'friend' with mock indignation. "We opened up the ship with you." He paused, and put the phone on speaker.

"I remember." The boy was cautious. "What do you want?"

"We were sorry to hear about your father," Elisa said.

"We want to help you with the scroll," Daniel added.

"How?" he asked, and Daniel and Elisa exchanged a look. *Does he still have it?*

"It is very valuable. It needs to be examined and tested. We think it is nearly twelve thousand years old." Elisa hoped he was at least a little bit interested in history, or archaeology.

"I thought everything in that shop was just junk. My father thought it was junk. Tourists are stupid, he said." Tomás was starting to open up now.

"I knew it was special when I saw you take it out of the old ship."

"Museum?" Daniel whispered to Elisa. She nodded.

"Could you take it to the Prague museum?" Daniel asked. "We could contact them and tell them to expect you. They will be very interested and will be able to look after it safely."

"What about the man who killed my father?" the boy asked nervously.

"That man is dead," Daniel said. "Could we contact the Prague museum?" Daniel pressed, hopefully. He was still worried Tomás would be tempted to sell it to a private collector.

"I'm not in Prague. I was scared. I'm staying with a friend. How do you know he's dead?"

"We both saw it happen. There's no doubt," Elisa said. "Let us help you. Please."

There was a long silence.

"Okay." He was starting to sound relieved. "I will come to London. You will meet me?"

"Of course," Elisa quickly replied. "At Heathrow?"

"No ... I'm in Amsterdam, I will come by train tomorrow."

"Okay. If you tell us which train you're on, we'll meet you when you get off."

"Okay. I will send you a message." Tomás ended the call.

Elisa and Daniel looked at each other, not quite knowing what to say.

Eventually Elisa broke the silence. "So, the scroll survived. I think we'd better start writing before this story is told by someone else!"

Back at her flat, Elisa spent two hours tracking down the right people at the British Museum in London, eventually getting through to a senior curator whose attention and imagination she was able to capture. He agreed he would look at the scroll.

The man also agreed the museum would offer an 'appropriate financial consideration' if the artefact proved to be of real value. A reasonable start. Daniel didn't want to ask Tomás where the scroll was, in case he scared the boy off. They could do that tomorrow.

"I wonder how Willow is getting on?" Daniel asked, remembering that the Plymouth survey would be well under way by now. Both searched, quickly finding news, although it was outside of the mainstream sites. No doubt they would get a better account when they spoke to Willow next. They read the main story together on Daniel's laptop.

Atlantis may finally have been found!

A joint survey sponsored by the University of Plymouth and the US National Oceanic and Atmospheric Administration has discovered evidence of ancient ruins deep in the Mid-Atlantic. The hydrographic survey has identified remarkable man-made features, including ruins of walls, building foundations, roads, stone tablets and stelae, in regular patterns over an area estimated to be at least four to six square kilometres in size.

Willow Peters, a scientist on board the vessel, has theorised that these ruins could have been part of a civilisation submerged by previously unknown volcanic activity associated with the formation of the Mid-Atlantic Ridge, at least several thousand years ago.

A detailed archaeological study of the site is being considered; however, at a depth of three thousand metres, the feasibility of such a study is unknown.

Elisa showed Daniel some of the other headlines she'd found, which included '*Atlantis enthusiasts excited by lost Atlantic island*', '*Archaeologists sceptical about alleged Atlantis ruins*', and '*Academic warns that alleged Atlantis find could simply be wreckage from a naval battle*'.

The following morning, they took the train into London, transferring to the tube for King's Cross St Pancras, where they waited at the Eurostar terminal. Tomás looked younger and more childlike than they remembered, as he exited the international terminal with an old backpack slung over his shoulders. He looked relieved to see them.

Elisa told him how sorry they were about his father, and slowly Tomás opened up more. He'd been scared for weeks, since the fire. He hadn't even told his friends in Amsterdam about the scroll. It seemed to be the thing that had got his father killed, but he knew it was important and valuable, and just didn't know what to do with it.

Elisa told him about the British Museum, and offered to go with him whenever he was ready to go and get the scroll.

"But I have it here!" he said, surprising them both. He opened his backpack and took a small plastic box from the bottom, showing them the scroll shining inside.

Elisa could have hugged him. "Do you want to go to the museum now? We could be there in less than half an hour."

Tomás seemed unsure.

"They've promised to keep it securely for you while it's analysed. They'll make you an offer for it, if it's assessed as valuable. And we think the analysis is going to make it *very* valuable!"

"Okay. We can do that," Tomás said.

93

In approximately one hour, Elisa and Daniel's flight would land. They had decided to get as far away from recent events as they could, and that a real, restful holiday was what they needed. A trip where nobody was trying to kill them, earthquakes were not likely, and they could just relax. Perhaps they would be able to start writing their story, just as Avery had suggested. For both of them, collaborating on a book seemed an exciting prospect.

The scroll was now with the British Museum, and already the early composition analysis had proved most interesting. It was made of an unusual alloy that included gold, copper, nickel, zinc oxide and a small percentage of carbon. It was a completely unknown alloy of gold that resembled rose gold, although had a different hardness and lustre. Its most interesting, yet inexplicable feature was that, because of the oxide and carbon, it would require a great deal of heat to manufacture. A much higher temperature, in fact, than was thought possible, even in the bronze age, which was many millennia later than when it was believed to have been made.

All in all, it was a remarkable find that had a lot of scientists talking, and *arguing*, at the museum. Its value was more difficult to estimate, but as its provenance improved, its value would improve. If evidence of the civilisation that created it was confirmed, it was expected to run to many hundreds of thousands of pounds, possibly into the millions.

The pilot announced they would soon begin their descent into Sydney.

"I'm so glad we decided to come here," Elisa said. "I just hadn't realised how much I've missed my parents."

"I'm looking forward to seeing Katie, too," said Daniel.

"It'll be nice to have Christmas with Mum and Dad; it's been quite a few years," Elisa said.

"I can't believe it will be Christmas in two days!" Daniel replied.

They had booked two nights at a hotel in The Rocks, one of Elisa's favourite places, filled with cafés, restaurants and old pubs.

The plane landed gently, and the crew announced it was a beautiful warm evening, calm and twenty-one degrees. They disembarked and navigated their way through the airport to the train, arriving at Circular Quay station half an hour later. By the time they checked in at the hotel it was seven-thirty, so they navigated the fifty metres down a cobbled path to the main street and found a cosy little Italian restaurant.

A glass of wine later, the jetlag from their twenty-two hour trip started to hit, so after dinner they went straight back to the hotel and slept for almost ten hours.

"Good morning!" Elisa said, as she climbed back under the covers. Daniel had just opened his eyes. "I've just looked out the window, and it's another glorious day!"

"Good morning," said Daniel sleepily. "You're perky this morning."

"I'm just so glad to be here. With you. I've missed it more than I'd realised."

Daniel pulled her close and kissed her. "I'm glad I'm here with you, too."

After a leisurely breakfast, they wandered around The Rocks, finding a lot of little curiosities, and narrow pathways between buildings that climbed up and down the hill. They toured the Sydney Observatory, walked under the huge base of the Sydney Harbour Bridge, ultimately winding their way around to the Australian Hotel on Cumberland Street, where Katie was meeting them for lunch. They wandered in to the old pub a little early, expecting to find a table and wait for Katie.

"Danny!" A young woman with short brown hair and light-brown eyes just like Daniel's waved at them. She jumped out of her seat and gave Daniel a bear hug. "So good to see you!"

"Katie! It's great to see you, too. This is Elisa."

Katie gave Elisa a hug. "It's good to meet you," she said.

"And you," Elisa replied. "Daniel's told me a bit about you. And your mum."

They chatted for a few minutes before taking a seat at the table. Daniel bought drinks while Elisa and Katie talked about him, and started to get to know each other. They soon became engrossed in their catch-up on each other's lives. Daniel and Elisa gave Katie an abridged version of their recent adventure, saving some of the detail for another time. As the pub filled with the lunchtime crowd, Daniel suggested they order their meals, and Katie jumped up to join him at the bar.

"I really like her, Danny, she's just lovely," Katie whispered to him. "She's a keeper."

"I know," he said.

Epilogue

As the plane taxied across to the terminal, Alice Reade reflected on the past year. It must have been almost two years since she had started to notice her son was in a rut and wasn't happy. He'd seemed to be just living one day to the next, rudderless and depressed. She also remembered his nonchalant response to the letter from Edward's solicitor. Of course, he couldn't have known it would be something that would change his life. That letter had started, or restarted, the whole adventure of the ancient tablet, a story that went all the way back to Alice's great-great-grandfather, Henry Hobbs. And what an adventure it had been! Leading Daniel on a chase around Europe, to follow evidence that led to a monumental discovery.

It had also led Daniel to the woman he loved, and he was happier than Alice had ever seen him. She was delighted for him. For them both. Elisa and Daniel had visited her after last Christmas, and it was obvious then that they were in love.

Their book was now on the bestseller list. Sales had started slowly, then its popularity increased when the British Museum published their findings on the golden scroll. But when the detailed survey of the Mid-Atlantic archaeological site was completed and it was declared a World Heritage

Site by UNESCO, the book's popularity had soared.

Alice was also heartened by the renewed relationship Daniel and Katie had. She had been worried for years about them losing touch; they'd been so close when Katie was still a child. But Katie was one of the reasons Daniel and Elisa had chosen to live in Sydney – that and Elisa being closer to her parents. *They have truly landed on their feet,* Alice thought, with Elisa having found her passion for writing, while working at Sydney University. Now she was writing her second book, a study of some unexplained ancient maps. Daniel had completed his Master of Teaching during the year, and he was now teaching at Sydney University. The success of their book had helped him negotiate an arrangement that allowed him and Elisa to spend time doing research overseas.

Alice was looking forward to staying with them at their home in Glebe, in inner Sydney, near the university. It looked charming in the photos. She was also looking forward to meeting Elisa's parents for the first time. *This would be a wonderful family Christmas with everyone together.*

Author's Note

First of all, I would like to thank:

My family for their patience, support and encouragement. Louise Kendall for advice and encouragement. Lorena Goldsmith of Daniel Goldsmith Associates for manuscript advice, and special thanks to Adrienne Charlton at AM Publishing for frank feedback, insightful advice and a sharp eye.

There are many others who have listened, advised and contributed in important ways, including Conor Occleshaw, Dianna Bodman, and my friend João Ricardo Vasconcelos for advice on Portuguese words and phrases.

Any residual mistakes are, of course, all mine.

The Zeno Map

The Zeno Map is an interesting curiosity. Like other ancient maps, such as those of Piri Reis and Oronteus Finaeus, it should not exist. It is one of a few that depict the apparently fictitious island of Frisland, in the Mid-Atlantic. Remarkably, for a non-existent island, it is rendered in great detail, including its rocky coastline and possible port in the south.

This surprising map, allegedly compiled in 1380, is reasonably accurate in its depiction of the coasts of Norway, Sweden, Denmark and Scotland. It also correctly shows the latitude and longitude of a number of islands. This is remarkable, because the device necessary to measure longitude, the marine chronometer, was not invented until almost four hundred years later, in 1761, by John Harrison. The Zeno brothers were also somehow able to map Greenland *free of glaciers*, which, according to scientists, have been there for millions of years.

After the Zeno map was (re)published in 1558, Frisland started to appear in other North Atlantic maps of the late 1500s. All these unexplained maps are reputed to have been compiled from much older sources, but no evidence of these ancient sources has yet been found.

My solution to this problem, the golden scroll, is pure fiction, as is the Guillaume de Machaut manuscript. The picture of the Zeno Map on page 181 is a public domain image, courtesy of Wikimedia Commons, https://commons.wikimedia.org/wiki/File:Zeno_1558.png, 30 August 2019.

Transatlantic Telegraph

The first attempt at laying a transatlantic telegraph cable was commenced in 1854 by Cyrus West Field and the Atlantic Telegraph Company. To the best of my knowledge, the only similarity between Field and my invented character, Cyrus Lee, is their shared first name, a more common name at that time than it is now. The project wasn't completed until 1858, when the cable landed in Newfoundland.

Unfortunately, it only operated for three weeks, but the venture had proved it was possible, and within the next decade the undertaking was successfully completed.

Mid-Atlantic Ridge

Early in the story I refer to the Mid-Atlantic Ridge having been discovered 'a few years' before 1854. I've taken a liberty here. While the existence of a ridge under the Atlantic Ocean was inferred by Matthew Fontaine Maury in 1850, the ridge itself was not discovered until 1872. A team of scientists led by Charles Wyville Thomson discovered a large rise in the middle of the Atlantic as they investigated the future location for a new transatlantic telegraph cable. The nature of the ridge was not fully confirmed until 1925, following the invention of sonar.

Daniel's Book

Daniel is reading a book called *Ancient Traces*[1] by Michael Baigent. I recommend this book to anyone interested in reading an unorthodox history of humankind, supported by a good deal of evidence. Reading *Ancient Traces* was part of the genesis of this novel.

Ancient Megalithic Sites

In this story I've referred to ancient sites such as Baalbek in Lebanon, and Sacsayhuamàn in Peru. These sites are real and remain genuine mysteries. Many academics, scientists and engineers assert that, even with modern technology, these feats of architecture and engineering could not be replicated. There are many other sites like these, such as Puma Punku in Bolivia, that also remain insufficiently explained.

Yonaguni is an interesting example. It continues to divide geologists and archaeologists as to whether it is natural or man-made, much like the debate between Owen and Marie in the story. It consists of massive, regularly shaped stone blocks, sitting approximately twenty-five metres below sea level off the Japanese coast.

Acoustic Technologies

The acoustic technology that Professor Avery Compton describes in this story is a reality. Fractal non-linear acoustic levitation is likely to keep physicists and engineers occupied for decades, in my view. For this story, I have scaled it up rather unreasonably. The theories Avery discusses with Daniel and Elisa, such as string theory and quantum physics, are also real and go back decades. For an easy-to-read and up-to-date view, I recommend *Reality is Not What it Seems*[2] by Carlo Rovelli.

Ancient Sea Levels

Theories on ancient sea level abound. I've referred to work that the US National Oceanic and Atmospheric Administration (NOAA) have done on Beringia. The name 'Beringia' was coined by Swedish botanist Eric Hultén in 1937, named after the Bering Sea. The existence of a land bridge is well documented and believed to be the route of human migration to the Americas from Asia between 12,000 and 20,000 years ago.

The work on the Strait of Dover is emergent and less widely accepted. It is believed that the English Channel was created by several events, the first being some 450,000 years ago, but that the final stage may have happened around 8,500 years ago, with rising sea levels submerging the last remaining portion of land.

Guillaume de Machaut

Machaut was a real historical figure, and a secretary or official in the court of King John of Bohemia, during the fourteenth century. He was widely travelled (with the king's court), and he was a writer. To the best of my knowledge, there was no 'Machaut manuscript'. The tourist museum in Prague, and the scroll, are also the products of my imagination. Machaut was better known for the poetry and music he composed than any other writings.

A final word

None of my characters are based on real people. Any resemblance is purely unintentional, and I hope no offence is caused.

I hope you've enjoyed reading *The Doomsday Tablet* as much as I enjoyed researching and writing it. My next novel, *The Sentinel's Map*, will be released later this year.

William Henshaw,
January 2020.

---

[1] Baigent, Michael, *Ancient Traces: Mysteries in Ancient and Early History.* London, 1998
[2] Rovelli, Carlo, *Reality Is Not What It Seems: The Journey to Quantum Gravity.* New York, 2017

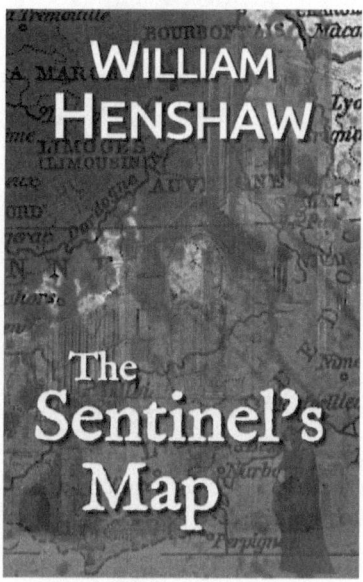

PROLOGUE

"Tell me, old man!"

The stricken man sat in his leather captain's chair, one of three antique chairs in the timber-panelled room.

It was warm; a small fire burned in the Victorian cast-iron fireplace. A black iron poker protruded from the red coals at an awkward angle, as if thrust drunkenly into the grate. Ash had spilled onto the flagstone hearth. A crystal tumbler of whisky sat on the leather-inset oak desk, a half-empty bottle resting just behind it.

The older man picked up the glass and drew a good measure of the liquor across his dry lips. His assailant, wearing a black robe over trousers and socks, towered over him; his shoes were presumably outside the house, a precaution that had enabled him to reach the room without being heard. He was dressed totally in black, including his strange and ominous headwear – a medieval executioner's mask.

The mask covered the man's head as far as his nose, where it split, allowing it to protrude. His mouth and chin were visible beneath. He had a broad nose and thick lips, and his neck was muscular. His face seemed to be expressionless, impassive. He was clean-shaven and spoke calmly, with an unexpected pitch of voice reminiscent of Peter Lorre. The older man reflected momentarily that this giant would be a generation too young to have heard of Peter Lorre.

The assailant suddenly struck out, knocking the tumbler and its contents across the room. It flew past the open safe and smashed against the wall.

"Tell me where it is," he repeated.

The man held the interloper's gaze unsteadily but remained silent as he attempted to place the accent. Eastern Europe, he decided.

He knew what he had to do. No matter his fear of what his attacker was about to do, he would not forget the words he'd repeated to himself over the years.

He had some idea what to expect from his assailant. Immediately after the man entered the room, he had silently picked up the poker and thrust it into the fire, then lifted him out of his chair by the throat and softly demanded that he open the safe. After some remonstration, he had agreed to comply.

The safe was set into the wall to the right of the desk, and the intruder had stepped politely out of the way to allow the man to reach it. Only when he pulled the door open did the intruder quickly approach to ensure there was no concealed weapon. He had slowly withdrawn a small bundle of banknotes and some papers and carefully placed them on the desk.

"Take whatever you want." He slumped back into his chair, his breathing shallow.

"I don't need this." He struck the man across the face, a brutally crunching blow with the back of his closed fist. "You know what I want," he went on quietly. "Tell me where it is and this will stop."

The man in the chair wished he still had his whisky. He knew this was not going to stop. Blood dripped from his nose onto his crisp white shirt.

"We've been hunting your kind for centuries. We know you have it." The aggressor leaned in close, and the older man could smell mint on his breath. It seemed incongruent. "Tell me now."

"I don't know what you're talking about," the man replied, with a tremor in his voice. "Take the money. It's all I have."

"I don't want money." The huge figure in black loomed over the chair, the upper part of his robe parting slightly to expose a tattoo of the crucifixion on his chest. He crossed himself and struck the older man hard under the chin. As his victim slumped groggily, he quickly retrieved the poker from the fire. He crossed himself again, and with his left hand, he gripped the man's throat with breathtaking force, driving his head into the back of the captain's chair. At the same time, he placed his left knee across the man's legs to further restrain him.

The older man could not move. Aside from the attacker's strength and weight, he was frozen with an unexpected mixture of impotent fear and a resolute determination. The intruder's impassive expression did not change as the glowing poker pressed into the old man's left eye. He screamed as he struggled desperately to turn his head away. He could barely breathe, but as he did, he could smell the burnt flesh of his eyelid. The pain seared through his body, and although his eyes were screwed shut, he was sure he glimpsed a wisp of smoke rising from his left eye socket.

He briefly lost consciousness, a blessing soon curtailed as the big man threw whisky in his face straight from the bottle.

"Tell me where it is and this will stop."

He could not speak. The pain in his left eye was excruciating. An awful smell of burnt flesh and liquor, tinged with the coppery scent of blood, filled his nostrils. Whisky was in his eyes, and each time he blinked he wanted to scream again.

The big man's face was just inches from his. He mustered all the strength he had left. "I don't know what you're talking about." His voice was weak and fearful; ethereal and unworldly. Nothing like the strong and confident voice he had trained and perfected throughout his life.

"Dei gratia," said the big man softly. He crossed himself again and pressed the poker into the man's chest. There was a sizzling sound as the poker burned the whisky, blood and skin. He kept pushing. *He seems to have boundless strength*, thought the older man, by now unable to move, his good eye blinded by the pain. The poker seared the flesh as it slowly penetrated his rib cage, finding its way through the pulmonary artery and right ventricle, ultimately coming to rest in the plush padding of the chair's ageing leather upholstery.

WILLIAM
HENSHAW

The
Relic

A strange relic is found deep under the Antarctic ice, but before it can be analysed it is lost in a mysterious plane crash on a remote island.

Anthropologist Peter Hennessy investigates the relic and its implications, while within days of the crash people on the island begin to die from an unknown illness.

Biological samples are brought from the island to Australia for analysis, and a rogue diplomat seizes his opportunity. Police are soon investigating murders.

As he explores further, Hennessy discovers medieval maps that depict Antarctica in impossible detail, and the mystery deepens...

A former colleague of Hennessy, Dr Nicole Palmer, is working on the seemingly unstoppable plague, and the pair soon find themselves in a race against time to prevent a deadly pandemic, and piece together how the relic is connected.

www.williamhenshaw.com